A TRAP FOR CATHERINE

A TRAP FOR CATHERINE

Juliette Benzoni

Catherine Series No. 6

This edition published in England in 2020 by
Telos Publishing Ltd,
139 Whitstable Road, Canterbury, Kent CT2 8EQ
www.telos.co.uk

Telos Publishing Ltd values feedback. Please e-mail us with any comments
you may have about this book to: feedback@telos.co.uk

ISBN: 978-1-84583-984-0

A Trap for Catherine © 1973, 2020 Juliette Benzoni

Original title: *Piège Pour Catherine*

Cover art: Martin Baines
Cover design: David J Howe

The moral rights of the author have been asserted.

British Library Cataloguing in Publication Data.
A catalogue record for this book is available from the British Library.

CONTENTS

This edition dedicated to Linda Compagnoni Walther

PART I:

THE BESIEGED CITY

1: Fire in the Valley

Bending low over her horse's neck, with fear riding hard on her heels, Catherine of Montsalvy fled homewards, thanking heaven for the impulse that had made her choose this half-broken stallion in preference to her beautiful but delicate palfrey, since his apparently inexhaustible staying power gave her a real chance to outdistance her pursuers.

Despite the steep and ill-defined road up to the plateau, Mansour literally flew, his long, white tail streaming, comet-like, behind him. His white coat must have been visible for miles in the sinister afterglow that was lighting the western sky with streaks of blood red, but Catherine knew already that she had been recognised and that it was vain to put her trust in concealment.

Close behind her, she could hear the heavier hoofbeats of Mâchefer, the horse belonging to her steward, Josse Rallard, who always accompanied her on these rides about her domains; but farther off, down in the darkness of the chestnut trees that filled the valley, there came a sound of other hurrying hooves, unseen but menacing; the hoofbeats of the *routiers* galloping in pursuit.

In that cold March of 1436 snow was still lying on the high plateau of the Châtaigneraie, to the south of Aurillac. It showed up here and there as light patches against the dark brown earth, and the north wind had frozen it to ice. The woman on the horse did her best to avoid it, expecting, each time she failed, to feel Mansour slip and fall, for then nothing could save her.

As she galloped, she glanced backwards now and then, watching for the glint of helmets in the valley and the clatter of arms.

Each time, she had to tear furiously at the blue veil she wore as the wind wrapped it over her eyes. She was casting one of these anxious looks behind when she heard Josse's voice call reassuringly:

'No need to look round now, Dame Catherine! We're gaining on them … We're winning …! See! There are the walls! We'll reach Montsalvy well ahead of them …'

He was right. The town walls, with their squat, unbeautiful towers, hacked from the living granite and the lava of long-dead volcanoes, their watchful battlements and narrow gates, well-supplied with iron grilles and oaken drawbridges, loomed black against the blazing sky, like some barbaric crown on the rim of the plateau. Those walls were crude enough, to be sure – crude and rustic below the encircling frieze of barrel staves – but they could withstand a siege and offer good protection to men of flesh and blood! And so Catherine and Josse had to reach them far enough ahead of the *routiers* for those stout gates to close behind them and the town be placed in a posture of defence. If not, the savage wave would pour in after the châtelaine and sweep away Montsalvy and its thousand inhabitants like a rising tide.

Catherine's heart tightened and missed a beat at the mere thought that this could happen. She had seen war too often and too close to have the smallest illusion as to the fate of the women and children of a conquered town when a host of soldiery, thirsting for gold, wine, blood and ravishment swept over them, giving free reign to all its basest instincts. If the Lady of Montsalvy trembled as she pressed her horse's flanks, it was less with thoughts of her peril than with the fear of coming too late to save her children and her people.

As a dying man sees his whole life pass before him in an instant, so Catherine seemed to see them rise up suddenly out of the muddy road before her: her son, Michel, four years old, with his round cheeks and permanently untidy thatch of fair hair; her ten-month old baby, Isabelle, who, much more than herself, ruled as a miniature despot over the castle, the town and even the abbey. She saw Sara, too, her old Sara who had watched over her from a child, when she had found refuge in the Court of Miracles in a Paris torn by rebellion. Sara was 53 now and she governed both the children and the household. Then there was Marie, Josse's wife, whom she had met in the Caliph's harem in Granada and who had fled with her; Donatienne and her husband, Saturnin Garrouste, the old bailiff of Montsalvy; and all the people of the town, as well as the Abbot, Bernard de Calmont d'Olt, the monastery with all its peaceable monks, so clever with their hands … a whole little world, the life and safety of which now hung on her courage and her wits. None of them must be allowed to fall into the clutches of the robber of Gévaudan.

Now, Catherine and Josse were racing over the summit of the plateau. A gentle slope led upwards, straight to the north gate of the little town, the Aurillac Gate, before which stood the few, bolder, houses of the little outlying suburb called the *barri* Saint-Antoine. The horses lengthened their stride now that the strain of the long climb was over. As he rode, Josse took from his belt the silver-banded cow's horn that never left him, and filled the evening air with the long calls that should let the watchers on the rampart know that danger threatened.

Almost neck and neck, the two riders dashed through the low-arched gateway, so furiously that they were unable to avoid the miller and his donkey. Fat Félicien and Grizzle were sent rolling upside down into the pile of dried cowdung used by the guard for firing.

Once inside, Catherine reined in her rearing mount with all her strength.

'Brigands!' she screamed, as her squire laid aside his horn. 'They're hard on our heels! Call in the out-folk! Raise the drawbridge! Lower the portcullis! I'm going to the monastery and to the Entraygues Gate!'

Josse had already sprung from his horse to give a hand to those who were hastening to the walls with stones and barrel staves to strengthen the battlements. Women were screeching like startled hens, crying 'Jesus!' and going on to list all the local saints as an added precaution while they ran about searching for their children. The portcullis came down with a horrible grating crash.

'I've been saying for months it needed greasing,' Josse muttered as he went with Félicien, who by now had extricated himself from his midden, to manipulate the great winch that controlled the bridge.

Catherine had already left them and was dashing along the main street toward the monastery, still crying her warning. Mud flew from under her pounding hooves, and pigs and chickens scattered in all directions.

Pastouret, the landlord of the Grand St Géraud, began hastily putting up his shutters and sending his two or three customers on their way.

Catherine hurtled breathlessly through the monastery's romanesque gateway and fell rather than dismounted at the Abbot's side, where he was working with his sleeves rolled up, pruning his roses and tending his medicinal herbs in the monastery's small garden. He looked round, showing her a thin, ascetic yet contented face in which the eyes seemed always to see farther and higher than those of other men.

'You come like a storm, with sound and fury, my child! What has happened?'

'Sound the tocsin, father!' Catherine cried, without preamble. 'The brigands are upon us! We must prepare to defend Montsalvy!'

Bernard de Calmont d'Olt looked at his châtelaine with unfeigned surprise. 'Brigands? But – there are no brigands here? Where are they from?'

'The Gévaudan! It is the Apchiers, reverend father. I recognised their banner! They are burning and pillaging! Climb your tower and you'll see the smoke and flames from the village of Pons!'

Dom Bernard was not a man to demand long explanations. He stuck his sickle into the rope that girdled his black habit and set off at a run for the church, calling to Catherine:

'Go back to the castle and look to the south gate! I'll take care of the rest!'

In another moment, the brazen voice of the monastery's great bell, Géraude, shattered the evening air, sending the frantic notes of the ancient alarm, still dreaded and never forgotten, foreboding misery and weeping, winging away on the bitter wind from the frozen peaks of extinct volcanoes. Catherine, hurrying along the short road leading from the monastery to the castle and the Valley Gate, felt her heart contract as she measured the warning beat. Like Joan, the Holy Maid, she had always loved church bells, and liked to feel the heart of her household and of her own life beating in time to the unchanging rhythm of their monastic sounds, from the chilly angelus of dawn to the quiet one of evening. But these bells, this age-old cry of anguish sent up by man to God, these she feared with every fibre of her being, for the sake of the burden of bodies and souls that rested on her slender shoulders.

'Arnaud!' she murmured silently. 'Why must I be alone? The demon of war has taken you again, and now I, too, must pay tribute to him!'

In a little while, the groups of frightened peasants would emerge from the darkened valleys, from under the shade of rocks and chestnut trees, and feel their way, with only Géraude to guide them, up to the sheltering walls, driving their sheep and goats before them, with their few possessions done up in bundles and loaded with wicker baskets full of chickens and grain, the women carrying their youngest, while those old enough to walk clutched at their skirts. They would all come in through the Entraygues Gate, those from the north making their way round the town by almost invisible paths, to escape the brigands whom, with the sure instinct of all mountain folk, they had already scented from afar. They would have to be given shelter, comfort and reassurance. They must be already on the way, making the most of the last gleam of daylight, and the bulk of Montsalvy's few men-at-arms must be posted to guard their entry.

Small though her little force was, Catherine was not really anxious for the safety of her town. The people of Montsalvy were quite capable of defending it; and, if it came to a fight, Bernard de Calmont's holy monks were a match for hardened warriors. But suppose the brigands settled down to lay siege to the place? The hard, upland winter was almost at an end and so, too, were their provisions, and there would be many mouths to feed!

Catherine stood for a moment at the Valley Gate, left open to admit the fugitives. It would not be closed until the last possible minute. It was dark under the gate and the shadows were deep, but out there beyond the stone ogive that housed the portcullis, the landscape still glimmered with a faint light before being plunged into the darkness that enveloped the valley of the Lot.

A torch was lighted under the dark archway and stuck in the wall, where its flame shone on the steel caps of the archers posted there by the sergeant, Nicolas Barral, to help pick out and identify the refugees.

At the sight of the châtelaine, Nicolas touched his hand to his helmet and grinned, showing his teeth below the long, black moustache that made him look like some old Gaulish warrior.

'I knew when I heard the bell! There are three men up there on the walls keeping a look-out on the Entraygues road and the field paths. You can look to the castle, Dame Catherine.'

'I'm going there now, Nicolas. But try to get in as many refugees as possible before you raise the bridge. I'm afraid those who do not get inside will be sacrificed!'

'Who are the enemy?'

'The Apchiers. By what I saw at Pons, they give no quarter.'

The sergeant shrugged, making the plates of his armour clash, and wiped his nose on his leather sleeve. 'They never do. The winter's drawing to an end and the wolves of the Gévaudan have gone hungry this many a day, I doubt not. I heard tell they were out round Nasbinals, and that the monks of the Aubrac had suffered somewhat at their hands. But I never thought they'd come as far as this! They never have before.'

'Yes,' Catherine corrected him bitterly. 'They were here last autumn. Bérault d'Apchier was at the christening of my daughter Isabelle.'

'A funny return for hospitality! Seems to me, Dame Catherine, they must have heard that Messire Arnaud is away again at the wars. They thought their chance had come, Montsalvy in the hands of a woman!'

'They did hear, Nicolas, and I know how! At Pons, I saw a man lighting a bonfire underneath a woman's feet as she hung by her hair from a tree. It was Gervais Malfrat!'

The sergeant spat on the ground and then wiped his mouth. 'The whoreson dog! You should have hanged him, Dame Catherine. Messire Arnaud would not have hesitated.'

Catherine said nothing but, raising her hand in a gesture of farewell, turned her horse toward the castle walls. It was almost two months now since Arnaud had left, in the depths of winter when the snow lay thick on everything and made the roads difficult, taking with him his lances, the flower of the County and the youngest of his men, all those who burned to win a name for themselves in battle. The Constable de Richemont, now appointed the King's Lieutenant for the Ile de France, was mustering his army for the attack on Paris that was to mark the opening of the spring campaign. The time had come at last to wrest the capital away from the English, for by all accounts there was great suffering there.

Naturally, when the word came, the Lord of Montsalvy had known not a moment's hesitation. He had gone, only too delighted, Catherine thought bitterly, to exchange the dull boredom of the Auvergne winter for the fierce intoxication of battle, which was the only life he really liked. On that triumphant night last autumn that had celebrated Isabelle's baptism, Arnaud had promised his wife that he would never leave her again; that when he went to war again, she could go with him. But, two months ago, Catherine had caught a chill. She had been feeling very ill and certainly in no fit state for a long ride in such bitter weather. And the Lady of Montsalvy had the odd impression that her lord had been not ill-pleased that circumstances should have released him from a promise he had clearly come to regard as little short of childish.

'You couldn't have come with me in any case,' he had told her, by way of consolation, as she watched tearfully while he tried on his armour. 'There will be fierce fighting. The English are clinging to the soil of France like a wild boar to his wallow. Besides, there are the children, the fief, our people! They all need their châtelaine, my sweet!'

'Do they not need their lord, too? They have lacked him long enough!'

Arnaud of Montsalvy's hard, handsome face had closed up, and his black brows had drawn together in a frown of annoyance. 'They would need me, if any serious danger threatened them. But, God be thanked, there are no enemies left in our hills that can be a threat to us. It is long since any English strongholds remained in Auvergne; and those who, out of friendship for Burgundy, might have leaned that way, dare not show themselves. As for the *routiers*, their time is past. There is no Aymerigot Marchès today to threaten our lands and our purses. But the King must take back the remainder of the lands God gave to him. And he cannot truly call himself King while Paris is still in English hands. I must go, but when the fighting is over and we celebrate our victory, then I shall send for you. Until then, I tell you, my heart, you are in no danger. Besides, I shall leave you Josse and my most experienced men ...'

The most experienced, perhaps, but also the oldest. Those who would much rather warm their rheumaticky joints at the guardroom fire with some mulled wine to drink than watch through the wet nights on the ramparts. The youngest was Nicolas Barral, their captain, and he was close on 40; full years in an age that did not run to the making of old bones. Admittedly there was also the region's spiritual leader, Bernard de Calmont d'Olt, and his thirty or so monks, and Arnaud knew precisely what stuff they were made of.

So, he had left Montsalvy one frosty morning, riding proudly on his black charger, his banner floating in the cutting wind off the plateau. Its sable and argent had been in striking contrast to the gaily-coloured pennants streaming from the lances of his knights. These knights were all of the noblest from the surrounding lands; and all of them considered it a high honour to follow the Count of Montsalvy to the relief of the capital: the Roquemaurels of Cassaniouze, the Master of Sénezergues, Archambaud de la Roque, the Fabreforts of Labesserette, the Sermurs, the Lord de la Salle and the Lord of Villemur, all with their own people about them and all as glad to be away to war as boys let out of school.

And Catherine, watching from the walls as they receded into the low cloud and gusting wind, had not once seen Arnaud turn round to bid her a last farewell; indeed, she had had the feeling that he would have spurred his horse to a gallop if he could, the sooner to be with his brothers in arms: La Hire, Xaintrailles, Chabannes, all the King's captains for whom life was worth living only when there were perils to be faced, blows to be struck and victories to be won. Between Catherine and her warlike husband, they wove a fine-meshed tapestry of blood and steel, the designs of which were picked out in brilliant colours against the blazing gold of a morning's triumph and the blue of the royal banners waving against the black lines of the foe. There were the long years of brotherhood, also, and memories in common, grave or happy, wounds taken in company and blood shed together, reddening the same turf and colouring the water in the same barber's basin.

The life of men among men! A life that belonged to them alone and in which no woman, not even the most deeply beloved, could be more than an intruder.

'His friends mean more to him than I do!' she had thought then.

Yet, the night before he had left, he had loved her with a kind of fury. He had taken her again and again, until they had had to strip the sweat-soaked sheets off the bed, falling tirelessly on the sweet flesh that offered itself to him and filling the shuttered room with his triumphant cries. Never had Catherine known him like that, and never had she experienced a keener or a more exhausting pleasure. Then, at the very height of her joy and satisfaction, a strange idea had germinated in Catherine's mind; and when, just as the abbey clock was chiming for matins, he had cast himself down beside her, panting, ready to sink, like an exhausted swimmer, into the depths of sleep, she had snuggled up to him and with her lips against the hard muscles of his chest, had murmured:

'You have never made love to me like that before ... Why?'

He had answered simply, in a voice already thickened with sleep: 'Because I felt like it ...! And so you shan't forget me when I'm gone.'

Then he had said no more but fallen asleep, clutching his wife's moist hand fast in his as if he meant not to let her go, even for an instant. And Catherine had known that she was right. Indeed, he had admitted it quite freely, for he was not a man to lie. The surest way to keep a young wife from forgetting her husband must surely be to fill up the time of waiting with the preoccupations of impending motherhood. A thoroughly masculine piece of reasoning, after all, and well in keeping with a husband of a jealous disposition! In the warm darkness within the closed curtains, Catherine had smiled ...

But that last, frenzied night had not borne fruit, and by dawn the smile had given way to barely-repressed tears. And now that the danger Arnaud had not believed in (being a man who had never learned to distrust his friends) was about to fall on Montsalvy, Catherine was glad enough that her husband's selfish, loving plan had come to naught. Lord, how would she have coped with morning sickness when called upon to play the part of a heroine in battle?

Catherine's hand moved in a little automatic gesture, brushing aside regrets like so many troublesome flies. Without realising it, she had passed the castle barbican, and now the confusion within struck her in the face.

The courtyard was humming like a hive in May. Serving women were running hither and thither, some carrying baskets of wet linen back from the wash, others ferrying buckets of water and jars of oil up to the ramparts and setting them down beside the great fires that the men were lighting up there under the direction of old Saturnin, the bailiff. The blacksmith and armourer were hard at work in one corner, raising a great clanging and sparking from the anvil.

Half-way between living-rooms and kitchen, near the ovens from which a few women were busy taking the steaming, golden-brown loaves, Catherine saw Sara standing with her hands folded over her ample white apron, dominating the tumult as calmly as if this were a day like any other. The wave and smile she gave her châtelaine were just the same as always, no more hurried or agitated. And yet, even before Catherine had given a single order, the castle was already preparing to put itself in a posture of defence.

This was the first time since its building that the castle would come under fire from an enemy. It had been completed for only a year. The Montsalvys had built it to replace the old keep of Puy de l'Arbre, destroyed by order of the King, with the large sums remitted to them annually by the merchant Jacques Cœur, to whom, in a moment of trouble, Catherine had entrusted the most precious of her jewels, the fabulous black diamond that was now among the treasures of Our Lady of Le Puy-en-Velay.

They had built this time close to the southern gate, and the crenellated mass backed onto the ramparts, making the walls two or even three times as thick in that part. In its starkness and majesty, with its thick curtain walls of grey granite well-furnished with stout oaken galleries, its tall, square keep flanked by slender turrets, towering massively above the high, carved windows of the new dwelling house and the tracery of gilded weathervanes, and the seven projecting towers strengthening its walls, it looked like nothing so much as one of those legendary dragons that lay coiled at the entrance to deep caverns, guarding the treasures within. But would it, when the time came, prove strong enough to withstand the enemy's fire, the shock of mangonels and trebuchets and whatever other engines of war might come against its walls?

When, earlier that day, Catherine had rounded a belt of woodland to come almost face to face with the wolves of Gévaudan as they went about their grim and fatal business, she had had no time to stop and estimate their strength. It had been all she could do to swing her horse round and fly before a cry was raised after her; and Josse, who had followed her, had seen no more. There was no telling what the Apchiers might have with them, and Catherine was afraid for her castle as she was for her people. It was, in a small way, her own, private achievement.

It was she who had laid the first stone, had talked over the plans with the Abbot Bernard and the brother architect of the abbey, in the days when no-one at Montsalvy, she least of all, believed that they would ever again set eyes on Messire Arnaud in this world. She had meant it to be impregnable, inaccessible; and yet, for that, she was well aware, it should have been built on some sheer crag so that its first guardians might be its loftiness and isolation. But most of all, she had insisted that it must be the protector of the town and the abbey, even at the cost of some sacrifice to its own defences. Attached as it was to the walls of Montsalvy, the castle had its weaknesses, well known to its châtelaine, and worst of them, for certain, was the ever-present danger of treachery.

Catherine had, of course, complete confidence in her twenty-five men-at-arms and in Nicolas Barral, their captain; but who could say if, among the eleven hundred odd souls within the town, there might not be one base enough to be tempted by Judas's thirty pieces of silver? There was one precedent already in the man Gervais Malfrat, whom she had had flogged from her walls because she could not bring herself to hang him, and who had gone straight to join Bérault d'Apchier ... That had been an ill-timed piece of clemency, beyond a doubt, and Arnaud would be furious if he knew of it, for Gervais Malfrat had deserved hanging a hundred times over. He was a thief, quick as a fox and as adept at worming his way into a girl's bed as into a hen roost. He stole from the father and left the daughters big with child yet, the odd thing was that although the former might rage and swear to have his skin, none of the girls ever complained. It was as if they were content with their lot, despite the shame it brought them.

But then there had been the latest one, pretty little Bertille, the clothier Martin's daughter. She had been unable to endure her shame, and they had fished her out of the Truyère one morning, as cold and pale as that ill-omened dawn. And for all her mother's grief and Catherine's entreaties, they had had to inter her not in consecrated ground but by the roadside, like one accursed! The only consolation that the châtelaine had been able to offer the girl's parents had been to dig the narrow grave close by the Hermit's Chapel, the ruined cell where, long ago, an erring monk had lived out his penance. The whole village had wept for Bertille. They said it was grief that had cast her into the arms of death, grief for the love that the wicked Gervais had planted in her heart, like a bolt from a crossbow, when he left her for another. They even said that he had driven her to kill herself out of cruelty, because he liked to see women suffer. They said, oh, so many things! So many things, and none of them proved.

Nevertheless, when the people of Montsalvy had swarmed into the castle bailey, brandishing scythes and pitchforks and yelling for blood, Catherine had commanded Nicolas Barral to take Gervais and keep him under guard. But even then, she had been unable to find the strength to condemn him to death, to set up a gibbet. She had sentenced Gervais only to be flogged and cast out of the gates at nightfall into the snow, to the mercy of God and the wolves.

She knew that, in doing so, she had offended Martin, the girl's father, who had wanted the seducer's skin. Yet how could she make him understand her horror of an angry mob? How could she tell him that she could not hang a man, because once, in a moment of anger, the people of Paris had hanged her own father, Gaucher Legoix, from the sign above his own goldsmith's shop?

The Abbot Bernard had approved her action. 'Thou shalt not kill,' he had said to her, by way of comfort. Indicating the black night and the whiteness underfoot, he had added: 'If God wills his death, he will die tonight of cold or exhaustion or by some wild beast. You were wise to leave Him to judge. I shall tell Martin so.'

And so everything had returned to normal. Only, Gervais had not died, and now Catherine blamed herself for a clemency she had come to regard as squeamishness, for if her village and her home and people were in danger of their lives through this man's wickedness, it was she, Catherine of Montsalvy, and she alone, who must bear the blame. Indeed, she came close to thinking that God's judgement in the matter had been a great deal weaker even than her own, and found it hard to see why she should pay for that too.

With a slightly rebellious sigh, Catherine urged her horse across the great courtyard of the castle, which was filled with the clash of arms, the sounds of hammering and the roar of flames. Like a well-trained animal, the great watchdog of Montsalvy was sharpening its teeth, ready to bite. The bell was still tolling and the sky was dark.

Catherine joined Sara, who was hustling the frightened kitchen maids, some of whom were in tears.

'Wouldn't you think,' exploded the one-time gypsy, 'that they were going to be raped within an hour! Before the bell had rung for three minutes, there were six of them hiding under the beds! You, there! Gasparde! Don't stand there gaping as though the sky was about to fall on you. Run to the barns and tell them to get ready fresh straw for bedding for the homeless. Here are the first of them coming in already!'

Thus adjured, the girl departed in a flurry of blue petticoats and yellow coif, while, true enough, at that very moment an ancient wooden-wheeled ox-cart entered the court, surmounted by a brood of screaming infants, huddled round a mother speechless with terror. Sara moved as if to go to them, but Catherine held her back.

'The children?'

'In bed. Donatienne is with them, and you would do well to join them. You look as if you'd seen the devil!'

'I have! He had a hundred heads in steel caps, all screaming, and a thousand arms laying about them indifferently at human flesh or wooden doors, and flinging torches into houses whence they had dragged the people out and flung them down into the mud to have their throats cut like sheep!'

Below her tall linen coif, the two horns of which, gave her a faintly diabolical air, Sara's black eyes studied the pale face shrewdly. 'What are you going to do?'

Catherine shrugged. 'Resist, of course! The Abbot is ready to help us, and it is up to me,' she added with a simple pride that was stronger than her fear, 'to set an example, since I am the Lady of Montsalvy! You attend to those who come to us for shelter. I am going back to the Aurillac Gate to see how matters stand. It is too late now for the brigands to encircle Montsalvy that night. They will never find the way. But they must be already on the plateau.'

She swung her horse round and set off back along the way she had come a few moments earlier, although much more slowly now, on account of the hurrying groups of peasants.

There was terror painted on every face. All, or nearly all, had already lived through the attack led by the mercenary Valette, the Lieutenant of the Castilian, Rodrigo de Villa-Andrade, four years earlier. Some had been tortured, others had seen those near to them die in agony, and it was their screams, their groans of anguish that filled the ears of the survivors now, behind the brazen clangour of the bell called Géraude.

They prayed aloud as they came, breaking off only to greet Catherine and beg her protection. She had a cheerful word of welcome for all of them, and seeing her so apparently calm, they felt their burden of fear weigh less heavily as they made their way to the castle or to the monastery.

As they entered, the town that, as night fell and the curfew sounded, generally seemed to curl itself up for sleep like a great black cat, now became filled with noise and light, so that it might have been thought a holiday but for the anxiety reflected in every face. Even the shop signs, creaking in the night breeze, seemed somehow menacing.

The walls above the Aurillac Gate, now duly barred, were crowded. Men, women, children, old folk and monks, all crammed together, were bawling such a stream of insult and abuse at their invisible assailants that it was quite deafening.

In the midst of them, Catherine caught sight of Josse, striving to quiet them, perhaps in order to parley. Hurriedly hitching her horse to a ring in the wall, Catherine picked up her skirts and hurled herself up the steep stone steps that led up to the ramparts. Someone saw her coming and called out:

'Here is Dame Catherine! Make way! Way for our Lady!'

She smiled at that, although the simple trust and loyal affection of it wrung her heart. It was true that for these good people she was their one earthly refuge; they depended on her for all their hopes of a decent life. For them, the châtelaine was in some degree an extension of that other Lady, infinitely more high and puissant, the Lady of Heaven who was their last hope and their ultimate refuge. And Catherine's heart was wrung, because at that moment she knew, when called upon to prove equal to that trust, just how great was her own weakness.

Dozens of hands reached out to help her up the last few steps, and somehow she found herself leaning over the battlements alongside the Abbot Bernard, whose face she saw was looking strangely set.

'I was going to send for you, Dame Catherine,' he muttered quickly. 'I have tried to parley with them, but these men will speak with none but you.'

'Then I will speak to them. Not that I expect them to listen.'

She leaned forward, resting both hands on the stone before her.

The gentle slope that ran down from the Puy de l'Arbre to the walls of Montsalvy was alive with men. The large though motley army of the Lords of Apchier was already beginning to make camp. Tents, clearly put together out of whatever stuff came to the robbers' hands, were being erected a few furlongs off, along the edge of the trees. Some were of goatskins, the badly-tanned hides showing the fur stiff with filth. Others showed strips of rich cloth, faded and grimed, alternating with large pieces of sacking. Fires had been lit, reflecting a red glow on the bearded faces of the men-at-arms. Some were already starting to prepare a meal. Slovenly serving men were skinning two freshly-killed boars and three sheep, and others were setting huge cauldrons on to boil on a tripod made of pikes, while a third gang rolled a cask out from one of the abandoned cottages. Strangely enough, none of the houses in the little outlying hamlet had yet been set on fire.

Catherine's glance came coldly to rest on the group of horsemen drawn up, motionless, on the far side of the ditch, looking up at the wall. One of them, the oldest and the stoutest, was a few paces in front of the rest. He uttered a sneering laugh when he saw the châtelaine.

'Well, Dame Catherine,' he cried, 'is this your hospitality? How is it that we find your gates made fast against us and all your people manning the walls when we come, my sons and I, in all friendship to pay you a visit?'

'One does not make a friendly visit with a troop of armed men, burning, slaying and pillaging, Bérault d'Apchier! The gates of Montsalvy would have opened to you and your sons, but they are closed to your soldiery and closed they will stay! Tell the truth, for once. What seek you here?'

The man laughed again, and Catherine thought that he was not called the Wolf of Gévaudan for nothing. It seemed to her that even the wolves might justly take offence at the comparison. He was ageing now, and bent from long hours in the saddle, but he was still as strong as a bear. Seated massively on his destrier, caparisoned in leather like himself, Bérault looked more like a brigand than the lord of a noble line that he was. The face that showed through beneath his raised visor was carved in rugged lines. The long, grey-stubbled chin gave him something of the look of an old lynx, and his eyes, of no particular colour, were unwinking and sunk deep in his head. His face, under its coating of dirt, was wine-red, and when he lifted his dark lips, it was to show a row of astonishingly blackened stumps that did duty for teeth.

The man was hideously ugly and appallingly dirty, but the armour and weapons covered by his torn and greasy surcoat were kept in shining order.

The three riders at his back were his sons. The two legitimate ones, Jehan and Francois, were like younger copies of their father: the same formidable strength, the same sullen, wolfish countenance, but with a fire burning in their dark eyes and a fresh ruddy tint to their full lips. In Gonnet, the bastard, the savagery to be seen in his half-brothers was mitigated by the suffering on the part of his mother, a gentle nun ravished from her burning convent and carried off to the baronial halls to serve their master's lust and bear his child and die. He was slimmer, fairer and more lithe, but cunning sat like a mask on his fine-drawn features, and his pale eyes had the cold glimmer of marsh lights. He was bareheaded, his fair locks lifting slightly in the night wind. He wore no sword, but a woodcutter's axe hung from his saddle-bow and, with it, a newly severed head that showed the use to which he put it. Catherine dared not look too closely at that head for fear that she should know it.

Receiving no answer, she repeated her question. 'I am waiting! What seek you here?'

The old man laughed, wiped his running nose on his gauntlet, cleared his throat and spat. 'Passage, gracious lady, only passage! Are you not mistress and guardian of the road to Entraygues and to Conques? All day long travellers pass by Montsalvy and pay toll. Wherefore are we denied?'

'Travellers do pass, indeed, by day, but not by night, nor has an armed band ever been allowed to pass through our town. If you wish to reach Entraygues, you must go by the valleys.'

'And break our horses' knees? I thank you, no! We would rather pass through Montsalvy.'

'Pass through, merely?' the Abbot asked.

'And pause awhile, perhaps. We are weary, hungry, and the weather is inclement still! Can't you give us a Christian welcome?'

'Christians do not carry such baggage as that!' the châtelaine exclaimed, pointing to Gonnet's hideous trophy. 'Go on your way, Bérault of Apchier, or rather go back whence you came. But I guess that there is nothing left to plunder or to burn where you have passed.'

'Not much,' the other admitted in his slow, thick voice. 'Is this all your welcome, Dame Catherine? Your husband gave us a better one not long since!'

'Your coming tonight shows that he was wrong. Get you gone. Montsalvy's gates do not open when its lord is absent! As you know full well he is, or you would not be here, would you?'

There was a gleam of evil triumph under Bérault's bushy brows. 'Of course we know. There are none now behind your walls but old men and monks and children. You need men, and I have come to offer you my protection.'

A murmur arose around Catherine. The people of Montsalvy who, until then, had listened in attentive silence to the exchange were beginning to show their teeth. A woman's voice called out boldly: 'Look at yourself in the mirror, Bérault! Do you think you're still a young gallant? We still have men better and stronger than you! And your protection ...'

Gauberte's advice as to what he might do with his protection drew a smile from Catherine and a roar of appreciation from all those around, who launched into a stream of jibes and insults that the Abbot tried vainly to stem. The people of Montsalvy hated the Wolf of Gévaudan even more than they feared him, and the severed head, still dripping blood down the legs of Gonnet's horse, roused them to still greater fury. Fists were shaken, and already stones were beginning to fly toward the four motionless horsemen. One, flung by a sure hand, struck Jehan on the helmet, and he spat out an oath.

Old Bérault rose in his stirrups and, beside himself with rage, let them know the true reason for his attack. 'I'll get in yet, you bunch of bragging swine, and slit your throats like the pigs you are! I want this town, and I'll have it, too, and you with it, you Burgundian whore! When that opinionated donkey Arnaud comes back from his wars, he'll find his gates shut against him, his town under my heel and his wife in my bed! If I still want her when my men have done with her! You asked what I came for, Catherine? I'll tell you. First your gold, and then yourself!'

With a movement of her hand, the Lady of Montsalvy silenced the murmuring crowd about her. The brigand's insults could not touch her. 'My gold, say you? What gold?'

'Don't play the innocent with me, my beauty! It was unwise of you to celebrate the baptism of your daughter Isabelle with such great festivities! No doubt it was splendid to entertain the old queen and the Constable, but it gave some of us a chance to estimate the wealth of your castle and its contents. Ah, they're a fine sight, all those great tapestries and silken sheets and huge dressers loaded with gold and silver plate! By my faith, I want my share!'

'By what right?'

'The right of the strongest, indeed! If you'd seen my tower at Apchier, you'd know I badly need new furnishings. But most of all, I need a bed, a big feather bed, all nice and soft and with plenty of warm covers on it, with a lovely blonde in it to keep me warm! And my men can make do meanwhile with the least raddled of those cackling hens you have around you!'

The people of Montsalvy had heard enough. Their patience was at an end. Before Catherine could open her mouth to speak, she found an archer on either side of her, each with a drawn bow. But before the arrows could be loosed to wash away the brigand's threats and insults in his own blood, the Abbot Bernard had sprung into the embrasure, with both arms spread wide. He knew that old Bérault's death would solve nothing and it was best to avoid the irrevocable as long as possible.

'Don't fire!' he cried. 'This is not the time to kill! Keep your tempers, for this man's sole aim is to make you lose them! As for you, Bérault d'Apchier, cease this offence to God and men! It is known, even in Gévaudan, that this land belongs to the Church as well as to the Count! This is a place of asylum, and he that attacks it, attacks God himself, for He is the ultimate suzerain here!'

'I've time enough to make my peace with God, monk! When I have these lands, I'll give Him a fine gift of the gold I get! I've a complaisant chaplain. Three paters and three aves and half a dozen masses and he'll make me white as a lamb, even if I've put to death every living creature in this rat's nest!'

'You've been told already, there is no gold! Messire Arnaud took with him all the money in the castle when he left with his men.'

'Then I'll make do with the furnishings,' Apchier said obstinately. 'Besides, spring is coming. Before long there will be companies of merchants travelling to the fairs in the south, pilgrims going to Conques and to the Spanish shrines. You may be an asylum, but you take tolls, too, eh, holy man? And there's money in tolls! So even if the magnificent Arnaud has taken it all with him – well, a season or two here could still be mighty interesting! Now do you understand?'

Yes, the Abbot understood, and Catherine too. The outlaw, unlike others of his kind, had come not to rob and burn and go away. He had quite simply come to stay, to batten at his leisure on the heavy traffic that, going from the uplands of Auvergne to the Valley of the Lot and the rich lands of the south, was bound to pass through Montsalvy.

A rush of anger brought Catherine up into the embrasure beside the Abbot. 'You are forgetting only one thing, brigand! The lord of these lands! You may conquer us, you may even take our town, though God grant you will not, but one day Arnaud of Montsalvy will return. His hand is heavier than yours, and then nothing will save you from his vengeance. Remember, the King loves him and the Constable is our friend.'

'Maybe. *If* he returns. But something seems to tell me that – he will not return! So we may as well settle the matter here and now.'

'He will not …?' The strangled cry died away on Catherine's lips. The Abbot was gripping her arm and muttering to her:

'Hush! Seem to pay no attention to his words! He's only trying to make you lose your head and do something foolish. But listen! There's no point in talking further.'

This was true. A veritable storm of shouting had broken out all along the ramparts, accompanied by a hail of stones that was forcing the *routiers* to withdraw. In addition, a fine, cold rain had now begun to fall. They rode off to their camp, which now stood half-way between the town and the Puy de l'Arbre, where the ruins of the old castle showed in the light of the cooking fires.

But although his sons rode off quite indifferent to the explosion of fury from the people, as though to them it was a matter of no importance, the old man turned back several times to shake his fist at the town.

Catherine came down from her perch and looked at the ring of faces around her. They showed red in the torchlight, still flushed with the anger that had roused the people of Montsalvy when they heard their lord and their lady so vilely insulted. But from all those faces came a single voice to assure the châtelaine of her people's loyalty:

'We'll hold out, Dame Catherine! Never fear, we've stout walls and stouter hearts! The old brigand'll soon be sorry he ever came here! He'll not take our town for himself tomorrow!'

Catherine smiled impulsively and clasped the hands nearest to her. It was Gauberte, the linen weaver, who asked suddenly:

'What did he mean by saying Messire Arnaud would not come back?'

There was silence. Fat Gauberte had uttered aloud the question they were all asking themselves, and the one that had been secretly tormenting Catherine. But the Abbot cut in quickly, seeing the anxiety creep back into her eyes at the unanswerable question.

'Fear not,' he said. 'We shall know soon enough, unless it was no more than a boast aimed at sapping our courage. If he has a plan, Bérault d'Apchier will be sure to make his threats quite plain, if only to oblige Dame Catherine to engage in dangerous sorties, knowing that in open country we stand no chance against him.'

Catherine wiped the sweat from her forehead with a hand that trembled still. 'If you had not been here, father, I think I should have been fool enough to attack him. And that's the last thing we must do! Now, I think we should hold a council of war to decide what steps to take. We are going to have to stand a siege. It may well be a hard one, and I need all your help …'

The crowd on the walls cleared slowly. Except for the armed guard, who would watch until daylight in case of a surprise attack, everyone went home to check the stores and pray to God to save the town and its inhabitants from the rapacious wolves of Gévaudan. Only the leading citizens made their way to the castle where the council of war was to take place.

They met in the Great Hall, where hung the tapestries of Arras and Aubusson that had so excited the greed of Bérault d'Apchier, as they were in the habit of doing every month, grouped around the lord's chair where, only a short time before, Arnaud of Montsalvy, in his black kid doublet with a chain of gold about his neck, would greet them with a jest or a roar of anger according to the circumstances. These assemblies generally took place toward the end of the morning, around a bright fire, and Messire Arnaud never failed to send round tankards of spiced wine to hearten his good townsmen for their work.

Not so that night. True, the fire blazed as always in the immense hearth, but the lofty roof timbers of the Great Hall, above the colourful array of banners stirring in the draught, were lost in the shadows of night, where the scanty torches in their iron rings threw no light.

Outside was none of the morning bustle of the castle, the giggling serving maids and cackling hens, but only the silence of a night heavy with menace, and the lord's chair was occupied not by the knight's six feet of muscular vigour but by the blue-clad form of a young woman who had never seemed to them more slender and frail.

True, at her side there was the black-robed Abbot Bernard, with his shaven crown and thin, contemplative face. He was as thin as a blade, and they knew his spirit to be like the finest tempered steel. But he was a churchman, a man of prayer, for whom renunciation and brotherly love were the ultimate weapons, while the time now was for brute force.

For her part, the Lady of Montsalvy watched them come in, one by one, marvelling to find them the same as every day and yet, at the same time, different. Her eyes rested in turn on their faces, weatherbeaten by sun and snow and gale. They were broad, high-coloured faces, framed for patient daily toil, with rugged features that seemed graven into deep lines by the harsh soil of Auvergne. Tonight, in their best black tunics, which they always donned 'to go up to the castle', with their long hair and their drooping moustaches hiding equally well savagely-bared teeth or a jovial grin, they looked startlingly like their remote forebears, those Arvernes who had founded an empire, invented the word 'independence' and afterwards opted definitively for loyalty.

The Arvernian emperors, the men of Luern and Bituit, who went into battle on silver chariots with a pack of hounds at their heels, must have looked like that, cut out in face and build for the terrain of schist and lava where they built their settlements.

The châtelaine looked at those faces, one by one, dwelling for a moment on each. There was Félicien Puech, the miller, round as a barrel, with the seams of his tunic straining over his paunch, and great hands, either one of which could easily lift a sack of flour. Auguste Malvezin, the chandler, who made the best wax candles in all the Carladès and whose cheeks shone as if they had been polished with his own wax. The giant Antoine Couderc, like a hairy cyclops with immensely long arms, who combined the offices of blacksmith and wheelwright, and whose eyes were like two cornflowers growing miraculously through the soot. Then there were the Cairou brothers, cloth weavers: Martin, the elder, the father of little Bertille who had died for love, and Noël, the husband of that Gauberte who had the sharpest tongue in all Montsalvy. Both were of medium height and sufficiently alike despite the six-year difference in their ages: the same thin, sharp-featured faces, the same drooping moustaches giving their narrow lips a sad, disdainful expression, the same backs bowed from bending over their work. But Noël's placid demeanour became, in his elder brother, a dull, latent violence, a bitter desire for vengeance on the villain for whose sake his child had undone herself and damned herself in the sight of heaven.

After them came the coppersmith, Joseph Delmas, a cheerful fellow who sang all day long as he tapped at his pots and pans. That night, however, Joseph was not singing:

'Mountain, be low and valleys rise,
'On Jeanneton I'd rest mine eyes ...'

They all filed in, silently as usual, and took their seats on the stools ranged in a semicircle about the lord's chair. In the centre sat the bailiff, Saturnin Garrouste, grave as ever, with his long chin and the deep, vertical lines that lifted a little on one side to give a quirk of private humour to the old man's face.

At a sign from the Abbot, they all rose, and with them Nicolas Barral and Brother Anthime, the abbey treasurer.

'My children,' intoned the Abbot, 'we are gathered here tonight to take council together, but council of a different kind from that to which we are accustomed. We are not here to discuss the price of cloth, some business relating to the tolls or a disease of rye, but a mortal peril to our town. And so, before we begin, we must ask God, in whose hands we are, to take pity on us and fight with us against the men of blood at our gates ...

'Our Father, who art in heaven ...'

Meekly they knelt there in the straw, their big hands grasping their woollen caps, and fervently repeated the ancient prayer, so that the last words were almost a cry, so well they expressed the secret fears of all of them: 'Deliver us from evil!'

Catherine, for her part, had prayed silently. Her mind wandered far beyond the prayer, and joined to her appeal to God was a passionate longing for some unlooked-for chance – a miracle it might be – to bring her husband home again, while knowing in her heart that there was nothing and no-one that could bring Arnaud back until Paris was returned to the true King of France.

Seated again on her high ebony chair, her hands folded quietly on her blue dress, she listened carefully as Brother Anthime enumerated the abbey's stores, and then Saturnin read out a list, handed to him earlier by Josse Rallard, of the reserves of the town and the castle. The total was not particularly encouraging. Packed as it was with refugees, the town could not hold out for more than two months without hunger making itself felt. And besides that, the harvest would suffer.

In a deathly silence, Saturnin rolled up his parchments and turned to the châtelaine. 'That's how matters stand, Dame Catherine. This gives us victuals for a few weeks … assuming we can hold out against direct attack.'

'Who says we shan't try to hold out?' Nicolas growled, his hand going to the hilt of his sword. 'We're all of us stout of limb and of heart and sure of eye! We'll defend our town, food or no!'

'I did not say otherwise,' the bailiff protested mildly. 'All I said was that the Apchiers are strong and our walls high but not insurmountable … and we may be overrun. Since when has it been counted cowardice to look truth in the face?'

'I know. But I'm telling you …'

Catherine rose to her feet, cutting short the incipient dispute. 'No need to argue,' she said. 'You're both of you right. We have courage, and to spare, but if we want to come out of this business without too much harm, we need help.'

'Lord, where are we to get it from?' fat Félicien sighed. 'From Aurillac? I hardly think so!'

'Nor I,' Saturnin agreed. 'Neither the Bailiff of the Mountains, nor the consuls, nor the Bishop of Aurillac will be interested in our troubles. They are all for my Lord Charles of Bourbon, now that his marriage has made him Count of Auvergne. Indeed, they say that Monseigneur Charles is ambitious – ambitious enough to have an eye to the throne! The people of Aurillac are no fools. They'll not go asking for trouble with the Duke for the Lord of Montsalvy's sake, not when he's gone off to aid the King. Besides that, the Bailiff of the Mountains isn't on the best of terms with the Bishop of Saint-Flour. He has an eye to his great position!'

Catherine looked at the old man with something like astonishment. Of all at Montsalvy, he was the quietest, most unassuming and peace-loving, and this had given him a certain reputation for wisdom, but she was discovering now that her bailiff knew how to keep his ears open for the affairs of the kingdom. He talked little but was an excellent listener, and no-one was more skilled at worming information out of the merchants who passed through, paying their tolls, when the season came round, on their way to the few fairs in the south that war had not curtailed. In fact he knew as much as Arnaud – who, before he had left, had expressed anxiety about the growing appetite of the Duke of Bourbon and feared to see a second La Trémoille, only nobler and more powerful, darken the kingdom's horizon.

'In any event,' she said calmly, 'our immediate overlord is not the Duke of Bourbon but Monseigneur Bernard of Armagnac, Count of Pardiac, for whom my husband held the castle of Carlat three years ago. It is to Carlat and nowhere else that we must look for aid ...'

She paused. The danger must be pressing indeed for her to think of Carlat. That formidable stronghold, set on its basalt crag, held cruel memories for her, from the day when Arnaud's cousin Marie de Comborn had tried, in a fit of jealousy, to kill their baby son, Michel, and Arnaud had later stabbed her like a noxious beast, to that other day of pain and anger when, in the village church, they had said the Mass for the Dead for the Lord of Montsalvy before he went to the leper colony, while Hugh Kennedy's bagpipes wailed from the rock above. But Carlat had been their refuge, too, when the owners of Montsalvy had been proscribed by the King and their castle reduced to ruins by Valette's mercenaries. And since that time a saint had passed by there to add sanctity and glory to the impregnable keep. Bonne de Berry, dowager Countess of Armagnac, divided her time between the castle and her winter residence at Rodez, and the whole region benefited from her presence. She had returned there at Christmas and had died there, on the last day of December, amid the grief of all who had struggled over the bad, snow-covered roads to follow her to her last resting place in the Franciscan Convent at Rodez.

Before she died, the Countess Bonne had given Carlat, which was her own personal property, to her youngest son, the Count of Pardiac, that same Cadet Bernard whose friendship for the Montsalvys had never failed. Now Bernard's wife, Eléonore de Bourbon, had made her home in the castle and held it during her husband's frequent absences.

Even if Cadet Bernard was not at home, Countess Eléonore would send help to the Montsalvys without a moment's hesitation if she knew they were in danger, for all that she was sister to Charles of Bourbon. When she had married Bernard, she had adopted his friendships and his hatreds.

'She must be told of this at once,' the Abbot agreed.

Catherine realised that, for the last few moments at least, she had been thinking aloud. 'The men of Armagnac could take the Apchiers in the rear and sweep them up like autumn leaves. Count Bernard maintains a strong garrison at Carlat, and they could spare a few companies of archers without leaving the castle undefended.'

'Good,' Antoine Couderc said. 'Then a messenger must be sent there, this very night! It's still possible to get out by the south gate before the town is surrounded. I'll go.'

He was already on his feet, so tall and black that it seemed as if a small mountain had sprouted suddenly in the middle of the room. Courage and eagerness flowed from him like milk boiling over in the pan. However, Noël Cairou, the weaver, forestalled him.

'No, not you, 'Toine! A besieged town needs a smith. We must have weapons! But we can do without a weaver for a while. I'll go!'

There were more protests. They all wanted to go, all of them eager in their generous natures to do something for their little town. Everyone was talking at once, until Abbot Bernard quelled the din with a lift of his hand.

'Be quiet! None of you shall go. I shall send one of our brothers. They all know the country well and can easily cover the eight leagues between here and Carlat. Moreover, if by any mischance our messenger should be caught by the Apchiers, his habit should, I think, protect him from the worst. Brother Anthime, go you to the abbey and ask Brother Amable to come here. Dame Catherine shall give him a note for the Countess and he can set out at once. It is a dark night. No-one will see him. He can leave by the postern gate.'

Everyone concurred in this solution, and gave it their voice with something like joyfulness. As soon as the decision had been taken, the intangible fear that, for all their courage, had clutched at their hearts, had vanished as if by magic.

The entrance of Sara with the traditional spiced wine, followed by a girl bearing cups, put the final touches to restoring a general cheerfulness. They relaxed and drank to Montsalvy, the châtelaine and the people of Carlat.

At that moment, the Wolf of Gévaudan shrank to the dimensions of a bad dream that fades with action. When everyone had been served, Sara went across to where Catherine, a little apart, was standing at a bronze lectern writing her letter.

'I'd never have thought to find them so merry with the enemy at our gates! Whatever's got into them?'

'Hope, merely,' the young woman said, smiling. 'We've decided to send a monk to Carlat to ask for help. And you know they'll not refuse it to us.'

'If he can only get there! That Bérault must have spies out everywhere! Aren't you afraid of your monk falling into his hands?'

'Brother Amable is cunning and fleet of foot. He can look after himself -- and it's a risk we have to take, my poor Sara. We have no choice.'

A moment later, the black-robed messenger was kneeling at the Abbot's feet to receive both Catherine's letter and a last blessing from his superior. Then Abbot Bernard and Nicolas Barral went with him to the postern gate, while the other councillors of Montsalvy returned to their homes and Catherine made up her mind at last to retire with Sara to her own apartments.

She entered her own chamber with a feeling of profound relief. The room was light and cheerful, and warm too, thanks to the better part of a chestnut trunk burning in the hearth. The leaded panes of coloured glass in the tall, narrow windows shone like precious stones in the light of the great fires burning in the castle courtyard. There were fires on the ramparts, too, as there would be every night as long as the siege lasted, to keep the pitch and oil hot against the chance of a surprise assault. Even now, the night air was full of their acrid smell, overcoming the scents of the earth.

Catherine was comforted, without quite knowing why, to find herself in her own place. Perhaps it was just because within these walls, and with her own people, she felt safe.

Sitting on the vast bed, she pulled off her tight headdress and, loosening her braids, began running her hands through the mass of her hair. Her head ached. She felt as if all her anxieties were crammed into an iron helmet, and the action gave her a childish feeling of release.

'Would you like me to plait it again for you?' Sara asked, coming back into the room with a bowl of hot milk cradled between her hands.

'No, no!' the young woman said quickly. 'I'm much too tired to go down to the Great Hall to sup. I'll go and kiss the children good night and then I'm going to bed and you can bring me something to eat.'

'Does your head still ache?'

'Yes, but with good reason this time, don't you think?'

Instead of answering, Sara took Catherine's head between her big brown hands and, plunging them into the silky thickness of her hair, began gently massaging the throbbing temples and skull.

A little frown creased her forehead, betraying the uneasiness she felt. Since Arnaud's departure, Catherine had been suffering frequent headaches. It was true that Sara could usually dispel them by this simple means, but even so, she did not like them, for they recalled unpleasant memories. As a young girl, Catherine had almost died from an attack of a mysterious brain fever, brought on by a terrible nervous shock, and Sara lived in dread of a recurrence.

For the moment, however, Catherine sat like a child, her eyes closed and her head relaxed, only sorry that her nurse's skilled fingers could not root out the thought that haunted her. Why had Bérault d'Apchier said that Arnaud would not return? Was it, as the Abbot had said, mere boasting? Or was there some real foundation for that horrible threat?

'Try to make your mind a blank for a moment,' Sara murmured, 'or I can't take away the pain.'

Since she had come to Montsalvy, the one-time gypsy had grown wiser still in the arts of healing human suffering. Medicinal herbs grew plentifully on the plateau, in the forests with their wealth of fungi of every kind, and in the deep, overgrown combes. And little by little Black Sara had become well known for two or three leagues round. Such was her reputation, in fact, that it had earned her the enmity of the local witch, a taciturn, cat-eyed old woman called La Ratapennade – meaning 'the Bat' – whose hovel lay deep in the woods toward Aubespeyre.

La Ratapennade, whose age and true name no-one now remembered, lived there in the best traditions of her kind, with an owl, a crow and a fair collection of toads and snakes whose venom served her as a base for some of her more sinister potions. It went without saying that the people of Montsalvy lived in terror of this old woman, whose malevolence was forever afflicting them with a whole range of disasters ranging from sickness in their cattle to impotence in their young men. But they took care not to ill-use her. Even Arnaud hesitated to do anything to her, in spite of the curses she had been known to put on those who incurred her displeasure, and he could only look forward to the day when old age would carry the crone to a better world where she could do no more harm to anyone. Meanwhile, although the villagers avoided the road that led to her dwelling, yet it would often happen that a basket of eggs, a loaf of bread or a fowl would be left there, by the turning, as a sop to one whose counsel might be sought, from a safe distance, on some moonless night.

People said she was rich and had a fortune hidden in the ditch along with her snakes, but such was the fear she inspired that not even the most desperate villain would have dared to try to rob her of it. There were even some who were her friends, like that very Gervais whom the châtelaine had driven out and who had now returned to bring ruin on Montsalvy.

As for the Abbot Bernard, he frowned at the mention of the witch's name but only sighed and crossed himself. Every attempt of his to bring the old woman back to God had failed, and he knew that there was little he could do against the strange powers of this creature of Satan, except to recommend his flock to trust instead to the infinitely more wholesome talent of Sara, who was gradually coming to figure as the physician of the district.

Catherine had finally succeeded in 'making her mind a blank' and her headache was passing. Then Sara said quietly:

'Did you know the page was not back yet?'

The châtelaine started and opened her eyes, her heart missing a beat. 'Bérenger?' she cried. 'He's not back? But why didn't you tell me before this?'

'I thought you knew … and in any case, I don't see what you can do at this hour …'

'Not back! Oh, my God!' Catherine exclaimed in horror. 'Where can the boy have got to? I confess I'd quite forgotten him …'

She had slipped away from Sara and was pacing up and down the room, hugging herself with her folded arms as if she were cold. 'Not back! she murmured to herself again, as if she could not quite comprehend it yet, and then added: 'But where can he be?'

She said no more after that, not daring to put into words the fear that had assailed her, lest her page should be in the Apchiers' hands.

Ever since he had first come to Montsalvy, six months before, Bérenger de Roquemaurel had seemed to bring a breath of fresh air into the house. The new page belonged to the family of Roquemaurel of Cassaniouze, whose castle, somewhat dilapidated but still strong, stood frowning like an old burgrave over the deep chasm of the Lot.

Bérenger, at 14 years old, belonged to a type as yet unknown among the nobility of Auvergne and the Rouergue. He believed that life was to be lived for something other than fighting and boar-hunts, family squabbles and extravagant feasts at which everyone gorged themselves to bursting and then drank themselves under the table. He was a dreamer, imaginative and peace-loving, but he was the only one of his kind for miles around, and no-one had any idea where he got it from.

His father, Ausbert, a great drinker of barley beer and a great wielder of the mace, forever on the look-out for a head to break or a petticoat to lift, was a man who, for strength and violence, might have stood as a model for the ancient Gaulish god Tutates, wielder of the thunderbolt. But he had met his match before the walls of La Charité-sur-Loire in the mercenary Perrinet Gressard. A well-aimed arrow had stilled his restless body for good.

His two elder sons, Amaury and Renaud, were a pair of straw-haired giants good for nothing but fighting and drinking. Their normal state was a kind of jovial boisterousness, and the whole valley spoke with a mixture of awe and terror of their massive drinking bouts, their occasional legendary feats of arms and the wicked pranks they played the year round on the canons of Saint Projet.

United by a fraternal solidarity that amounted to collusion and was as good as love, the Roquemaurel brothers had only three ideas in their heads: devotion to their mother, Mathilde, a colourful virago who reminded Catherine a good deal of her friend Ermengarde de Châteauvillain; attachment to their own castle; and a ferocious hatred for their cousins of Vieillevie, 'a grasping brood who'd skin a flea for its hide,' and whose monopoly of the river ferries enabled them to cheat and exploit travellers. For the moment, however, the two brothers had entrusted Roquemaurel to Dame Mathilde, enlisted their lances under the banner of Montsalvy and gone off happily to show 'those scurvy dogs of Paris, more English than the English, what the nobles of Auvergne can do!'

Beside these larger-than-life figures, Bérenger was like the ugly duckling. He resembled them in nothing but his size, for he too was big and strong for his age. In other respects, he was brown as a chestnut with a gentle, happy, boyish face, and he made no secret of his dislike of the business of arms. His tastes, and everyone at Roquemaurel wondered where on earth he could have got them, were for music and poetry and nature, and his hero was his namesake, the troubadour Bérenger de Palasol. Since he was equally set against the cloister (Bérenger had made this quite plain to them by coolly setting fire to the monastery where they had taken him in the hope of making a bishop of him, in order to regain his liberty), his family had agreed to despatch him to Arnaud of Montsalvy, whose reputation as a warrior was well established, in a last effort to let him make something of himself.

Montsalvy had agreed, but as he was about to leave for Paris, he had put off young Roquemaurel's military education until his return. He had simply handed him over to his old master of arms, Donat de Galauba, to get some rudimentary idea of the knightly life hammered into his independent head.

'There will be other campaigns,' Arnaud had told his wife. 'The battle for Paris is going to be too fierce to take a boy as wholly inexperienced as he is.'

Bérenger had therefore remained at Montsalvy, where he passed his days pleasantly enough, roaming the countryside like a minstrel with his lute on his back, composing ballads and songs that he sang to Catherine in the evenings. From the very first day, he had counted the châtelaine his official muse; a role for which her beauty and charm made her naturally fitted. But in his heart of hearts, Bérenger's secret adoration was given to his cousin, Hauvette de Montarnal, 15 years old and frail as a lily. It was for her sake, in fact, that he had fought so fiercely against the life of a monk, although he would have let his tongue be torn out rather than confess it. For Montarnal and Vieillevie were virtually all one, since the famous river crossing lay between the ramparts of the one and the tower of the other, forming a two-way traffic, and Bérenger had sensibly decided to wait awhile before informing his family of this latest eccentricity of his. As things stood just then, his back would undoubtedly have suffered for it, since Mathilde, Renaud and Amaury were all equally heavy-handed. So he waited philosophically for better days, and meanwhile his wanderings took him often enough towards the deep valley of the Lot.

Catherine de Montsalvy was fond of her page, just as he was. He reminded her a little of her childhood friend Landry Pigasse. Moreover, the songs he composed were as fresh as a bunch of primroses. She could not think how she had managed to forget about Bérenger all this time. The dreadful shock of the early evening was some excuse, but not, she judged, sufficient, and if the unfortunate lad had fallen into the hands of Apchier's soldiery, she dreaded to think what might be happening to him.

She repeated her anxious question as she stood over Sara, who was busy delving in a chest for the gown of plain grey velvet trimmed with miniver that she would put on Catherine after getting her out of her wet dress.

'Where can he be? He spends all day rambling about the woods and never says where he is going.'

'He nearly always goes in the same direction,' Sara observed dispassionately, all her attention concentrated on shaking out the gown. 'Down to the valley.'

'That's true. He likes fishing in the river.'

'Huh! That's as may be. But it's an odd kind of fishing. He hardly ever brings back a fish, but he often enough comes home as wet as if he'd thrown himself in the river. In any case, he should have been back long before this. Géraude sounded the alarm clear enough. Though it's a fair step to the valley.'

Catherine's eyes narrowed to two slits of violet. 'What are you trying to tell me, Sara? This is no time for riddles.'

The gypsy gave a shrug. 'That the Montarnal child has a fire in her eyes, for all she keeps her lids so modestly lowered, and something under her gown to make the most starry-eyed dreamer lose his head; and that your page may amuse himself by singing the praises of Dame Catherine's violet eyes – for which he may yet come in for the flat of Messire Arnaud's hand – but all the same, he's in love, and no good will come of it. If ever the Lord of Montarnal comes to hear of this sudden passion for the River Lot, that boy may well find himself deeper in it than he bargained for!'

'Bérenger in love? Why didn't you tell me this before?'

'Because much good it would have done! At the mention of the word love, you melt like butter in the sun. But today the matter is more serious. The boy can't have had time to reach here …'

'Go and fetch me Nicolas Barral! We have to try to find him tonight! By tomorrow, the town will be completely surrounded and Bérenger will never be able to get in.'

Sara did not argue but went in search of the captain, whom she found by one of the watchfires on the walls. But Nicolas, when summoned to the châtelaine's presence, declared himself powerless to hunt for the page just then.

'It's too dark out there, Dame Catherine. The Devil himself would never find him. All I can do is leave someone on guard at the postern. The page will call out to have it opened. But if he isn't back by first light, I'll see if I can try a brief sortie to cover the ground nearest the gate. Are you quite sure he went toward Vieillevie?'

'That's what Sara says.'

'Then it must be so. She's never mistaken.'

This was said with a seriousness and a degree of respect that made Catherine open her eyes. This was certainly a day of surprises! Was she about to discover that her captain of archers was in love with Sara? It would not be so astonishing, after all. Maturity had given the woman she thought of as her nurse a generous and shapely fullness of body that might well appeal to these lusty, mountain-bred men.

Nicolas returned to his post, and Catherine allowed Sara to strip off her dress and shift and the long band of fine linen she was in the habit of binding round her breasts for riding. Then, with a little pleasurable shiver, she slipped into the long, fur-lined gown and felt its silky softness caress her bare skin from neck to ankle. It was the most comfortable of all her gowns, and the one she liked to wear after a long day hunting or out in the open air. Yet, fond of it as she was, tonight she wished almost at once that she had not put it on. That gown, with the daring slit up one side, was made for lovers' meetings, and it held too many memories for her – too many and too sweet! The sensual touch of the fur against her skin brought back, almost unbearably, the memory of another touch, while caught up in the velvet folds along with her own woman's scent there was another; a man's smell that, tonight, was too poignant. The old boar had dared to tell her 'he' would never return – that never again would this room be haunted by his voice, his hands, his body ...

'Take it off!' Catherine cried suddenly. 'Give me another gown – whichever you like. I don't care. Only, not this one!'

She gritted her teeth to keep herself from screaming and shut her eyes tightly to keep back the tears, her whole body shaken suddenly in an agony of love and fear. She wanted to rush out of the room, fling herself on her horse and gallop away into the night, away from her fears; to gallop without halt or stay until she escaped from the nightmare that held her prisoner; to gallop until she found her husband and could fall into his arms, even if it were only to die there.

But already Sara had started forward, horrified by her cry, and almost snatched off the grey gown. For a second, she stared into the younger woman's tense face as she stood there, naked and trembling. No explanations were needed: Sara knew her too well.

She reached out for the soft shoulders, shuddering in the grip of a spasm of nerves, and shook them gently. 'Hush, now,' she said, with a deep tenderness, and then, with sudden force: 'He will come back!'

'No – no! Bérault d'Apchier flung it in my teeth. I'll never see Arnaud again! That's why he dared to attack us.'

'It's a clumsy ruse to trap you, and you ought to be ashamed of yourself for falling into it! He will come back, I tell you. I! You've more to suffer yet through him.'

'Suffer? If he comes back alive, how can he make me suffer?'

But Sara would say no more. Instead, she dropped over Catherine's head a robe made of the thick white woollen stuff, woven by the women of Valenciennes, for which the Lady of Montsalvy never wanted, thanks to the good offices of the merchant, Jacques Cœur. Gradually, as she drew the silken ties briskly together at neck and wrists, Sara felt Catherine's momentary panic subsiding.

'There. Now you look like a nun! Just what is needed tonight,' Sara said, laughing. 'Now go and kiss the little ones goodnight. I'll bring you some chestnuts seethed in milk, flavoured with vanilla and lots of sugar – that is, if Michel hasn't eaten it all.'

Soothed, Catherine suffered herself to be led into the adjoining room, which belonged to Sara and the children. There was a fire burning there, and also, beside the big red-curtained bed, a tiny oil lamp, its flame glowing softly on the fair head of the little boy who lay fast asleep, lost in the vast expanse of snowy sheets and purple counterpane. His thick blond curls shone like gold shavings, and his long, dark lashes softly shadowed his round cheeks. The thumb he had been sucking when he went to sleep had fallen out, leaving his mouth slightly open, and his other hand lay on the sheet, the small, rosy fingers spread wide, like a starfish.

Her heart melting with love, Catherine picked up the small wrist and kissed it softly before tucking it carefully back underneath the warm blankets. Then she turned to her daughter.

On the other side of the nightlight, in the big chestnut wood cradle, rocked by hand, in which Arnaud himself had uttered his first cries, ten-month-old Isabelle de Montsalvy slept with enormous dignity. She looked astonishingly like her father. She had the same black eyes. Her tiny, dimpled face already bore all the more commanding features of her father's countenance, and the long, silky lock that curled from under her cap of fine lawn almost down to her little nose was a most beautiful black. Isabelle lay with clenched fists, sleeping with immense concentration, but her appearance was misleading, for awake she was the happiest of babies, the pet of the whole household, a fact of which she took full advantage. It was clear already that she was a girl who would know how to look after herself, and if ever, gazing into her son's dreamy eyes, Catherine was troubled by a passing fear that he was too soft and gentle, she was amply reassured as far as Isabelle was concerned. The saucy look in her eye spoke for her.

Catherine knelt down between the bed and the cradle and prayed, passionately, that no danger might come near this room or touch those beds and the childish heads entrusted to her sole protection. 'Oh God, grant, I implore you, grant that nothing may happen to them! They are so little! And war is such a dreadful, cruel thing – and so blind!'

Her prayer overflowed the confines of the room to take in all the mothers and children who had come that evening, at the summons of the bell, to seek shelter for their fragile lives within the walls of Montsalvy. She had given orders for them to be housed as well and as comfortably as possible, feeling herself a sister to those other mothers. Châtelaine or shepherdess, there was the same old fear in the vitals in the face of weapons and the idea of children in danger. Men might feel that fear too, but it was not as strong as their inbred love of battle.

The calls of the watchmen, ringing from tower to tower, came to her like an answer to her anguished appeal. Nicolas's men were keeping good watch on the town walls, and before long, perhaps, the Count of Armagnac's men-at-arms would come riding up to drive away the predatory wolves. Bérault d'Apchier's motley horde would never stand against them, and the mothers of Montsalvy might once more sleep in peace and, forgetting their alarms, go back to their homes in safety.

On which comforting thought, Catherine crossed herself for the last time and, rising, left the children's room.

2: Azalaïs

'The messenger ...! He's dead! They've killed him!'

Sara's anguished voice tore through the last remaining mists of sleep as Catherine lingered in her warm bed.

Instantly, the châtelaine was plunged back into the midst of the grim world from which she had struggled so to find release the night before. She opened her eyes to see Sara's face bent over her, so petrified with horror that it resembled grey granite. Catherine spoke with an effort:

'What did you say?'

'Brother Amable has been murdered! Bérault's men have taken him and slain him!'

'How do you know? Have they found his body?'

Sara uttered a derisive snort. 'His body? The whole town's crowding to the walls to look at it this very moment! Bérault d'Apchier's hanged him from a butcher's hook at the corner of the first house in Barri Saint Antoine! Poor wretch, he's stuck as full of arrows as a hedgehog – and your letter pinned to his chest with one of them.'

Sara's legs seemed to give way suddenly with the shock, and the poor woman sank down on to a chest, wringing her trembling hands together.

'They are devils!' she groaned, in a voice that was not her own, a voice so altered that Catherine did not recognise it. 'Instruments of Satan! They will devour us all ...'

The other woman was already out of bed and rummaging in a coffer for a dress. She paused for a moment and stared with disbelief. 'Sara! You're afraid! You!'

It was not a question but an appalled statement of fact. Never in all her life, even in their worst moments, could Catherine recall having seen her old friend look like this, with this ashen face, these trembling lips and this hunted expression. It was so wildly unexpected that she felt herself wavering also, for if her chief support were to fail, how would she sustain her own courage through the darkest hours?

Herself on the verge of tears, she repeated the words, desperately, as if she could not yet quite believe them: 'You're afraid!'

Sara hid her face in her hands and wept, as much from shame as from terror. 'Forgive me! I know I'm a disappointment to you …. but if you had seen …'

'I'm going to see!'

In a sudden burst of fury, Catherine slipped on a dress at random, thrust her feet into a pair of soft boots, and without even pausing to bind up her hair, ran from the room and down the broad spiral stair, out into the open air.

She swept like a gale through the vast courtyard, the pale mass of her hair billowing down her back, her eyes unseeing, and almost knocked over Josse, who was just coming in. She did not hear what he said to her. She was already out in the street, running as fast as she could, with her skirts caught up as high as her knees to speed her progress. She was borne up by a fury greater than anything she had ever experienced. She did not know why she was running, or what she meant to do, but she was driven onward by an unknown force that dragged her out of her usual self and turned her into a different creature, full of rage and violence, to be satisfied only by blood.

Storming up onto the walls, she broke through the silent people thronging the battlements, who gave way instinctively before her. The crowd here was strange to her also: every face was tinged with the same grey as Sara's, every eye was blank and every voice was silent.

Someone muttered on a curious croaking note: 'The man of God! He's dead!'

Dead he was, indeed, just as Sara had said. The unhappy monk dangled from his butcher's hook, stuck full of arrows, a grotesque and terrifying figure in his black habit, stiff with dried blood, with his big feet, the toes contracted in his dying spasm. Those few words uttered by an anonymous voice brought home to the Lady of Montsalvy the terror that held her people rigid. The victim was a man of God. The enormity of the crime was beyond all comprehension. It left these simple souls numbed and speechless.

A couple of soldiers were loitering near the corpse, looking up at the stunned town, smirking and picking their teeth.

Beside herself, Catherine screamed into the thin, cutting wind of the plateau: 'Yes, he's dead! They've killed him for us! And are you going to stand there and do nothing?'

Before anyone could guess what she meant to do, she had snatched a bow from one of the guards. Anger gave her strength to bend it easily, stiff as it was, and the arrow, hissing like an angry snake, flew straight for the throat of one of the two mercenaries. He fell, blood choking his scream. She reached for a second arrow for the other man, but Josse got there before her, and that man too dropped beside his companion.

The people of Montsalvy woke at that. The evil spell of fear was gone. A stream of arrows and crossbow bolts flew from the walls, forcing those of Apchier's men who had come running up to fall back to their camp. In a little while the open space that lay between the walls and the besiegers' camp was empty but for the remains of the murdered monk and his guards.

'Cease firing!' Josse cried. 'No sense in wasting ammunition.'

'But we can't leave poor Brother Amable hanging there to rot under our very noses, like a trapped fox left to moulder in the wind and rain!' a voice protested indignantly.

Gauberte thrust her way through the crowd like a ship in a high sea, her great coif billowing like a sail. She seemed to have constituted herself the town's spokeswoman, like the chorus in an ancient play, and she towered over Catherine, taller by a head – which, already large enough in itself, appeared still more so by reason of the black braids, each as thick as a child's arm, coiled over her ears. Facing the châtelaine in her favourite stance, hands on hips, the linen weaver went on:

'He was a holy man, as gentle as God's own lamb, and he died for us! He deserves to have a decent Christian burial, not to be scoffed at by those impudent scoundrels, and if no-one will go and cut him down, I swear on my mother's crucifix I'll go myself! Just let someone open the gate for me!'

Catherine hesitated. To sally forth from the walls, even in some strength, meant risking a battle in the open, in which the besieged would be at a disadvantage. In particular, there was the danger that the enemy would overrun them and sweep on into the town. On the other hand, Gauberte was right: they could not leave the monk's body in the hands of his killers without shame.

Sensing that she was about to carry her point, Gauberte pressed it home, half-beseeching, half-demanding. 'Well, m'lady? What are we to do? Will you …'

She was interrupted by the deep voice of the monastery bell ringing the knell for the dead. It broke through Catherine's deliberations. Everyone turned automatically to look down into the town, from whence, at the same time, rose the sound of a funeral chant.

'The monks!' someone said. 'Look! They are all coming out!'

It was true. Two by two, the Augustinian friars of the abbey were making their way toward the St Antoine Gate. Their hands folded inside their wide sleeves, hoods pulled down over their faces so that only their mouths were visible, they were chanting aloud the prayers for the dead. At their head, flanked by two brothers bearing tall wax candles, walked the Abbot Bernard. Wearing a purple chasuble embroidered with a silver cross, his mitre on his head, he held aloft in both hands the monstrance, the host shining in a sunburst of golden rays. All knelt at his approach.

Reaching the lowered portcullis, the abbot paused in his chanting and made a sign for it to be raised. Up on the walls, all eyes were turned questioningly to Catherine.

This time, she did not hesitate. One did not bar the way to God!

'Open!' she cried. 'But let the archers on the walls stand ready to shoot. Arm the crossbows. If anyone makes a move toward the Abbot, fire without waiting for the command!'

The grinding of the portcullis going up rasped everyone's nerves. It was taking a great risk. Would men who had murdered the monk in cold blood fall back before the Holy Sacrament? In another moment, perhaps, the enemy might be upon them. They would fall, shrieking, on the defenceless town of Montsalvy, every man sheathing his weapon in living flesh. The funeral chant would be followed almost at once by the screams of the dying, and then it would be the end ... With a roar like the crack of doom, the drawbridge dropped into place.

Catherine reached quickly for the bow that she had laid down on the parapet beside her. Coolly, she fitted an arrow to it.

'If Bérault d'Apchier shows himself, he is mine,' she said, in a voice of perfect calm.

Resting one foot on the low stone embrasure, she drew back the bowstring slowly, leaving herself a fair margin. The slim ash bow bent slightly. She stayed like that, waiting.

The camp below was curiously silent. No-one was to be seen there. Nothing stirred. Only, behind the palisade of branches covered with fresh hides that the attackers had erected as a protection for their tents, there was a sense of men watching with keen eyes and bated breath. The bodies of the two soldiers lay spread-eagled on the ground not far from the dead monk.

The procession crossed the bridge. The chanting died away for a moment, muffled by the walls and by the barbican, and then rolled out again in the full forecast of the divine wrath to come.

'*Dies irae, dies illa*
'*Solve saeclum in favilla ...*'

But they had ceased to advance. At a word from their superior, they even seemed to be retiring.

'Back inside the walls. Take up the drawbridge!'

Catherine's bowstring slackened and she peered down in amazement. Outside the walls now were none but the Abbot, a thin, fragile figure holding both hands uplifted to the grey sky bearing a golden sun, and three monks, two of whom carried a litter and the third a ladder. And, as the abbot had commanded, the drawbridge was being slowly raised.

'He won't endanger the town,' Josse breathed, standing, grim-faced, at Catherine's shoulder. 'But it's a fearful risk!'

'Go and tell them not to raise the bridge. We, too, should share the risks!

And post armed men at the windows of the houses nearest the gates!'

The one-time vagrant sped away, and Catherine turned back to the Abbot.

He was walking forward, unhurriedly, the litter at his heels. The wind flattened the amethyst-coloured chasuble against his thin body, like a flag against a flagpole. Overhead, the clouds, driven by the west wind, scudded toward the lonely wastes of the Aubrac, away beyond the thundering gorge of the Truyère, eternally shrouded in mist. They raced so low over the plateau that it seemed they were trying to hide the audacious little priest who would go out to hunt a wild beast with a human face, carrying a bright golden sun between his hands.

As he reached the corpse, there was a movement inside the camp. A massive figure appeared at a gap in the palisade and stood there, motionless. Catherine recognised it for Bérault d'Apchier and swung her bow a little toward him, for he was armed. His long arms rested on a great naked sword, but he came no farther forward.

'Begone, Abbot!' he cried. 'And meddle not with my justice!'

'This is one of my sons whom you have put to death, Bérault d'Apchier. I come to claim him! And this is your God, nailed to the cross by such as you. Strike at it if you dare, and then seek out some forest deep enough, some wilderness secret enough to hide your wickedness and shame, for you will be accursed on Earth and in heaven to the end of time! Come, then! What are you waiting for…? See! It is gold I bear; the gold you love and have come so far to find! It is within your grasp! You have only to raise that great sword that serves you so well.'

Leaving the three monks to cut down the body and arrange it, as best they could given the arrows projecting from it, on the litter, the Abbot advanced boldly toward the camp, still holding aloft the monstrance. But as he advanced, so the aged ruffian seemed to shrink before him like the devil in the old story, dwarfed by a stoup of holy water. He was shaking like an autumn leaf in the wind, and for a moment it looked as though he would yield to the old, half-forgotten forces of his childhood and bend those knees grown stiff with pride and rheumatism. Then, behind him, there appeared the figures of his sons, the bastard, and the sardonic face of Gervais Malfrat. Pride kept him upright despite his fears of the hereafter – which, at his age, was creeping uncomfortably close.

'Begone, Abbot!' he said again, but in a very different tone that was not without a hint of weariness. 'Take your monk! All cats are grey in the dark. He was dead by the time we saw what he was. But don't think I'm sorry! We'll meet again one day, and you will not have God to shield you!'

'I shall always have Him for my shield, for each day my hands touch His Body and His Blood. He is with me even when you cannot see Him, as He is with this peaceful town you would destroy.'

'Destroy? No! I would make it mine, and mine it shall be!'

But the Abbot Bernard was no longer listening. He had folded the golden sun to his breast as a mother shelters her child, and he held it there with both hands crossed over it as he retraced his steps toward the silent town, the people of which had observed the scene with breathless anxiety.

The monks and their litter passed slowly through the gate. Last of all came the Abbot, his head bent in prayer over the holy thing he carried. The gates closed after them.

None of those at the entrance to the camp had stirred, but in the town a great clamour of joy and relief broke out as soon as the portcullis was down.

'Shoot, Dame Catherine,' Josse whispered. 'You have the stinking dog in range! Shoot and rid us of him!'

She gave a sigh of mingled weariness and regret and laid her bow aside with a shake of her head. 'No. The Abbot would never forgive me. Bérault did not touch him. Perhaps, if he still fears God, he may not fight us after all. Let him think it over …'

'Think? He and his men are greedy for meat and for gold. They'll not give up until they're satisfied. If you think they'll go away, you're much mistaken, Dame Catherine. Believe me, they'll attack!'

'Well, let them. We'll drive them off somehow.'

But the attack did not come that day. Bérault d'Apchier used his time completing the ringing of the town. All morning, the people of Montsalvy watched the enemy slowly encircling it, weaving through the rocks and scrub like steel snakes, setting a guard on all the roads, with more tents and more cooking fires in sheltered nooks and crannies. The foot soldiers dug themselves in there, and men were hard at work in the woods that clothed the hillsides, felling trees to make ladders and making bundles of brushwood to cast into the ditches. The handsome pines that had stood guard so proudly over the threatened town lost their crowns and fell with a rending crash, filling the air all around with a warm, resinous smell like springtime.

Catherine spent most of the day on the walls. With Josse Rallard and Nicolas Barral hard on her heels, she went the rounds of the battlements and watchtowers, inspecting the hoardings, checking the reserves of stones, arrows, wood and weapons and the various likely points of attack.

Abbot Bernard's bold success in recovering the body of their unlucky messenger at the risk of his own life had heartened them all and steeled their resolution, supposing anything of the kind was needed. The deep, almost religious horror that had held them for a moment had disappeared. They all felt in their hearts that when the time came God would be fighting on their side, and Catherine especially was now confident that it would not be hard for them to get the better of their enemies.

Only one thing really remained to trouble her, and this was the continued absence of her page, but she trusted vaguely that he might have had time and sense enough to seek shelter in his mother's house.

Sara made up for her moment of weakness by throwing herself more than ever into the work of the castle, supervising the normal running of the household and at the same time seeing to it that the refugees were provided with everything that could ease the discomfort of their temporary homelessness. She had even offered the Abbot her assistance in laying out Brother Amable's body for burial, for she was skilled in the removal of arrowheads with the aid of oil and a knife. Now, washed in wine and shrouded in a length of fine linen, the broken body was lying in the crypt of the abbey church awaiting interment later that night, in order that none of the monks should be prevented from taking their share, with the other inhabitants, in the defence of the town during the day.

In a little while, there would be nothing left for the beleaguered garrison to do but wait and watch the enemy's movements. Little by little, the town settled down to a state of siege, and the inhabitants began to go about their normal business again, except when their presence was required to man the walls.

While Guillaume Bastide, the baker, went off to fire an extra ovenful of loaves for the refugees, Gauberte, at the well, was giving the townswomen and their country cousins a good talking-to, for she had noticed in one or two of them a tendency to bewail their fate and the failure of the hopes they had placed in Brother Amable.

'So the monk was caught,' Noël Cairou's wife conceded. 'That doesn't mean we'll get no help, for all that. For one thing, we'll certainly try to get another messenger through; and, for another, it'll be a fine thing if the folk at Carlat don't get to hear of our troubles. And, God be thanked, we're not such fools, nor so ill-provided, that we can't hold out for weeks against these wicked beasts.'

'We're short of men,' objected Marie Bru, one of the refugees who could not forget that she had been forced to leave her little farm at Sainte-Font to the mercy of the marauders. 'And those villains are a strong force, well-armed and accustomed to fighting.'

Gauberte looked down her nose at the dissenter and her coif quivered ominously. 'We may be short of men, but we've stout walls, as you were glad enough to find, eh, Marie? We've weapons, too, and then there are us women! I'll tell you one thing. When I saw that scoundrel Gervais Malfrat, who ruined my niece, Bertille, strutting alongside that old brigand, I was ripe for murder! So they won't have to ask me twice if they ever need me on the walls, and I'll do my share of killing, I can promise you!'

'It's all very well for you; you're as strong as an ox,' Marie said, refusing to be carried away by the prevailing mood of heroism. 'I couldn't even lift a sword!'

'And who said anything about swords, little simpleton? When you're harvesting the rye at Sainte-Font, you can manage a sickle well enough, can't you?'

'Yes, but ...'

'A bill weighs no more and is easier to use. You just stick it in and push, that's all!'

This brilliant exposition was an instant success with the women. As they drew up their buckets of water they all fell to speculating on the type of weapons that would suit them best, and when Catherine joined them on her way down from the walls, the linen coifs were swelling with warlike suggestions. Only one had not joined in, and she stood leaning against the carved stone rim of the well, listening with a faint smile on her lips.

She was a tall, dark girl and might well have been called the belle of the town, although in fact she was not altogether a local girl. Her skin had the golden smoothness of a nectarine, and the velvety blackness of her eyes made one think of Spain.

She had come to Montsalvy some ten years earlier with her mother, a widowed lacemaker from Le Puy, who had married, as her second husband, the carpenter Augustin Fabre. The mother's health was never good, and an unusually severe winter had soon carried her off, but Augustin had grown fond of the little girl and reared her as his own daughter. Indeed, it was hard to see what would have become of her otherwise. As time went by, Azalaïs had come to take her mother's place. She was an excellent housekeeper and, having learned from the dead woman the delicate art of manipulating the tiny bobbins to create their airy wonders, it was natural for her to carry on her mother's work. It was not long before she surpassed her teacher, and in time she acquired the patronage of every castle or house of any size in the district. Noble ladies even came from Aurillac to buy her lace, with an agreeable sense of procuring contraband goods, since in this way they could have all the skill of the lacemakers of Velay on their own doorsteps, without the trouble and expense of going to Le Puy and dealing with the middlemen who controlled the whole of the workers' output.

The Lady of Montsalvy, more than any, had ordered numerous beautiful pieces from her, but while she admired the girl's skill and artistry, the lacemaker was pretty well the only woman in the town with whom her relations were impersonal to the point of coolness. Not that any of the women of Montsalvy liked Azalaïs. It may have been the bold way she had of eyeing the boys and even married men, or the low, sweet chuckle, like the cooing of a turtle dove, that would escape her when the young men crowded round to lead her into the dance, or possibly again the way she would let the neck of her gown gape lower than was proper on hot days as she sat at her window, bent over her pillow of red silk.

Beautiful, clever and by no means penniless, Azalaïs might have married a hundred times over, but although she was evidently not indifferent to them, none of the young men who wooed had ever won her.

'I'll give myself only for love, and the man I love must be worthy of me; I mean he must be ready to do anything for my sake,' she would say with a droop of the dusky lashes that many a youth had dreamed of underlining with the dark shadows of sleepless nights.

In this way, she had reached the age of 25 and remained unwed. Augustin encouraged her in this resolve, fearful of losing his housekeeper if she were to marry.

'None of these hobbledehoys is worthy of you, my pearl,' he would tell her, stroking her velvet cheek. 'You deserve a lord!'

Naturally enough, this kind of talk made Augustin not at all popular with the young men, but the old ones only shrugged philosophically and counselled patience. The day would come when Azalaïs, tired of waiting for her lord, would see that time was running out and youth could not last forever. Then she would make up her mind to take a husband.

Catherine, like everyone else, had heard of the matrimonial dreams that Augustin cherished for his adopted daughter. Donatienne, old Sébastien's sober spouse, had reported them with a good deal of indignation, but Josse's wife, Marie Rallard, who had acquired an astonishing understanding of the female heart during the time she had spent in the harem in Granada, went straight to the point.

'Augustin says "a lord" – but his daughter thinks of Messire Arnaud. You've only to see how she looks at him when he rides through the town. Like a cat at a cream pot! And when she makes her curtsy to him, it's a wonder she doesn't fall flat on her face!'

'You're talking nonsense, Marie,' Catherine had said quickly. 'She'd never dare aim so high!'

'Girls like her have a good head for heights. Her heart won't fail her, for she's afraid of nothing!'

The châtelaine had felt a twinge of uneasiness, in spite of herself. She was sure of her husband's love, and she did not fear such traps as a village girl might lay for him. Yet Azalaïs reminded her of the two women she had feared most in her life: Arnaud's cousin, Marie de Combron, who had loved him to the point of murder, and the Moorish Princess Zobeïda, who had kept him prisoner for so long. Azalaïs had the rapaciousness of the first and the naked sensuality of the second, as well as the same jet-black hair and amber-coloured skin. Now and then, when the lace-maker came to the castle to deliver a kerchief, or the veil for a pointed headdress, Catherine would catch herself wondering if she were not perhaps a third incarnation of some she-devil determined to snatch away her love.

Marie and Zobeïda, it was true, had both met their deaths in the same way, at Arnaud's hand, struck down by the dagger with the silver hawk that had always been a sure talisman to Catherine; but who could foretell a man's reactions?

Had Catherine been born in a baronial hall, she would have paid no attention to the girl. She would have scorned the idea of a possible rivalry with a girl who was no more to her than a vassal among all the rest. But the daughter of Gaucher Legoix, the worthy goldsmith of the Pont au Change, shared none of this contempt. She knew, from her own experience, the miracles and the madness that love could work on quite modest origins. She had never made the mistake of underestimating her opponents, nor had she ever been given any cause to regret it.

Since her husband's departure, the Lady of Montsalvy had to some extent forgotten the vague fears aroused by Azalaïs's moist lips and smouldering eyes; and in the peril to her town, all such thoughts had been swept away completely. Even so, she had been unable to repress a slight frown, finding the lacemaker among Gauberte's audience. It might have been partly because Azalaïs was holding herself coolly a little apart, as usual, in the midst of the other women's excitement, and perhaps it also had something to do with the faintly mocking half-smile with which she regarded them, as though what became of them or of the town itself was no concern of hers.

The excitement in the little group redoubled with the châtelaine's arrival. In this hour of peril, she was the soul of Montsalvy, and not one of the women but felt secretly flattered that that soul belonged to one of their own gender.

They flowed into a warm, friendly circle around her on pretence of seeking the latest news about the movements of the enemy. Like their menfolk the night before, they marvelled compassionately at how fragile she seemed for her great task; yet they knew her equal to performing any wonders. Hadn't she sought her husband even in the infidel sultan's palace, and hadn't she brought him home, safe and well, when everyone knew he had escaped from a leper house? No-one in Montsalvy would believe that Messire Arnaud had never really been a leper. For all of them it was a miracle, a miracle owing to the great charity of Monseigneur St James, perhaps, but also in some part to Dame Catherine's unconquerable love.

They loved her for her beauty, for her gentleness and courage, but also for this uncommon love, worthy of the finest chivalric romances, that she had inspired and returned a hundredfold. And not one of the women who crowded about her but could still hear Bérault d'Apchier's jeering voice prophesying death to Arnaud of Montsalvy.

Each one of them shared, secretly, the fear they could sense lay deep in his young wife's heart, but at the same time they respected her for the gallant way she hid it and could smile at them, as she was doing now, as she answered their questions.

It was not easy. They were all talking at once, wanting to know if the enemy had completed their encirclement, if they seemed about to launch an immediate assault and if their strength was as great as they had thought.

Gauberte's powerful voice made itself heard above the rest. 'Not only that,' she said, 'but poor Brother Amable's untimely end hasn't helped matters. Oughtn't we to be thinking, perhaps, of sending someone else, another messenger?'

'And how would you be thinking of sending him,' countered Babette Malvezin, 'now that we can't so much as open a gate without risking a volley of arrows? Toss him over the walls and pray to God he lands far enough off?'

Gauberte shrugged, and bellowed back with splendid scorn: 'There's the tunnel under the castle, you poor ninny! What's that for if not an occasion like this?'

It was a fact that when Catherine and Abbot Bernard had rebuilt the old castle of the Puy de l'Arbre at the very gates of Montsalvy itself they had not neglected to endow it with the time-honoured means of escape in time of siege, in the shape of an underground passage. The tunnel started, in the traditional way, below the keep and emerged into the open country in the shelter of a jumble of rocks and tangled undergrowth that had been carefully left to look as natural as possible.

This tunnel was a masterpiece of its kind, having been provided with an exceedingly efficient system of internal defences, in case of an enemy's discovering the outside entrance and attempting by that way to force an entry into the castle. However, this was clearly not the kind of information to be trumpeted from the housetops.

Motioning to the linen weaver to speak more softly, Catherine said hastily: 'We've thought of that, but for heaven's sake, Gauberte, keep your voice down. You could be overheard.'

'Who by, m'lady? The enemy aren't lurking in our houses.'

Catherine smiled, 'No, but your voice carries a long way, my dear. You could lead an army, like the Maid; and indeed I know how greatly you revere her ...'

Her voice was drowned in a thunderous hammering. It came from one of the houses near the well; the one occupied by Azalaïs's adoptive father, Augustin. The door to his workshop stood wide open, in spite of the damp chill in the air, and they could see the wood chips flying inside.

Catherine looked at the lacemaker. 'Your father seems to be hard at work. What is he making?'

'A coffin. The first ... for Brother Amable.'

'The first? Is he hoping for more?'

Azalaïs smiled her slow smile, but her shrewd eyes rested on the châtelaine with scarcely-veiled insolence.

'There will be many more, Dame Catherine, and you know it! Whether the siege continues or the town is carried quickly by assault, my father will not lack work. You know there will be many dead on your account.'

Silence fell, like a blanket of fog. Catherine wondered if she could have heard correctly, while Gauberte and her friends stared at one another, unable to believe their ears. But the châtelaine recovered quickly. She frowned.

'What do you mean by that?'

'No more than what the Lord of Apchier said – if I understood him right? What he wants, Dame Catherine, is gold – and he wants you! Gold I don't doubt you could give him, but what of yourself? It's to keep you safe the men of this town are going to die, isn't it? You alone – since Messire Arnaud isn't coming back! '

As she spoke, she raised her full water jar from the well's rim and hoisted it, with a graceful twist of her hips, on to her shoulder. She was still smiling, clearly enjoying the effect of her cruel words, which – as she well knew – had struck at Catherine just where she was most vulnerable. But before she had time to leave the well, a pair of well-delivered blows to the face, with the full force of Gauberte's 180 pounds behind them, sent her rolling on the ground amid the shattered fragments of her pitcher. Gauberte followed up this attack in person, and as Azalaïs started to struggle dazedly to her feet she was felled once again, while the linen weaver grasped her hair to pin her to the ground.

'Gauberte!' shrieked Catherine, appalled by the fury that convulsed the big woman's features. 'Let her go!'

But Gauberte was past hearing. She had her knee in the girl's belly and was pulling her plaits with one hand while she spat in her face. 'If I didn't know your poor dead mother for a saint, Azalaïs,' she scolded, 'I'd say a sow brought you forth! You're very concerned about the men of this town all of a sudden! Yet you act hoity-toity enough with any boy that's fool enough to talk love to you. What you want's a lord, eh? And since you can't have Messire Arnaud, you thought to yourself that one of those Apchier wolves might do as well, eh? Is that what you want? Well, is it? Is it?'

With her free hand, Gauberte dealt the girl a blow of such savage fury that Catherine thought she would knock her unconscious.

'We must part them, Babette!' she screamed at the woman beside her. 'Gauberte will kill her!'

'Bah!' The chandler's wife snorted. 'That might be no such bad thing either! My youngest shed tears enough on her account after St John's Eve. But it's for you to say, Dame Catherine.'

Assisted, without enthusiasm, by the other women, for none of those worthy housewives could feel much concern over the pretty lacemaker's fate, they succeeded in dragging the foaming Gauberte off her victim, and

Marie Bru even went so far as to help Azalaïs to her feet.

The lacemaker scrambled up, sobbing, her face flaming from the blows she had received and blood running from her arm where a piece of the broken pot had cut her. Her dress was soaking wet and covered in mud, and her coat split down the back. Her pitiable appearance did nothing, however, to calm Gauberte's rage, and it was all that they could do to hold her back, so furiously she struggled.

'Let me go!' she raged. 'I'll drag the trollop in the mud! Drag her in the mud until she begs our lady's pardon!'

And when the women clinging to her arms still refused to let her go, she bellowed after her enemy's retreating form, as Marie led the girl back to her house:

'You hear, slut? You'll beg her pardon!'

Augustin the carpenter, drawn by the noise that had finally made itself heard above the din he was making himself, had appeared in the doorway of his shop, a hammer in one hand, a bunch of dowel pins in the other, just in time to come face to face with his adopted daughter being escorted home, soaking wet and suffering from obvious ill-usage.

Marie Bru tried to explain. 'It's nothing,' she said, scenting a fresh outburst. 'She and Gauberte had words ...'

Augustin put her aside without listening and advanced toward the group of women. With his eyes almost starting from his head and his face nearly as red as the woollen cap crammed down over his ears, the heavy mallet gripped tight in one hand, he was a sight to make anyone quail, but it took more than that to impress Gauberte, especially when roused.

'Ask pardon for what she dared to say to Dame Catherine,' she cried. 'No offence, Augustin, but that Azalaïs of yours is a downright little hussy! A good hiding from you, now and then, might have knocked some of the nonsense out of her!'

'And what was it she dared to say, eh? Or don't you dare to tell me?'

'I hardly like ...'

Augustin continued his advance and, seeing the hammer swinging dangerously in his brawny grip, the women who had hold of Gauberte fell back a touch, with a little moan of fright, expecting him to fall on them at any second.

Catherine, too, released her hold, but only to step quickly between Gauberte and the angry joiner. 'That's enough,' she said curtly. 'It's my turn to speak now, and you will both of you listen to me. Put that hammer back in your belt, Augustin; and you, Gauberte, calm yourself!'

At the sight of her the carpenter paused, hesitated an instant, glanced stealthily at her and then, with a bad grace, tugged off his cap. 'I've a right to know what's happened to my girl,' he growled.

'Agreed,' Gauberte said, her good humour returning as her temper cooled. 'And you've likewise a right to know what she said. As to what happened to her, I'll tell you. I did what you've never had the nerve to do: I boxed her ears for her! And what's more, I'll do it again, unless you do it yourself. She said you'd make a pretty penny out of all the coffins that would be needed for those who were going to be killed on Dame Catherine's account! What do you say to that?'

'She can't have said that!'

'Yes, Augustin, she did say just that,' Catherine intervened. 'She believes that I, and I alone, am the cause of all that you and this town will have to suffer! Is that your opinion also?'

'N-no, of course not! No-one would want the Apchiers for lords! They are hard and cruel. Only, if Messire Arnaud were never to come home ...'

'You'd see no reason to fight for his wife and children,' Catherine finished clearly, feeling the colour ebb from her face.

She stared at the man's stubborn countenance. It was clear that he blamed her for what had just passed, although a kind of inbred respect prevented him from saying so to her face. Once again, it was Gauberte, quite incapable at any time of standing aside from an argument, who resolved the situation.

'Messire Arnaud will return,' she said firmly. 'And even if he didn't, he has a son, and we have Abbot Bernard to share the lordship. We need no Apchiers! And now you may tell your daughter that before we give up Dame Catherine, since that's what you seem to be thinking in your family, we'll send her out of the gates, stark naked, and see what the lords she's so fond of make of her then!'

'That will do,' Catherine broke in. 'Augustin, I bear your daughter no ill-will. I daresay she is frightened, and that may excuse her. Do you, for your part, bear no grudge against Gauberte? She did what she did out of friendship for me. Now, be friends.'

Fabre muttered ungraciously that he bore no malice, while Gauberte, on her side, mumbled that Azalaïs need fear nothing from her provided she kept her tongue. Catherine was satisfied with that. The incident was closed and everyone went about their business. The women picked up their pitchers and, each bobbing a final curtsy to the châtelaine, made their way back to their kitchens, still discussing what had happened.

Catherine turned her steps toward the abbey, where she was due for a meeting with Montsalvy's spiritual leader. Gauberte, also on her way home, walked with her.

In spite of the many proofs of affection that had just been lavished on her, the Countess was feeling sad and heavy-hearted, because she had discovered a small crack in the solid bulk of the town's loyalty and devotion. Small it certainly was, and not perhaps very dangerous, yet it was still too much at a time when the whole town should have been welded into a single heart and will.

Admittedly, Catherine had cherished few illusions as to what Azalaïs's feelings toward herself must be, ever since that winter's morning in the castle courtyard when she had caught the glance the lacemaker had given her husband. She had known then that Marie was right and that the girl must hate her. But that her adoptive father thought the same was an unpleasant discovery, because it led naturally to the idea that Augustin and his daughter might not be alone in their opinions. In any event, she must make sure that such ideas did not spread, and keep an eye on the lacemaker.

Gauberte, who had been observing the châtelaine in silence, broke in on these gloomy reflections with her usual abruptness. 'Don't you go bothering your head with imagining things, now, Dame Catherine! That Augustin's so besotted over his Azalaïs that he's never noticed she's as nasty a little piece as ever the sun shone on. Everything she says is Gospel truth – but when it comes to that kind of talk, he's on his own!'

'Are you really sure?'

'Sure? Holy Mother of God! Why, the very idea's an insult to the rest of us! Besides, what have we to do with Azalaïs's funny ideas? She's not a native of these parts!'

'Neither am I,' Catherine said gently.

'You?'

Gauberte stopped dead in her tracks, set down her pitcher and shook her head with such a pitying look that Catherine began to wonder if the other woman thought she was simple-minded.

'… You! Holy Virgin! You belong here more than if you'd sprung from our old earth, like this pebble here.' Here Gauberte bent and scooped up a pebble from the road. 'You may have been born in Paris, but how much of that remains? You and Messire Arnaud, you're one flesh, one heart! And if he's not from these parts, I'd like to know who is! And but for you, we'd not have Messire Arnaud now … So get along with you, Dame Catherine. Whether you like it or not, you're the cornerstone in the walls of Montsalvy, and nothing and no-ne can ever tear you out – or deny it, either!'

'Thank you, Gauberte. But I think it will be best for everyone if Azalaïs holds her tongue in future, and she must be watched. We can't have attitudes like hers in a town under siege.'

'Don't worry, Dame Catherine, we'll keep an eye on that young beauty. One false step, I tell you, and you put her under arrest, even if it does upset that poor fool Augustin. Never fear, m'lady. The word shall go round.'

By this time they had reached the abbey gate. Without giving Catherine time to register her feelings, Gauberte dropped a hurried curtsy and, turning, strode off rapidly in the direction of her own house.

Blinking back her tears and yet, at the same time, feeling curiously warmed, the younger woman entered the monastery gates and was greeted by the brother porter with the information that she would find Abbot Bernard in the chapter house.

'He's giving the little lord his lesson,' he added, smiling broadly.

'A lesson? Today?'

'Yes indeed! The reverend father doesn't regard a siege as an excuse for wasting time.'

How like the Abbot, Catherine thought. When they might expect at any instant to find the town being stormed by hordes of enemies and his own church was probably filled, at that very moment, with people praying for heavenly intervention, he went on calmly giving little Michel his lessons just as if nothing were the matter.

As she approached the chapter house, Catherine could hear her son's voice reciting a snatch of poetry that was seasonal, if nothing else.

> 'April am I, of all months most brave,
> 'And ever held of men in high honour,
> 'For in my time, our ransomed souls to save,
> 'By reason of his pain and great dolour,
> 'Was pierced with a lance our Saviour
> 'and Maker of this world ...'

The door, creaking under Catherine's hand, broke in on the clear, childish voice. Perched, short legs dangling, on a stool opposite the Abbot, who stood listening with his chin propped in one hand, Michel, interrupted in mid-flow, turned a reproachful, chubby face upon his mother.

'Oh!' he remarked, with apparent displeasure. 'My lady mother! Did you have to come in here just now?'

'Shouldn't I?'

'No, you shouldn't! I hope you didn't hear?'

Deducing from the anxiety with which this question was put that the little boy had been practising a poem to be recited to her on Easter morning, in addition to the customary good wishes, Catherine smiled at him innocently.

'Was there anything to hear? The door was closed as I came along. I didn't hear a thing. I'm sorry if I've disturbed you ...'

'Oh, that's all right,' Michel conceded magnanimously. 'Just so long as you didn't hear.'

'That will be the end of lessons for today, Michel,' the Abbot said, laying a hand on the fair, curly head. 'You've been a good boy, and now I think you may run along and find Sara.'

At once the little boy jumped down from his stool and ran to fling his baby arms round his mother's legs.

'Please ... need I go home right now?'

'Why? Where do you want to go?'

'To see Auguste! He's beginning to make the wax ready for the big Easter candle today, and he told me I could go.'

Catherine picked him up and held him close to her, kissing the plump, downy cheeks adoringly.

'Go, then, my son. But don't get in Auguste's way, and don't be too long or Sara will be anxious.'

He promised readily and, in his haste to be gone to watch Auguste Malvezin at his marvellous waxworking, deposited a smacking kiss on the end of her nose. Then he wriggled out of her arms and ran off, followed by the indulgent smiles of his mother and the Abbot.

'He has all his father's eager curiosity,' the Abbot said.

'He's a real Montsalvy,' was Catherine's proud answer. 'I'm not sure he isn't more like his uncle Michel than his father. He's gentler than my husband, and not so fond of violence. But then he's very little still ... But I must say I'm surprised at some of you people – you, especially. We are in peril, and yet you go on giving little Michel his lessons, and Auguste is busy making the Easter candle! Sweet Jesus, what will have become of us by Easter? We may not even be alive!'

'You think not? You do not place much trust in God, my daughter. It's scarcely more than two weeks now to Easter! The celebrations may be a little more subdued than usual, I grant you, but I hope we shall all be here to give praise to God.'

'I pray He may hear it! I came to talk to you about what we should do now that poor Brother ... I thought perhaps the tunnel under the castle ...'

'To be sure! We'll use it when we send our next messenger.'

'But who will be willing to risk his life like that? Brother Amable's dreadful end might well put fear into the stoutest heart.'

'Never fear, my child. I already have the man we need. One of the lads from La Croix du Coq came to offer himself. He wants to go tonight.'

'So soon? But why?'

'Because of the spring sowing. It's been raining all day and may freeze tonight, but as soon as the land dries out we must get on with the harrowing. Then there's cabbages and roots to be sown. If the siege drags on, then all the vital April work will never get done and the harvest will suffer. There's not a man here that wouldn't risk his life to save his land.'

'It has been suggested that there is another – easier – way to save Montsalvy.'

'And that is?'

'To give Bérault d'Apchier what he wants: the wealth of the castle and ...'

'And yourself? What nonsense! Who's been putting such ideas into your head?'

She told him, giving him a rapid sketch of the scene at the well. The abbot listened with undisguised impatience.

'Gauberte is right,' he exclaimed, when she had finished. 'She's got a better head on her shoulders than poor, silly Azalaïs. As for Augustin, he is much to blame for putting such thoughts into the girl's head. They are neither suitable to her condition, nor very wise! I've been thinking for some time that she would bear watching. I don't like the company she keeps.'

'What company? A boy?'

'No, it might be better if it were. La Ratapennade! She's been seen several times just recently in the neighbourhood of her hut. If we're not careful we'll find the poor creature is willing to risk her immortal soul in order to achieve her demented ambitions! Meanwhile, I hope you aren't going to let yourself be upset by these two and their crazy ideas? Don't you know that if you gave yourself up, your husband would leave not one stone of this place standing on another? Do you not know how terrible is his anger?'

'Yes, I know … if he ever comes back!'

'Again?'

Catherine bowed her head, ashamed of her weakness.

'Forgive me. I can't stop myself worrying about it. I'm afraid, father – more afraid than you can possibly imagine! Not for myself, no … but for him!'

'Only for him? Have you found your page yet?'

She shook her head and, fumbling in her purse for her handkerchief, wiped away the tears that spangled her lashes, and blew her nose. She guessed that by talking to her about Bérenger the abbot was chiefly trying to turn her thoughts away from the unknown dangers threatening Arnaud.

'I don't think you should worry too much about him,' the Abbot continued. 'He would have seen what was going on on his way home. He must have turned back and made for Roquemaurel. He may even have warned Dame Mathilde and help will come to us that way.'

'I doubt it. Amaury and Renaud left few men at home. That old castle of theirs practically defends itself, you know. But I'd like to know Bérenger is safe.'

'Come and pray with me for a little while, my dear. That is the best comfort I can offer you. God must surely be in the way of performing wonders for you by now! Let us go and ask him to work a few more …'

They went together into the church, where the prayers for deliverance were being said. The building was filled with a sound like a hive of bees; a sound made up of the muffled voices of a hundred or more women and children who knelt there before the high altar. An aged monk was conducting the office, his thin, cracked tones alternating with the deeper, more robust voices of his congregation.

The nailed feet of the great painted wooden Christ on the wall were lost in the combined radiance of so many lighted candles that the dying God seemed to be rising from a blazing pyre and great pools of yellow wax lay on the old, uneven flagstones, gleaming like ice in the sun.

The Abbot proceeded to his throne, and Catherine made her way to the lord's place, around which most of the castle servants were already gathered.

She saw Marie Rallard's fair face framed in the hood of a black cloak and smiled and beckoned to her. She felt suddenly that she did not want to be alone. Her role of châtelaine left her frightened and uneasy, even in God's presence. She knew that Marie had not come, like the other women, to implore heaven to turn away its wrath. She was not afraid: that showed in her limpid gaze. She had lived through too many perils between her birthplace in Burgundy and the harem in Granada to be thrown into a panic by a provincial siege.

From the time she had spent with the Moors, Marie had acquired a certain fatalism, a quiet acceptance of the often incongruous whims of fate, together with an amazing adaptability. Looking at her as she was now, piously kneeling, with a coif of fine lawn bound demurely about her rosy face, and her hair braided up under a wimple so that she had the air of a little nun, with her eyelids lowered and her lips moving in silent prayer, Catherine could scarcely believe it was the same woman she had first seen sprawled on silken cushions beside the blue waters of a bathing pool that reflected back her voluptuous nakedness. Then she had been called Aïcha; before that she had been Marie Vermeil; and now, by love's miracle, she was Dame Marie Rallard, respectable married lady and waiting woman to the châtelaine, with the whole of the castle wardrobe in her charge.

Never, since leaving Granada, had Marie so much as alluded to that strange time when she had been merely one among the many pretty creatures who existed for no other reason than to serve the pleasures of a king. From the moment she had given her hand to Josse Rallard she had thrown off her life as an odalisque, as a serpent sloughs its skin, and slipped with astonishing ease into that of a young girl in love and a contented wife.

Now, she was innocently grateful to the Lord of Montsalvy, because, when he had mustered his men for the march to Paris, he had left her her husband.

Leaving Marie to tell her beads devoutly, Catherine buried her face in her clasped hands with a smothered sigh; but she was not praying. She seemed unable to. The incident with the lacemaker was still too vivid, and seemed in some way to poison her thoughts. In spite of the Abbot's words, she felt strangely troubled. There had been a grain of truth in the vicious words Azalaïs had flung at her, and if it were a fact that Apchier was after nothing but her own person and property, then the first deaths, which were bound to come unless help arrived swiftly, would weigh heavily on her conscience.

Undeniably, the *routier* also meant to get his hands on the tolls, so as to milk future travellers at his leisure, but perhaps if he were to get what he wanted, the people's lives would be spared. And then again …

Catherine sat through the prayers, tormenting herself with such demoralizing thoughts as these, turning the problem over and over in her mind, but without finding a solution. She was discovering all at once that it was not easy, when you were born of the people and still felt yourself so much a part of them, to take on the thoughts and feelings of a noble lady for whom the sacrifice of human lives was a natural thing.

She knew, of course, that Arnaud would feel nothing but contempt for her scruples. He would shrug them off with a laugh. But then, if he were here, the problem would not arise. It was her problem, hers alone, and probably the most difficult one she had ever had to face.

'O Lord, please send us help!' she whispered, deciding at last to put her trust in heaven. 'Don't let the burden get too heavy! Already, one man has died …'

Late that same night, long after Brother Amable's remains had been consigned to the earth in the presence of the Lady of Montsalvy, robed in deepest black, and as many of the town's inhabitants as were not required for guard duty on the walls, a man descended the ladder going down to the underground cellars that lay buried deep below the keep.

He carried a torch, a dagger and a letter. Before he vanished into the thick, subterranean darkness, he smiled at Josse, who had come thus far with him; and then, with a wink and a wave, he was gone.

He was never again seen alive …

3: The Tunnel

The assault took place at dawn. Taking advantage of the cold hour before the morning watch, when men's defences, numbed by long wakefulness, were at their lowest ebb, Bérault d'Apchier set his troops to storm the walls in the two places that seemed to him most vulnerable.

During the night, the besiegers had succeeded in silently filling in a part of the ditch, already very nearly dry, with bundles of brushwood, and as soon as the sky began to lighten in the east the scaling ladders were brought up to these two points.

These operations had been carried out as secretly as possible but, even so, not without attracting the attention of the watch; and when, led by the bastard, Gonnet, the soldiers began swarming up the ladders, they were met with such a hail of stones and boiling oil that they were forced back down again.

Gonnet himself was badly burned on one shoulder and withdrew, howling like an injured wolf and shaking his fist in trembling fury at the town's inhabitants. Two hours later, the farm at Sainte-Font was burned to the ground.

Catherine stood on the walls, with half her people gathered round her, and watched it burn with a thick black smoke that was drawn out by the wind into long, dirty streaks against the grey of the sky. Marie Bru huddled within the circle of her husband's arm, crying with great, despairing sobs that went to Catherine's heart, while he kept patting her shoulder in an automatic way, unable to drag his eyes from the calamity.

'We'll make it all up to you, Marie,' Catherine said gently. 'When these brigands have gone, we'll rebuild it ...'

'Of course we will,' Saturnin said cheerfully. 'We'll all get down to it! And help won't be long now. We've heard no news of our messenger, so he must have got through.'

Catherine threw him a grateful glance. He could not have said anything better. Meanwhile, as some comfort to Marie, she gave her three gold crowns.

The next day there was a second attack, just as firmly repulsed, and this time the farm at La Croix du Coq was burned.

At the council held that evening in the castle, the spiced wine tasted a little bitter on the lips of those in whose charge the town lay.

'At the rate of one farm per assault per day,' said Félicien Puech, the miller, expressing the thoughts of all of them, 'there'll be nothing but scorched earth left around our town by Easter Sunday.'

'Help will be here long before that,' countered Nicolas Barral. 'Jeannet ought to be at Carlat by this time. I'll wager my helmet to a cabbage stalk that before two days are out we see a troop of Monseigneur Cadet Bernard's* good lances, sent to our aid by Dame Eléonore, his wife.'

But neither that day nor the next were any lances seen, and signs of anxiety began to show in the little community. Even when Félicien brought the sergeant an outsized cabbage stalk and requested him, with apparent seriousness, for his helmet in exchange, he raised only a few, rather perfunctory smiles. The people of Montsalvy were feeling less and less inclined to laugh.

What did come, however, was the rain. It started on Palm Sunday, in the middle of the night, and settled in as if it had come to stay. Nor was it one of those fine, persistent spring rains, penetrating deep into the fruitful earth, swelling the seed, making the grasses and the tender shoots of wheat and rye stand up strong and tall, and opening the downy buds on the chestnut trees. It came in great sweeping torrents, borne on the gusty breath of an angry gale, washing away the soil from the hillsides and carrying it in black streams down to the valley bottoms, laying bare the rock wherever there were no trees to anchor it with their roots and tearing off whole branches in rags and tatters where they were.

Then came the hail in hard, icy lumps as big as walnuts, battering pitilessly at the washed-out fields, crushing the hopeful shoots and destroying the first, faint hope of a harvest to come.

The people of Montsalvy stood on their walls, soaked to the skin but dry-eyed, and watched the rain pelting down on their sodden fields. The next winter would be hard and probably hungry; but who could be sure of living until the next winter? The threat that overhung the town had not departed. The besiegers were still there, in the midst of a sea of mud, huddled under tents that were pierced through with hailstones, if the wind had not already carried them away over the treetops as easily as a girl's bonnet over a windmill.

Compelled by the weather to abandon their direct attacks, they had only grown more sullen and determined. The leaders, of course, had taken up

---

* Popular nickname for Bernard of Armagnac, Count of Pardiac.

their quarters in the abandoned houses of the two small, outlying hamlets, but the bulk of the army made do as best they could, grinding their teeth at the thought of the stout roofs and warm beds inside those well-sealed walls.

Catherine and Abbot Bernard spent themselves tirelessly, despite an ever-increasing anxiety, to keep up the courage of their flock, who now spoke little except in proverbs.

'When April is angry, it's worst of all,' one would sigh.

'If it rains on Palm Sunday, it will rain at haytime and at harvest,' said another.

Everyone seemed able to dredge up some old adage from the depths of his memory, each one gloomier than the one before. They had reached a stage now where the siege itself almost faded into the background. To these people of the soil, injury to the soil took precedence over all else, and the town's two co-seigneurs had their work cut out to combat the belief, arising naturally out of the torrential rains, that heaven had declared against them.

'We'll find a way of making good all that has been destroyed,' the châtelaine insisted, thinking of her friend Jacques Cœur and the fortunes built up by his mercantile ventures. 'At least this rain has stopped the enemy from burning more farms.'

'Yes, God is on our side,' the Abbot added, coming to her assistance. 'Don't you see, He's keeping the enemy at bay? With Him fighting for you, and keeping you safe, why are you quibbling about a few acres of wheat or barley? You can't make an omelette without breaking eggs!'

All the same, the Abbot ordered great public prayers to be said; and never, within living memory, had Holy Week been kept with such fervour – or been so wet!

The members of the Brotherhood of the Passion, who had made it a point of honour to hold their customary procession on Maundy Thursday, emerged from their tall red-and-black-dyed hoods, which gave them a closer affinity with Red Indians or blue Bedouin.

Sara wore her fingers to the bone pounding up cabbage leaves in clay to anoint the rheumaticky joints of all the old people in the town.

Most people spent what time was left over from praying or tending, under their makeshift shelters, the fires kept burning continually to heat the pitch for their defence and light the wall walks for the watch at night as they gazed along the northward road, hoping to catch a glimpse of the gleaming lances and bright, waving pennants of Armagnac. But the horizon remained dull and empty, unillumined by the smallest glimmer of hope.

When a week had gone by since Jeannet's departure, the people of Montsalvy began to think that something must have happened to their messenger. Confirmation came in an unexpected fashion.

Easter Sunday fell on 8 April, St Hugh's day, and dawned as dismal and wet as the preceding ones. The sky was so heavy and lowering that the world seemed wrapped in a sodden blanket, as if the sun had deserted it altogether for another planet.

Catherine, like everyone else, had risen from her bed at the crack of dawn to honour the resurrection of Our Lord. Festivities, of course, were out of the question, but Abbot Bernard was to conduct high mass later that morning, and afterwards towns people and refugees alike would be entertained by castle and abbey jointly to a meal that, although by no means a feast, would take on a sense of something a little special from the very fact of being eaten together.

On account of this meal, Sara, Donatienne and Marie were as busy about the castle's enormous kitchens as they had ever been in happier days.

Catherine was on the point of joining them to add her own contribution to the work when Saturnin found her. He, usually so grave, was for once quite out of breath and almost grinning, for it seemed to him that the news he brought was the best of all Easter gifts. In fact he looked so happy that Catherine's heart missed a beat.

'Help? Has help arrived?'

'Not that we looked for, Dame Catherine, but help all the same.'

Outside the Entraygues Gate, a small body of men was at that moment breaking through the besiegers' lines, weak enough at that point, in all conscience, and cutting their way toward the town.

'A small force? How many men?'

'About twenty, I think. They bear no distinctive blazons but they fight well. Nicolas is waiting your command to raise the portcullis.'

'I'm coming. There's no time to lose. Unless …' She kept the rest of her thought to herself. Bérault d'Apchier was a man capable of any kind of trickery. How could they be sure that this body of men who fought well but with no distinctive blazons might not be the most effective kind of trap to open the town gates from inside?'

All the same, she ran to the gate, where a fight was indeed going on. Some twenty horsemen, armed at all points, having hacked themselves a passage through Apchier's unsuspecting lines, were now falling back toward the town, fighting a vigorous retreating action against an enemy that was growing greater minute by minute.

Catherine had pelted up to the battlements and now she cried out: 'Who are you?'

'In God's name, open up!' came a breathless voice. 'It's me! Bérenger.'

The voice in question emanated from a weird assortment of ill-co-ordinated pieces of armour belonging to one of the riders in the centre of the troop. This remarkable warrior was wielding a gigantic battleaxe in a manner quite as dangerous to those of his own side as to the enemy, distributing blows more or less at random, with a good deal more enthusiasm than expertise. But the sound of her page's familiar voice was enough to fill Catherine with a joy she would scarcely have believed possible only a moment before. It was a joy that spread to all the defenders of the gate.

Even before she could open her mouth to give the order, Nicolas Barral and two of his men had leaped to the windlass to raise the portcullis and send the drawbridge crashing down. Meanwhile, a rank of archers posted in the battlements kept up a constant hail of arrows on the enemy.

The entry of the little troop was over with a speed that was almost uncanny. Almost before the hollow clatter of their hooves had died away, the drawbridge was up again. The enemy's arrows and crossbow bolts thudded harmlessly into its massive oaken timbers while, with a hideous clank of iron, Bérenger de Roquemaurel heaved off a helmet far too big for him and tumbled off his horse almost into the sergeant's arms, very nearly putting his eye out with the helmet in the process.

'Christ's blood, boy!' Barral swore. 'We'll make a fighting man of you yet! Why, how pale you look after that nice little warm-up!'

'I've never been so frightened in my life,' the boy declared ingenuously, and indeed his teeth were chattering. 'Oh, my lady! How good it is to see you,' he added, vainly endeavouring to adapt his metal carapace to a graceful bow. 'I came as quickly as I could, but I had a good deal of trouble, one way and another. I hope you've not had to suffer too much so far?'

'No, Bérenger, all is well – or very nearly. But you, where have you sprung from?'

'From home. My mother sends you her best love and she will pray for you. And – and from Carlat!'

'From Carlat? But – these men?' She indicated the armed troop now assembled within the closed gates and dismounting heavily.

'They too. They are all that the governor, Messire Aymon de Pouget, can spare you. He's desolated, but the Countess Eléonore has just left for Tours, where it seems they're getting ready for the marriage of my Lord Dauphin to the Lady Margaret of Scotland, and the Sire de Pouget can't send more men to aid you without leaving his own garrison perilously depleted. That's why he wouldn't have them wear any insignia, so that these stinking dogs who dared attack you shan't guess that Carlat is less well defended.'

He who appeared to be the leader of the new arrivals came to bow the knee before Catherine, assuring her that he and his men were ready and willing to die for her; but she could summon up only a pallid smile of thanks.

The disappointment was too great. Twenty men! Only twenty, when she had hoped for at least two hundred! With such a small force, she would never succeed in prising loose the iron grip that threatened to crush the life out of her home.

Her trouble and dismay were written so clearly on her face that Barral hastened to intervene, fearing their effect on the people who were already running up to hear the news.

'You must have these men taken to the castle, Dame Catherine, for rest and refreshment, for they have fought well. And what about this young paladin?' he added, dealing the page a slap on the back that set him coughing. Then, in an undertone, 'Best if the news doesn't spread too fast. Only the council ought to know about it for the present – and the Abbot.'

The Abbot appeared at that moment, striding cheerfully through the puddles, heedless of the rain streaming down on his splendid festive robes.

Given a discreet picture of the situation, he entered into it without a blink, loudly proclaiming his delight at the page's unexpected return to them. Then he hurried everyone off to the castle, saying no more than that an exceptional meeting of the council would take place in the abbey chapter-house directly after mass.

As the rain chose that moment to come down still more heavily than before, everyone scattered to get under shelter and discuss the unlooked-for arrivals. They seemed to everyone an excellent omen regarding heaven's future intentions.

While Nicolas Barral took charge of the reinforcements, Catherine carried Bérenger off into the castle and handed him over to Sara.

The hero of the hour was led off to the bath house and stripped, washed, scalded, drubbed, dried and laid out on a broad stone table to be energetically kneaded and massaged with aromatic oils by no less a person than Sara herself.*

Seated on a stool at a little distance, her hands clasped in her lap and her brows drawn together in an anxious frown, Catherine listened to the page's account of his adventures, an account punctuated by frequent anguished groans that Sara's pummelling elicited from her victim.

Bérenger had been coming up slowly through the woods after his 'fishing' expedition when the tolling of the bell warned him that something untoward was happening at Montsalvy. He was still a good way off and it was already getting dark. By the time he drew near to the town, night had fallen. The Entraygues Gate was closed and he could see soldiers creeping toward it, so he had continued round the town, seen the Apchiers' camp and heard the robber-baron's threats.

'I didn't want to put you in danger by trying to get in, so I hid in the ruins of the Puy de l'Arbre. From there I was able to watch what was going on in the enemy camp ... I saw the monk die, alas, and it put such terror in

---

* In the castles of the Middle Ages, the women of the house were always in charge of steam washing the lord, his son and his principal officers. It was to make a guest feel welcome to entrust him to the care of the ladies.

me, Dame Catherine, that I fled as far as I could go.' He managed a pathetic little smile. 'I'm afraid I'll never be very brave. My brothers would be ashamed if they could have seen me.'

'Far from it, Bérenger,' said Catherine gravely. 'If they'd have seen you just now, they could not but have been proud of you. You fought like a champion!'

'So just you stop your moaning, gallant knight,' Sara put in quickly. 'Who ever saw a paladin so thin-skinned!'

'You're not massaging me, Sara. You're kneading me like dough! Where was I? Oh yes, I was running away … Well, all that day, I hid in the gully away beyond Sainte-Font, waiting for nightfall. My idea was to try to reach the entrance to the secret tunnel, you see, and get into the castle that way.'

'The secret tunnel?' Catherine said. 'You know about it, then?'

Bérenger grinned, half afraid, half contrite, as Sara wrapped him up in a sheet of fine linen to remove the surplus oil.

'There's one very much like it at home. It wasn't difficult to find when I looked in the cellars under the keep. And the guards helped me to use it sometimes to leave the castle …'

'To go night fishing,' Sara finished for him ruthlessly. 'You must have thought us very simple, Messire Bérenger, if you imagined your escapades were unnoticed.'

'That will do, Sara,' Catherine broke in quickly. 'This is no time to quarrel with him about that. Go on, Bérenger. Why didn't you come back?'

'It was late when I approached, well after ten o'clock, and pitch dark. The place seemed to be deserted, but even so I was careful to move cautiously, keeping in the shade of the bushes. And it was as well I did, for when I came within a few yards of it, I heard men's voices. One was complaining about the length of the wait. Then another said: "Patience. It won't be long now. I was told they'd be sending another messenger tonight, by the tunnel."'

The two women listening exclaimed together: 'Told? But by whom?'

'That was all I heard. Then a third voice broke in, telling them roughly to keep silence, and everything was quiet once more. So I made myself as small as I could and waited with them. But, however much I tried to hold my breath, my heart was thudding so against my ribs that it seemed the whole county must hear it. And all the time, I was trying desperately to think of some way to warn the man coming down the tunnel. I didn't have long to think about it, though, because it all happened horribly quickly. Someone rose out of the tumbled rocks hiding the entrance. I saw a movement in the bushes and a darker shadow coming nearer, taking a cautious step or two. But, before he could take another, the men who had been lying hidden sprang out upon him with a yell of triumph and he was overborne and carried off …'

'Killed?'

'No. Only gagged and bound. I saw them go off after a few minutes, laughing and jesting. They were carrying a kind of long, narrow bundle that must have been your messenger. But as they passed the rock where I was hidden, I was able to see who was guiding them. It was …'

'Gervais, I'll be bound!' Sara cried. 'The trouble that wretched man has caused us! He's the only one in the Apchiers' camp who could have known about the entrance to the secret passage.'

'The only one?' Catherine said, with a bitter smile. 'I begin to wonder. The number of people who seem to know of our tunnel is quite terrifying, when you think that it was supposed to be a secret. First Gauberte, blabbing it out at the top of her voice by the well, and now this vile Gervais! I repent more and more that I ever spared his life! There are times when clemency is almost a crime! But go on, Bérenger. What did you do then?'

'I ran home, first of all, to ask my mother's advice, and perhaps get help from her. She's a very wise and sensible person, and she's fond of you. It put her into a furious passion to hear how you were placed, and she was quite desperate, because my brothers had left nobody at Roquemaurel but five men almost too old to bear arms and the maids. All the others had gone off to Paris with them in search of glory. Glory! I ask you! Some of them will never come back, and of those that do, half of them will have lost an eye, or an arm or leg, or …'

'Bérenger!' the châtelaine said firmly. 'I know all your views on the matter of war, but what concerns me at the moment is the rest of your adventures. There'll be time for philosophising later.'

The page flushed and looked a little shamefaced. 'I'm sorry, my lady,' he said, allowing Sara to finish drawing a pair of green and black two-coloured hose over his long shanks and knobbly knees. 'I forgot you were in a hurry to hear. Well, my mother said: "It would be to Carlat that Dame Catherine and the Abbot Bernard were sending their messenger. Well, they'll never do it, so it's for you, Bérenger, to try to do it for them. And for goodness' sake do your best not to let the family down for once!" Then she gave me a hunk of bread, some bacon and a flask of wine, with one of the two farm horses she had left, and her blessing. The horse got a double ration of oats and a wallop over the crupper to make him trot, and we were off …

'We went a long way round so as not to run the risk of being caught by any of the Apchiers' scouts, and eventually came to Carlat, where we found matters as I've told you.'

There was a silence. Neither Catherine nor the page had anything to add. The two women had accepted the fact that the looked-for aid from their suzerain would not come to them now, and one single question was uppermost in both their minds. It was a grave and pressing one, because of the subtle dangers it implied. Who, inside Montsalvy, was in touch with Gervais Malfrat and could betray their own people like this?

All through mass, that question remained fixed like a hook in the part of Catherine's heart that was most vulnerable. As she knelt on her red velvet cushion, swathed in the snowy folds of the great veil of white lace she had fastened to her velvet hennin, the same violet colour as her eyes, in honour of the Resurrection, her hands clasped before her, she asked herself which one of the faces she could see from her place opposite the Abbot's seat was the face of a traitor ... or was it, perhaps, a woman?

The idea was Sara's. She had thrown it out, with a shrug, not bothering to hide her contempt. 'Only a girl would pass information to Gervais. He knows how to get round them!'

A girl? A woman? It might be. Catherine racked her memory for a face or a name that might have been associated with Gervais at the time he was driven out, but she could think of none: none save poor little Bertille. And yet one had to be found. Montsalvy's peril was too great to allow the continued existence of this maggot lodged in its very flesh. But who was it? The Countess knew every one of those before her intimately.

A small town with a lord that loved his lands well enough not to stand on ceremony was like one big family. They had their share of violent men, and plenty who were obstinate or stupid, rancorous or downright spiteful, but no-one who was capable of this wickedness. They were all upright and honest, clean in spirit, as they were in body today in their holiday garments, put on despite the siege.

Yet there was someone ...

At the council meeting that was held, as the Abbot had proclaimed, in the great chapter-house immediately following the *Ite missa est*, the revelations of the page's narrative were listened to in deathly silence. Every face was drawn and tight-lipped, and in every pair of eyes Catherine could read the same incredulous horror. A traitor in their midst? It was impossible!

'A traitor, no! But a traitress, yes!' cried Martin Cairou, his hatred flaring up at the mere mention of Gervais's name and leading him, by instinct, to the same conclusion as Sara. 'Only a besotted wench would sell her own people to that rogue! Whom was he courting when he did that wrong to my girl? I seem to call to mind he was taking a good deal of notice of your Jeannette,' he added, shooting a glance at Joseph Delmas, who rose instantly to the bait.

'Now, see here, Martin, what are you trying to say? That my Jeannette is the kind of abandoned, godless hussy who could stick a knife in her own parents' backs? You've suffered a hard blow, I know, and I'm sorry for you, but you're going too far! Gervais would go after any girl with her nose and her eyes in the right place! So why should it be my Jeannette any more than your brother's girl, Vivette, or Auguste's Babette?'

The Auvergnat is a hot-blooded creature and ticklish where his honour is concerned. Instantly, Noël Cairou and Auguste Malvezin flung themselves into the fray, and within a matter of seconds the council chamber had become the centre of such a hubbub of shouted insults and protestations that it seemed as if at any moment real violence would break out. The Abbot exchanged a speaking glance with Catherine, then got up from his chair and, wading into the midst of them, seized hold of Martin and Joseph who, roaring like madmen, were already coming to blows, and dragged them apart with a strength no-one would have suspected him of possessing.

'That's enough!' he cried. 'Are you out of your minds to fight thus, on Easter Sunday and in God's own house? Can't you see that by doing so you're only playing into the enemy's hands?'

'That might be so if it were nothing more than a rumour, a piece of malicious whispering. But we're dealing with a fact, reverend father! There is a traitor amongst us, and it's up to us to find him – or her!'

'You won't do it by fighting one another,' Catherine said. An idea had just come to her. 'But there may be a way …'

More, even, than the Abbot's intervention, her calm voice with its promise of a way to get to the bottom of the mystery soothed them. There was an immediate silence as everyone turned to look at her expectantly.

'A way?' the Abbot said. 'How?'

Catherine gazed slowly round the circle of faces turned toward her, as though trying to assure herself in advance of their agreement. Then she spoke quietly.

'We must let it be known that we are going to send another messenger down the tunnel. We'll keep what happened to Jeannet strictly to ourselves. Poor lad, he must be dead by now, but if the enemy have not let us know that, it must be because they want us to go on hoping for rescue. We'll simply give out that we're getting impatient and are therefore sending to Carlat to beg Countess Eléonore to make haste. Then, in the next few nights, someone else will go down the tunnel after Jeannet. Only this time he'll not go alone. A strong escort shall go with him.'

'I don't see what you're getting at, Dame Catherine,' the Abbot said. 'Why send a force down now that we know we've nothing to hope for from Carlat?'

'This is what I'm getting at. Bérault d'Apchier will send a few men, just as he did the other night, to intercept our latest messenger. According to what Bérenger told me, the last party consisted of four men, one of whom was Gervais. Our messenger will serve as a kind of bait. As soon as Apchier's men fall on him, our men will fall on them in turn, but not to kill them. I want prisoners, and I want them alive. Especially if one of them is Gervais Malfrat!'

'And what will you do with these men?'

'She'll hang Gervais, that's for sure,' Martin cried. 'And I'll do the office of hangman!'

'Possibly. But first of all I mean to make them talk – by whatever means!'

Catherine's words fell on the ears of the men present with the cold clarity of axe blows. Such deliberate menace was in her voice that the men regarded their châtelaine in amazement. She stood before them, as slim and straight as a sword blade and as inflexible, and they felt suddenly as if they had never before seen her properly, perhaps because never before had they seen that fierce, implacable look in her soft eyes.

She had announced her decision and nothing and no-one was going to make her alter it.

'By whatever means?' the Abbot said, with the faintest inflection of disbelief.

She rounded on him then, her cheeks on fire and her mouth hard. 'Yes, by any means whatever! Including torture! You need not look at me like that, father. I know what you are thinking. I am a woman, and it is not my nature to be cruel! I hate such methods! But remember, there are two things I must know, because all our lives depend on it. One is the name of the viper in our midst – and the other, the precise nature of the danger threatening my husband.'

'Do you expect to learn both those things from the men you take prisoner?'

'Yes. If one of them is Gervais. He is in Bérault's confidence, and if he directed the taking of the first messenger, there is no reason why he shouldn't direct the capture of the second as well. I want to get my hands on that man, because he is the root cause of all our troubles. And this time, reverend father, he can look for neither mercy nor pity at my hands!'

A roar of approval greeted this statement. There had been a hardness in her voice that conveyed to those men of Montsalvy something of Arnaud's decisive tones, and they found it reassuring. What they had feared to find in Catherine were the weaknesses of nervousness, indecision and squeamishness inherent in her woman's nature. Now that she was speaking like a leader of men, they were ready to follow her to the ends of the earth.

Gratitude sent Martin Cairou to kneel impulsively at her feet. His face haggard but his eyes filled with tears of joy, he seized the ermined hem of her gown and raised it to his lips.

'My lady!' he cried. 'When we've captured this accursed villain, you won't have far to look for a man to torture him! I'll do it, and by the memory of my dead child I promise you he'll talk!'

'No, Martin. I will not give that task to you. A torturer is not an avenger. He must be cold and indifferent. You have too much hatred, and your hatred would get the better of you. You would kill him.'

'No... no, I swear it!'

'In any case, if he is the coward I think him, we may not have to go to such extremes.'

She raised him gently but firmly, gazing deep into the distraught father's eyes with all their old gentleness in her own.

'Do not insist. This time, justice shall be done, and done to the full. Let it be enough for you to know that he shall hang – and you will be there to see it. Now, my friends, we must decide on the remaining details of our plan.'

This took a long time, and it was not until much later that members of the town council were able to join the guests crowding round the strings of sausages, the dried hams and cheeses in the great hall of the castle.

Catherine and the Abbot stood together for a moment, alone in the empty chamber, listening to the eager buzz of conversation that greeted the councillors as they emerged from the abbey.

Abbot Bernard sighed deeply. Then, rising from his chair, he slipped his hands inside his wide sleeves and made his way to where the châtelaine stood waiting, with her head a little bowed.

It was evident that she meant to stand by her decision, although she knew precisely what he was going to say to her.

'You have spoken perilous words, Dame Catherine. Do you think it wise thus to rouse the violence that is in them?'

'It was not I who chose the path of violence, father. They are the attackers. Besides, what weapons more in keeping with Christ's law have you to offer when the treason is within, when the enemy knows the secret of our movements as soon as we do ourselves? If the tunnel were not so well and strongly defended, Bérault d'Apchier would be already here, inside the citadel, thanks to the wretch who keeps him informed! Can you tell me he would not use violence, or that his hands when he came would be filled with lilies and olive branches?'

'I know, Dame Catherine. I know you are right, but these dreadful weapons – torture – the gallows – are they the proper tools for you, a woman, to use?'

She drew herself up to her full height, seeming even taller by reason of the steeple of purple velvet that crowned her golden hair.

'At the moment, Abbot, I am no longer a woman. I am the Lord of Montsalvy, its surety and defender! If I am attacked, I defend myself. What do you think Messire Arnaud would have done in our place?'

There was a brief silence. Then the Abbot muttered a faint, mirthless laugh, shrugged and looked away. 'Much worse, I know. But he is himself and you are – you!'

'No,' she cried, all her passionate feeling quivering in her voice. 'We are one! And you know that better than anyone! So forget Dame Catherine, my Lord Abbot, and let Arnaud of Montsalvy do what he must.'

She could still hear that proud statement of her faith, that cry of love affirming with the ardour of despair the total unity with the man she loved, for whom she had fought with superhuman strength ever since the day of their first meeting on a Flanders roadside; and it still rang in her head that night as she went the rounds of the watch upon the walls for one last check before she went to bed.

She was tired and worried, for in making this grave decision on her own, virtually against the Abbot's advice, she had taken on at the same time the crushing burden of responsibility, with no-one to share it. But Arnaud did not like shared responsibilities, and his wishes must remain the prime consideration even in his absence.

The rain had ceased at last, round about nightfall, but an icy wind had sprung up in its place. It whistled through the gaps in the shuttering and drove clouds across the sky like frantic sheep before a mad shepherd. It would almost certainly freeze that night, and what the torrential rains had spared would be finished off by the frost. It would be a hard winter to come, whatever happened, and as soon as the enemy had been driven off she must write at once to Bourges to tell Jacques Cœur of their difficulties and ask him to purchase corn and fodder, sugar and wine and all the other things they would need out of the huge sums he remitted regularly to the Lady of Montsalvy on account of the investment that she had once made and that had enabled the merchant to make a fresh start after the shipwreck that had ruined him.

Jacques, she knew, would readily understand her renunciation of the gold, the precious spices and silks with which he usually supplied her but which would be worse than useless to a starving countryside. Probably the hardest part would be to find the grain, when the staple food was still so scarce in so many parts of France ...

Catherine strolled on slowly, wrapped in a thick black cloak from which only her head emerged, covered by a simple scarf, making her way right round the curtain wall and moving from the pools of firelight to long stretches of darkness where it was hard to distinguish the figures of the men on watch from the solid bulk of the merlons by which they stood.

She was greeted everywhere with a cheerfulness engendered by the feast she had provided earlier in the day. Someone offered her a cup of mulled wine, and she smiled and shook her head as she went on her solitary way, lost in her own thoughts, trying to find some answer to the problems that had fallen so heavily on her.

She had just quit the tower that looked toward Pons and was proceeding along the dark passage linking it to the gatehouse tower when, just as she passed the black opening of one of the stairways cut into the thickness of the wall, she had a sudden feeling that she was being observed. Someone was breathing close by. Thinking it was one of the men-at-arms who was taking shelter there against the icy draught whistling through the covered way, she turned her head to give him a goodnight when something caught her abruptly by the shoulders and she was flung forwards.

She let out a cry that changed to a scream of pure terror as she saw that the planks covering one of the machicolations had been removed. A great gap loomed right at her feet, through which rose the damp exhalations from the moat below. Toward this abyss she was being thrust relentlessly.

'Help! He –'

The hands holding her increased their pressure. She reached out desperately, searching for a handhold, but her fingers slipped on the smooth stones and a brutal blow on the back sent her sprawling.

By good luck, she fell across the open gap. From shoulder to knee there was nothing but emptiness below her, but somehow she managed to stiffen her body and cling on to the remaining boards. She screamed again, as loudly as she could, while her invisible enemy kicked at her back, seeking to thrust her down the hole. She felt a sudden and much sharper pain in one shoulder. But her cries had been heard. Running footsteps approached. The blows on her back ceased and a light shone into the passage.

'Dame Catherine!' The old master-of-arms, Donat de Galauba, came running up, two other men at his back. 'What's happened?'

He bent down to raise the fallen woman whose grip was weakening fast.

'Take care!' one of the other men said quickly. 'The hoarding underneath her is open. You might easily send her straight through.'

'Hurry!' Catherine moaned. 'I – I'm falling!'

Swiftly putting aside the great black cloak that had concealed the opening, Donat gripped her firmly round the waist. At the same time, one of his men took a firm hold of his belt to prevent her weight from dragging him into the void, while the other edged his way along the wall to release Catherine's cramped and stiffened fingers.

Gently, they lifted her up, and turning her over, laid her down at a little distance. Her face was chalk white, and the eyes looking up into the old master-of-arms' face were wide with horror.

'He was there – hiding in the stairway. He fell on me from behind.'

'Who was it? Did you see?'

'No – no, I couldn't recognise him. He tried to throw me down but, thanks be to God, I fell the way you found me … Then he kicked me … hammered at me … I don't know.'

Donat drew out one of his supporting hands from beneath her and showed it to her. It was wet with blood. 'You're hurt! We must get you to the castle at once. Sara will know what to do for you.'

She shook her head impatiently. 'Hurt? I don't know - I didn't notice. But hurry – leave me here. It can't be serious! You must catch the man! '

'My men have gone after him. Lie still and don't worry.'

But the shock had been more than her nerves could stand. She clung to the old man, sobbing and wailing incoherently: 'But I must know … I need to know who … Someone hates me, Donat … Someone hates me and I want to know ...'

Very gently, like a father comforting his child, he stroked her damp forehead. 'No-one here hates you, Dame Catherine. We knew already that we had a traitor. From there to murderer is a short step. But we'll find him, don't you worry ...'

However, it seemed this was more easily said than done. The two soldiers returned empty-handed. The stairway led down to a dark, narrow alley that ran alongside the abbey wall, linking the covered marketplace with the massively buttressed tithe barn. The whole area was deserted at this time of night, and a person could easily melt into the shadows with no trouble at all. But although they had not found the attacker, the two men had spread the news of the attack on Catherine, and she was escorted back to the castle by an angry and highly vocal little crowd. This saw her restored, half-fainting, to the care of Sara and Donatienne, who lost no time in getting her to bed.

She came to herself again under Sara's ministrations. The wound in her shoulder was cleaned and dressed with a poultice of plantain leaves. Fortunately, the injury was not serious. The folds of Catherine's ample black cloak had deflected the would-be murderer's hurried stroke, which had, in any event, been aimed less to kill than to make her let go her hold and precipitate her into the void.

On the face of it, it looked as though he had wanted her death to appear an accident.

Catherine opened her eyes to see the three faces of Donatienne, Sara and Marie grouped round her bed like some allegorical portrayal of the three ages of human life. The old woman wore an expression of outraged solemnity. Sara's face was closed and set, but Catherine knew the boiling volcano of sheer anger that underlay her apparent calm. Only Marie's sweet face was streaked with tears.

To reassure them and to take away the anxiety she read in those three, so dissimilar pairs of eyes, Catherine forced herself to smile at them. 'It's nothing,' she said. 'I was more frightened than hurt.'

'And you're still frightened,' Sara grumbled. 'Who wouldn't be? Here, in this town, where everybody loves you and admires you for your many virtues, who would ever think there could be anyone so base ...?'

'As to tire of admiring my many virtues, as you call them? I'm only a woman, Sara, my dear, like any other. And even though you might not understand it, because you love me, it's quite natural that I should have enemies – little as I like the idea.'

'Whoever attacked you is more than an enemy,' Marie exclaimed. 'That man hates you!'

At this point, Donatienne emerged from her disapproving silence. She gave the impression that in attacking Catherine the unknown assailant had been guilty of a personal affront to herself. 'No-one here has any just cause to hate our lady,' she said categorically. 'Myself, I think the man was acting under orders, and his private feelings had nothing to do with it. In other words, he doesn't so much hate Dame Catherine as love the Apchiers. They must have thought that, with our lady out of the way, the Abbot, not being a man of war and as mild and gentle as a true saint, would make little trouble about accepting a new lord, especially if ...'

She broke off in some embarrassment as the thought that had been in her mind for days past now rose naturally to her lips. It was Catherine who finished it for her, grimly.

'Especially if, as Bérault prophesied, my lord should never return from these wars.'

She sat up on her pillows, so suddenly that she cried out from the pain in her wounded shoulder. Ignoring the pain, she stared round at the three faces turned toward her.

'I want you all to promise, if anything should happen to me– No, no! No arguments. It's quite possible. My mysterious attacker has failed once, but he might easily try again, indeed probably will, given time ...'

'That he won't have!' Marie cried fiercely. 'Josse is scouring the town at this very moment, searching every house, questioning everybody and making them all tell what they know! He was nearly mad when they brought you in just now. He said he had sworn on his life to Messire Arnaud that in his absence no harm should come to Dame Catherine or the children, and if the murderer had succeeded in his aim, there would have been nothing left for him but to die!'

'That's the last thing he should do,' Catherine said severely. 'If I were dead, that's just when Michel and Isabelle would stand in most need of friends to protect them. In fact, that is what I wanted to talk to you about. Promise me that if I should die you will do all in your power to save my children. Hide them in the town, because if Montsalvy falls into Bérault's hands, he will not spare my babies. Hide them – I know, with Gauberte's! She is loyal to me, and she already has ten of her own. Two more won't even be noticed. Then, when things are quiet again, take them to Angers, to Queen Yolande. She will see that they are brought up properly and their rights maintained – and their parents avenged! Swear this!'

Donatienne and Marie raised their hands at once, but Sara, who had been drying hers on a linen towel, threw it aside angrily and took two or three agitated turns about the room. Her brown face was much flushed, and there was a tell-tale brightness about her black eyes.

'You're not dead yet, as far as I can see,' she snapped out. 'Here you are dictating your last wishes as if we were simple-minded! Do you think it needs an oath to keep us to our duty if ...'

She stopped short suddenly, and stared at Catherine out of wide, tear-filled eyes. Then, like some great, dark bird, she sank to her knees beside the bed and buried her face in the covers.

'I forbid you to speak of your death!' she sobbed. 'I forbid it! If you died – do you think your old Sara could go on breathing God's pure air and beholding His sun, when you had gone down into the dark? Impossible! I could not! Don't ask me to swear … I could not keep my promise!'

She was sobbing openly now, and Catherine, moved beyond words by this desperate proof of her old friend's devotion, drew the woman's head down on to her breast and rocked her like a little child. The knot in her throat made speech impossible.

For years now, Sara had been like a second mother to her. She had shared everything with Catherine, the worst moments as well as the best, and had risked her life many times for the one she called her child. There were even times when it seemed to Catherine that the gypsy woman she had first met in the Court of Miracles in a time of great trouble held a bigger place in her heart than her own mother, now far away in Burgundy. It made her a little ashamed, although she had long known that the heart cannot always control its feelings and will not always beat as it is directed.

By the time Josse came in, a few minutes later, the other two women had caught the infection and Catherine's room was filled with weeping.

Josse stood looking gravely at the four women, his face drawn with a trouble that was all the deeper because it was unacknowledged. He rested one hand briefly on Marie's shoulder in a familiar, protective gesture, smiling at her with his curious half-moon smile that lifted the corners of his mouth without opening his lips. Then he bowed to his mistress, who had put Sara gently away from her and seemed to be waiting for him to speak.

'Apparently you have to deal with a phantom, Dame Catherine, capable of melting into stone walls. No-one has seen or heard anything! The man must be a cunning devil. Either that or he has accomplices.'

Catherine tensed. Josse's words had widened the crack that Bérenger's tale had opened in the wall of loyalty she had thought so secure about her.

Accomplices? It was possible … Who could say if her attacker and the traitor were one and the same? After all, those closest to her believed that traitor was a woman. That made two enemies, and all the more to be feared because they were cloaked by the mantle of trust!

An anguished bitterness flooded over Catherine. She closed her eyes tightly to keep back fresh tears, of discouragement this time. What was the good of struggling if even her own friends were fighting against her?

Josse moved forward to within arm's length of the bed and recalled her to herself with a gentle pressure of his fingers on the hand she clenched convulsively on the sheet. She looked up at once.

'Yes, Josse?'

'You're tired, and I'm sorry, but Nicolas wants to know if the decision taken in council today still stands, and if you are still determined …'

'More than ever! We'll make it tomorrow night. Find me a man capable of – of making our captives talk, if we catch any. Only not Martin Cairou. He is too full of hate. I'll await the outcome myself in the chamber below the keep. I want to know as soon as possible.'

'In the keep? But will you be fit to leave your bed by tomorrow?'

The fires of anger had dried the tears from her eyes. A slight touch of feverishness showed itself in two red spots high on her pale cheeks, but the eyes that stared up at her steward held a look of such inflexible determination that no other answer was possible.

Josse Rallard understood. With a deep bow, he left the chamber.

4: The Worm in the Bud

'Dear my Lady,' Bérenger said, greatly daring, 'you should not be here. It's cold and wet and you have not been well. See, your hands are trembling …'

It was true. Despite her thick grey velvet dress and squirrel-furred pelisse, Catherine's teeth were chattering. Her flushed cheeks and over-bright eyes betrayed her feverishness, but she insisted on remaining where she was in the low, heavily-vaulted chamber on which the cold lay like a leaden cope in spite of the brazier glowing redly by the stool on which she sat.

It was a gloomy place. Lying underneath the keep and covering its whole extent, it opened into two passages leading to the dungeons that, so far, had been used to hold nothing worse than casks and salting tubs; for, being cut out of the rock, they made admirable cellars.

Catherine had not had them built for fun. No castle worthy of the name could afford to be without some such places of detention.

In the centre of the room, under the flowered keystone with the iron ring set in it, was a large, open trapdoor through which could be seen the first steps of a ladder descending into darkness. This ladder led to another room, the same size as the first, which was generally supposed to be an oubliette. But it was in fact the entrance to the secret tunnel. It followed the course of what had at some time been an underground stream, running out far below the plateau. It was further defended by mighty iron grilles, impossible to force without giving the alarm to the guard who watched day and night in the underground chamber in case the enemy should discover the secret entrance.

Tonight, however, the châtelaine and her page were alone, in an utter silence, broken only by an occasional crackle from the brazier and, now and then, by Bérenger's nervous breathing.

It was almost an hour since, guided by Josse, who had taken on himself the dangerous role of the messenger, a number of the men of the town had vanished into the subterranean darkness. Nicolas Barral was their leader, and they had been armed for the venture as well as was possible without making them too noisy. Besides Nicolas and two of his company, the expedition was made up of the two Malvezin brothers, Jacques and Auguste; Guillaume Bastide, the baker with the head of a bull; and the gigantic farrier, Antoine Couderc. All carried axes and daggers. Antoine alone had nothing but the great hammer he used in his forge.

'I couldn't manage anything else; but this, this is something I know how to use!' he said. 'And I'll get a few of them with it, believe me! It'll be some consolation for our own dead!'

The attack that Bérault d'Apchier had launched against the town at daybreak had been murderous. Infuriated by day after day of inaction while the rain had poured down, the *routiers* had hurled themselves at the ladders with such violence that it had been all the townspeople could do to repulse them. At one point, the barbican at the Aurillac Gate had been all but carried, only old Donat de Galauba had seen the danger and rushed to its defence with a handful of village lads he had been trying to drill into soldiers ever since the siege began. Fired by his example, the boys had performed miracles, but three of them had fallen on the walls; and Donat himself, his throat pierced by a bolt from a crossbow, had ended there, in the heat of battle, a loyal and honourable life devoted to the house of Montsalvy. At this moment he was lying, in his well-worn armour, in the middle of the Great Hall of the castle, upon the banner of Montsalvy, which, all his life, he had fought so valiantly to defend.

Catherine herself had placed his great sword beneath his folded hands and laid his gauntlets and golden spurs on a velvet cushion at his feet. She had done so with piety and also with a kind of tenderness, and she had wept for the old servant who, she could not help thinking, had died for her. But hatred and anger had grown with tears and sorrow, and it was a Catherine more fiercely determined than ever who had given the signal for the start of that night's expedition.

'I must have prisoners,' she had repeated to Nicolas. 'One, at least, provided it's the right one!'

Now she waited, struggling to overcome her fever and her weakness. Her shoulder was very sore in spite of Sara's compresses and the ointment she had spread on it, and it hurt her to move her arm.

'They are so long! My God, they are so long!' she muttered through her teeth. 'Pray heaven nothing has gone wrong!'

The page, who was hardly daring to breathe for fear of disturbing his mistress in her anxious reveries, took his courage in both hands. 'Would you like me to go and see, Dame Catherine? I could go down to the entrance to the tunnel and listen if I can hear them coming?'

She forced herself to smile, well knowing what that offer must have cost his naturally cautious spirit. 'There's no point. It's too dark down there. You'd only break your neck and do no good to anyone ...'

'I could take one of the torches ...'

'No, Bérenger, stay where you are. Your place is with me. Besides, I think I can hear footsteps ...'

'Yes ... but they're coming from above, not from the tunnel.'

A moment later, Abbot Bernard appeared at the bottom of the steps leading from the keep, accompanied by the two Cairou brothers. At the sight of Catherine, huddled in her furs with only her drawn face emerging, he shook his head with an exclamation of mingled pity and disapproval.

'I thought I'd find you here! Really, my dear, you are not being sensible. Why don't you let Josse and Nicolas manage the business? They are perfectly capable of doing so to your complete satisfaction. Don't you trust them?'

'You know I do! But this is a matter of justice, and that is my responsibility. It is my duty – and my right!'

'It is mine also. Let me take your place, Catherine. You are in a high fever and can hardly stand! Go up and leave it to me. You will not be disappointed, I promise you. Only, for your own sake, do as I ask. You are looking dreadful!'

Catherine was so tired that she might well have allowed herself to be persuaded, but at that moment a terrific din broke out below their feet and Nicolas's steel-capped head popped up out of the ground.

'We've done it. Dame Catherine!' he announced, still panting from the effort of the fight. 'We've got him!'

Instantly, Catherine was on her feet. Her face was if anything paler than before, but a new flame burned in her eyes.

'Gervais?' she whispered. 'You have taken him?'

'They're bringing him now.'

Then the central trapdoor seemed to erupt, like a volcano, with a lava-flow of steel-clad men, all trying to clamber through at the same time and all talking at once. The cellar, so silent only a moment before, was filled with noise and movement.

A man, his hands bound behind his back, was thrust roughly forward by the smith's huge hand, and fell sprawling at the châtelaine's feet. His face, under the blood that dappled it from a wound in his head, was ashen. Nothing, at that moment, remained of Gervais Malfrat's swaggering conceit, as he found himself, alone and unarmed, in the centre of a group of human beings whose hatred he must have felt like the wave of hot air from a furnace.

In general, he was a well set-up young man, with reddish hair, a pale, freckled skin and eyes that were midway between brown and a deep yellow. He was proud of his fine physique and liked to show off his muscles to the local girls at feasts and holidays. But now terror seemed to have shrunk him to half his normal size, and he crouched there with his face in the dust, like a capon newly trussed for the spit, not daring even to lift his eyes to those around him for fear of what he might read in their faces.

As they flung him to the floor, Martin Cairou's expression had been transformed by a fearful joy. He made as if to hurl himself on the prisoner, but Abbot Bernard grasped him firmly by the arm and held him back.

'No, Martin! Wait! This man belongs not to you alone, but to all of us.'

'He belongs to Bertille! A life for a life, my Lord Abbot.'

'Come now, do not make me sorry that I allowed you to come.'

'That might not be such a bad idea,' Catherine said thoughtfully.

She stood for a moment, speculatively regarding the man who lay panting at her feet, then turned to Nicolas, who was flushed with pride and evidently awaiting his meed of praise.

'You brought only one prisoner, Sergeant? Was this man alone?'

'You must be joking, Dame Catherine! There were eight of them!'

'Then where are the others?'

'Dead. We're not so well stocked with victuals we can afford to feed captured vultures!'

'I don't think this one will last long enough to cost us very much,' Catherine said.

Her words, and the implication behind them, redoubled Gervais's terrors. He ventured to lift vacant eyes to the châtelaine.

'Mercy!' he stammered. 'Don't kill me …'

His face was livid, and beads of sweat rolled down his unshaven cheeks, while the saliva dribbled from his slack lips in his abject paroxysm of fear.

Catherine gave a shudder of disgust. 'What reason should I have to spare you? I have already spared you once, and that was once too often, for you repaid me by bringing this pack of famished wolves down on us.'

'Not I!'

'Not you?' Bertille's father cried. 'Leave him to me, Dame Catherine! He'll sing another song in a few minutes' time, I promise you!'

'I mean,' Gervais amended hastily, 'it was not I who put it into Apchier's head to come here. He had it in his mind ever since the great feast last autumn. But I knew nothing of that when they found me up there, on the Aubrac, half-frozen and nigh dead with hunger.'

'But it was you who told them Messire Arnaud was away and his men with him,' Abbot Bernard said. 'It comes to the same thing. Worse, maybe, because but for you the women and children and old men of our town would not now be in peril.'

Gervais squirmed toward him. 'Reverend Abbot – you are a man of God … a man of mercy … have pity on me! I'm young! I do not want to die! Tell them to spare my life!'

'And what of poor Brother Amable?' the smith snarled. 'He wasn't so old either! Did you implore your Apchier friends to spare his life?'

'There was nothing I could do! Who am I to advise such lords? To them, I am nothing but a peasant.'

'To us, also,' the smith growled. 'But they must think you a serviceable peasant to judge by the arrogant way you were strutting out there on the night they came.'

'And the second messenger, Jeannet – the one you lay in wait for at the tunnel's mouth, just as you did tonight,' Bastide went on. 'I suppose he's still alive and well?'

Arrowlike, the accusations were falling thick and fast now on the wretched Gervais, who huddled more and more abjectly beneath the storm, grovelling with his head bowed between his shoulders as though against a swarm of wasps, not even trying to defend or justify himself.

For a little, Catherine let it go on, without interfering. The hatred and anger emanating from the circle of men was putting the final touch to the prisoner's state of terror, and this was what she wanted.

She sat on her stool, hugging her furs about her, silent and shivering, and keeping her eyes averted from the rag of humanity crouched at her feet. Such cowardice sickened her. Yet from this cowed and terrorised craven, she still had to drag the truth …

When she sensed that he was ready, she lifted her hand and, with this simple gesture, silenced her companions. Then she put out her foot and touched the shoulder of the man lying before her.

'Now listen to me, Gervais Malfrat! You have seen these men, heard what they say. They all hate you, and not one of them but would like to put you to all the torments of hell before they let your miserable soul escape from your body. Even so, you can still save yourself a world of suffering …'

Gervais looked up at once. She read a faint hope in his staring eyes.

'You'll spare me again, gracious lady …? Only tell me, tell me, tell me quickly what you want of me!'

She saw that he was ready to talk, to tell them anything so long as he thought he could still save his life. It would have been easy to promise, but she refused to lie, even to such a vile wretch as this, or stoop to such a ruse. Regardless of the possible cost, she put him right at once.

'No, Gervais. I am not going to spare you, because it is no longer in my power to do so. You are not my prisoner, you belong to the people of this town, and none of them would understand it if we allowed you to continue your immoral life. But you shall have a quick death if you answer two questions … only two.'

'Why not my life? Grant me my life, Dame Catherine, or I will answer nothing! What do I care what you want to know if I must die just the same!'

'There are deaths and deaths, Gervais. There is the rope, the arrow, the axe and the knife, which kill in an instant … or there is the strappado, the tongs, the molten lead, the red-hot irons – with those a man may last for hours, for days sometimes, and they can make him scream and cry out for death and long for it as a boon!'

As each dreadful word fell from Catherine's lips, Gervais uttered a moan, ending at last in a long howl of: 'No! No ... Not that!'

'Then talk. If not, I swear by the honour of the name I bear that I will hand you over to be tortured, Gervais Malfrat.'

But even now, terror had not altogether darkened the wretch's wits. A cunning expression passed over his haggard face.

'You make yourself out to be more cruel than you are, Dame Catherine. I know as well as you that there is no torturer in Montsalvy.'

'There is me!' Martin Cairou cried, unable to contain himself longer. 'Give him to me, my lady! He'll talk, I promise you, and I'll not bate his agonies for all his screams and prayers ...! Wait! I'll show you.'

Bending swiftly, the clothworker seized a long iron poker that lay by the brazier and thrust it into the fire amid a deathly hush.

They could hear Gervais' panting breath.

'Look at that man,' Catherine said. 'He hates you. His child embraced death on your account. For days and nights now – nights especially – he has dreamed of having you at his mercy, to make you suffer an eternity of pain in the hope that so he might, in part, appease his own. You are quite right when you say we have no torturer at Montsalvy, but that is because we have never needed one. But for you, there will be one, and one that you yourself have made ... Now will you talk?'

The iron rod was glowing, incandescent, in the fire. Martin grasped it firmly, while Antoine Couderc and Guillaume Bastide moved as one to seize Gervais, whose howls were like a wolf's at the point of death, while his straining muscles were stretched taut in expectation of the agony to come.

'No-oo-oo!'

Martin took a step forward. Catherine caught him by the arm and held him back, then spoke to Gervais, who was struggling wildly in the grip of his guards, so that the Malvezin brothers were obliged to go to their assistance.

'Speak! Or in another moment you will be stripped of your clothes and fastened to that ring in the roof, and then we will leave you to Martin!'

'What – what do you want to know? '

'Two things, as I told you. First, the name of your accomplice. There is a traitor somewhere in this town, from whom you had your information. I want his name!'

'And the – the second thing?'

'Bérault d'Apchier has been shouting aloud that the Lord of Montsalvy will never return. I want to know what he is plotting, to be so sure! I want to know what it is that threatens my husband!'

'I told you, my lady ... I'm too small a fish to be honoured with Apchier's secrets ...'

Before he could go on, Catherine said, without raising her voice: 'Take off his clothes and hang him by the wrists from that ring ...'

'No! For pity's sake! No! Don't hurt me! I'll talk ... I'll tell you all I know!'

'One moment,' Abbot Bernard broke in. 'I will write down all that you have to say. You are before a tribunal here, Gervais. I shall be its clerk.'

Calmly, he produced from his scapula a rolled sheet of paper[*] and a goose feather and unhooked from his belt a small inkwell. Then he signed to one of the men to make his armoured back a writing desk.

'There,' he said with satisfaction. 'We are ready to listen.'

Glancing in turn at the waiting Abbot with his quill poised, at the châtelaine, sitting chin in hand and watching him with relentless eyes, and at Bertille's father, replacing his poker in the fire, Gervais croaked out: 'Gonnet ... Apchier's bastard, is no longer in the camp. He left on the morning of Easter Thursday for Paris ...'

'You're lying!' Nicolas cried. 'The bastard was burned on the shoulder during the first assault. He could not go!'

'I swear to you he's gone,' Gervais cried. 'They've tough hides in that family! Besides, it was his shoulder that was hurt, not his arse! He could ride a horse ...'

'I believe you,' Catherine broke in impatiently. 'Go on – tell us what he went to Paris to do.'

'To find Messire Arnaud. Not that they told me, of course, but you hear a lot of things through the walls of a tent at night, if you keep your ears open ...'

He was interrupted again, this time by a burst of laughter from Nicolas.

'If you expect us to believe your bastard has gone off to assassinate Messire Arnaud right in the middle of the Constable's army, either you take us for fools or that Gonnet of yours has a taste for martyrdom! Setting aside the fact that our master's got the use of both his arms, he has a guard about him that the King might envy. No-one cuts down a Montsalvy when a La Hire, a Xaintrailles, a Bueil and Chabannes are by – not unless he wants to leave his skin behind him!'

'I didn't say he was going to murder him ... not outright, at any rate. The Apchiers are too clever for that. Gonnet is going to Paris – to fight alongside the captains. He'll claim he's come to serve the King to try to win himself a pair of spurs. That's what he'll say, and Messire Arnaud won't think it at all unnatural. He knows Gonnet is a bastard and will have nothing much to look for from his father, seeing that Bérault d'Apchier has two legitimate

---

[*] Paper mills had been in existence for nearly a century: witness that of Richard de Bas, near Ambert. which dates from 1356.

sons. No-one will wonder at it if a lad brought up to the trade of arms should try to carve himself a place in the sun, will they?'

Catherine strained her wits to try to unravel her enemy's dark plot, the meaning of which still eluded her.

'You mean,' she said, not so much questioning as thinking aloud, 'that by going to my husband, Gonnet is going to try to gain his protection and, by offering to fight under his banner, win his confidence?'

'Something like that ...'

'He'll not find it easy! My lord has no great love for the Apchiers, legitimate or not. He simply tried to keep on neighbourly terms with them, but that is all.'

'He does not love them, but he will listen to Gonnet. The bastard's not such a fool as to try and make himself out a plaster saint. For one thing, he'll acquit himself well in battle. He'll have no trouble there, for he is brave. But Messire Arnaud will pay attention to him soon enough when he learns that the old brigand, his father, and his brothers are laying siege to Montsalvy.'

'What? He's going to warn him?'

'Of course. You see, Dame Catherine, Gonnet will arrive at the Constable's camp all hot with pretended anger: his father and brothers have fallen on Montsalvy as a gift from heaven but have refused to share with him. He has been driven off, beaten, even wounded, for he'll make the most of his injury and claim he had it in a fight with one of his brothers. He's burning for revenge. So he ran away and came to warn the lawful owner of the wrong that was being done him, in the hope of making a friend, and preferably a grateful one. Messire Arnaud will find that kind of talk quite natural coming from Gonnet d'Apchier ...'

Gervais needed no urging now to make him speak. Driven on by the hope that the Dame of Montsalvy might yet be grateful enough to spare his life, he omitted no detail in his explanation.

Catherine listened, her eyes wide with horror. For all her fever, she felt an icy chill creep through her veins as she glimpsed the hideous blackness, the loathsome pit that was opening before her feet and her husband's, although as yet unable to measure its depth. The men around her were conscious of something of the same sensation, and it was Nicolas Barral who put the next question.

'What does the bastard hope to gain by telling Messire Arnaud what is happening here?'

'That he will leave the army at once to return here. Gonnet will go with him, of course, supposedly to enjoy his vengeance. There will no longer be all those soldiers and captains about him, and so, on the road ...'

'If he returns at all, he'll hardly come alone!' Couderc burst out indignantly. 'He might not have his gallant friends or the Constable's army, but he'll have his own men with him on the road home, he'll have his knights and all our lads, who'll be only too ready to warm an Apchier's hide for him, true or false! Do you think they'll let your Gonnet strike him down and do nothing?'

'Gonnet carries with him a poison – a poison that acts slowly and does not alter the taste of wine. When they halt for the night, and the knights are drinking a cup of wine or two to refresh themselves from the weariness of the road, it won't be hard for the bastard to slip it into Messire Arnaud's cup, with plenty of time afterwards to disappear.'

A spontaneous growl of anger burst from every throat and rolled round the vaulted chamber, echoing Catherine's cry of anguish.

As one man, the sergeant, the smith and the brothers Malvezin threw themselves on Gervais with the object of choking him to death. The Abbot was only just in time to get between them and the prisoner and prevent him from being slain on the spot.

'Wait!' he said. 'The man has not finished yet. Let him be! It is not he who must be kept from doing harm at this moment!' Turning to the man crouched in the shelter of his black habit, he added: 'Tell me, Gervais, if Gonnet d'Apchier possesses a poison so strong and so secret, why doesn't he use it as soon as he finds Messire? He would have time to vanish just as easily in Paris?'

'To be sure, Reverend Father, but what Bérault d'Apchier wants is not only Messire Arnaud's death – but also his disgrace.'

'What?'

'If the Lord of Montsalvy leaves the siege of Paris, abandons the army to return home, how will he be judged by his peers? I don't know how Gonnet means to do it, but he will see to it that his departure will look like flight – or treachery. "It's always possible," he said, "to leave some compromising thing behind, and I'll not miss my chance." And when Messire Arnaud disappears soon afterwards, Bérault d'Apchier will have no trouble in possessing himself, with the utmost propriety and lawfulness, of the traitor's goods. It won't be the first time King Charles VII has struck at the house of Montsalvy!'

This time there were no cries of indignation, no comment even. Anger and revulsion held each man present dumb with astonishment.

Catherine rose and looked around her proudly. 'Then we have nothing to fear. My lord knows his duty too well – and places too much trust in all of you, his vassals, and in me, his wife, to desert in the face of the enemy only to fly to our assistance! Even if he knew that Montsalvy was burning, he would not leave the army while there was still a campaign to be fought, and this time more than ever, because it is Paris, the capital city of this kingdom, which must be wrested from the English and given back to our King! Your Gonnet is wasting his time,' she added, turning to Gervais. 'The Lord of Montsalvy will not desert his post, not even to save us from peril! At the most, he will ask the Constable for leave to send what men can be spared from his own company.'

The young woman's words had the effect of a jet of oil sprayed on boiling water. Every man breathed again, every face relaxed, and some even exchanged grins of triumphant delight.

'To be sure!' Guillaume Bastide said. 'Messire Arnaud will do what he can, as an honourable knight, to help us, and the bastard will have his pains for nothing!'

'Aye,' Nicolas agreed gruffly. 'He wasn't born yesterday. Tho Apchiers' tricks aren't subtle enough to catch him.'

Gervais was suddenly angry. In some extraordinary way, the bound man seemed to find it intolerable that what he had said should be dismissed so lightly. He had no thought now of bargaining with his information. Carried away by a blind fury he shouted: 'You stupid churls! What cause have you to preen yourselves like turkey cocks, strutting and crowing with pride? I'm telling you he'll go with Gonnet! He'll set out for home! Because he'll have no choice. How do you think your Messire Arnaud will react when Gonnet tells him his wife is Jean d'Apchier's mistress, that she brought her lover here to deliver the town up to him ... and when he gives him proof that they have lain together?'

There was a deathly silence. They stared at one another, unable to believe their ears, while Catherine, her face as grey as her gown, stood rooted to the spot with staring eyes ... Then, gazing straight ahead of her at a fixed spot on the wall, she said in a flat voice that seemed not to belong to her: 'Proof ...? What proof?'

Appalled by the effect of his word, Gervais made no answer, dared not even move. At that, as if she had been suddenly released, she sprang on him and, seizing him by the collar of his grimy jerkin, began to shake him wildly.

'What proof?' she cried. 'Speak! What proof ...? Tell me before I skin you alive!'

Moaning with terror, Gervais slipped from her grasp and lay, face down, on the ground before her, stammering 'One of your shifts ... and a letter also ... a love letter ... or a piece of one!'

But Catherine had overestimated her own strength. She was exhausted, and the violence of the spring that had carried her to Gervais had reawakened the pain in her shoulder. She opened her mouth to speak, but no sound came. Her eyes rolled, her arms flailed helplessly for a moment, and she sank, unconscious, to the stone floor beside the prisoner.

At that, they all moved at once, Bérenger, who throughout the violent scene had stood as still and silent as a statue, dropped to his knees to raise her head, but already Nicolas Barral had stooped and, sliding one arm beneath Catherine's shoulders and the other under her knees, had lifted her as easily as if she had been a featherweight.

'That's all it needed,' he growled furiously. 'She ought never to have been present when we questioned him. It's enough to kill her,' he added, looking down with pity at the bloodless face with heavy black rings round the eyes as it lay against his shoulder.

Abbot Bernard shook his head. 'We should have had to tell her in any case. Take her to her chamber, Nicolas, and give her into Sara's keeping. Tell her what has passed and then come back. I still need you here.'

'What shall we do with this?' Couderc asked, with a jerk of his head toward Gervais. 'Hang him out of hand?'

The Abbot also regarded the prisoner, with no hint of mercy in the eyes, which were in general so gentle and kindly. Clearly the man, as much as the diabolical plan he had just revealed, filled him with revulsion.

'No,' he said coldly. 'We'll go on. Gervais still has many things to tell us. The name of the traitor within our walls, for one. We had forgotten that for a moment, learning of the danger that threatens Messire Arnaud, but now it becomes more urgent than ever to discover it.'

The other Lord of Montsalvy took his seat on the stool that Catherine had vacated. On his lap, he smoothed the paper on which he had inscribed the prisoner's previous confessions, and he sighed.

'You must answer me now, Gervais. But do not deceive yourself. My conditions are the same as Dame Catherine's. With this difference only: that I shall add to it absolution from your sins if your repentance is sincere … before I hang you.'

An hour later, while Catherine, watched over by Sara, slept deeply under the effects of a soothing drug liberally administered, while Gervais, in chains, was inaugurating one of the castle dungeons from which three salting tubs had been hastily removed, and Abbot Bernard, an anxious frown on his face, was walking back to his monastery to await the next stage of events, Nicolas Barral, escorted by four soldiers, was knocking on the door of Augustin Fabre, the carpenter. Getting no answer, he broke down the door, the noise bringing an assortment of scared, night-capped faces to windows and doors all around, each accompanied by the gleam of knife or axe, caught up hurriedly in the belief that this was a surprise attack.

Ever since the siege had begun, the people of Montsalvy had got into the way of sleeping with their weapons within reach. In Gauberte Cairou's house, even, the whetstone turned continually. Everything down to her spindle was as sharp as a lance's point, and in her nightly dreams she aspired to rival the glory of the Maid of Orléans, who was her private heroine.

Day was just breaking. Cocks were crowing shrilly on all sides. For the first time in many days, the skies were clear of cloud and the morning star stone there like a great blue diamond.

It was at the sky that the newly-wakened townspeople glanced first. In that direction, at least, their troubles seemed to be over. Their second glances were all for Fabre's violated house, from which Nicolas and his men were just emerging, baffled. The house was empty. Augustin and Azalaïs had vanished inexplicably.

Immediately, the sergeant and his men were surrounded by an eager crowd, longing to know what was happening. It was a crowd soon joined by Gauberte, whose house was at a little distance. She came running with a sheepskin thrown over her shift and brandishing her spindle.

Then the four men who had taken part in the night's ambush came up on their way back from the castle. Soon, the little square was filled with half-dressed people, all talking at once and waving an assortment of weaponry, none of them knowing quite why.

Nicolas realised that he would have to provide some explanation or watch the gathering turn into a riot. Clambering up on to the rim of the well, he stood on the stone sill and, with arms spread out like a conductor, tried to quell the din. This was not easy, because everyone was shouting all the louder because he or she did not know what it was all about. But Gauberte's curiosity was not to be stifled. Climbing up beside Nicolas, she uttered two or three bellows of such piercing quality that silence fell as if by magic, for there was not a pair of lungs in all Montsalvy that could rival hers!

She let her eyes roam over the crowd with a satisfied expression. 'There you are, Nicolas. Now tell us what's going on!'

Schooling himself, not without difficulty, to the making of a speech, the sergeant described the events of the night, leaving nothing out. He told them of the confessions extracted from the terrified Gervais, of the trap laid for Arnaud de Montsalvy, of Catherine's fainting and finally of how, driven to the last ditch by the Abbot's merciless questioning, Gervais had at last named as his accomplices the carpenter, his daughter and the local witch, La Ratapennade, who had provided the poison Gonnet d'Apchier had taken with him. Last of all, he told how Augustin Fabre, a victim of the highly unpaternal feelings inspired in him by his dead wife's daughter, had fallen entirely under Azalaïs's domination. According to Gervais, the lacemaker's provocative beauty had made of the once honest and peaceable man a slave to his monstrous desires, whom the girl could play like a puppet – and would mock at when, in the days before he was driven out, she had met Gervais behind the mill. For, by flattering the girl's ambition, by dangling before her eager eyes the prospect of a future she believed him perfectly capable of realising, by playing up to her vanity, Gervais Malfrat, skilled in the game of love, had not found it hard to win what she so scornfully denied to other young men.

Fabre, naturally, was unaware that Azalaïs was the rogue's mistress, and it was he who, acting on his strange daughter's orders, had tried to murder the Lady of Montsalvy on the ramparts. In exchange for this service, she had promised to give herself to him at last. The thought of it must have driven the poor man mad until, to possess the body whose grace haunted his nights, he would as readily have stabbed Abbot Bernard in the middle of high mass.

As for Azalaïs herself, it was she who had not only given Gervais one of Catherine's shifts, which she had acquired for the purpose of mending a tear in the lace, but had also written the infamous 'love letter', by counterfeiting the châtelaine's own hand. Gifted with a genuine artistic talent, as well as considerable quickness, the lacemaker was able to draw as well as write, and this twofold ability had made it easy for her to go one step further into forgery. All these things, like other messages to Gervais, had been lowered by Fabre with a rope at night while he was supposedly on guard at a convenient angle of the walls.

The outcry that greeted Nicolas's disclosures was so fierce that the watchers on the ramparts leaned down to see. The little square was boiling like a witch's cauldron, with tossing heads and flashing eyes and arms waving a motley collection of implements that might, at a pinch, be useful weapons.

Once again, it was Gauberte who spoke for all of them. 'We want Augustin and Azalaïs!' she roared.

Brandishing her spindle with as much conviction as if she had been Joan of Arc with her banner of the lilies, she leaped down from the well and bore down on the carpenter's house, drawing after her a tumultuous crowd that poured somehow into the workshop, despite the sergeant's swearing by all the saints in heaven that he had gone over everything already with a fine-tooth comb. He was even obliged to intervene to prevent Gauberte and her angry followers from setting fire to the house, which was packed to the eaves with people, and probably sending half the town up in flames with it.

In any case, they were compelled to accept the evidence. Warned mysteriously of the danger that would threaten them if Gervais Malfrat were captured, Azalaïs and her father had chosen flight and vanished as if by magic, leaving no trace, not even any sign of hurry. The carpenter's house, when Nicolas and his men had broken down the door, had been in perfect order. The beds were made and all the crockery in its place. Only their clothes and a few personal belongings were gone.

When Gauberte and her followers emerged again into the square, they were very quiet. Everyone was trying to think how Fabre and Azalaïs could have vanished so completely. Also, how they could have been warned of what had taken place at the council, at which the carpenter had not been present.

'We must find out who warned them,' Nicolas concluded. 'Someone among us has been letting his tongue wag, that's for sure …'

He turned his steel-capped head slowly, and his eyes sought out all those members of the council who were present in the crowd, those who had taken part in the night's events as well as the rest; but nobody failed to meet his gaze.

'Good,' he said at last. 'Then we'll have a search. See you look everywhere,' he said to his men, 'and overlook no cellar or loft, not even stables or hencoops. They must be found!'

'We'll help,' Gauberte declared. 'This is something that concerns all of us. Come on, lads! Let's have a few volunteers to help the men-at-arms!'

Volunteers came flocking by the dozen. Everyone was eager to pursue a traitor who was now revealed as being also an attempted murderer. But before Nicolas could organise the hastily-formed squads of volunteers, a cry from one of the watch rose in the red morning sky.

'Come and look!'

It was Auguste, one of the Malvezin brothers, who had called. He was kneeling in an embrasure with his spear propped against the wall beside him and staring down, pointing at something at the foot of the wall. In a moment, the rampart was crowded with people, craning to look down in their turn. A simultaneous gasp rose from every throat. There, on the edge of the ditch, lay the broken body of Augustin Fabre, his face turned up toward the sky and his eyes wide open. A crossbow bolt protruded from his breast.

Out of habit rather than respect, the nightcapped heads were uncovered.

'How did he come there?' someone asked. 'And where is his daughter?'

The first of these questions was answered almost at once. At the far end of the battlements, just before the bulge formed by one of the towers, a rope was hanging down the wall.

'He must have fallen!' someone breathed with awe. 'A man of his age, he'd no business to go climbing down walls like that!'

'And the bolt?' Auguste Malvezin retorted. 'Did he pick that up as he fell?'

'Someone must have fired at him. Perhaps they didn't know he was working for them?'

All of them were clearly shocked by Fabre's death. It was still only a short time since he had been one of their own, his defection unsuspected by anybody. Their hushed voices held a respectful note that disgusted Gauberte.

'Here!' she exclaimed. 'He's all by himself in the ditch! There should be two of them. What's happened to the lovely Azalaïs? It's hard to see how she could have gone the same road …'

'Why not? She's like a cat, that girl! There's such a devil in her, she could slip through a needle's eye or slide down a mountainside without hurting herself! I always said she was a bit of a witch,' Auguste finished bitterly.

The truth was that he had long sighed after the lovely lace-maker and had got nothing for his pains but mockery and laughter, and he resented it.

Barral pushed back his steel cap and scratched his head, not taking his eyes from the shattered body, which seemed to exercise a kind of fascination for him. He sighed.

'Auguste's right. Something tells me we'll not be seeing her again. Anyhow, there's poor Fabre lying dead before heaven, and no-one to give him a decent burial.'

And indeed, the body looked utterly pathetic lying there, more tragically forsaken than any they had seen. He had fallen on the muddy bank of the ditch, mid-way between the town where he had given his soul away to a devil in female form and the enemy camp, quiet at this hour, from which he had looked for something other than his death wound.

But the *routiers* were going about their normal daily tasks of lighting fires and cooking food, making the most of the fine weather to dry their garments and clean up a little, regardless of the pitiful corpse.

The sun had burst above the horizon and leaped up the sky, deluging the ravaged countryside with a flood of golden rays. Except for the bloody remains, there was nothing to show that between the camp, now buzzing with activity, and the city, lying momentarily at peace, fear, anger, greed and hatred had drawn an iron curtain.

But there was the corpse, with its gaping wound, its face contorted in its final agony, and everything slipped back into place and meaning.

'Let's hope those damned dogs will bury him,' Gauberte sighed at last. 'After all, he was betrayed himself as much as he betrayed us, and he's paid dearly for it. Best ask the Abbot for a bit of a prayer for his poor soul, because he wasn't the most guilty.'

Then, hugging her sheepskin round her, as if suddenly feeling the chill of death, the big linen-weaver tucked her spindle under her arm and, without another word to anyone, went off home to feed her family.

The crowd on the ramparts melted away silently, leaving only the men on guard to resume their monotonous rounds.

Meanwhile, in the castle, Catherine was awaking to a bitter reality that even the sun, flooding brilliantly through the stained glass of her chamber, failed to illuminate.

She learned from Sara that Abbot Bernard was asking to see her.

'I can tell him to come back later if you don't feel well enough,' Sara offered. 'You've given us all a fine fright already!'

'No. It's no good. I must speak to him, also. If he had not come, I should have sent for him.'

'Only tell me how you feel.'

The young woman's smile was infinitely sad.

'Better, I promise you. Whatever you gave me has done me good. But then, you know, this is no time to be wallowing in self-pity, or coddling myself between sheets. If Gonnet d'Apchier succeeds in carrying out his plan, it would be better for me if I died at once!'

'Let me be the judge of that. I'll go and fetch the Abbot.'

'No. Help me to my oratory. In what we have to say, it is best that God should make a third, for I have never had such need of His aid. Just bring me something hot. I need to gather my strength.'

Sara would have much preferred Catherine to stay in her bed, but she did not insist. She knew it would be a waste of time. Catherine certainly looked very ill and drawn, but there was about the corner of her mouth a stubborn line that the one-time gypsy knew well. When that appeared, Sara sensed that Catherine must be left to herself to go the length of her will, even if that meant driving herself to exhaustion or even beyond.

So she went out and led Abbot Bernard to the little private chapel, then returned bearing a basin of hot milk sweetened with honey, which she held out without a word.

In the short time since she had left the room, Catherine had dragged herself out of bed. As she ventured her first, tottering steps across the black-and-red-tiled floor, she felt her head swim and experienced another of the sudden blinding stabs of pain that so alarmed Sara. But she pulled herself together, obstinately determined to get the better of her weakness. For the sake of her own safety and Arnaud's, and most of all for the sake of their mutual happiness, she had to master her unwilling body, which was usually so supple and obedient but now refused to help her just when she most needed it. Both their lives depended on her alone, and she had to be able to fight. Later, when the storm was past – if it ever passed – then she could think of herself, of her own health and her sorely-tried nerves.

She stood, clinging to one of the bedposts, resisting the temptation of her pillows because of the fear that she might not be able to get up again, and waited for the dizzy spell to pass and the whirling walls to subside.

When all was still at last, like a roundabout coming to rest, she moved slowly to pick up her brown dress with the squirrel's fur trimming, and huddled herself into it somehow.

From the next room, she could hear little Michel's voice replying firmly to baby Isabelle's merry prattle. Big brother had taken it on himself to initiate his little sister into the rudiments of conversation and was devoting himself to his task with the precocious earnestness he brought to everything he did.

Catherine's heart melted, and she was tempted to go to them for the joy of holding them in her arms and reforging her own courage in their artless affection, but she resisted it for fear of frightening them. The tragic mask she saw in her mirror was not a sight for children's eyes. She moved softly to close more thoroughly the door between the rooms, drank the milk that Sara was holding ready for her, watching her closely, and then walked to her private chapel with steps the apparent firmness of which cost her all her willpower. Sara made no move even to offer the support of her arm. That, too, would have been useless.

The oratory was in one of the towers. Entering, Catherine found Abbot Bernard kneeling before the little granite altar on which a big cross of gold glowed beneath the blue and yellow of the arched window.

As a chapel, it was very small, made for the solitary meditation of a noble lady, but it contained, in addition to the cross of goldsmith's work, Catherine's most precious treasure: an Annunciation by her friend of earlier days, the painter Jean Van Eyck.

On a narrow panel of poplar wood, the artist had depicted a tiny Virgin, astonishingly pure and virginal in the extravagant folds of a wide gown of blue faille over which her hair fell in golden curls, held lightly by a jewelled fillet on her brow. Her face was a little averted, her hand raised in a pretty, timid gesture, and she seemed to be avoiding the eyes of the splendid and mildly quizzical Angel who, with elusive smile and kindly look, was offering her a flower, gently inclining his head of long, shining curls crowned with a golden diadem. The Angel's robe and his great, geometrically patterned wings, all seeded with glittering gems, made a gorgeous vision alongside the comparative simplicity of the little Virgin; but the Virgin possessed Catherine's face and huge amethyst-coloured eyes, and her incomparable golden hair. It was a young, shy, loving Catherine, like the girl who, one evening on the Peronne road, in her Uncle Mathieu's company, had found Arnaud of Montsalvy, unconscious and bleeding in his black, mud-spattered armour. And it was because of this that the quick-tempered captain had opened his gates last Christmas morning to the messenger from Burgundy who had dismounted in the snowy courtyard. The man had been not alone with the picture he carried, in its careful wrappings of thick wool and fine linen, before him like a baby. He had had a strong escort of men-at-arms, who must have been the first Burgundian horsemen to ride over French soil since the peace of Arras.

Arnaud's first impulse had certainly been one of anger. Duke Philippe's name alone had still the power to throw him into a passion, and the sight of his arms was ever like a red rag to an enraged bull. But the letter accompanying the gift had been not in the Prince's hand. It had been Jean Van Eyck himself who had written.

'One who is ever your faithful friend rejoices that he may now tell you so without being held a traitor, and wish you a happy Christmas in a land where brothers have ceased to hate one another. Accept, I beg you, this Annunciation in your likeness in the hope that it may foretell peace indeed. In its execution, your humble servant has relied on his memory – and his heart. Jean.'

The picture was charming, and the letter also. Catherine had accepted both with tears in her eyes, although she could not help observing with a blush: 'I am no longer so young – or so beautiful.'

'Young, you will always be,' Arnaud had said gruffly, 'and each day you grow more beautiful. Yet I am glad to welcome this young girl into my house, because it is thus you should have entered it if I had been less of a fool!'

And so the Annunciation had taken its place in the oratory where, morning and evening, Catherine went to kneel before it for a moment. It was one way of rediscovering her youth, and always it gave her the same joy. Little Michel, for his part, adored the picture in which his mother and the Queen of Heaven were confused on the wooden panel as they were a little in his mind.

As she came into the tiny chapel, Catherine's eyes went naturally to the picture, to the Angel's smile, and the daily spell worked once again. She felt better and stronger and more independent, as if the heavenly youth had instilled in her a little of his own zest for living.

She moved silently to kneel beside the Abbot, clasping her cold hands on the velvet back of her prie-Dieu.

Sensing her presence, he turned to look at her and frowned.

'You're very pale. Shouldn't you have stayed in bed?'

'I blame myself already for the time that has been wasted by my weakness last night. I can't stay in bed now, not knowing what I do! I don't know if I shall ever be able to sleep again until this fear is over! You see, father, when I heard what those – people were conspiring to do to ruin us, I felt as if I had died and ...'

'Stop trying to find excuses for your weakness, Dame Catherine. I myself reeled for a moment, I confess, at such base perfidy, but it may well have been the anger that I felt enabled me to continue where you left off, without weakening ... and without pity. Gervais Malfrat admitted everything we wished to know, without the slightest trouble. And his skin is still intact.'

In a few words, Bernard de Calmont d'Olt put the châtelaine in possession of the facts that were already known to her vassals, including Augustin Fabre's unfortunate end.

'It remains,' he said, by way of conclusion, 'for us to try to find Azalaïs, if that may still be done ... and to decide Gervais' fate. Do you stand by your sentence of death?'

'You know I have no choice, reverend father! No-one here would understand it if I pardoned him, and none would forgive me. I think our men would feel betrayed. And it would only make Martin Cairou do the thing himself, for no power on earth could stop him. So I should be putting his soul in jeopardy if I yielded to pity, for which there is, in any case, no justification. Gervais will hang tonight.'

'I cannot say that you are wrong, and I know what it must cost you. I will send one of my brothers to the dungeon in a little while to help him prepare for death. But that is not what is really worrying you, is it?'

'No,' she murmured dully. 'The danger to my husband is too great! Even now, the Bastard of Apchier is on his way to Paris, carrying the thing you know of. We must stop him! Suppose he has too long a start!'

'Four days. Not too much to overtake him if heaven is on our side and Gonnet meets with obstacles on the road. God knows there are plenty of those in this benighted country! But our own messenger will not be immune from the same obstacles. I'll not conceal from you, my dear, that I have been turning the problem over and over in my mind ever since Gervais confessed – and it is made worse by the fact that we cannot, like the Apchiers, leave the town just when we wish. Unfortunately, we are under siege!'

'It looks as though the siege did not prevent Azalaïs from leaving us. What a woman has succeeded in doing surely a man can do as well?'

'That is precisely what several of your men have already been to tell me – young Bérenger first and foremost. That young man who turns pale at the thought of a battle is nonetheless ready to go after as formidable a warrior as the Bastard all by himself to save Messire Arnaud. He insists he'll have no difficulty in getting down from the ramparts on the end of a rope. I left him panting in the courtyard, awaiting your answer.'

'My answer?' Catherine said bitterly. 'Go and ask Fabre while his body lies there, rotting before our eyes, left to the mercy of the weather and the beasts! Bérenger is only a child. I will not sacrifice him.'

'Anyone who tries to get down from these walls will have small chance of survival. The enemy keeps a good watch and – Listen!'

A hideous clamour had broken out below, made up of the clash of arms and voices shouting on all sides. The enemy had launched an attack, probably in the hope of making the most of the slight relief brought by the reappearance of the sun.

For a moment, the priest and the châtelaine listened in silence, then, almost simultaneously, they crossed themselves.

Catherine sighed. 'There will be more dead and wounded,' she said. 'How long can we hold out?'

'Not very long, I fear. A little while ago, I went up to the belfry of the church to study the enemy camp. They have a company at work cutting down trees, and their carpenters are busy. They are building siege towers. Others were killing such cattle as we could not bring inside the walls and flaying them to stretch their hides over the wooden framework for protection against our fires. We must have help soon, or we will have to parley … and probably yield!'

The young woman's pale face grew paler still. Yield? She knew the conditions for that already, and while she could see the contents of her house fall into the Apchiers' hands almost with indifference, her own person was a different matter. Surrender would mean signing her own death warrant, because she would never consent to enter the bed of the Wolf of the Gévaudan.

'In that case,' she sighed, 'there is only one solution. I must take the same way as the lacemaker. It makes little difference whether I die there or by my own hand to escape Bérault, and if I succeed no-one will carry greater weight with my husband. My presence, I imagine, will give the lie to Gonnet's accusations.'

The Abbot nodded, looking more careworn than ever. 'I was expecting you to make that suggestion. But, Dame Catherine, apart from the fact that no-one here would accept such a sacrifice, in your present weak state it would be madness.'

'I am better – and no-one need know. But seeing that I'm still not very strong, why not use the means employed by St Paul to leave Damascus?'

Unexpectedly at such a tense moment, Abbot Bernard laughed. 'Let yourself down in a basket? I admit I'd never have thought of it! No, Dame Catherine, it's not possible. But I may have a better suggestion …'

Surprised, she looked at him more closely. There was a light of battle in his grey eyes and a new determination on his face.

'You admit, then, that I am right to want to try to reach Arnaud myself?'

He was grave again immediately and, laying his hand on her arm, said slowly: 'I not only admit it – if you had not suggested it yourself, I would have begged you to do so. There's no use deceiving ourselves any longer. Any help, unless it comes from Aurillac and the Bailiff of the Mountains, is bound to come too late. Bérault of Apchier must not find you here when the day comes that I must let him in. You must go, but you shall not go alone. Your children cannot stay here, either. The risk is too great.'

'I'd thought of hiding them in one or two families, with Sara to keep an eye on them …'

'No. Your absence will enrage Bérault quite enough. His first thought will be to seek them out and use them as a bargaining counter to make you return. He is cunning, and there are some simple means of identification. No, my dear, you must listen to me. Leave here with your children, with Sara and even Bérenger. Go to Carlat, where you can leave the children with Sara. They will be safe there. Then you can go on to Paris and bring us help from there. No-one is better able to obtain from the King and the Constable a company of men for which your husband may be too proud to ask. You will come back to us with an army, especially if Paris falls – and sweep the place clean!'

As the Abbot talked, Catherine's imagination began to follow his plan. Forgetting pain and weariness, she saw herself riding the roads as she had in the past, reaching Paris, denouncing the Apchiers and their bastard and meeting her old friends once again, and especially Tristan l'Hermite, in whom the Constable de Richemont had such confidence. She saw herself kneeling again before King Charles and demanding justice, a justice he would not deny her, and then returning to Montsalvy to drive away the brigands and bring back peace and happiness ...

Was it the sun that now flooded into the little chapel? She was invaded by the warmth and joy of it ... But it faded almost at once.

Outside, the noise of battle still continued, bringing her back to reality. How could she go, taking with her all she held most dear, and leave the town, her town, to the suffering that awaited it? The Abbot had just said that Bérault d'Apchier would seek to avenge their mother's flight upon her children. Who could tell how he would react if he found the whole family fled? How many poor souls would pay the price for his rage? And how, afterwards, could Catherine ever look in the face the relatives of those who had paid thus for her? For her, when she had deserted them in the thick of the fray?

The Abbot's thin hand pressing more urgently on her shoulder forced her attention back to him.

'The other day, you told me not to look upon you as a woman but as the Lord of Montsalvy. Today, I say to you, I am co-ruler of this town, and as well as bodies, I have charge of souls. I know what I am doing when I ask you to leave, because you alone can put an end to the ordeal that lies ahead of us. You must trust me. We shall hold out as long as possible, be sure of that! But if we are compelled to open our gates, then Bérault d'Apchier will have to deal with me – with God – and he will give way before God's curse as he gave way before the Host on the day our Brother Amable died. I used to know how to fight, once, and although I have renounced weapons of war, I think I still know how to talk to men. Believe me, I shall find it easier to control Bérault d'Apchier if you are not here and when I have only his greed to reckon with. He'll not dare to lay hands on me, especially since he will not know what may be the outcome of your escape. I'll give him all the gold I can find, let him pillage the monastery, your castle and the richest houses in the place, but he will also listen to reason.'

'What kind of reason do you expect to make a brigand like that listen to?'

'Robbers' reason. I'll make him fear punishment, reprisals from the King, and he'll see that the more crimes he commits, the heavier will be the cost! If I'm not much mistaken, he'll be satisfied with a substantial profit. Go, and do not fear. Besides, the town is not without resources. We have not fallen into Bérault's hands yet.'

And indeed, triumphant shouts could now be heard coming from the ramparts, together with coarse pleasantries roared out to the enemy at the tops of men's voices. The assault must have been repelled yet again. Certainly, the people of Montsalvy knew how to fight.

For the first time, a faint smile lit the châtelaine's strained face.

'It is hard to gainsay you, reverend father, when you are determined to have your way. You do indeed know how to talk to men, and to women also! Even so, I must point out to you that there is a strange contradiction in your words. You reject my idea of copying St Paul – and yet you tell me to go and take my children, Sara and Bérenger. But how? By what road? Can you offer us wings so that we may fly away from the top of the keep?'

A broad, delighted smile spread over the Abbot's thin face. 'In other words, you think I'm mad? Well, I'll admit that appearances are against me. But come, I have something to show you.'

'Something? What is it?'

'Come, and you shall see.'

Spurred on by a curiosity stronger than herself, Catherine gathered up her dress in both hands and was half out of the low doorway before she paused suddenly and, looking back, let her eyes rest on the Annunciation, on her shy little Virgin and her mischievous Angel.

'If Bérault d'Apchier must plunder my house, my Lord Abbot, I beg you, take that picture and hide it. I care more for that than for the rest. It will be enough to wrap it up and hide it in a cellar, but I could not bear to think of it in robbers' hands.'

'Don't worry. I'll look after it … There are some things that only pure hands may touch.'

5: Abbot Bernard's Secret

Catherine followed the Abbot through the crowded courtyard of the monastery. A dozen or so wounded from the recent attack had been brought in and were being carried into the guest house where the monks were busy tending them.

Sara was there too, with a mountain of lint, jars of wine and oil and her best ointments.

But the priest and the châtelaine went on their way, pausing only to inquire into the seriousness of the injuries and to bestow the one a blessing here and there and the other a kind word. Then they passed through the archway into the quiet and emptiness of the cloister.

Here, the noises of the town and even those emanating from elsewhere in the monastery were stilled, as though kept at bay by the low stone arches surrounding an open space planted with miniature box trees.

The Abbot led his companion along one side of the cloister until they came to the walk that backed on to the apse of the church. There, Catherine saw that a large paving stone had been taken up and was raised on one edge beside the rectangular opening so revealed.

As she came nearer, she could see the top of a flight of steps descending into the ground beneath the cloister.

She turned inquiring eyes to Abbot Bernard, who laid a finger on his lips. He vanished briefly into the sacristy and returned carrying a lighted lantern.

'Come, daughter. You will understand without much explanation from me.'

He went first down the steps, holding up the lantern to light the way and giving his other hand to Catherine to help her down. It was not, in fact, very far: after about twenty steps their feet touched the earthen floor of a narrow tunnel apparently right underneath the church itself.

Guided by the priest, who still kept hold of her hand, Catherine groped her way after him. The air was damp and cold and smelled distinctly musty, making breathing difficult, but after a few yards the ground seemed to fall away and they came to another flight of steps, steeper than the first and probably longer, because the light did not reach to the bottom.

Before embarking on it, the Abbot paused and raised his lantern to study the face of his companion.

'How are you feeling?' he asked, a trifle anxiously. 'I hope I haven't overtaxed your strength. Can you go on?'

She smiled. 'Of course! I'm much too keen to see what you have to show me. Curiosity, father. With that, you could take a dying woman to the ends of the earth!'

He smiled back at her and lowered the lantern. 'Come, then.'

He began to descend the second set of steps, merely tightening his grip on her hand a little. As they went on, muffled sounds began to be audible, combined with the trickle of running water.

'Is that the spring we can hear?' Catherine asked. 'The one that runs under the church?'

'That's right. In a moment, we will come to the well.'

In the choir of the monastery church was a wooden trapdoor covering a deep well, the source of which was unknown, although its level never varied. The monks had naturally been careful not to block it, for this well was infinitely precious both in case of fire and in the event of a siege such as the present, when at least the people of the town were sure not to die of thirst. Moreover, the water was extraordinarily pure and cold, even in the heat of summer.

Meanwhile, the noises rising from the depths were growing louder, and Catherine said anxiously: 'I can hear the water running, but what are those other sounds?'

'Be patient a few minutes more and you shall see ...'

Catherine did not insist, unwilling to spoil the holy man's pleasure, for clearly he had a surprise in store for her, most probably a mysterious way out of the town. But, if that were so, why had he not revealed it sooner? However, these private reflections were soon interrupted by a fresh subject for curiosity. The flickering lantern-light revealed that the wall on one side of the stair was painted with frescoes; or had been so, at least, at some time in the past. Large, irregular patches of coloured plaster could be seen, depicting rigid folds of drapery and strange, stylised fish apparently caught in a net.

Then they came to the bottom of the steps and the Abbot held up the lantern and turned round, very slowly.

'Look,' was all he said.

Catherine obeyed. Her eyes followed the lantern's beam, and she uttered an exclamation of surprise.

She was in a crypt that had evidently been carved out of the living rock forming the better part of the walls. But this rock glittered with veins of purple and mauve that indicated the presence of seams of amethyst and formed a background at once splendid and barbaric, against which was set the chancel of chapel framed in a semicircular arch and two half-round pilasters.

Within were more of the frescoes, not so badly damaged as those on the steps, in which a procession of primitive angels with long, pointed wings mingled with the symbols of the four Evangelists. Strangest of all, however, was the chapel's end wall, where the angels and symbols led up to an amazing golden sun, the stiff rays of which were embossed with all the gems existing in such profusion in the ancient volcanic subsoil of Auvergne. Aquamarine and peridot, rose quartz and amethyst, topaz and citrine, all gleaming softly out of the shadows as the light from the lantern caught them, and all gleaming for nothing; for in the midst of the sun was a hollow niche, empty but for a thick coating of dust. Before this niche was a table of green basalt peppered with olivines, a kind of barbaric altar, still showing the dark stains left by the candles that had once burned there.

From the empty niche and the altar, snatched momentarily from the black night of the tomb by one feebly flickering lantern, there emanated so much sadness, such a powerful sense of desolation, that Catherine shivered.

'What a strange place! Why have I never heard of this chapel?'

'Because there is no-one here, beside myself, the latest Abbot of Montsalvy, who could have told you. Because no-one here – not even your husband – knows of it. This is the secret of Montsalvy, the reason for its existence, and also its lost soul ... You see, it is empty. At the heart of that sun, which stands for the world, there is nothing – has been nothing for almost two hundred years. But there remains a legend, a legend that still lives in the hearts of the old, and of some that are younger. They believe it to be nothing more than a legend and smile at it; but in their heart of hearts they think there may be some truth in it, even though they will not admit it and never speak of it. They believe in a secret, lost in the dark of ages; but they hope in some vague way that it lies buried somewhere, in some forgotten cave or in some deep abyss. If they knew that it had been reft from us long ago and that nothing remains to us but a deserted shrine, the disappointment would be too much for them. That is why, although each Abbot of Montsalvy hands the secret on to his successor on his deathbed, they never reveal it to a living soul.'

'Then why to me?'

The Abbot smiled, and in that smile Catherine was able, for the first time, to read the measure of his affection and esteem for her.

'Perhaps because you are not of these parts, but also because you can understand and have a spirit high and well-tempered enough to bear the revelation of a treasure lost, even the most signal and precious treasure! It will not turn you from treading your own road and holding your head high … In any case, it was necessary, for the road I have in mind passes this way.'

Catherine was fascinated by the fantastic sun and could not take her eyes from it. No-one had ever told her of the legend the Abbot had mentioned, perhaps because, as a châtelaine, she was still a too recent arrival. But Arnaud must have known it, and he, also, had said nothing … There was some mystery there.

'Father,' she said bluntly, 'will you tell me what it is?'

'Yes, I will tell you, but not now. We must not linger here. We might be looked for. Come, you have not yet seen what is most important to you.'

He was already walking toward a narrow opening contrived in one of the pilasters. A stone door had been left open, and from within came the muffled sounds that had continued all this while. But Catherine held him back.

'The well?' she asked. 'Where is it? I can't see it.'

'There,' the Abbot said, indicating a narrow, barred opening below the steps. 'If you take a light and peer through that hole you will see the water right before your eyes; but I do not think it is worth the trouble.'

Without another word, he stepped through the doorway. It led to a long tunnel that seemed to rise in a gradual slope toward the surface. The sound of running water was much louder here, as if a stream were flowing behind the wall on their left. Every now and then there was a broad, low step made of a flat slab of shale like the rest of the passage. Heaps of rubble lay at regular intervals.

All at once, a yellow light shone out. It came from two torches stuck in the wall, and by their light Catherine saw two monks firmed with picks and shovels. With sleeves rolled up, they were energetically attacking a rock-fall that completely blocked the tunnel.

As they went, they were wheeling the debris away in a barrow and forming heaps. This time, the Abbot did not wait to be asked for an explanation. He stopped and pointed to the workers.

'This tunnel,' he explained, 'used to link the abbey with the old Castle of Montsalvy at the Puy de l'Arbre. It came out under the chapel by a mechanism like that controlling the stone in the cloister and the doorway in the pillar. But when the King's men destroyed and burned the castle, four years ago, it was all broken, and the ruins partly blocked the passage. My brothers, as you see, are busy opening it up again. That is how you will leave the town; and very soon, I hope, because we are almost at the end. Tonight, perhaps, or the next. It must be soon.'

Catherine watched the toiling men in silence for a moment. One of them was Brother Anthime, the monastery treasurer, and well known to her. The other was Brother Joseph, who was probably the strongest and the gentlest of the monks, but was also deaf and dumb.

'Brother Joseph!' she breathed. 'Did you choose him because of his infirmity – because of the secret?'

'Yes. And Brother Anthime will succeed me, if God spares him, as head of this abbey. I may reveal it to him. In any case, he is of the stuff of martyrs, and would not talk even under torture.'

Catherine nodded. 'I see,' she said. 'But there is still one thing that bothers me. The Apchiers' camp lies between the town walls and the ruins on the Puy de l'Arbre. How can you be sure of not attracting our attackers' notice when you break the surface? The noise of the picks alone …'

'No. We are too far down to be heard here. As for the surface – we shan't go all the way. It would be too dangerous. At the level of the sixth step in the stairway there is a rocky passage. It was hollowed out long ago by the stream that feeds the well, and it still flows along the bottom, but it is possible to follow it up to a hidden cave where the stream bubbles up from under the earth. You can get out through that cave without being seen by the enemy. Brother Anthime will go with you. He'll take you along the Goul and then by the Embène valley, from which you will be able to reach Carlat. After that, he will return here. You will have to walk, of course, and it will not be an easy journey – eight leagues by mule tracks – but I don't think you will fear that. Do you understand now?'

'Yes, Father, I understand … and I shall never be able to thank you enough,' she added, giving him a smile that was very near to tears. 'I shall not disappoint you. I shall bring you relief!'

'There, I know that! Let us go back now. It is time you thought of getting some rest. You will need all your strength.'

Without more words, they made their way back by the way they had come. The flagstone in the cloister opened as if by magic to the pressure of the priest's hand, and closed again without a sound.

The sun bathing the cloister and shining on the grey slate roofs seemed to jump up at them like a pet dog, and with it came the sounds of the town.

Catherine, like the Abbot, walked with lowered eyes and hands tucked into her wide sleeves. She was thinking of the strange, underground world she had just seen and of the road to freedom it had shown her.

She saw again the strange, derelict chapel, bereft of an immense and mysterious presence she could not define but both loved and feared, thanks to the extreme, almost mystic sensibility that was hers.

She was obsessed by the Abbot's secret, and as they walked together toward the monastery gate, she looked up at him suddenly.

'When can I leave, father? Tonight?'

'Tomorrow night would be better. Brother Anthime will need time to complete his work and to reconnoitre the way. When you have gone, if the danger becomes very great, I will try to get the women and children to go, those of them who will. I shall only have to conceal the chapel, and we will see to that as soon as the passage is open again.'

'A whole night and day to wait? Father, remember Gonnet is on his way.'

'I know, but we cannot risk failure. If the enemy were to catch you, we should all be lost, once and for all! Be patient, my daughter. To help you, I will come to you this evening, when we have buried the dead, and tell you the great unknown story of our town. You, at least, must know it, so that it may not be altogether lost, for it may be that when you return you will find neither myself nor Brother Anthime here ...'

'Father!' Catherine cried, in sudden alarm.

But his peaceful smile quieted her.

'Come now. I did not say it was certain, only that it was possible. We are all in God's hands, Dame Catherine, and you will still be so when you have left this town. You will need His help as much as we, and more perhaps. My tale will make it easier for you to be brave, for you will understand that the Lord cannot altogether desert a land that has been so blessed. Goodbye for the present, my daughter. And in the meantime, make your preparations, but tell no-one, except those you will take with you. Only when you have gone will I make known what we have decided.'

'But that will look as if I am running away!' she protested at once. 'Surely the least I can do is to call a meeting of the council and tell them?'

'That would not be the least but quite certainly the last thing you would do. Don't forget that Augustin Fabre was warned of the plan afoot to capture Gervais. Whoever talked did so out of friendship or foolishness – I know not which – but we cannot doubt that he was a member of the council. We cannot take the risk. But do not worry. When I have spoken to them, no-one will even dream that you have run away. You promise to say nothing?'

'Of course. But it will not be easy. I love them ...'

'Love them. They deserve it. But many of them are like children, their heads are filled with light, but it is a light that wavers sometimes. You must love them without weakness to ensure their happiness, and not always tell them why ...'

Children? Catherine had no time to estimate the worth of this remark, or render due appreciation to its author, for at that moment Josse Rallard hurtled up to them as though shot from a gun. He was evidently beside himself, and his hair and clothes were as dishevelled as if he had been in a fight.

'Good God, where have you been?' he cried. 'I've been hunting for you for an age! Something dreadful has happened ...'

'What is it? Has the enemy launched another attack?'

'If that were all! Yes – Bérault d'Apchier has mounted a fresh assault, and we're beating it off. But those who are not busy on the ramparts are attacking the castle – your own keep!'

'The keep!' the Abbot exclaimed. 'But why? What do they want?'

Josse's wide mouth split to the ears in a hideous grimace, which was his version of a sardonic grin.

'It's not hard to guess. They're after Gervais' skin! They're crying out that it's a scandal that he's not been hanged yet. Martin's their leader – and they've brought a ram!'

Catherine and the Abbot hardly heard the last words. They were already running toward the castle, from whence came a murderous roaring punctuated by the thud of the ram striking the heavy, iron-studded gate.

It was not long before the weaker Catherine was outdistanced and, with a stitch in her side, she was forced to lean on the arm of Josse, who had followed them. Meanwhile, Abbot Bernard was running as if all the devils in hell were at his heels.

In fact, it was a kind of hell that lay in front of him as he ran, for a howling, screaming mob was pounding against the brand new walls of the keep like a high tide. Still at the same pace, the Abbot darted through the postern and when Catherine and Josse in their turn emerged into the outer bailey he had already thrust his way through the throng and, with his arms flung wide, interposed his thin body in its black habit between the heavy doors and the ram that, swung by eight pairs of muscular arms whose strength was scarcely enough to hold it against the blind fury of the crowd behind, threatened at any moment to surge forward and crush him.

Martin Cairou's voice rose angrily above the din. 'Out of the way, Abbot! This is none of your business.'

'Your soul is my business, Martin, and you're in danger of losing it! What would you do?'

'Justice! It's been delayed too long. We want to hang the miscreant Gervais! Out of the way, I say, or we'll carry on with the ram!'

With vigorous assistance from Josse, who carved a rough passage for her through the excited crowd, Catherine succeeded in getting to the Abbot. One swift glance showed her that the danger was very real. Taking advantage of the enemy attack, Martin had recruited his forces from two distinct types: on the one hand, there were the roughest farm hands, herdsmen and butchers, and on the other the kind of idle layabouts to be found in every tavern anywhere in the world, and Pastouret's was no exception.

There were eyes gathered round the ram in which the gleam was too bright to be inspired solely by the sacred love of justice, and the châtelaine could not be sure that no lurking thought of plunder underlay their eagerness. Martin had known what he was doing when he got such men to back him. She addressed him severely.

'Justice is for me to exact, Martin Cairou! Back! Call your men off, or take care lest justice should be done to you. You have dared to bear arms against the home of your absent lord, and that while the whole town is in peril! That is a treasonable crime, and you risk hanging for it! Do you know that?'

The clothworker let go of the head of the ram, a king-beam taken from the castle workshop, and moved to stand before the châtelaine. Legs well apart, thumbs hooked in the leather bell that girded his black tunic, he faced her boldly, yet not without a certain dignity.

'Hang me!' he cried. 'But give me what I ask! I shall die happy if, before I breathe my last, I see the body of the man who wronged my daughter and betrayed this town!'

Grief as well as hatred throbbed in his harsh voice, and with it a despair so real and poignant that, ignoring his rebellion, the Lady of Montsalvy took a step forward to the man whose honesty and loyalty she knew. Gently, she laid her hand on the black tunic, speckled with tiny strands of hemp.

'Martin, I promised you that you should have justice, total justice. Why such haste? Why – all this?' she added, indicating the beam and the mob gathered round it.

'Go up to the walls, Dame Catherine, and look at the enemy. They, too, are tired of waiting! They are cutting down our trees, and from the wood they are making siege engines – a cat – a ram more powerful than this to break down our gates, a tower to reach as high and higher than our ramparts! Our danger grows from hour to hour, and by tomorrow we may be overrun and swept away by a furious onslaught! Men are dying! Three this morning, not counting Messire Donat who'll be buried tonight and those who may be falling by the Comtale Tower at this very moment. And meanwhile, in his prison, Malfrat lives still, safe from harm, and praying to the devil, his master, that his friends may come in time to save him. He is waiting! And you are waiting, too – for what?'

There was a deep, expectant silence during which everyone held their breath. Catherine hesitated. Her pride urged her to fight on, to try to quell the revolt by the sheer power of her will, for she disliked seeming to yield to force.

Undecided, she turned to look at the Abbot, but his head was bowed, his hands clasped his pectoral cross, and she saw from the movement of his lips that he was praying. In that instant, she understood that he did not wish to influence her, that he was leaving her to take on her own a decision that, as a priest, he could not endorse.

Finally, she looked at Martin's tortured face and, knowing that she had to go away from them, leave them facing danger – to save them, maybe, but leave them all the same, like lost children – she felt that one man's life was nothing compared with their bewilderment and despair. They had earned an indisputable right to the harsh justice they were demanding.

She raised her head and met the weaver's eyes, which did not flinch.

'Gervais Malfrat will hang tonight, at sunset,' she declared in a firm voice.

And, while their joy burst around her, Catherine gathered up her skirts and, plunging through the crowd, which opened up before her, sped toward the lord's dwelling and vanished inside.

Without slackening her pace, she ran all the way to her own bed and threw herself down on it, shaken by a convulsive sobbing that came, not from any feeling of pity for Gervais Malfrat, who had amply merited his fate, but from a dreadful sense of weakness and inadequacy. She was not made for this terrible role of a captain of war, the mistress of a great fief, with all the merciless responsibilities it carried with it! And while she knew herself capable of killing a man without hesitation under the stress of anger or necessity, she was finding out that it is always a dreadful thing to sign a death warrant.

She wept for a long time, finding a kind of solace in this explosion of her over-strained nerves. But when, at last, she raised her poor, ravaged face and swollen eyes, it was to see, through the hair obscuring her vision, Sara and Josse watching her in silence. It acted on her like a counter-irritant. Ashamed of being caught out in her moment of greatest weakness, she sprang up, flinging back her hair, and addressed them impatiently.

'Well? What are you doing here? Why are you looking at me like that?'

With the air of one accustomed, Sara sat down on the bed and began dabbing her eyes with a cloth dipped in cold water.

'You had to have your cry out. It was what you needed. But now, Abbot Bernard wants us to go this very night. He thinks by midnight it will be possible, and bids you hold yourself in readiness. In any case, he will come, as he promised, after the dead are buried. We must have put some distance behind us by dawn, because he may be forced to begin negotiating sooner than he thought ...'

'Oh ...! He has told you?'

'Yes,' Josse said, 'and we can see he's right. In our – your present position, the only possible solution is for you to go. You must reach Messire Arnaud as soon as possible! And then we shall be saved.'

'You agree with him because you are my friends,' Catherine said miserably. 'But the people here? What will they say? That I have fled, and deserted them?'

'No, stupid,' Sara growled. 'They'll not only understand, they'll bless you and pray for you! Especially since, once you are at Aurillac, there will be nothing to stop you seeing the consuls, and the bishop and the Bailiff of the Mountains, and trying to force them to help us. There's no-one like you when it comes to managing an awkward man!'

'Don't worry, Dame Catherine,' Josse added. 'Everything will be all right. Only ...' He reddened suddenly and looked away, while his fingers plucked nervously at the gold cord fastening the curtains of the bed.

'Only what?'

Suddenly making up his mind, he looked at her with that curious smile of his that concealed a very deep reticence. 'I wanted to ask you take Marie with you. She can stay at Carlat with Dame Sara. Look, I trust the lord Abbot absolutely. I know that with him here, Bérault d'Apchier and his men will be kept in check, even if we do have to surrender, and that he'll do the right thing ... only – you never know! And Marie is – so sweet! She's had enough of that as it is!'

The deep love he bore his young wife could be felt in every halting phrase, but so great was his love for his little Marie that the very depth of his feeling made him a little ashamed, as if he felt that he, the one-time Paris street hustler, with wits and fingers both too nimble, was unworthy of such a pure and lofty emotion. He hardly dared to put it into words.

'I will take Marie,' Catherine said, going to him and embracing him warmly. 'I'll take her if she will agree to come, which is by no means certain. Marie loves you, Josse. She will not readily agree to leave you.'

'For once,' he said, with an embarrassed smile, 'I mean to use my authority as a husband. I hope she will obey – especially if you will order her, too?'

This idea, and the form in which it was put, amused Catherine.

'I'll do what you ask, Josse. Don't you worry, Marie will go with me.'

'I shan't be easy until she is out of here!'

That night, the abbey bell tolled to rest the valiant soul of Messire Donat de Galauba and three more, of humbler condition, who like him had fallen in defence of Montsalvy.

Then, when the stones of the castle chapel had been laid once more over the old master-at-arms who, years before, had placed a little wooden sword in Arnaud's childish hand, and when those whose duty did not take them to mount guard on the walls were fast within doors to rest and thank God for sparing their lives one day more, Catherine and her friends withdrew to their own apartments to make their preparations for departure.

Abbot Bernard accompanied the châtelaine. The hour was fixed for midnight, and so the two friends sat together, for one last time, before the hearth in the great hall, as they had so often done before when the Lord of Montsalvy was at home. But that night they were alone, the châtelaine and the Abbot, each seated in a tall chair of ebony, bathed in the warmth of the fire, on the edge of the wide pool of ruddy light that drove back the shadows of the vast, empty hall – so empty and so dark in its recesses that Catherine felt herself already removed from it.

For a while, they were silent, each looking into the burning of the fire for the stuff of their own thoughts. Outside, the murmurings of the town were still, and even the sounds of war were quiet. There was nothing to be heard but the calls of the watchmen on the walls, and more distantly, the singing of the enemy, who were making merry on the proceeds of a profitable pillaging expedition in the direction of Junhac. For Catherine it was a vigil …

In a little while, she would go as she had done so many times before and put on the boots and the doublet and hose of a man. She would clasp a heavy leather belt about her hips and hang from it a leather purse containing a small quantity of gold – not much – and no jewels except the emerald incised with the arms of Yolande of Aragon, which never left her hand. For if Abbot Bernard were forced to negotiate, was it not necessary that he should be able to cram the ever-rapacious stomach of the brigand Bérault? It was even possible that by offering him more than he had hoped to gain he might be persuaded to take his vultures away. In that cause the whole wealth of the castle should be sacrificed …

It was the châtelaine who broke the silence, which was becoming oppressive.

'You promised me a story', she said softly. 'I think it is time …'

'We have two whole hours yet, but you are right: it is time …'

And as if his silence had been occupied in the sole business of selecting his words, Abbot Bernard began at once:

'We are, as you have long known, a sanctuary. As a place of asylum, delineated by four Occitan crosses facing to the four points of the compass, our lands provided a haven of mercy and charity against savagery and brutality. Here, the poor, the homeless, victims of war, thieves, all those unfortunates harried by an unkind fate, could find rest and comfort before traversing their harsh roads again, unless they elected to remain here. And we are still such a privileged place – or should be! But we are no longer, in a true sense, the Mount of Salvation, the holy mountain rising from the flanks of the Auvergne, the ancient place of refuge to which, in all ages, men flying from the Infidel, whether Norman or Saracen, have come to find shelter. There were many monasteries and convents between Limagne and Rouergue, but we were, at one time, the holiest of them all – and the most secret, for we could not proclaim the relic that made us holy, still less display it, or it would have been swiftly torn from us.

'It all began a very long time ago, before even the Venerable Gausbert founded this monastery, to be, ostensibly at least, the guardian of the perilous passes and a refuge for benighted travellers and lost souls alike.

'One night, toward the end of the year 999, while the whole land and all of Europe also waited in fear for the fateful hour of the Millennium that, it had been foretold, was to mark the ending of this world, a man, a traveller, came to this spot, then almost a desert. His name was Mandulf, and he came from Rome …'

The Abbot broke off as Sara entered, bearing a tray with the familiar spiced wine and a few girdle cakes, sweetened with honey and still warm. This she set down on the hearthstone and then poked up the fire vigorously until, becoming suddenly aware of the silence that had fallen at her entry, she glanced round, first at the motionless Abbot and then at Catherine, who sat with bright eyes and a flush on her cheeks, as though in expectation. She rose and shook out her apron.

'I'll leave you,' she said, and sighed. 'It seems I've come at the wrong moment. But you must eat something, both of you; and you, Catherine, especially. You've a long night ahead …'

The younger woman regarded her absently. 'Is everything ready?'

'Yes. Marie and Bérenger are finishing their preparations now, and mine are all done. The children are fast asleep. They'll hardly wake when we pick them up. I'll come back in a little while.'

She took herself off, a trifle put out that neither Catherine nor the Abbot had made a move to stop her going. But Catherine was too absorbed in her companion's tale.

'What then?' she asked. 'Go on.'

He smiled at her eagerness. She was like a child listening to a good story. Michel was just the same, and Catherine, at that moment, was astonishingly like him.

'In Rome,' he went on, 'a son of our own country had just mounted the throne of St Peter. He had taken the name of Sylvester II, but before that he was that strange monk Gerbert, about whose fantastic life you have already heard many, many times – and much of it highly exaggerated. The truth is that when he entered the Abbey of St Géraud at Aurillac he was nothing but a shepherd lad from the mountains. But he was a strange boy, and familiar with many of nature's secrets from his earliest youth, thanks to his own curiosity and the lonely life he lived.

'At the abbey, he flung himself into his studies with an incredible appetite for learning. But he very soon outdid his teachers, and before very long he was so learned and so brilliant that the good monks began to eye him askance and wonder if he had made some pact with the devil, to know so many things that no-one could have taught him.

'Then Gerbert left the monastery to travel the great world, which was the only school equal to his universal mind. He wanted to go farther, higher and deeper all at once. He went to Catalonia. But it was not chance that led him to that land, where the Moors had been so short a time before him. He wanted to wrest from it the secrets of the old Visigothic kings, Arians and heretics, but the learned repositories of ancient secrets. In this, he had a definite objective. For in his native Auvergne, old men still told of the great fear there had been, five centuries earlier, at the approach of Euric, the Clovis of the Visigoths and the man who had conquered Portugal, northern Spain, Navarre and the southern part of Gaul, laid siege to Clermont and defeated the Bretons at Bourges.

'Euric was a dedicated Arian but not hostile to Christianity, indeed he made St Leon his closest counsellor, and he never stirred without a mysterious treasure that he carried with him everywhere, like a captured king, and about which he maintained a strong guard, as if his own life depended on keeping the object at his side. Legend has it that he had in his side a hideous ulcer that broke out afresh if ever he was obliged to part from his treasure for a moment.

'When he died at Arles, in 484, his son, Alaric, succeeded to the throne. He was an out-and-out heretic and might well have done away with his father's marvellous treasure if his father-in-law, Theodoric the Great, King of Italy, had not taken it and carried it off to his capital at Ravenna. Alaric died young, slain by Clovis at the battle of Vouillé, and Theodoric ruled over the territory of the Visigoths during the minority of his grandson Amalaric. But he kept the famous relic for himself, for Amalaric was even worse than his father, a wild beast whose wife, Clothilde, later died as a result of his brutality. But the treasure vanished with Theodoric, who had it placed secretly in the monumental tomb that, like a pharaoh of Egypt, he had built for himself at Ravenna ... where, long afterwards, Gerbert, then Archbishop of Ravenna, was to find it ...

'For a long time, this monk of ours had pursued his studies, his researches and his career patiently. In Rheims, where he became a teacher, he educated a king and later rose to be archbishop, while his reputation as a magician and a man gifted with supernatural powers grew with the honours heaped upon him. But he was obsessed with the idea of Euric's treasure, and hoped one day to lay his hands on it. That happened when he was appointed to the See of Ravenna; but he remained there only a short time and, soon afterwards, he was elected Pope.

'On his elevation to the pontificate, he was reluctant to keep in Rome the object for which he had searched all his life. He feared that once again, after his death, the worst might befall it, for it was in Rome that the Barbarians of Alaric I[*] had got possession of it. Instead, knowing the deep faith and indestructible loyalty of his native Auvergne, which he would never see again, he wished to make it a gift of this thing. He therefore entrusted it to a man he could trust, to that very Mandulf who had been born in the same volcanic landscape and had long been his friend.

---

[*] Euric's ancestor, who sacked Rome in AD 410.

'Mandulf returned here. He knew this country well, having been born here, and instead of placing the relic in the monastery of St Géraud as Gerbert had counselled him, he preferred a deeper and surer hiding place. The place he chose was an ancient *oppidum* or township on the Puy de l'Arbre. Moreover, the land belonged to St Géraud. From the ruins, he built a strong castle and carved out the underground passage and the secret chapel. After that it remained only to build a monastery, so that the treasure might be guarded by consecrated hands. This was done by Gausbert, who carried on Mandulf's work, and our holy house was raised above the buried chapel.'

Here, Abbot Bernard paused a moment for breath and also, perhaps, to recover from the emotion it roused in him thus to describe the foundation of his abbey.

Catherine, who had listened to him without daring to utter a sound, took advantage of the pause to ask the burning question: 'But Reverend Father, this treasure, this object – this relic – what was it? It must have been unbelievably precious ...'

'More even than you can imagine! Yet it was nothing more than a rather ordinary vessel, a plain silver cup, tarnished with age – but it was the one from which Our Lord, at the Last Supper ...'

Catherine was trembling. 'You mean that what was in the chapel was – that it was the Grail?'

The Abbot smiled sadly, with a kind of resignation, and shrugged. 'So it is called. Yes, it was the Grail, the true Grail, which was neither carved out of a single, enormous emerald nor made of some unearthly material. Before Christ used it, it was just a cup like any other; just one of many in a house in Jerusalem. It was the divine touch, the miracle of the first mass that made it an outstanding treasure, unique in the world. After the Passion, Joseph of Arimathea gave it to Peter when he went out to preach the Gospel to the world, and it was under the Fisherman's rough woollen robe that it crossed the seas and began its travels to our poor land. Some have claimed that Joseph of Arimathea used it at the foot of the Cross to catch the blood of the Crucified, but that is not true. The time it held the divine blood was before, when Jesus offered the cup to his assembled disciples ... Yes, Dame Catherine, what was in our keeping was the Grail, for that was what Mandulf brought to our mountains on that winter's evening. And our Montsalvy is none other than the legendary mountain of Salvation! But, alas – we have it no longer!'

'What became of it? It was so well hidden ... How could it have gone from the chapel?'

'It was taken from us. Oh, not by a thief – no ordinary thief, at least. You see, as time went by, there grew up all over France an order of men also adept at penetrating the best-guarded secrets: the Knights Templar. They established a powerful commandery at Carlat and soon acquired a knowledge of all the legends associated with the region. How did the Templars reach the truth about Montsalvy? By what magic – or what collusion?

'I do not know; but one day in the year 1274, the Abbot of the time, Guillaume de Pétrole, saw the Commander of Carlat approaching at the head of a strong force. This mighty and impressive company was escorting the new Grand Master of the Temple, Guillaume de Beaujeu, who was on his way from the Council of Lyon to England, in order to recover the vast debts owed to the Order by King Edward.

'Guillaume de Beaujeu shut himself up in the church with the Abbot of Montsalvy, who was extremely nervous and apprehensive in the face of so elevated a personage. All the same, their interview lasted a long time, a very long time, and we can picture the poor Abbot defending his position foot by foot. In fact, we know nothing of the arguments the Grand Master used. Did he invoke the dangers of mysticism, the state of the Order, grown too rich and too powerful, so that deviations were now frequent? Or was it the sufferings of the Holy Land, fallen almost totally into the power of the Infidel? Whatever it was, the underground chapel was empty when the Grand Master resumed his journey northward …

'Since then, the cup has vanished without our being able to discover any trace of it. We would need another Gerbert!'

The last words were accompanied by a regretful sigh, and followed by another silence. Catherine had listened, fascinated, and in an excitement that surprised herself. But these strange events had found an echo in her own spirit. This was the second time in her life that the Knights Templar had crossed her path.

She had used them and the bait of their fabulous treasure to lure her enemy, Georges de la Trémoille, into the trap at Chinon. She saw herself again, with her dyed skin, disguised as the gypsy Tchalaï, chained in a deep dungeon in the castle of Amboise, condemned to death, yet still feeding a fat and greedy man wonderful lies in the shape of a mirage of gold that had led him to his downfall. What she had told him then was an ancient tradition of the Montsalvy family, one of whom had been a highly valued member of the Order at the time of its fall. He it was who had been charged with placing its incredible riches in safe-keeping. It was, to say the least of it, a coincidence.

'It's strange,' she murmured, 'that you should never have heard anything more. My husband told me, a long time ago now, that when King Philippe put down the Templars, one of his ancestors was entrusted with the task of placing the treasures of the Order in safe-keeping. It seems to me that the cup must surely have been among them. I can't believe their treasure was composed entirely of gold and earthly riches. There must have been some sacred objects, records, secrets …'

'And you are quite right. It was, in fact, Hughes de Montsalvy who, with

Guichard de Beaujeu, the grand-nephew of the Grand Master Guillaume, was honoured with this formidable trust. But he died soon afterwards, in somewhat mysterious circumstances, while in hiding far from here in an effort to escape the dread hand of the King. The secret of the treasure died with him, and we have never been able to discover whether, among that treasure, was the thing we had lost. But was the cup still in the Templars' possession? Or did the Grand Master's action in so rudely tearing it from its secret hiding place for his own purposes draw down the wrath of Heaven on the Order? I do not know. But the fact remains that Guillaume de Beaujeu was the first of the last three Grand Masters, that he was a kinsman of Jacques de Molay, and that between that night at Montsalvy and the arrest in 1307 there elapsed a space of no more than 33 years, the exact duration of Christ's earthly life!'

The coincidence was a strange one. Catherine nodded; then, bending, she took one of the cakes from the hearth. It was still slightly warm, and she nibbled it thoughtfully while the Abbot refilled their wine-cups. The aroma of the spiced wine pervaded the fireside. But Catherine ate and drank mechanically. Her mind was still far away, in the mists of the past, where the priest's words had led her, and he heard her murmur: 'If we could only find it – bring it back here …'

He answered, very gently, so as not to break the private dream that was providing the young woman with a last moment's respite before what would undoubtedly be a grim ordeal.

'No-one would be happier than I, but it is long since that I gave up hope of ever seeing it. You see, Dame Catherine, I believe it lies now in a concealment too deep and unsullied for the hand of man to reach it, short of a miracle. And it may be best that it should be so, for men have searched for it and will continue to search, while there are any left who still prefer a noble dream to the reality of this world, who need the absolute and impossible in order to feel at ease in their human form. Fundamentally, this quest is a poetic form of the search for God Himself, and …'

He broke off as Sara appeared once again in the doorway. This time, however, she did not enter, but only observed: 'It is time. The abbey clock has just struck midnight. Didn't you hear it?'

'No,' Catherine smiled. 'We were miles away, you see.'

'Maybe; but the time has come to take another journey! Come. I have your clothes all ready.'

Abbot Bernard rose. 'I will leave you. Meet me again in a little while at the side door of the abbey. I will leave it ajar. I will go now and see that everything is in readiness.'

He was gone like a shadow into the darker shadows of the great, empty hall.

Half an hour later, a little procession passed unobtrusively out of the castle. Catherine went first, dressed in her black boy's clothes, and accompanied by Marie, dressed in the same fashion. At her belt she carried a well-filled leather purse and a dagger. But the dagger was one she had donned as a matter of necessity and with complete indifference, for the one with the silver sparrowhawk that had been her companion on so many perilous adventures had been lost during the dramatic events at Granada, when Arnaud had been dragged off to prison for killing the Caliph's sister, Zobeïda, who would have put Catherine to death.

Next came Sara, carrying baby Isabelle in a big basket that had been furnished as a temporary cradle. The baby was sleeping in it as comfortably as in the little bed she had just left.

Bérenger followed, with Michel on his back in a big corn sack with a pillow in it. The little boy had hardly opened his eyes and went to sleep again with no trouble at all.

Catherine and Marie each carried a bag containing the basic necessities for all of them.

Josse brought up the rear. He was to go with them as far as the abbey to ensure that they reached it unobserved.

Fortunately, the distance was not very far, but they kept close to the walls all the same. The night was dark and comparatively mild. A light wind was blowing out on the high plateau, bringing with it, for the first time, scents of spring that, in normal times, they would all have greeted with delight. But now their hearts were too full to leave room for any cheerful thoughts, and Catherine walked with her face muffled in her cloak, not looking about her but brooding instead on the pain she felt at leaving her own town in secret, almost like a criminal. In spite of all that everyone had said, she could not rid herself of the feeling that she was deserting.

When they reached the abbey, Josse clasped his wife in his arms without a word, gripped the others by the hand and then turned and made his way back to the castle without looking round. The darkness swallowed him up almost at once. Catherine felt Marie, at her side, grow tense, and heard her give a quiet sniff. She knew that the girl was crying.

'We'll be back soon,' she whispered to comfort her.

'I know – but I'm afraid! I would so much rather have stayed with him ...'

'He won't have it. You'd be in his way, Marie. In the days to come, Josse will need to feel free. And I'm not worried about him in the least, I promise you. He's a man who knows how to look after himself! Come, now! Carlat is not so far, and you may be back before me.'

With an arm round the younger woman's shoulders, she thrust at the door with her foot. It opened without a sound, revealing the black habits of the Abbot and Brother Anthime coming to meet them.

The whole party entered the courtyard and made for the cloisters, where the paving stone over the stairway was already raised in readiness. The monastery was in darkness. No lights gleamed, and the church and belfry stood out faintly against the night sky.

A thin beam of light shone out as the Abbot took up a dark lantern that had been left beside the steps. He held it up and studied the drawn faces, carved into tragic relief by the shadows, one by one.

'Go down now,' he said quietly. 'Brother Anthime will lead you. May God protect you on the road before you. You have eight leagues to cover before you reach Carlat; and you, Dame Catherine, have much farther to travel. We shall not linger over our farewells, for they are apt to sap the courage. I will pray to the Lord that we may meet again soon ...'

He raised two fingers in a gesture of benediction that lasted until the last of the fugitives had vanished underground. Then, when he was assured that all had reached the level of the first passage, he replaced the stone and made his way to his private oratory, there to remain all night in prayer for those who had gone and for those who had been laid to rest earlier that night; and also for Gervais Malfrat, who had been hanged before the burial service and whose body now swung gently in the night wind from the gibbet that had been set up on the Comtale Tower, so that the enemy might be in no doubt as to what had happened.

He, in particular, stood in great need of prayer. He had died as he had lived, like a coward, weeping and begging for his life and struggling so that Nicolas Barral had had to knock him out to get the rope round his neck.

Finally, Bernard prayed also for someone else, for La Ratapennade, the evil old witch, skulking in her hovel in the woods, whence she continued to threaten the people of the town. He did not pray for grace for her – that was scarcely possible, for the devil does not easily release what he holds – but that death might no longer pass her by but would take her in her lair before Arnaud de Montsalvy came home. For then, Abbot Bernard knew well, nothing and no-one could save the old woman from the stake. And that was a sight the priest could not endure.

Meanwhile, the travellers were pursuing their journey underground to emerge, without incident, at the end of half an hour. When they came to the cave at the far end of the passage, Catherine took a deep breath, filling her lungs with the fresh air and her ears with the cheerful voice of the Goul stream rushing down into the valley below.

Brother Anthime spoke in her ear. 'Are you all right? The Father Abbot was anxious about your wound ...'

'I've not felt better for a long time, Brother! Once I can fight, I ask nothing more. Now I must go to find, if not my husband, at least Gonnet d'Apchier, who is threatening him; and believe me, I shall succeed!'

Resolutely, she took up one of the staves that the Abbot had had placed at the cave entrance to make walking easier, and began to descend the path

115

leading down to the bed of the stream.

It was no use turning for one last look back, for the town and the enemy camp were both completely hidden behind the rocky shoulder of the hill.

PART II

THE PRISONER IN
THE BASTILLE

6: The Spectre of Paris

As she came near to the lofty walls of the Jacobin convent by the Porte St Jacques, Catherine turned her horse's head toward a little knoll surmounted by a wayside shrine that stood among the vines. Then, throwing back the hood that had been drawn down almost to her eyes, she let the rain whip her face and gazed at Paris.

It was twenty-three years now since she had last seen the city of her birth. Twenty-three years almost to the month since she had seen her quiet, carefree bourgeois life disintegrate in blood, tears and suffering as a result of the Cabochian riots that had cost the life of her father, the goldsmith Gaucher Legoix, and of young Michel de Montsalvy, Arnaud's elder brother, as well as so many more, and had taken the first step on the road of her strange, brilliant and wholly unexpected destiny.

Behind her, Catherine could hear the quick, eager breathing of her youthful companion.

'Paris!' he murmured. 'So this is the capital city of the kingdom that has been for so long in English hands, and has now been liberated by my lord Constable almost without a blow struck!'

This news had reached them as they rode up to Orléans. A messenger of the Royal Stables, riding like the wind for Issoudun, where King Charles VII lay at that time, had shouted the glad news to them on the morning breeze.

'Nowell! Nowell! The Constable de Richemont has entered Paris! The city is ours!'

It had been a horrible, murky day, dripping with a fine, persistent rain that soaked through everything, but the rider's cry had reached the two tired travellers like a breath of spring, or like a cup of dew to a plant dying of thirst.

For the journey had been long and hard.

At the time of that wonderful encounter, Catherine and her page had been on the road for fifteen days, having left Carlat on the morning after their arrival, on horses provided by the governor, Messire Aymon de Pouget, to whose protection the Lady of Montsalvy had confided her

119

children, Sara and Marie.

Despite the fatigues of a journey of eight leagues on foot from the time of their midnight escape from Montsalvy, Catherine would delay no longer in setting out in pursuit of Gonnet d'Apchier. Her shoulder was much better, thanks to Sara's energetic care; and her own natural vigour, stimulated by the joy of being able to act as a free agent once more and by the danger running ahead of her, had restored all her powers.

In the courtyard at Carlat, she had mounted the horse a squire was holding for her with a sense of almost savage freedom, an intoxicating feeling of strength renewed. She was no longer the anxious châtelaine burdened with responsibilities too heavy for her shoulders. Once again she was Catherine of the open road, a woman accustomed to grasp life by the horns, like the drovers of Auvergne, and bring it to its knees. Now, it was between her and Gonnet d'Apchier: one of the two must admit defeat, and Catherine was determined it would not be her.

Even so, in spite of the impatience that consumed her, she had paused long enough at Aurillac to try to persuade the consuls to send some help to her town in its peril. But she had soon realised that whatever faint hopes she had pinned to them must be abandoned, for she had found the city, its bishops and consuls shivering with terror at the prospect of a visit from that greatest of all scourges, Catherine's old acquaintance, Rodrigo de Villa Andrade, who after spending the winter ravaging and plundering the Limousin was now apparently preparing to lay siege to the powerful fortresses of Périgord, Domme and Mareuil, where the English were still firmly entrenched and had long been defying the Comte d'Armagnac's forces.

'We cannot spare a single archer or a sack of grain,' the consuls had answered her with one voice. 'It may well be that we shall have bitter need of them ourselves! We'll be lucky if we can buy the Castilian off with gold!'

Catherine had known then that, even if Villa Andrade never showed his face at Aurillac, the people of the episcopal city would not lift a finger to help Montsalvy. Like everyone else in Auvergne and Languedoc, she knew that Villa Andrade had assembled the leaders of every band of *routiers* in the Midi at Mont Lozère the previous autumn and had made with them a pact of mutual aid and assistance that boded ill for any peace-loving town. The four Apchiers had been present at that fiendish council, and the men of Aurillac knew well enough that the best way of attracting the Castilian's attention to themselves would be to attack one of his associates. Their one desire was to see the enemy reach the Dordogne without seeking to investigate the financial state of the bishop and consuls. A cautious neutrality was therefore indicated.

The Lady of Montsalvy had turned her back on these circumspect citizens with a shrug and set out on a last attempt. She came to Murat, hoping to find there Jean de la Roque, the Lord of Sénézergues and Bailiff of the Mountains of Auvergne. The Bailiff's lands marched with those of Montsalvy, and the towers of his castle, perched far up the side of a gorge, could be glimpsed as one went from Montsalvy to Roquemaurel.

Catherine had thought that the old alliance, born of a common fear, might perhaps work for her and speak more strongly than policy. But she had knocked in vain at the gate of the Bailiff of the Mountains. They had told her that Jean de la Roque had gone to le Puy en Velay, to celebrate Easter there, accompanying his wife, Marguerite d'Escars, who had made a vow to Our Lady. He would not be back for several weeks, since he meant to take advantage of the pilgrimage to visit a number of his kinsfolk.

'Then we had better not look for help in these parts,' Catherine had sighed to Bérenger. 'We shall do more good by going straight to the King than galloping up and down every mountain track after Messire de la Roque.'

'Is that what you were thinking of doing, Dame Catherine? I thought you were more anxious to catch up with that confounded bastard? And it seems to me we're wasting time!'

'I ought to do it, Bérenger. I've no right to neglect that slightest chance of sending help to Abbot Bernard and our brave men! As to the time, we've not lost much, because we're following the same road that Gonnet d'Apchier took.'

Even after a week, the bastard's trail was all too plain to see, for it was a trail marked in blood. Burned cottages, cattle hacked and disembowelled and left to rot by the wayside, charred bodies strung up over the blackened remains of a fire or pitiful, headless trunks given a rough burial beneath a heap of stones: all this told its sinister story of the passage of the twenty-year-old youth who was like a man in form but in nothing else.

The people Catherine spoke to confirmed that it was Gonnet indeed. They were not too frightened to approach the fair, good-looking rider, dressed all in black and accompanied by an overgrown youth, who questioned them so civilly and whose gloved hand left a gleam of silver on the horny palms. Mountain shepherds and peasants from the valleys seemed all to have still in the depths of their staring eyes the dreadful picture of the bastard, the boy with his pale hair and pale eyes who carried at his saddle bow a woodman's axe and a severed head that was replaced from time to time by a fresh one.

Six savage-looking men followed him, like wolves running at the heels of their fiendish leader, and woe to the lonely farmstead, the peasant astray with his flocks or the girls coming home from some nearby church or well: Gonnet and his men knew no way but by torture and death to procure the necessities of their journey and to beguile the tedium of the way.

They seemed to be in no hurry, and by the time the walls of Clermont loomed out of the evening mist on the edge of the vast expanse of the Limagne, Catherine found that she had already gained two days on her enemy, and flung herself with renewed ardour on his trail. Unfortunately, chance, which had favoured her consistently so far, seemed to have deserted her now, for when they came in sight of the tower of Saint Pourçain, the travellers saw, floating from it, the most unexpected and unwelcome of banners: a red ground with the bars and crescents of that very Villa Andrade whom the consuls of Aurillac believed to be on the point of descending on their own city.

In fact, after a hard and somewhat disappointing campaign in the Limousin, the prince of plunderers had chosen to turn back to the wide, easy valley of the Allier and had taken up his quarters in the ancient, half-ruined abbey, where the unlucky prior, Jacques le Loup, bore with him as best he might, which was to say very ill. But he had no choice.

From the still-blooming city on the banks of the Sioule, Rodrigo reached out with his claws to all the country for several leagues about, and Gonnet d'Apchier's misdeeds were no longer distinguishable in the general devastation brought about by his *routiers*. Catherine was compelled, in consequence, to make a wide detour in order to avoid falling into hands that would not readily have let her go again.

Despairingly, she was turning aside toward Montluçon when a remark of Bérenger's gave her fresh heart. Young Roquemaurel had said little since they set out. With his beloved lute on his back, he followed after his mistress, doing his best to conceal the aching stiffness caused by endless hours in the saddle, and now and then he would try to enliven their journey with a song.

This was almost his only venture into speech, for Catherine rode in silence, lost in her own thoughts. On the other hand, he looked keenly at all that went on about him and used his ears well. Everything was new to the boy, whose world had been so far limited to the piece of country lying between the walls of Aurillac and the valley of the Lot.

Thus it happened that when Catherine explained to him, with tears in her eyes, why they must avoid the city lying before them and turn west instead of continuing their journey northwards, Bérenger merely observed calmly:

'If I understood you rightly when we left Aurillac, you said that the Apchiers were on good terms with this Castilian, being allied to him by the oath or whatever that was sworn at Mont Lozère?'

'That's so.'

'Then even if we have to go by a longer road, the fact that this Rodrigo is here may not serve us such a bad turn. He'll have welcomed his fellow brigand with honour and friendship. He'll be bound to feast him, and perhaps offer him some entertainment in the form of a profitable excursion or two. That takes time, and since the bastard doesn't know that we are on his heels, he's in no hurry. Thanks to this chief of Skinners, we may make up some of our lost time; and, if we hurry, we might even reach Paris at the same time as he does ...'

Catherine could almost have hugged her page. And it was with increased vigour that she pressed forward on the road that would lead her, by way of Bourges and Orléans, to the besieged capital. Certainly, her best course was to stop worrying about the way Gonnet had taken and try to overtake him.

The encounter with the royal messenger had combined with this to lend her wings. They had passed through Orléans unrecognised, pausing no longer than was necessary to give horses and riders a few hours of much-needed rest, although Catherine had many friends in the city.

The news of the liberation of Paris had filled her heart with a new joy and hope: now that great city was restored once more to its rightful sovereign, surely it would be possible for the master of Montsalvy to speed back to his own lands and drive away the invader?

It was true that many places about the capital were still in English hands, but for these mopping-up operations, the Constable could do without Arnaud.

At Corbeil, they had come upon the advanced posts of the King's army. Richemont's troops had recaptured the town a short while before, in the course of an encircling movement. And now Paris, Paris itself, lay stretched before Catherine's eyes and those of her companion, with its piled rooftops tumbling down from the heights of the Faubourg St Jacques into the watery mist, pierced here and there by floating church spires and towers, which lay over the Seine and its islands.

Deep in Catherine's memory a voice stirred, a voice long silenced now. It belonged to Barnaby, the Cockleshell Man from the Court of Miracles, who had loved her like a father and who had died for her at last. It was long ago now ... And yet she could still recall so clearly that July day when they had sailed together up the Seine in a barge loaded with pottery on the way to Dijon and Uncle Mathieu's house, where Gaucher Legoix's widow and daughters were to find a second home.

It was strange but, the moment she saw Paris again, she found herself remembering also those lines of Eustache Deschamps that the Cockleshell man had sent floating with such joy and such pride, out over the sunny river:

> 'She is crowned the Queen of Cities
> 'Wellspring of religion and learning,
> 'Standing on the River Seine,
> 'Vines, woods, fields and meadows,
> 'All the goodly things of this mortal life
> 'Has she more than other cities do.
> 'All strangers now and evermore shall love her,

'For loveliness and jollity
'There is no city to rival her.
'None can compare to Paris …'

A sign from Bérenger brought Catherine back to reality, and she realised that she must have been thinking aloud when she heard him murmur:

'The dreadful thing about poets is that they always look on the bright side of things, and you cannot trust them! This city is so sad!'

It was true, and Catherine had to admit that she herself would not have recognised the city of her birth. The streets had been stained with blood when she left it, and yet she had retained a glowing memory of it, for the eyes of children are more tender and luminous even than those of poets.

Alas, the city that lay before her eyes was no longer anything like her memories, or the poet's verse. To be sure, Paris was still vast and impressive, but a closer look gave one the curious impression of being faced with a simulacrum, a phantom city, insubstantial despite the smoke coiling from its chimneys.

The grey, misty weather may have had something to do with this discouraging impression, but it also had the advantage of blurring the outlines of things and obscuring the facts. And the facts, as the eye gradually discerned, were that the great Capetian walls were dangerously cracked, with here and there a place where the masonry had collapsed and no-one, apparently, had troubled to build it up again.

The Porte St Michel, on Catherine's left, was in such a state that it had been simply blocked up with rubble and shored together with baulks of timber and thick planks nailed across. The tower, now for the first time in thirteen years flying the banner of the lilies, had lost a good part of its battlements, while above the walls a number of roofs showed the bare framework of joists stripped of their tiles.

Catherine sighed and, leaving her vantage point, turned her horse toward the Porte St Jacques, which at this hour of the morning was wide open, with a guard of archers.

A file of ragged beggars was just passing through, making for the great monastery at the gate of which a Dominican friar had appeared with a basket of bread. But as she came closer, Catherine saw that these people were nothing like the more or less professional beggars she had known in the kingdom of the King of Thune. They were, for the most part, women and children, with a sprinkling of old couples supporting one another's steps, and poverty was etched deep into their faces, so that many might have been almost any age.

The monastery bell began to ring. As if it were a signal, the other belfries of Paris began to echo the sound. Then Catherine remembered that the date was 1 May and it was time for mass. For a moment she hesitated, half-inclined to enter the monastery church, but eagerness to find her husband and be done with the threats of misunderstanding that hung over them was stronger.

She urged her horse forward under the dark archway of the gate. There was a strong smell of rancid cooking fat and urine, which made her wrinkle her nostrils, but she drew up nevertheless before the guard post. It was manned by two lounging soldiers, one of whom sat on a stool picking his teeth and staring idly up at the blackened beams overhead, while the other leaned against the doorpost aiming blobs of spittle earnestly at a large stone.

The latter, Catherine addressed.

'I desire to see my Lord Constable. Where may I find him?' she inquired.

The man paused in his occupation, pushed back his steel cap and contemplated the two riders with unconcealed interest. The results of his scrutiny could not have been very favourable, for he began to laugh, revealing a set of teeth he would have done better to keep hidden.

'Ho, indeed! Well, you certainly don't mince matters, my young friend! See the Constable? Is that all? Well, you know, we don't go showing our captain to all and sundry, just like that. We'll have to see now ...'

'I did not ask you how I could see Messire de Richemont. I asked you where I could find him. Answer me, and stop trying to tell me what I already know!'

The young woman's incisive tone caused the archer to revise his first impression of the newcomers, which had taken in only their exhausted and travel-stained appearance. He now perceived that, beneath the dust, their clothes were rich and the soft-voiced young gentleman bore himself like one accustomed to obedience.

He straightened his cap and, drawing himself up, answered gruffly: 'Monseigneur lodges in Rue Percée, at the Hôtel du Porc-Epic, near the church of St Paul ...'

'I know where it is,' Catherine said, giving her horse its head. 'Thank you, my friend.'

'Here, wait! Lord, young sir, you are in a hurry! If you go to the Constable's lodging, you'll likely not find him ...'

'Why not?'

'Why, because he's not there, to be sure!'

'Then where is he, if you please?'

'At the Priory of St-Martin-des-Champs, along with all his captains and half his army, as well as a great crowd of the people of this city. There's a ceremony ...'

But Catherine did not stay to ask what ceremony this might be. The soldier had uttered the magic word 'captains'. That meant that Arnaud, too, would be there.

Tossing a coin to the guard, who caught it, swift as a cat, she rode gladly out from under the shadow of the fortified gate and began to make her way down the Rue St Jacques through the fine, persistent rain.

'Is it far to this priory?' asked Bérenger, who had been hoping that they would find some shelter soon.

'The other side of the city, but it's quite straight. We've only to follow this street, cross the Seine and then go on until we come to the walls …'

'I see,' the boy said resignedly. 'A league or so!'

But he stopped complaining before the sight that met his eyes. Catherine had some magical words of her own to utter.

'You ought to be pleased with this street, Bérenger. This is the famous Montagne Ste Geneviève, the scholars' quarter, and here, on either side of the street, are the colleges. This one is the Collège des Cholets; over there, on the right, is the Collège du Mans; and there, straight in front of you, is the celebrated Collège du Plessis, which is so highly spoken of!'

Bérenger gazed wide-eyed at the grim, dilapidated buildings – which, as far as outward graces went, looked half prison and half monastery – but he saw neither the damp-stained walls nor the unglazed windows, nor the heaps of refuse that choked the central kennel and were piled in unattractive mounds at the foot of the walls.

To him, it was the home of wit and learning, a place dedicated to the acquisition of knowledge and, at the same time, to a degree of freedom. The youngster from Auvergne was very near believing himself on the threshold of paradise.

There appeared to be some disturbance in paradise, however, for just outside the Collège du Plessis a student, recognisable by his short black gown, his hungry look and the writing-case hanging beside the noticeably thin purse at his belt, was haranguing an audience of his fellows and a sprinkling of idle citizens. The youth, who was about twenty years old, with a head of carroty hair and a form as long as a fast day, had climbed up on the mounting block outside the Barillet tavern and was holding forth earnestly, clutching with one hand to the timbering of the house to keep his footing on his narrow perch.

He could not have been in the habit of getting enough to eat, because he was as thin as a wasp about the middle, and his long but not unattractive face revealed a strong bone structure but very little flesh. Its chief ornament was an extremely large and arrogant nose, together with a pair of remarkably lively dark grey eyes set deep under irregular, bushy brows of which the left, being raised considerably higher than its fellow, gave to his face a permanent, somewhat ironic expression.

But although the student's belly might be clearly empty, this in no way detracted from the power of his voice. This organ would have been worthy of a herald, and the echoes of it rolled majestically back and forth across the narrow street like some great cathedral bell. Like any self-respecting student, the speaker was naturally discontented, and it did not take Catherine long to discover that he was inciting his hearers to revolt.

'What do you think the Constable de Richemont and his men are about this morning, good people? Some pious deed? Some noble work? Not a bit of it! They are going to pay homage to one of our worst enemies! These past days, they have given thanks to God, as was right; formed procession after procession; sung mass after mass; and that was very good, because it is proper to render unto God that which is His. And at the same time, they have begun to restore order to our city; to rebuild the northern walls; and that, too, is good! But what is less good is the honours they are now preparing to render to the decaying bones of that wild beast who formerly drove out our friends the Burgundians and brought a reign of terror to us citizens of Paris! Who can endure to see the incense burned today to that Devil's emissary, the accursed Constable d'Armagnac, at whose hands we have all suffered so severely?'

One of the townsmen, who had been listening with his head in the air and his hands clasped behind his back, began to laugh and interrupted him.

'Us? You're overdoing it, my friend! You're talking of things past and done with twenty years and more! You can't have suffered much yourself!'

'Even in my mother's womb, I knew the meaning of injustice!' the boy declared superbly. 'And, young as I was, I knew the day we dealt justly with the Armagnac dog was a great day! And, what's more, we scholars mean to keep faith with our friend and father, Monseigneur Philippe, Duke of Burgundy, whom God preserve, and we shall ...'

But the citizen had not done yet.

'Well, and who talks of breaking faith with him? You're behind the times, Gauthier de Chazay, or else you've no eyes in your head! Haven't you seen Messire Jean de Villiers de l'Isle Adam who commands the Burgundian troops here, helping to drive out the English, riding with his banner beside Monseigneur de Richemont in these last days? If the Constable is paying honour to one of his predecessors today, it is by full and courteous agreement with Burgundy.'

'Agreement in principle, a lip-service paid to consent! The Lord de l'Isle Adam will not take it on himself to be the first to sully the brand new parchment, while the ink on the Treaty of Arras is not yet dry! I'm sure he agreed unwillingly and would be glad to hear the voices of sensible men raised against it! Come with me, all of you! We, too, will go to St-Martin-des-Champs and let them know what we think of this sacrilege ...'

Catherine, who had at first listened to the lad's diatribe with some indignation, felt her attitude undergo a curious change when the citizen uttered the student's name.

He was called Gauthier, a name that had long been and would always remain dear to her heart, because it was the name of the best friend she had ever had. There was something else as well, a vague resemblance, perhaps – the height (although the difference in breadth was as great as that between a king-beam and a broomstick) and the colour and texture of the hair, which was as thick and red as the Norman Gauthier's. He, too, had had grey eyes, although their colour had been much lighter …

Then there was the violence, the youthful ardour, the eagerness to fall upon any obstacle that filled his thin form, just as they had once radiated from the powerful frame of the forester of Louviers.

It was another link. Finally, there was the name, Chazay, which meant something to her, something that her keen recollection brought back to her almost without thinking. She saw herself again, five years earlier, a few days after Joan of Arc's death at the stake, shut up with Sara and Gauthier in the broiling summer weather within the walls of plague-ridden Chartres. A man had helped them escape by way of the tanneries, leading them to the grating across the stream. He was a thin, humorous character, dressed in red, who went by the name of Anselme l'Argotier. He had told them that he came from Chazay, near St-Aubin-des-Bois, a village nearby.

Was it from the same Chazay that the excitable scholar took his name?

There was, of course, no answer to this unspoken question. Then, suddenly, Catherine had the feeling that the young man was on the point of committing some outrageous folly, but that nothing and nobody was going to stop him seeing it through.

So, when he sprang down from his block, shouting like a Philistine at the assault on Gaza, and drawing after him a handful of students as famished-looking as himself, Catherine determined to follow, especially since they were all going in the same direction and the observation of the students' actions would not take her out of her way.

The citizens, for their part, were returning to their own houses with discontented shrugs, by no means pleased to have stood in the rain for such an unprofitable speech.

However, as the little crowd moved off, the weather seemed to change in its favour. The rain eased off and ceased, until soon the only water left was on the leaves of the trees and in thin streams trickling from gutters and spouts.

Young Gauthier led his followers at a headlong pace, but the two mounted travellers were able to keep up with them in perfect comfort. In any case, it would have been impossible to overtake the students, who had now linked arms right across the street from wall to wall.

They gave vent to their feelings on the way, by bawling out loud if somewhat outdated war cries.

'Long live Burgundy! Death to Armagnac!'

None of this produced much effect on the good people making their way to St-Benoît-le-Bétourné for mass, who regarded the ragged, long-haired band with the mistrustful and faintly uneasy commiseration generally reserved for lunatics who might turn dangerous at any moment. They crossed themselves in a random way and hastened to gain the shelter of the church doors, from which the sound of the organ could already be heard.

Certainly no-one seemed to have any idea of disputing the students' reactionary sentiments.

Things took a turn for the worse after they had crossed the Petit Pont and entered the Cité. Nearing the Palais, the rioters came suddenly face to face with a squad of archers of the Watch making for the Petit Châtelet, and not alone, for in their midst walked a magnificent dark girl. Her hands were bound behind her back, the black mass of her hair fell over her shoulders, but she walked proudly, holding her head high, oblivious of the breasts swelling proudly from the torn bosom of her low-cut gown of crimson velvet and not even trying to cover them with her hair. Far from it, she was smiling at every man she met and bandying witticisms to make a beggar blush, while her eyes met theirs with a bold, bright, provoking glance. At the sight of her, the students' rage swelled to a fury.

'Marion!' Gauthier de Chazay roared out. 'Marion l'Ydole! What have you done?'

'Nothing, my darling, only offered a little comfort to suffering mankind! But a fat mercer's wife at Les Innocents caught me in the storeroom with her son, a young spark of 15 who was tired of his virginity and asked me very nicely to help him be rid of it! It's not the sort of thing you can say no to, especially in these hard times, but the old woman screeched for the Watch.'

One of the archers dealt her a blow between the shoulder blades that took her breath away and left her doubled up with the pain of it.

'Get a move on, trollop, or else …'

He had no time to finish his threat. Already young Chazay had flung up his arm and was hurling himself upon the men of the Watch crying: 'Come on, lads! Let's show these brutes the students of the Collège of Navarre don't stand aside and see their friends maltreated!'

In another moment, the fight had become a free-for-all. The archers, on their side, had their weapons, although these were useless to them in hand-to-hand fighting, and their leather jacks reinforced with plates of steel, but the students were borne up by their own fury and laid about them like madmen.

Even so, the fight was far too one-sided. The ground was soon strewn with the prostrate forms of half a dozen students with bleeding noses and broken heads. The rest took to their heels, and when peace was restored, Catherine, who had watched the battle with more amusement than actual alarm, saw that the prisoner had vanished in the scuffle, but that young Gauthier had now taken her place. Securely pinioned by two of the watch, he was bellowing abuse at the top of his voice and claiming immunity as a member of the University, while a third man-at-arms completed the task of binding him firmly.

'I'm going to complain!' he shouted. 'The Rector will have something to say about this, and my Lord Bishop will take up my case! You have no right …!'

'Students have all the rights, we know that,' retorted the sergeant in charge of the squad. 'But they've no right to go attacking the Watch and helping prisoners to escape! And I'd advise your Rector to keep quiet unless he's asking for trouble! Our New Provost, Messire Philippe de Ternant, is not an easy man to cross! '

Catherine started at the name, for it was a Burgundian one. She had met the Sire de Ternant often in the old days at Dijon or at Bruges, because he was one of Duke Philippe's intimates. He was a ruthless man, certainly, but also one of unusual courage and integrity. So he was now the Provost of Paris? A Paris liberated by King Charles's troops? Decidedly matters had changed, and it seemed as if the implacable civil war that had set Armagnacs and Burgundians at one another's throats for so many years was coming to an end at last.

Thinking that she might be able to be of some use to the student troublemaker, she approached the sergeant, who was re-forming his men.

'What are you going to do with your prisoner, sergeant?' she asked.

The man turned and looked at her, then, apparently satisfied with what he saw, smiled and shrugged.

'What we do with all his kind when they make too much noise, young sir. Put him in the cooler for a while. There's nothing like it for a hothead. A dungeon cell, cold water and black bread work wonders for them.'

'Cold water and black bread? But he's so thin already …'

'So are we all! When my Lord Constable entered Paris we'd been starving for weeks; but it was still the students who ate the least, except when they managed to steal something. Quick march! Black bread's better than no bread at all! Get along there, keep moving!'

Catherine did not insist. She watched the gangling figure vanish under the arched gateway of the Petit Châtelet, promising herself to put in a word for him at the first opportunity. But as she turned away to mount her horse again, she noticed Bérenger. He was sitting on his horse as though turned to stone, still staring at the entrance to the prison, although there was no longer anything to see.

'Bérenger? Well, let's get on …'

He turned his head, and she saw that his eyes were shining like candles.

'Is there nothing we can do for him?' he sighed. 'A student in prison! Wit and learning, the light of the world basely incarcerated between four walls! It's intolerable to think of!'

Catherine bit back a smile. The tragic words, combined with the page's delightful southern accent, were almost irresistible.

'I didn't know,' she said, 'that you had such a deep admiration for the members of the University. Of course, you're a poet ...'

'Yes, but I'm so ignorant! How I wish I could have studied! Unfortunately, my people regard books as degenerate instruments of the devil!'

'How odd! Yet I seem to have heard that the canons of St Projet were very learned and that there was something to be learned from them! So why did you leave them – and setting fire to the place into the bargain?'

'I wanted to be a student, not a monk! But at St Projet you couldn't have one without the other.'

'I see. Well, my friend, we'll see if we can't get you some more teaching when we are home again. Abbot Bernard seems to me to be the ideal person. Meanwhile, we've better things to do, and if you'll only drag yourself away from the attractions of this place, I promise you that I'll try to rescue this light of the world who makes such a deal of noise and interests you so much!'

Instantly, Bérenger spurred his horse and trotted away eagerly. They crossed the Seine by the Pont Notre Dame, because Catherine could not feel that her courage was strong enough yet to cross the Pont au Change where her happy, carefree childhood had been passed, only to end so tragically in blood and horror. In any case, it was the shortest way to reach the place where she was sure of finding Arnaud with the Constable. She was seized by an enormous, irresistible urgency.

As they approached St-Martin-des-Champs they met a great crowd of people. A veritable river of humanity was surging about the battered walls of the Priory, channelled into the Rue St Martin by the cordon of troops across the street, which kept them from reaching the great door.

The people trampled about in the mud but made no attempt to break through the barrier. Flowing along the wall between the two corner turrets, they turned into the Rue du Vert-Bois and made their way round the conventual buildings into the Cour St Martin. This was attached to the Priory, and here stood its prison and scaffold, for the Prior of St-Martin-des-Champs possessed rights of high and low justice.

Even so, there was not much progress to be made, because another stream of people was coming from the opposite direction, from the faubourgs and villages outside the walls of Charles V and the Porte St Martin at no great distance from the monastery.

Thanks to their mounts, Catherine and Bérenger were able to steer a course through this human sea, which opened to them under protest but opened nevertheless, to avoid being trodden on by the horses' hooves.

The two travellers rode straight up to the line of soldiers, beyond whom could be seen rows of troops drawn up in good order, with banners and a host of knights in armour and splendidly-robed churchmen. Plumed helmets and heraldic tabards mingled brilliantly with the long black and purple robes of the priests.

Catherine addressed herself boldly to the officer in charge of the cordon.

'I must see my Lord Constable at once,' she said haughtily. 'I am the Countess of Montsalvy, and I should be glad if you would make way for me, for I have travelled far.'

The officer stepped up to her, frowning, evidently by no means convinced.

'You claim to be a woman?' he said, scornfully surveying the slender black-clad figure with its thick coating of dust and travel-stained cloak.

'I claim to be what I am, the Countess Catherine de Montsalvy, lady-in-waiting to the Queen of Sicily! If you do not believe me ...' With a swift movement she pulled back the silken hood that covered her head and neck so that only the oval of her face showed. The golden hair braided tightly round her head gleamed suddenly in the brightening daylight. Then, snatching off her right glove, she thrust her hand under the officer's nose. On it shone, unanswerably, the emerald cut with Queen Yolande's arms.

The effect was magical. The officer swept off his helm and bowed as gracefully as his armour permitted.

'Pardon me, my lady, but I am obliged to be vigilant. Monseigneur's orders are strict. Now, however, I beg you to look on me as one ready to serve you. I am Gilles de Saint Simon, the Constable's lieutenant, and your obedient servant.'

'I do not ask obedience, messire,' she said, with a smile that won his heart on the spot. 'I would only pray you to let me pass.'

'Of course. But you will have to dismount and leave your horses with one of my men. Ho, you there, make way!'

The pikes that the men were holding at the slope to form a barrier were raised, and two soldiers stepped aside to let the newcomers through. The lieutenant extended his hand gallantly to help the traveller dismount.

'You must be patient for a little, my lady. You cannot approach the Constable immediately. The procession is forming up inside the church and will appear at any moment.'

'I'll wait,' Catherine said. 'But I was told that all the captains were present at this ceremony. Can you tell me where my husband is?'

Her eyes were on the lines of men-at-arms and on the little knot of officers, so that she was not looking at her companion and did not see his quick frown.

'Captain de Montsalvy?' he said at last, after a moment's pause. 'But – did you not know?'

'Know what? Has something happened to him? He is not ...'

'Dead? No, my lady, God forbid, nor even wounded. But ...'

Catherine let out a sigh like a gale of wind. For a moment, she had pictured the worst, the enemy arrow penetrating the chink in the armour, the descending flail or the axe smashing through the helm, or even Gonnet's insidious poison, if the bastard had arrived sooner than expected … and she had felt the blood drain from her face. But Saint Simon hurried on: 'You are quite pale! Did I frighten you so much? Then I pray you pardon me, my lady; but in good faith I thought you would know…'

'But I know nothing, messire, nothing at all! I am but this moment come from Auvergne. So, tell me …'

The Priory bells tolled out suddenly, interrupting her. They were so close and made so much noise that everyone was deafened instantly. At the same moment, the doors creaked open to reveal the inner courtyard and a blaze of candles borne by solemn, penitential monks with lowered hoods.

The blazing mass of candles moved forward under the grey stone arch, while from the black frieze habits with their black girdles broke a mighty *De Profundis*. Next came a banner depicting a centurion gazing heavenwards while dividing his cloak in two to share it with a ragged beggarman of remarkably well-to-do appearance. The painted and embroidered silken image was surrounded by a flock of choirboys whose white surplices and piping trebles formed a startling contrast to the deep voices of the monks. After this came the cross, a tall, heavy bronze crucifix that a powerfully-built priest was just able to hold erect between his two hands.

Immediately behind it came the Bishop of Paris, Messire Jacques du Chastelier, a venerable old man with long, white hair and hands almost transparent, so much enfeebled by the recent privations he had undergone that the heavy golden cope seemed a burden like the cross upon his fragile shoulders.

The Prior of St Martin, equally thin but a good deal younger, supported him unobtrusively, and they were followed by the remainder of the clergy, dressed in mourning robes of black and silver against which the episcopal cope stood out like the sun.

It was a colourful picture and a rich one, in spite of the marks of suffering imprinted on every face, but Catherine paid little heed to it. Standing on tiptoe behind the row of soldiers, which had closed up automatically as the procession passed, she was searching for a glimpse of the Constable and his captains, so as to read from her husband's face what it was that had happened to him.

But the victors' procession had not yet emerged from the church. What came next was the Provost of Paris, Messire Philippe de Ternant, whom Catherine knew at a glance. His glance passed over the wretched crowd with lofty indifference and came to rest on some distant prospect of interest only to himself. Beside the arms of the capital, he bore, arrogantly, those of Philippe of Burgundy.

Catherine fretted at the slowness of the procession, and the moment the bells paused for an instant in their clamour, she turned to her neighbour.

'Will you tell me what has happened to my husband?'

'Be patient for a moment, lady. We cannot talk here, and besides, I think I may have said too much …'

It was evident that he was regretting it, but Catherine did not mean to be kept in the dark any longer.

'I dare say, messire,' she agreed coldly. 'But you have certainly said too much not to finish now. And if you don't want me to make a frightful scene by running up to Monseigneur de Richemont in the middle of this procession of yours …'

Saint Simon blenched.

'You wouldn't do that!'

'Obviously you do not know me! But I'll be merciful. Only answer me two questions. First, is my husband in that church at the moment with the rest of the Constable's captains?'

'No.'

'Where is he?'

The young officer swallowed and glanced desperately up at the belfry, as if begging for the clangour to break out again and drown his words. But since nothing of the sort occurred, he took the plunge.

'In the Bastille. These two weeks past. But don't ask me why,' he added hastily. 'You must ask Monseigneur to tell you that! Now, for heaven's sake, be quiet! I can see the monks looking at us.'

But there was no need to urge Catherine to be silent. What she had just heard had left her speechless. Arnaud in the Bastille? Arnaud under arrest? And by order of the Constable, as it seemed? It was absurd, fantastic! It was pure lunacy. What could he have done, what terrible crime could he have committed to have deserved this?

She felt suddenly lost, overwhelmed by the crowd, imprisoned among the soldiers, the prominent citizens of Paris now filing past her, grave and solemn in their long red gowns with the insignia of the city emblazoned on one shoulder, the crowd hemming her in on all sides. She turned her head, looking frantically for a way out, a gap through which she might wriggle to hurry to the Bastille, where they might be able to tell her without the need to wait for the end of this interminable ceremony.

As she looked round, her eyes met Bérenger's. He looked shocked, yet seemed to be almost smiling.

'What the devil can you find to smile at?' she snarled at him. 'Do you know what the Bastille is?'

'A strong prison, I should think,' the page said. 'It's a great pity Messire Arnaud should be in it, but perhaps not as bad as you think, Dame Catherine.'

'And why not, may I ask?'

'Because it means he's little to fear from Gonnet d'Apchier. For even if the bastard got here before us, he can't have reached my lord, not if he's been in this Bastille for two weeks ... That's something, at any rate!'

Catherine's anxious frown relaxed a little at the page's logic. There was much in what he said; and, after all, if Arnaud's hasty temper, which she knew all too well, had incurred the Constable's anger, it would surely not be serious enough to endanger his life.

'I don't suppose,' the page went on, 'that you'll have much trouble in finding out what you want to know. Everyone at home knows how much in favour you are with the court. You need only be patient for a little while – until the ceremony is over.'

Somewhat calmed by this, Catherine endeavoured to interest herself in the spectacle, since she had no means of avoiding it. She watched with good grace the passage of the Echevins, led by the new Provost of Merchants, Michel de Lallier, that intrepid citizen who all his life had fought stubbornly against the English, continually striving and conspiring in secret to restore Paris to her rightful king. According to the whispers Catherine could hear behind her back, it was he who, on the morning of 13 April, had flung open the Porte St Jacques to the Constable's troops, while at the Porte St Denis, at the other end of the city, his son, Jean de Lallier, created a diversion to draw the English away in the belief of a French attack.

Once inside the city, Richemont had only to sweep all before him. In a gratitude he shared with the people of Paris, who were once more discovering the taste of bread, the Constable had promptly raised the old man to his present, well-deserved honours, and this was Lallier's hour of glory, for at the sight of him, the crowd burst into praises and blessings.

'Look!' Saint Simon breathed. 'There's the Constable!'

'He's my daughter's godfather,' Catherine retorted. 'I've known him forever!'

Yet she felt a genuine relief at seeing him. She was glad of the sight of that hideously scarred face, seamed with a score of wounds that yet could not entirely rob of its attractivenes the blue gaze of a pair of eyes as clear and candid as a child's. A square-built man, almost as broad as he was high, but athletic, also, and without an ounce of fat on him, the Breton prince wore his armour as easily as a page's silken tabard, and his tanned face was still alight with the joy of victory, despite the solemn nature of the ceremony.

There were a number of captains about him, but except for the Bastard of Orléans, his close friend who walked beside him, Catherine recognised none of them. There were Bretons and Burgundians but neither La Hire nor Xaintrailles, those old friends, nor any other of his usual companions.

Catherine's alarm, which Bérenger had momentarily soothed, revived once more. Arnaud in the Bastille, La Hire and Xaintrailles absent: what did it all mean?

She was not given long to wonder. The young lieutenant was grasping her hand.

'Come,' he said. 'We can follow the procession now.'

They tacked themselves, in fact, onto the tail of the procession, meeting, naturally, with no opposition from the soldiers forming the cordon, and followed as far as the Cour St Martin.

This was a vast square in the midst of which stood an elm tree in all the brilliance of its young foliage; but the tree was the only cheerful note in an otherwise grim spot.

The whole of one side was occupied by a prison with a pillory standing before its doors. The remaining sides were taken up with piggeries and by an immense and malodorous midden.

It seemed, however, that it was this midden that was the focus of attention for all the noble company drawn up before it. It was surrounded by a cordon of troops, and a number of soldiers stood to attention in front of it; but instead of lances, pikes or bills they carried dung forks and long hooks. They seemed to be waiting for a signal.

Several open coffins, decked with embroidered silken shrouds, stood to one side, not far from a group of persons dressed in deep mourning, to whom Richemont bowed courteously.

The Bishop and the Prior moved forward to the foot of the heap of dung; and, to Catherine's astonishment, the aged prelate lifted his hand and blessed it, before beginning to intone the prayer for the dead.

'What is all this about?' Catherine asked in a whisper. 'I thought the ceremony was intended to do honour to the Constable d'Armagnac ...'

'Precisely,' Saint Simon responded calmly. 'He is in there.'

'In where?'

'Why, in the midden, of course. That's where the good people of Paris threw him after they murdered him in 1418, when they went over to the Duke of Burgundy. They took a long strip of skin off his back and then they slew him and threw him onto this dung heap. He was not the only one, either! The Chancellor of France at that time, Messire Henri de Marle, along with his son, the Bishop of Coutances and two more men of note, Maître Jean Paris and Maître Raymond de la Guerre, must be in there with him. Monseigneur de Richemont has commanded that they are to be removed from their unworthy resting place and given Christian burial at last. The Burgundians have agreed, of course. You can see Messire Jean Villiers de l'Isle Adam standing by the Constable. He was the first to raise the banner of France over the Porte St Jacques. He is here in some ways to do penance; for, all things considered, it was he, when he took Paris, who brought Monseigneur d'Armagnac to the piteous state in which we shall see him.' He glanced at Catherine in sudden doubt and added, 'But it may be no fit sight for a lady.'

'I'm not squeamish,' Catherine retorted, 'and I shan't leave this place until I've spoken with the Constable! Besides,' she added stoutly, 'I dare say I've seen worse. And what of that person in the mourning clothes I see over there? Surely that is a woman?'

'That is the Dame de Marle, the Chancellor's widow and the Bishop's mother. It is a cruel ordeal for her, but she insisted on coming!'

Catherine threw the woman a glance filled with compassion. She remembered now having heard in Dijon of the horrors that had been perpetrated in Paris when the Burgundians took the city from the Armagnacs. It had been told as a matter for rejoicing then. She remembered, also, seeing what looked like a long strip of reddish parchment fastened to the banner of Jean IV of Armagnac, son of the murdered Constable and Cadet Bernard's brother: the piece of skin taken from his father's back, which the Burgundians had sent to him.

Then, it had not taken her long to forget the reported horrors, and even the hideous relic also, whereas now, looking at that enormous midden into which the soldiers were already thrusting their forks, she found herself face to face with the atrocities of civil war that had darkened her childhood and, in combination with another foreign war, had brought the country to within an inch of disaster.

It was so stupid, all this bloodshed and suffering; stupid and pointless if, after all these years and all this violence, the man who had authorised a massacre could now stand calmly by, watching with every indication of respect, while the bodies of his victims were extricated from the dunghill into which he had caused them to be thrown.

Nearly a hundred years of war, of fratricidal conflict, assassination, ambush, political manoeuvring, and mingled glory, shame and wretchedness, to achieve this! More, to restore this ravaged land, gnawed to the bone and dying on its feet, to the road back to health, it had taken Joan's blazing holocaust, the terrible and yet triumphant glow of that pyre in Rouen.

The soldiers were still hard at their disgusting task. In spite of the fresh breeze that fluttered the silken banners and the Bishop's long, white hair, the stench was becoming unbearable. It escaped in sickening waves from the great forkfuls of dripping filth that the men dug out of the thick, black mass. They would have to dig deep, because in 18 years the midden had had time to grow to mountainous proportions.

It took a long time. When, at last, the first skeleton was revealed, plenty of handkerchiefs had been brought out, and pomander balls were concealed in a good many hands.

Catherine, like most people, was holding her handkerchief to her nose; but the square of thin cambric, with only the faintest scent of verbena still clinging to it, was wholly inadequate, and she could feel her colour fading.

Saint Simon was right: not only was this no sight for a woman, it was altogether unendurable.

She shut her eyes rather than look at the ghastly remnants of humanity as the monks wrapped them in a white silk shroud and laid them in one of the coffins; then she opened them again and turned her head away, instinctively seeking a way of escape … She felt horribly weak all of a sudden and longed to get away, knowing that if she did not, she would very soon make a fool of herself by fainting in the midst of all these people, and in the presence of that other woman who was standing rigid and apparently unaffected beneath her black veils.

Feeling herself stifling, she tugged at the hood that once more covered her head, and pulling it off, brushed a shaking hand across her brow. As she did so, her eyes met those of a man in armour who was standing a few paces from the Constable and gazing at her with an expression of joyful amazement. He had his helmet under his arm, and it was all she could do not to cry his name aloud as she recognised him.

Tristan! Tristan l'Hermite!

She had not seen him at first. He had come not with the procession but a little later, and she had scarcely noticed the tall figure moving slowly but watchfully among the rows of spectators.

It was the first time she had ever seen Tristan in full armour. In addition, his fair hair, which he had worn rather long at their last meeting, was now cropped short into the neat cap dictated by the wearing of a helmet.

He, likewise, had realised the identity of the slim, black-clad gentleman standing next to Saint Simon, and was already making his way through the crowd toward the entrance to the court, and signalling to Catherine to do the same.

A quick word to the lieutenant, and with his help she succeeded, not without difficulty, in forcing a way through to where Tristan was standing in the angle of one of the church buttresses. There, she cast herself bodily onto his chest.

'You're just the very person I needed! Tristan! Tristan dear! How lovely to see you again!'

Tristan deposited a smacking kiss on either cheek, then held her away from him at arm's length, the better to look at her.

'It's I who should say that! Not that I ought to be surprised! I know you too well not to expect you to come hurrying from the depths of Auvergne as soon as you heard the news. What beats me is how you could have heard it so quickly. Who the devil can have told you? Xaintrailles?'

Catherine stared back at him anxiously. The smile that lightened his heavy Flemish features a little gave a touch of animation to a face already becoming known for its unyielding impassively, but it did not reach his eyes, which were of a blue so pale as to resemble chips of ice. They looked sterner than Catherine had ever seen them, at least when bent on her, and she felt all her earlier forebodings come flooding back. What could Arnaud have done that would make it necessary for her to be warned?

'I've only just this minute learned of my husband's arrest, and I still don't know why.'

'Then why are you here?'

'To seek help. My home is being besieged by a robber-baron, Bérault d'Apchier, and his sons. They are after our lands, our people, our goods and even our very lives, for the Apchiers have sent a bastard son of theirs here to gain Arnaud's trust, the better to murder him!'

The smile had vanished from Tristan's face, but the sternness in his eyes had turned to anger.

'The Apchiers! I've heard of them. Another tribe of noble brigands! I know they were at Mont Lozère with the Castilian. When we've flung the English back into the sea, I'll deal with them! But for the present ...'

'For the present,' Catherine broke in, beginning to feel that her friend's welcome was not altogether as warm as it might be, 'I want to know what Arnaud has done and why they have put him in the Bastille.'

'He killed a man.'

'He killed – what then? What does an army storming a city, what do the defenders within, what do the soldiers, the captains, princes and commoners do in these cruel times but kill and kill and kill again?'

'I know all that as well as you. But there is killing and killing. Come,' he added, becoming aware that their talk was acquiring an interested audience, 'we can't stay here. Who is this boy with you?'

'My page, Bérenger de Roquemaurel de Cassaniouze. He is a poet – but he can fight well enough if needed!'

'It's not a question of fighting just at present but of finding somewhere quieter we can talk. Saint Simon, let my lord Constable know discreetly that I've gone and take my place, will you? But on no account mention this lady to him. I'll take her to him myself when the time is right. Archers, make way there!'

The familiar lump of anxiety was knotting itself in Catherine's throat. What did all this mean? Why was Saint Simon not on any account to mention her name to the Constable? And why was Tristan going to take her to him? Arnaud had killed someone. But who? How? If he had killed the King himself they could hardly make more of a mystery of it.

She followed the Fleming with a pounding heart. Bérenger trotted after her, silent as an owl.

Catherine's impression that Tristan l'Hermite had become a person of importance was strengthened as she saw with what alacrity the men-at-arms made way for them and brought their horses. Tristan mounted a big roan stallion and led the little party away without a word.

Since he seemed disinclined to talk, Catherine elected to ride a few paces behind him. The happiness of a short while ago had dropped from her. Now, she felt uneasy, missing the solicitude, undemonstrative but effective, she had been used to expect from her old comrade in adventure. It was almost as if he were angry with her. But why? Was the man Arnaud had killed of such importance? On the other hand, she was quite sure that Arnaud was not the man to strike without reason, and if his temper was certainly hasty at times, it was never immoderately so.

The three rode in silence down the Rue St Martin as far as the church of St Jacques de la Boucherie, and Catherine's uneasiness increased all the way.

They encountered a large number of soldiers, for the city was still too recently delivered for military rule to have been relaxed; but all of them at the sight of Tristan l'Hermite displayed a degree of respect that had been hitherto unknown, and evidently held a considerable element of fear. Yet there was nothing in his outward appearance to indicate any particular rank or status. His polished steel armour was plain, and unadorned by even the most unassuming coronet. Only the lions and ermines on his tunic showed his connection with the Breton prince; but surely there was nothing in all this to justify the kind of apprehension visible on every face.

Nevertheless, Catherine's disquiet grew with every step her horse took. Fear grew in her until she could bear it no longer, made all the worse because, although she hardly dared admit it even to herself, she was afraid of Tristan now.

She had the uncomfortable feeling that her old friend had become hardened and remote, that he seemed to be hiding behind this steely blue statue with the cold eyes that warned off any attempt at recollection of the past. Then there were the streets themselves and the slow procession of houses as they passed along. Most of them cried out poverty, neglect and suffering, with their unglazed windows, many of which had broken frames to show, their sagging roofs and doors torn off their hinges gaping open on empty, silent rooms where a few lean cats, survivors of the recent great hunger, were the sole inhabitants.

Since its occupation by the English, Paris had lost a quarter of its population, or some 45,000 people. The greatest city in the world had been bled almost white.

There remained, in the midst of this desolation, still a few houses with well-maintained faces, shining windows, gilded weather-vanes and rooftops glistening like the scales of a freshly-caught fish; but these few, the very splendour of which proclaimed their owners' complaisant attitude to the foreign invader, only added by contrast to the melancholy of this ghost-city.

Yet, little by little, life was returning. Men were at work here and there, clambering among scaffolding or on the tops of ladders, filling in cracks, replastering between the timbering of a wall or building up the broken framework of a roof. Sounds of sawing and hammering, with occasional snatches of song, rang through the streets as far as the walls where the Constable's masons were already busy mending the breaches and restoring the ruins.

It was like the solemn prelude to a rebirth that, now that Richemont had announced the King's pardon and had it proclaimed from every square and crossroad in the capital that had so long denied him, had begun to seem a real thing at last. Amnestied thus, and redeemed also by the courage they themselves had shown in attacking the English garrison, the people of Paris were setting to work once more.

But Catherine looked on all this as if the people and objects were transparent. Even the poverty and desolation that rose around her at every step found no echo in her mind, for she scarcely saw them. Her eyes soon turned away to rest once more on the back of the man riding ahead of her, as though they had the power to read what was inscribed in Tristan's heart and memory.

This enforced delay of his was so painful that she could have screamed out loud, right there in the street, for nothing – only to relax the tension of her nerves, perhaps to compel him to speak. Lord God! Was it so hard to say, that it needed all these precautions?

Tristan l'Hermite was a man well able to speak out clearly and to the point; he had no need to pick and choose his words – unless what he had to tell her was so dreadful – so appalling! Good God, would this journey through the spectral city never end?

They were passing through the Place de Grève, where the newly-built scaffold struck a depressingly fresh note alongside the Maison aux Piliers, which could have done with some renovation of its own, when Catherine heard her page sigh: 'Is this really Paris? I'd imagined it all so very differently …'

'It was Paris, and it will soon be Paris again,' she said, a trifle irritably, since at that moment the fate of Paris did not interest her in the least. Then, relenting, she added, to please him, 'The city will be once more what it was when I was a child: the most beautiful, the richest and most learned – and the vainest and cruellest also!'

Her voice broke a little on the last words, and it came to Bérenger that perhaps her childhood recollections were not all as pleasant as he could have wished for her. He relapsed into the silence from which the pathetic appearance of the city had roused him.

Besides, they had arrived.

Tristan l'Hermite dismounted outside an inn in the Rue St Antoine. Facing the massive walls of a well-guarded mansion between the Rue de Roi de Sicile and the remains of the ancient walls of Philippe Auguste, it retained an air of prosperity, and it signs, displaying a spread eagle, had been newly repainted and gilded.

'You'll lodge here,' Tristan informed Catherine as he aided her to dismount. 'The Eagle has been famous for more than a century, and it was much frequented by the English captains, so it hasn't suffered too much from poverty. You'll be as well off here as anywhere. Ah, here comes Master Renaudot now ...'

The innkeeper was hurrying up to them, wiping his hands on his white apron and starting to bow. He took one look at Tristan and bent double in an obeisance in which Catherine detected all the respect shown by the troops, but with possibly somewhat less of awe.

'My lord Provost!' he exclaimed. 'It is indeed an honour to see you here! What may I do for you?'

'Provost?' Catherine said in astonishment. 'You too? But of what?'

For the first time, he smiled at her, and a glint of amusement lit the coldness of his eyes.

'You think the title's getting rather commonplace, do you? Don't worry, there are only three of us here: Messire Philippe de Ternant, Maître Michel de Lallier and I, Provost- Marshal, at your service! Which means that I have charge of all matters concerning discipline in the King's armies. I might add that Monseigneur de Richemont has also conferred on me the titles of Grand Master of Artillery and Captain of Conflans Ste Honorine, but I've no intention of sticking to guns that are none of my business. I prefer my provostship!'

'So that's why the men-at-arms salute you so respectfully – and a trifle nervously!'

'Precisely. They are afraid of me because I maintain inflexibly the law and discipline without which no army can exist, and the Constable expects his to be a model of its kind.'

'Inflexibly? Always?'

'Always. I might as well tell you at once, so that we will be able to talk freely: it was I who arrested Captain de Montsalvy.'

'You! Our friend?'

'Friendship has nothing to do with it, Catherine. I was only doing my duty. But come inside. Master Renaudot will be glad to give us dinner while the maids are getting your room ready. Fortunately, he still has some tasty meats left, and a few casks of excellent wine that he had the forethought to keep safe by walling up part of his cellar. That's one more wall our entry into Paris has brought down!'

The innkeeper's ruddy face broke into a gratified smile.

'Those cross-channel gentry are poor judges of wine. Except for that Bordeaux of theirs, they've no idea how to appreciate a real wine, and I've made a point of keeping the last of the Beaune or the Nuits as I've got through the good offices of a cousin of mine that's sommelier to Monseigneur the Duke of Burgundy himself. But I'll be happy to let you have a taste of it!'

'Bring us a good measure, my friend! These travellers have had a long journey and stand in need of refreshment.'

In another minute, Catherine, Tristan and Bérenger were seated at table before the huge fireplace in the inn, with strings of onions and well-smoked hams hanging from the beams above their heads. Before them, beside a variety of pewter cups and plates, were ranged a loaf of bread, some salted herrings, a roast goose and a dish of waffles the very smell of which was enough to proclaim Renaudot's talents as a master-cook. There were also two pitchers of wine, one of Romanée, the other of Aunis.*

Bérenger flung himself on this feast with a 15-year-old's appetite augmented by 150 leagues on horseback, but Catherine, although she was very nearly as hungry and would gladly have eaten, would take nothing but a cup of wine, and that only because she was conscious of a weakness that made her fear to faint. But she wanted a full and clear explanation, and she knew how easily, around a well-furnished table, problems could be minimised and made to seem less serious than they were.

Tristan l'Hermite was amazed at her abstinence, because he had always marvelled at Catherine's appetite.

'But aren't you hungry? Eat, my dear. We can talk afterwards.'

'My hunger can wait, but my anxiety can't. It's much more important to me to know what's been happening than it is to eat – as you very well know! But you are leaving me in suspense, to imagine God knows what! The worst, you may be sure! And if I let you have your way, you'd go on playing with me! It's not the way of a friend!'

Her tone was stiff and trembled a little with anger. The Provost did not miss it, and the old warmth came into his face. He put out his hand, grasped Catherine's where it lay on the table and squeezed it, disregarding her clenched fist.

'I am still your friend,' he assured her warmly.

'Are you?'

'You have no cause to doubt it. And I forbid you to do so!'

She shrugged her shoulders wearily.

'Can friendship exist between the Provost-Marshal and the wife of a murderer? For that was what you gave me to understand, wasn't it?'

Tristan, who, perhaps for the sake of something to do, had begun to carve the goose that Bérenger was regarding with covetous eyes, lifted his head and his knife and stared at Catherine with astonishment. Then, abruptly, he

---

* Nowadays, the Aunis grapes are used in the manufacture of Cognac.

burst out laughing.

'By St Quentin, St Omer and every other saint in Flanders, Catherine, you'll never change! Your imagination is always running way ahead of your pretty nose, and just as freely as in the days when you dressed up as a gypsy and dyed your hair black to mount an attack on that fat devil La Trémoille and lead him to his ruin! You run on and on! But, good God, have I ever given you cause to doubt my friendship?'

'Cause, no – but plenty of temptation! You know me very well, certainly, and yet you seem to be trying to gain time, as though it were so hard to tell me straight out, in plain words, just what it is my husband has done!'

'I have told you. He killed a man. But from that to calling him a murderer is a very different matter! In doing what he did, he was acting rather in the interests of justice.'

'And are you putting those who uphold justice in the Bastille nowadays?'

'Unless you stop interrupting me like this, I'll not say another word!'

'I'm sorry.'

'The fact is that he is in trouble over this killing mainly because it was an act of serious disobedience and a flagrant breach of discipline and clear orders. The reason I've kept you in suspense a little is precisely because I was trying to think of a way of breaking it to you without sending you into a passion. I want you to understand my position – and also the Constable's, because I acted only on his orders.'

'The Constable!' Catherine muttered bitterly. 'He, too, used to call himself our friend! He is my daughter's godfather, and yet he could command ...'

'God's blood, can't you understand that he's the commander-in-chief of the King's army first and the Demoiselle de Montsalvy's godfather second! He is a leader to whom even Princes of the Blood owe absolute obedience! Your Arnaud's not the King's brother, to my knowledge, yet he disobeyed an explicit order!'

He saw Catherine's eyes fill with tears and her fingers toying nervously with a pellet of bread and added gruffly: 'Now stop taking it out on your stomach and let me cut you some of this delicious-looking fowl. And don't imagine you're betraying your honour because we've taken bread and salt together! Get some food inside you, in God's name, and then listen to me!'

Beaten, she submitted, and while he filled his guest's plate, Tristan described to her at last what had taken place, that morning of 17 April, not far from the Bastille.

'When the city was in our hands and its former masters had quite given up all hope, they had no thought but to sell their lives dearly, and they ran to shut themselves up within the walls of the Bastille, which seemed to them the stoutest in all Paris. There were about 500 of them, part English and part citizens devoted to their cause, and they included, besides Sir Robert

Willoughby and his men, the Seigneur Louis de Luxembourg, Chancellor to the King of England, the Bishop of Lisieux, Pierre Cauchon and also some notable citizens among whom was one Guillaume Legoix, Master Butcher of the Rue d'Enfer ...'

Catherine started with surprise and cried out: 'Pierre Cauchon? Guillaume Legoix? Are you sure?'

'Of course, quite sure. Why? Do you know them?'

'Know them? Oh, God, yes! I know them!'

'How can that be? Well enough for Cauchon. Everyone in France knows of the wicked part he played in bringing Joan the Maid to her death – but Legoix?'

'You need not think that country life has made me stupid, Tristan,' Catherine broke in impatiently. 'If I tell you I know them, I mean I know them personally – and to my cost, alas! There are many things in my life of which you know nothing. This is one of them. On the night after Joan's death, after we and a handful of brave souls had tried to save her, Cauchon had Arnaud and me sewn into a leather sack and thrown into the Seine. We escaped only by the grace of God and the courage of one of our friends. As for Guillaume Legoix – he is my cousin.'

Instantly Tristan l'Hermite's face became a mask of astonishment.

'Your cousin?' he said blankly. 'How can that be?'

'Because before I was Catherine de Montsalvy I was Catherine Legoix, quite simply. My father and Guillaume Legoix were first cousins. Only, my cousin is also the man who, at the time of the great Cabochian riots 23 years ago in April 1413, murdered my husband's elder brother, Michel de Montsalvy, then squire to the Duchesse de Guyenne ...'

'Who is now the Constable's wife.'

'Exactly. Michel died outside our house, where I had hidden him. The crowd tore him to pieces, and Legoix – Legoix finished him off – with a cleaver. There was blood – blood everywhere – and I saw that horror with my own eyes when I was 13 years old. I nearly went mad, but by the mercy of God I was unconscious when the rabble hanged my father and set fire to our house. My mother and I - we found refuge in the Court of Miracles, but Caboche carried off my sister and raped her! It was there I met my dear Sara ... She nursed me – saved me ...'

The thread of memory spun itself again with the words. The images of long ago sprang to life before Catherine's eyes, and deep in her heart she found, like a treasure long buried, that first freshness of her youthful feelings.

Twenty-three years ago! Twenty-three years since her childish heart had leapt to its first cry of love, so soon to be followed by a scream of agony! Truly, it was like yesterday that she had seen Michel beaten down before her eyes, when she had risked everything to snatch him from death. She had loved him spontaneously, at the first glance, as a flower opens to the rising sun. In a single moment, he had become the whole world to her, and she felt as though she too had perished in his ghastly death.

After that, for a long, long time it had seemed to her that her heart had suffered an injury from which it would never recover. Until one evening on the road from Bruges when the broken web of destiny had been made suddenly whole again by throwing almost at her feet the one being capable of making her forget the tender, tragic love of her thirteenth year and replacing it in an instant with a mad, burning and wholly wonderful passion.

Warm, salt tears coursed silently down the woman's face from her closed eyes to the corners of her quivering lips. The man and boy watched her, scarcely daring to breathe for fear of interrupting her painful reverie. They glanced at one another, not liking to remind her of their presence, convinced, both of them, that Catherine had forgotten them.

But already the present had hold of her again and, without opening her eyes, she asked hoarsely: 'It was him, wasn't it – it was Guillaume Legoix whom my husband killed?'

It was not really a question. The answer was all there in her deep, intimate knowledge of her husband's passionate nature.

'Yes. Although we were able to intervene in time to stop him killing Cauchon also. He had stabbed the butcher and was already holding the bishop down on the ground with a knee in his chest and his hands about his throat.'

Catherine's eyes flew open suddenly, and she exploded into speech, without an instant's transition.

'So, you came in time! And I suppose you're proud of it? Proud to have saved the life of that swine, that monster who burned Joan! Well, not merely should you not have stopped him, you yourselves should have hanged him from the nearest gibbet! As for my husband, let me tell you that not only do I not blame him for what he did, but I should have done the same – and worse, perhaps, because it was no more than simple justice, pure straightforward justice, and thoroughly well-deserved! What man worthy of the name could stand by with folded arms and look the other way when his brother's murderer walked past? Not my husband, that I do know! The Montsalvys have blood in their veins – warm, red blood that they do not hesitate to spill generously for king and country!'

'I've never said otherwise,' Tristan countered harshly, 'and the whole army has long been aware of your husband's impetuous temper. But why did he say nothing of your connection with this Legoix and the wrong he had done you? When arrested he would only roar that Legoix was not fit to live, and that he had done nothing but justice!'

'If he had said it, would it have altered his position at all? And do you think that kinship could have been a source of pride to him? You know, Tristan, my husband does not like to think that his wife was born in a goldsmith's shop on the Pont au Change, to a craftsman with the heart and hands of an angel but no noble quarterings to his name.'

'Then he's wrong,' Tristan said forcefully. 'Although I can understand it. For my part, I think it makes me love you more! But these great nobles are intolerably proud. They're too ready to forget that their own noble ancestors, in Merovingian times, were often no more than clodhopping barbarians just a little more vicious than their neighbours. Aristocracy is a mighty catching disease! Not only have they not got over it, they've passed it on to their descendants in a more virulent form. Rights of high and low justice! That's their most cherished privilege – and it's that that drove Messire Arnaud to strike in defiance of the Constable's orders.'

Catherine smiled faintly. 'Then tell me how it happened, won't you?'

'Oh, that's easy. The very first night after we liberated the city, the Constable had his mind on those 500 gentry barricaded inside the Bastille. He wasn't feeling too friendly toward them – especially to Luxembourg and Cauchon. He wanted to catch them in their lair and take them by storm. He was counting also on the fact that there was very little food inside the fortress. But Michel de Lallier and other worthies who had opened the gates came to my lord and entreated him to be merciful.

'"If they wish to yield themselves, lord," they said, "do not refuse them. It was a great thing for you to have retaken Paris. Take thankfully what God has given you ..."

'The Constable has a noble mind, and he yielded in this. He let it be known that he would grant such conditions as they asked. On Sunday, 15 April, the treaty was signed, under my lord's name and seal. It granted all those within the Bastille their lives and goods safe, on condition that they left Paris.

'Two days later, on the Tuesday morning, they themselves opened the gates and came out, and made toward the river. There was a huge crowd hooting and jeering at them, and inevitably there were a good many itching to hurl something more substantial, but the Constable had let it be known that any who broke his given word would be punished with death. Also there was a certain amount of respect felt for Lord Willoughby, who was a veteran of Agincourt and Verneuil. He insisted that the laws of chivalry must be kept. But when that great Guillaume Legoix went past him, all pallid and sweating with fear, Montsalvy saw red. The man was loping along, looking about him in terror and clutching to his chest a bulging sack containing all that he had been able to save of his worldly goods.

'I must admit there was nothing about the man to inspire mercy or compassion or any other noble impulse. In fact, Catherine, I'll go even further and say that in Montsalvy's place I should have acted just the same –

and I should have been wrong, because orders are orders and your husband ignored them.

'At first, he just looked at Legoix and did not stir. Then, as the fellow saw that the troops were holding back the crowd to leave a passage for them he smiled, smirking a little, and Arnaud lost control. He tore his dagger from its sheath and fell upon the butcher crying: "Curse you, remember Michel de Montsalvy!" Then he buried the weapon in his breast. Legoix dropped like a stone, struck to the heart.

'Then the captain turned to Cauchon, who was standing staring with horror, and because the dagger was slippery with blood and with his steel gauntlets he could not grasp it, he sprang at him and would have throttled him with his hands.'

'You know the rest. He was taken straight to the Bertaudière Tower and imprisoned.'

'It's a shame!' Catherine cried.

'And did no-one speak up for him?' echoed Bérenger, who had now finished eating. 'Of all the men of Auvergne who came with him, did not one man stir to defend him?'

The Provost gave a small, mirthless laugh.

'In fact we nearly had a battle on our hands, my lad! Monseigneur himself had to call them to order; for, like a good Breton, he knows all about thick heads and hot blood. Even so, the knights of Montsalvy drew off, showing their teeth like whipped hounds. They've been sulking ever since. They've withdrawn to their quarters, and there they stay, refusing to take any part in their service. They're quite a problem, believe me, and the Constable doesn't know what to do about them. There are two of them, in particular, a pair of fair-haired giants who roll their rs like a bed of gravel in a stream, who are threatening to tear down the Bastille stone by stone! Their names are Renaud and Amaury de ...'

'Roquemaurel!' Bérenger finished for him, visibly delighted. 'They are my brothers, Messire Provost, and if they are threatening to tear down that Bastille of yours, you'd better look out! They're quite capable of doing it!'

Catherine drained her cup, made a little face as though the wine were bitter and then shrugged.

'I'm only surprised that no-one has yet thought of sending them home. It's dangerous to ill-use one of their own before their eyes!'

'It's what we long to do!' Tristan snapped. 'But they won't go! In any case, I might as well tell you at once, we've no money. The troops have had no pay for a long time, and that gives them something of an advantage.'

Catherine got up with a sigh and went to the window to stand for a moment looking out on the distorted vision of the street to be glimpsed through the green bottle glass windows.

'When you need men and can't pay them, you have to treat them with a little more respect. Surely the easiest way out of the difficulty would be to wipe the slate clean over the matter of my husband's killing and let our friends have their captain back? Don't you think the motive that drove Arnaud to disobey orders was a sufficiently worthy and noble one? What more do you want? He was avenging his brother – and my father!'

'Do you think the Constable doesn't know that? If it were with him alone, the Sire de Montsalvy would never have climbed the steps of the Bertaudière! But there is the army, always hot at hand; and there is Paris to be impressed – and finally, there is Legoix's widow who, relying on the Constable's word, is demanding the head of her husband's murderer.'

'What?'

Catherine swung round. Her face had gone so white against the blackness of her clothes that Tristan thought he saw a ghost. Her drawn face, clenched teeth and staring eyes were so alarming that he sprang toward her, frightened that she was going to fall flat on the stone floor. His arms went round her and she made no move to thrust him off, for her whole body seemed to have become rigid, and only her eyes blazed at him furiously.

'Arnaud's head!' she cried. 'The head of a Montsalvy for the slaying of a murdering butcher! How could such a thing be endured? Have you all gone mad? Or have I? Perhaps – yes, perhaps after all it is I who am going mad! Arnaud – my God! Surely I must be going to wake from this nightmare? You are mad! You are all mad! Raving mad! You ought to be locked up!'

She had put her hands to her head and was shaking it as though trying to free herself of the agony inside. Tears were pouring from her eyes and making rivulets down her dusty cheeks. She was weeping and crying out at once, struggling against the man striving to hold her. Her overstretched nerves, tested for too long, gave way at last, leaving her at the mercy of an uncontrollable emotional storm.

Bérenger had leapt to his feet and was making horrified attempts to help Tristan bring Catherine to her senses. Having no very clear idea what ought to be done in such a case, his clumsy efforts were proving more of a hindrance than a help to the Provost.

Maître Renaudot, drawn by the noise, came hurrying in, distractedly waving a dripping ladle. But he took in the situation at a glance.

'Water, Messire Provost,' was his advice. 'What she needs is a jug of cold water full in the face. There's nothing better!'

Bèrenger swooped on an empty pitcher and ran to fill it at the butt standing in a corner. Then, mentally begging his mistress to pardon such audacity, he flung the contents straight at her.

The screams and sobs stopped short. Gasping, Catherine stared at each of the three men in silence, opened her mouth to speak and then, without managing to utter a sound, closed her eyes and sank back, exhausted, into Tristan's arms.

He picked her up.

'Is her room ready?' he asked.

Renaudot hurried forward.

'Yes, yes indeed! This way, Messire … I'll show you …'

In a moment, Catherine was lying stretched on a downy quilt on a soft bed. Her eyes were closed but she was not unconscious. She could hear and feel all that was going on around her, although she had not strength enough to give the smallest sign of life. Even her thoughts were thin and wavering, and she felt as if she were floating in a merciful fog; but, more than anything, she felt more tired than she had ever felt in all her life.

Tristan and Bérenger, on either side of the bed, regarded her in perplexity, uncertain what to do. The page looked up, considering the man opposite.

'It was a hard journey, Messire,' he said. 'She was in such haste to be here that she drove herself beyond her strength, especially after the strain of the siege. And now, instead of the joy and comfort she had hoped for – there is this catastrophe! What are you going to do for her?'

It was not so much a question as a challenge, and Tristan l'Hermite did not fail to recognise the aggressive note in the page's voice. He shrugged.

'Give her over to the innkeeper's wife to get her undressed and into bed and watch over her. She must have sleep. And it would do you no harm to get some sleep either, my lad. You can hardly keep your eyes open. I'm going to see the Constable and tell him all this. He likes Dame Catherine, he'll certainly agree to see her and hear what she has to say. She is the only one who can do anything for her husband.'

'Is – is Monseigneur very angry with Messire Arnaud?'

Tristan l'Hermite's face hardened and a deep frown grew between his fair brows.

'Very,' he admitted. 'No-one likes to see his given word flouted so publicly, and the Constable is not a Breton for nothing. The Lady of Montsalvy will have her work cut out to get him to pardon the culprit.'

'But surely,' the page cried, very near to tears, 'he's not going to have the Count of Montsalvy put to death for such a little thing!'

Tristan hesitated, subjecting the boy to a searching look that measured his strength of character and capacity for self-control. At last he said, 'A little thing? A prince's word? For all the great service he has done, it would not surprise me if this were to cost Montsalvy his head.'

'Then take care!' the page cried with sudden fire. 'For there is not a man of spirit in all Auvergne who'd not take arms against the Constable if he dared take the life of a man respected by all – merely for doing justice!'

'Oh, a revolt? I see.'

'It might well become a revolution, because the common people will take their side. Tell Monseigneur to think twice before he strikes at the Count, for if he does, he will be striking at the whole region! It might be worth letting a butcher's wife, grown fat on treasonable gold, scream her fill!'

The page's ferocity drew a smile from the Provost. He raised his hand and gave him a buffet on the shoulder that made him stagger.

'In truth, what a counsel you make, Messire de Roquemaurel! You're of a different sort from your brothers, but no less effective. I'll be sure to tell him – the more so since I, too, love these madcap Montsalvys, he and she! Stay here, lad, and sleep. Recruit your strength and keep an eye on your mistress. I'll be back this evening to see how she does and tell her how things stand.'

He moved toward the door. Outside, the stairs could be heard creaking under the not inconsiderable bulk of Dame Renaudot, who was coming up, puffing a little as was to be expected of one weighing very nearly two hundred pounds. But in the doorway, Tristan turned, frowning a little.

'Better tell her not to reveal to the Constable and his like the – er – family ties between her and that accursed Legoix. No-one at court knows that she comes of common stock. For the sake of the Montsalvy name and honour, it's as well they should continue in ignorance.'

Bérenger shrugged. 'I thought aristocracy was a disease?' he said cheekily.

'No doubt. But it's the one disease from which the sufferers fiercely refuse to be cured. And you can't imagine how much they despise those who haven't got it!'

7: The Justice of Arthur de Richemont

Thinking that the Lady of Montsalvy's arrival might encourage them to abandon their angry withdrawal, Tristan l'Hermite made haste to convey the news to the men of Auvergne.

After leaving the Eagle, he went straight to the tavern called the Grand Godet, off the Place de Grève, where several of their leaders had their lodging. The bill of fare there might no longer boast roast hedgehog, cow's udders or 'jellied wood eels' (otherwise grass snake), as it had during the worst of the famine, but it was still very thin of cheer. On the other hand, the dry white wine of Aunis was incomparable, and the two Roquemaurel brothers, with their inveterate companion Gontran de Fabrefort, another chip off the same block as themselves, had been not slow to discover its virtues.

In acting as he did, the Provost was aware of serving his master's interests, in digging the rebels out of their retreat, as well as the interests of his friends the Montsalvys, by providing Catherine with a strong escort against the time when she would have to confront Richemont.

The interview was not a long one. The brief, heartfelt advice that Tristan had to deliver was decently washed down with liquid refreshment as befitting a talk between gentlemen, and when he rose to take his leave he was sped on his way by a series of genial thumps on the back from Renaud de Roquemaurel and a vast and vinous embrace from Fabrefort, who hugged him mightily and called him brother. They arranged to meet again on the following morning.

His official business completed, Tristan directed his steps toward the Hôtel des Tournelles, the elegant residence of the Dukes of Orléans, not far from the Bastille, where he paid a discreet visit to an extremely elevated person on whose support he knew he could count in the present situation. He emerged after half an hour looking much more cheerful than when he had gone in and, humming a drinking song fervently if inaccurately under his breath, turned his horse's head at last in the direction of the Hôtel du Porc-Epic, formerly the property of the Duke of Burgundy but bestowed by Philip the Good on the Constable in place of the Hôtel de Richemont in the Rue Hautefeuille, near the Cordeliers, which had been commandeered by the English in 1425 and of which little now remained.

The result of all these comings and goings was that next morning, as the bells of St Catherine du Val des Escholiers were ringing tierce*, Maître Renaudot began to wonder if a riot could be taking place outside his house; for, at that precise moment, a troop of spirited percherons deposited at the inn door a company of high-handed swaggering and remarkably noisy gentlemen.

They were all talking at once in deep voices accustomed to competing with mountain storms and emerging from torsos inured to grappling with bears. The innkeeper knew by their accents that all were Auvergnats. Some, indeed, had emerged from their own fastnesses for the first time in their lives in honour of the liberation of Paris, and these spoke nothing but their own patois, the ancient Auvernian tongue that was such an apt mixture of granite and sunshine.

But the French spoken by one pair of blond giants, the second a scarcely smaller copy of the first, was faultless and unanswerable. As easily as if he had been a wicker basket, Amaury de Roquemaurel took Renaudot by the ears and bore him gently into the inn, informing him that he was to go and tell the Lady of Montsalvy that her escort was waiting to conduct her to the Constable.

The innkeeper offered no objection and, having no wish to repeat an experience that was painful to say the least, scrambled down from the table where the giant had deposited him and scuttled for the stairs with the tears streaming down his face. He missed his footing, fell flat on his face and, weeping harder than ever, vanished into the upper regions. But he had no need to deliver his message. He found the young woman already at her door. She smiled at him.

'Go and tell them I am coming down, Maître Renaudot. Indeed, they need not have sent you. From the noise they made, one would have to be deaf – the whole district must know by now that I am going to Monseigneur de Richemont! But I must beg you to pardon their eagerness. I am afraid they are a little rough.'

Renaudot smiled back at her through his tears, and with a good deal of unconcealed admiration, for the woman before him bore no resemblance to the exhausted young traveller of the day before.

Learning at dawn from a message left by Tristan the previous night that

---

* About 9.00am.

Richemont would receive her at dinner time*, she had made a long and careful *toilette*, donning one of the two dresses she had brought with her in her slender baggage. She was much too familiar with the ways of the world, and especially of courts, to make the mistake of presenting herself in the wretched guise of a suppliant come straight from her provincial retreat.

At all times, her outstanding beauty had been her best weapon, and now that she was past 35, nothing had changed except that she had mellowed and grown more bewitching than ever. In this, she might say that her adventures had helped her, because when she looked at other women of her age, prematurely worn-out by child-bearing and aged by neglect or ignorance of bodily care, Catherine blessed the time she had spent in Granada in the house of the fat Ethiopian woman known as Fatima, from whom she had learned many strict principles and precious recipes that enabled her to face the passing years fearlessly.

This morning, she accepted as her due the innkeeper's dazzled gaze. Every trace of grief and weariness had been erased, and Catherine knew that she was beautiful and fashionable in a long gown of black velvet belted high below her breasts and with no other ornament than a band of snowy ermine edging the low, pointed neckline that descended to her waist at the back, the long, narrow sleeves and the hem of the dress that swept out behind in a three-foot train.

On the queenly crown of her magnificent, silky golden hair, she wore a little truncated steeple of white satin, tilted very far back and serving merely to support a cloud of marvellous Malines lace, a present from Jacques Cœur.

By way of ornament, in addition to the chased emerald that gleamed on her hand, she wore another, similar stone, but larger and brighter still, shimmering in the hollow of her breasts, on a gold chain as slender as a stroke drawn by a pen. The green stones with the whiteness of the ermine brought out the golden tones of her skin, while the velvet, worn next to her skin, delineated bust, shoulders and arms with absolute precision.

Renaudot, deeply impressed, retreated backwards, marvelling, toward the stairs, as if he had seen a ghost, and would probably have fallen a second time had Catherine not checked him with a question.

'Have you seen my page?'

'Young Bérenger? No, noble lady. I saw him go out a while ago, just after daybreak, but I've not seen him since.'

'Where can he be?'

'I do not know, my lady, upon my honour, but he seemed in a great

---

* Which at this period was eaten round about 11.00am.

hurry'

Catherine gave a sigh of vexation. Carrying a lady's train on ceremonial occasions formed part of a page's duties. Until now, it was not a service that Catherine had required of Bérenger, since life at Montsalvy, for all its elegancies, was an informal affair. Now, just when she needed him, her page had managed to slip away without warning. God alone knew when he was likely to return, always supposing he did not lose himself altogether in a Paris that was totally unfamiliar to him.

Resigning herself to doing without a companion whom she had come to value, Catherine decided to join her boisterous escort, feeling some slight qualms about the figure she would cut in the midst of a set of fire-eating ruffians who were both loud and quarrelsome.

Richemont might not be pleased with a tearful wife accompanied by such a blustering escort. On the other hand, there could be no doubt that an escort made up of the Roquemaurels, Fabrefort, Ladinhac, Sermur and other men of Auvergne would carry an undeniable weight in argument, especially in their present mood. Richemont might well think twice before goading such men into a revolt that would do no-one any good.

Before leaving her room, Catherine had prayed for a long time to Our Lady of Le Puy-en-Velay, for whom, ever since setting out for Compostella in Galicia, she had retained a special reverence, and in whom she placed an absolute trust. Strong in this trust, she descended the remainder of Renaudot's noisy staircase and stepped into the room below, where a sudden silence greeted her entry.

As though touched by an enchanter's magic wand, the knights froze in whatever attitude they happened to be in at the moment of her appearance. Some had their mouths open, others a cup of wine half-way to their lips, but all were held rigid by the woman's sheer beauty, made more exquisite and startling by the background of the inn.

In spite of the pain it caused her to see gathered together in some degree of cheerfulness the men she had watched riding away with Arnaud, she smiled at them all in turn, dividing her general greeting equally among them.

'I bid you all welcome, gentlemen, and I want to tell you what a comfort it is to me to see you all assembled here to defend my cause ...'

'Your cause is also our cause, Dame Catherine,' Renaud de Roquemaurel said gruffly. 'I might even claim that it is ours first, for if the worst should happen and Montsalvy suffer, which of us fighting men would continue to serve a prince who denies us justice – and pays so badly!'

'Even so, I thank you, Renaud. But who told you I was here?'

'That great Flemish clod who's the Constable's watchdog!' the Sire de Ladinhac threw in, with a contempt that annoyed Catherine.

'Messire l'Hermite is an old friend of ours,' she retorted curtly. 'Your presence here is proof of that. And I can't advise you too strongly, Messire Alban, to think more carefully before you speak of one who is both Grand Master of Artillery and Provost-Marshal.'

'Ha, the artillery's not up to much! A lot of bronze mouths shooting off at random! A good troop of horse is worth much more, or ...'

Catherine had no desire to become embroiled in an argument concerning the relative merits of guns and cavalry, and so, abandoning all hope of Bérenger's arrival, she glanced around her, saying: 'It is nearly time for the audience, gentlemen. Which of you will give me his arm to the Constable?'

Immediately, there was a noisy rush. All were eager to offer their services, and the resulting competition might have ended in a fight had a clear, cold voice not risen above the tumult.

'With your permission, Messires, I shall do that.'

There was instant silence as the turbulent crowd parted, like the Red Sea before Moses. Through the passage thus created, a man came walking alone and unarmed.

He was magnificently dressed in a green velvet doublet and close-fitting black hose thrust into high, kid-lined boots. On top of this he wore, with an air, a great gold-embroidered gown of black velvet, its wide sleeves slashed to show the green taffeta lining beneath. A heavy gold chain around his neck and a green velvet hat with a pin like a gold griffon added the finishing touches to an outfit that the provincial knights in their stained leather and mail beheld with an admiration untinged by either criticism or envy.

All of them, indeed, felt both liking and respect for the man whom the entire army called, with affectionate brutality, the Bastard, as if he had been the only one of his kind, but whose real name was Jean d'Orléans, although he would go down in history as the Count of Dunois.[*] But to women, who played a large part in his life, he was, above all, an unusually attractive, because a very charming, brave and gentle man.

Also, although in his case the royal arms were crossed with the bar sinister, the son of Louis d'Orléans, who had been done to death by the Barbette Gate, and the lovely Mariette d'Enghien, held princely rank.

In the absence of his half-brother Charles, the lawful duke, still held prisoner in England, it was he who governed the city and lands of Orléans, to the satisfaction of all.

Catherine de Montsalvy had known her husband's famous brother-in-

---

[*] The Bastard was not in fact made Count of Dunois until 1439, but he is called by that name here in the interests of clarity.

arms for a very long time and had never doubted his quality. The curtsy she made to him now would have satisfied the king himself.

Dunois came to her and, bowing, took her hand to assist her to rise, then kissed it gracefully.

'It is time, Catherine,' he said, as simply as if they had parted only the night before. 'We must go, unless we want to be late.'

So it was he who was to go with her to the formidable Breton prince? Suddenly flushed with happiness at the prospect of a support she would never have dared to ask for, she bestowed on him a smile sparkling with gratitude.

'You do me such honour, Monseigneur, that I do not know how to thank you. Only tell me how you knew that I was here?'

'In the same way as these gentlemen: from Tristan l'Hermite, who must have been blowing your trumpet very thoroughly, I think. He's a man who will do his duty rigidly, even if it breaks his heart, but he is also a true friend. As to the honour, my dear, that's not so very great. You've always known I thought of Arnaud as a brother!'

'All the same, your support gives me courage. With that, I am sure ...'

'Don't cherish any illusions, Dame Catherine. I've been pleading Montsalvy's cause continually ever since that business outside the Bastille, and so far to no good end! So it's I who should consider your arrival as a gift from heaven, because your beauty and grace are still irresistible and may have power to soften our Constable's hard heart. Come now, we must not keep him waiting.'

Raising high the hand he still held, and placing his other on his hip as though about to lead her into the dance, the Bastard conducted Catherine out to the street.

'Follow us, gentlemen!' he threw over his shoulder.

The troop formed up behind them, as solid and compact as a wall of masonry.

From the inn of the Eagle to the Hôtel du Porc-Epic, the fortified gateway of which opened onto the side of the old royal Hôtel Saint-Pol, was not a long way. One had only to cross the Rue St Antoine.

Ever since dawn, the weather had made up its mind to be perfect. The sun, high in the clean-washed sky, looked brand new. It was so bright that even the muddy little puddles that lay between the cracks of the wide Capetian paving stones glittered like gold. Out in the street, which at this point was unusually wide, the people of Paris, unaccustomed to fine weather, were taking their first, faltering steps among the din of the street traders, crying their wares and calling on housewives to buy water, wood or mustard.

It was not yet the joyous clamour it had once been, when the street had been crowded with hurrying townsfolk, merchants in rich, furred gowns, needy monks, persistent beggars, noble ladies tripping unsteadily on wooden pattens to keep their skirts out of the dirt, and shameless hussies in invitingly low-cut bodices. Then poverty had walked side by side with luxury, to the embarrassment of neither. Today, the street was struggling back to life again after so many years of bitter depression, and stretching its wings to try its strength.

People paused to watch the curious procession of bronzed and weatherbeaten fighting men escorting a pair as pretty as a picture. It was like some fantastic wedding party. But then they recognised the Bastard and greeted him warmly, while all eyes were drawn to the beauty of his companion. They left a flattering trail of cheers and applause in their wake, but Catherine neither heard nor saw. As they had reached the centre of the Rue St Antoine, she had caught sight of the dark towers of the Bastille looming threateningly above the proud and empty shell of what had been the royal palace of Saint-Pol, and her heart was wrung with anguish for her husband, immured within that massive keep of stone. And the thought came into her mind that perhaps it was all going to begin again, just as it had happened before amid the same scenes ...

She saw herself again, an urchin with stiffly braided hair and bony knees, amidst a mob of rioters in one of the rooms of that now silent palace, watching with disbelieving eyes as a bloodstained butcher tore from a weeping princess's arms a youth as beautiful as an archangel but doomed to the gallows. In that moment, her whole life had been changed. Her 13-year-old eyes had rested on Michel's face and her world had turned upside down.

Now, in another room in another royal palace not far from there, she was going to plead with Arthur de Richemont for the brother of that murdered archangel, the man she had loved above all else, just as in an earlier, tragic Parisian springtime the woman who was then the youthful Duchesse de Guyenne had pleaded with her own father, the implacable Jean Sans Peur, for the life of Michel de Montsalvy. The duchess had pleaded in vain. Would she, Catherine, have better fortune? The precedent was not encouraging.

As she passed through the gateway, with its crowned porcupine carved in the stone, Catherine could not repress a shudder. Her companion noticed it and glanced at her anxiously.

'Are you cold? I think you're shivering.'

'No, my lord. Not cold. Frightened.'

'You? Afraid? There was a time, Catherine, when you were not afraid of torture, or even the gallows. You were going to it very proudly when the Maid saved you.'

'Because then the threat was only to myself! But I'm not brave when someone I love is concerned. And I love my lord Arnaud more than myself; you know that!'

'I know,' he agreed seriously. 'And I also know what feats that love can accomplish. But be comforted; what you are going to face here is not an enemy but a prince who wishes you well.'

'It's for that very reason I am so afraid. I should fear the worst enemy less than a friend angered. What's more, I do not like this house. It brings bad luck.'

The Bastard stared, somewhat disconcerted by the unexpected pronouncement.

'Bad luck? You can't be serious! What do you mean?'

'Just what I say. I was born not far from here, my lord, and I know that all the owners of this house have died untimely deaths.'

'Nonsense!'

'Didn't you know? Think: after Hughes Aubriot, its builder, who perished at Montfaucon, there was Jean de Montaigu, dragged to the scaffold and hanged; and Pierre de Giac, who sold his hand to the devil, which hand the Constable had cut off before he was sewn into a sack and thrown in the Auron. Then there was your own father, Duke Louis of Orléans, who gave it his symbol of the porcupine, murdered; the Prince of Bavaria, died under suspicious circumstances; Duke Jean of Burgundy, murdered ...'

'Good God! Don't talk of such things! Remember Richemont is a Breton, and superstitious! In any case, the risk is his. You don't own the house, as far as I know.'

'No. But so much violence leaves its mark ... There is an atmosphere. This is not a merciful house.'

The Bastard took out a handkerchief and mopped his brow with a sigh.

'Well, my dear, you can congratulate yourself on an unrivalled talent for raising people's spirits. Here have I been trying to comfort you, and you start upsetting me with ghost stories ... Ah! Messire du Pan!'

The Constable's steward had appeared just as Catherine and her companion were about to mount the stairs leading to the great hall. Dunois welcomed him with visible relief.

'Will you announce this lady and me, Messire? It sounds as if there's a deal of company within?'

The upper storey was buzzing with the sound of many voices, like a hive of bees in summertime. But the steward bowed, smilingly.

'Too much company, indeed. Monseigneur's orders are that I am to take my lady into the garden, whither he has retired with his council.'

Catherine suppressed a sigh of relief. She had feared that Richemont might compel her to state her case in public, as though in a court room where, because of the large numbers of people present, she might have found herself condemned out of hand.

The amount of noise inside the building had made her fear this from first entering it. She therefore smiled on the Sire du Pan, who was politely waiting to show her the way. Even so, there was nearly trouble when he tried to separate Catherine from her escort and forbid the gentlemen of Auvergne's entry into the garden.

'My lord Constable wishes to hear the Countess of Montsalvy in private, gentlemen. He has said that he wishes to keep this unfortunate business a family affair as far as possible, on account of the close ties between himself and the Montsalvys.'

Amaury de Roquemaurel took a step forward so that he stood towering a full head above the steward.

'We are Arnaud de Montsalvy's brothers in arms, Sir Steward, and that makes us, too, members of the family! Therefore, we too shall go in! Whether you like it or not! Indeed, we do not like the ways you have here at court of dealing with family matters. We are one with Dame Catherine, and it may be she will have need of us!'

'Let them in, Du Pan,' Dunois intervened. 'They'll stay at the edge of the orchard and won't interfere without need. I'll vouch for that.'

'In that case, I yield. Be so good as to follow me ...'

The garden, descending in a gentle slope to the Seine, was flooded with sunshine. It was a fresh and charming spot, a large orchard of old cherry trees, covered now in this late spring with white blossom, while the new grass beneath was enamelled with primroses, violets and anemones. Clumps of purple lilac formed soft, shady bowers for a number of seats of weathered stone, and the lazy surface of the river glinted between the branches.

Richemont was awaiting Catherine in one of these arbours. He was seated on one of the stone benches, dressed all in dark grey velvet, unadorned, talking quietly with the various gentlemen about him.

In addition to Tristan l'Hermite, who stood a little way apart, his attention concentrated on the movements of a blackbird hopping along the ground, there were the Burgundian leader, Jean de Villiers de l'Isle Adam; the new Provost of Paris, Messire Philippe de Ternant, with the other master of the city, Michel de Lallier; and one of the most distinguished Breton captains, Jean de Rostrenen.

The men of Auvergne remained docilely at the entrance to the orchard, while Jean d'Orléans led Catherine forward to the Constable. She bowed before him as if he had been the King himself.

The conversation had ceased at her approach, and although her head remained modestly bent, she knew that all eyes were upon her. There was a moment's silence, as quickly broken by the joyous trilling of a bird on a nearby branch, a sound quite out of keeping with the gravity of the occasion. It was followed by the harsh and unwelcoming tones of the

Constable.

'So, Madame de Montsalvy, you have come! I was scarcely expecting you; and, to be quite honest with you, I'm not at all glad to see you. I may say it's the first time.'

It was not a hopeful beginning. However, Richemont had risen courteously to greet his visitor and now motioned to her to sit beside him on the bench.

Catherine ignored the invitation, forcing herself to be brave. The Constable's tone had told her that it would be a hard fight. This was not going to be a matter of polite conversation. Therefore, it was better to face it openly, with no subterfuges.

Speaking with the licence of a woman and a very great lady, she answered him as stiffly: 'Neither am I glad to be here, my lord! I came to Paris to complain most bitterly of the wrong done to me. I did not look to be compelled, as soon as I arrived, to come here to implore your mercy. But coming as a plaintiff, I find myself transformed by some magic into the accused!'

'You stand accused of nothing!'

'Whoever accuses my lord Arnaud, accuses me!'

'Well, then, let's say you stand accused of trying to wrest from me a pardon I have no desire to grant. As for your complaint – may I know the cause?'

'Do not pretend ignorance, my lord. I see here Messire l'Hermite, who cannot have failed to inform you why I came. But if you insist on having it from my own lips, my complaint is of the wrong done to me and mine, to my lands, my town and my people. My complaint is that Bérault d'Apchier and his sons, in defiance of all justice, have taken advantage of my husband's absence, with all his best knights, to lay siege to Montsalvy. Even now it may have fallen and be crying to heaven in its agony! I complain that I could get no help either from the consuls or the Bishop of Aurillac, because they feared an attack from Villa Andrade, who is now at Saint-Pourcain, or from your Bailiff of the Mountains, who would rather go on a pilgrimage with his wife than keep watch as his duty demands! Lastly, I complain that the master and natural protector of this sorely-tried land has been flung unjustly into prison, when without him I and mine are doomed to death and destruction!'

Catherine's voice swelled with anger to a ringing tone, and the garden was not so very big. No sooner had the news of Montsalvy's peril reached the ears of the Roquemaurels and their comrades than they lost all semblance of the unnatural restraint that had held them.

There was a rush, and in an instant the orchard was full of sound and fury. Catherine and the Bastard, who had remained at her side as though to stress that she was under his protection, found themselves at the centre of a fire-breathing horde.

Jean d'Orléans did his best to control them, but the captains of Auvergne were in no mood to suffer further management.

'Montsalvy is attacked, and you, Monseigneur, knew it yesterday while we, the true sons of that soil, were kept in ignorance!' protested Renaud de Roquemaurel. 'What are we doing here, havering over the well-deserved death of a villain, when hundreds of men, women and children are in peril? What good is it to win Paris from the English if you let brigands ravage the rest of the kingdom? Give us Montsalvy, Lord Constable! Give us our captain and let us go! We have wasted too much time!'

The Constable put up his hand to quell the uproar.

'Peace, gentlemen! This thing is not as simple as it seems. Believe me, I was both grieved and angered to learn what was passing in the High Auvergne, and as soon as possible I will send help ...'

'As soon as possible?' Fabrefort protested. 'In other words, when every brave man has perished within the walls of Montsalvy and Bérault d'Apchier has had plenty of time to dig himself in there! And did you hear what Dame Catherine said besides? The Castilian is at Saint-Pourain and the people of Aurillac go in fear of his coming! What is Paris to us if we go home to find our castles taken, our villages burned and our women raped? We'll not stay here a moment longer!'

'Then go! I'm not keeping you!'

'We're going,' Roquemaurel retorted. 'But not alone! We want Arnaud de Montsalvy, and we'll get him even if we have to tear him out of your Bastille by force! You'll have to cross swords with your own troops, my lord Constable!'

'You see nothing but your own interests!' Richemont cried. 'You forget that in a freshly-conquered city justice must be stricter and more inflexible than anywhere. My orders were clear and the penalty in no doubt. The Lord of Montsalvy knew that and chose to ignore it.'

'How can a man stand by and do nothing when his brother's murderer walks by?' Dunois said. 'There's not one of us who wouldn't have done the same!'

'Do not say so, Sir Bastard,' countered Richemont. 'No one knows better than you how to obey orders. How can the people of Paris trust me, and see that I alone am master here and responsible in the King's name, if I pass over the first serious case of disobedience? Have you forgotten that I pledged my word?'

'Arnaud de Montsalvy's head is worth more than your word!' Catherine snapped. Then, as Richemont paled and fell back as if she had struck him, she fell on her knees. 'Forgive me!' she cried, 'I spoke more than I meant. Do not hold it against me. I have been half mad since I heard of my husband's peril – and the cause!'

'A prisoner has been killed,' the Breton answered stubbornly, 'when I had promised him his life. Do you think I wasn't longing to string up that greasy swine Cauchon, whose insane fury sent the Maid to her death? Yet I contained myself!'

'Did you know he was in the Bastille?'

'N-no, I did not know at the start of the negotiations; but if I had, it would have made no difference. I had to free all or none. Get up, Dame Catherine. I don't like to see you at my feet like that!'

'It is the proper place for a suppliant, Monseigneur. You must let me be! Besides, I will not rise until you grant me what I ask! All that you have told me, I already knew. I knew how grave was my husband's crime, for he dared to defy your word – the word of a prince who is the soul of honour!'

A man who had not so far spoken stepped forward. It was the Provost of the Merchants. Michel de Lallier gave a small, apologetic bow and said with a sigh: 'Unfortunately, lady, the people of Paris are not yet well acquainted with Monseigneur de Richemont. But their recollections of the Armagnacs, and especially of the Constable d'Armagnac, are by no means happy. It is true that they have returned of their own accord to their natural lord, King Charles of France, whom God preserve, but how will they take it if the man who is his representative is to take such liberties at this early stage? The prince gave his word to me, as Provost of the Merchants, and to my Echevins. It is not within my power to release him from it.'

'But why? Why?' Catherine moaned, ready to weep.

'Because I am bound to deal justly with Legoix's widow. Her neighbours plundered her house and maltreated her, but she was to have gone with her husband, and now she has nothing left.'

'Will she be any richer or happier for my husband's death?'

'Lady,' the old man said, 'you cannot understand. You are a high and noble dame to whom the common people are so little ...'

'Guillaume Legoix did not belong to the common people. He was a grand bourgeois, a rich man!'

'That is as may be, but still he was no more than a bourgeois, like me and most of our fellow townsmen. Paris, my lady, is made up largely of the bourgeois and the common people. We have very few nobles. Great lords are far removed from us, occupied as they are with war and tourneys. It is true that Guillaume Legoix slew the Lord of Montsalvy's brother, but it was in time of war, my lady ...'

In a moment, Catherine was on her feet, facing the Provost.

'Of war? No, Messire, not in time of war! Time of rebellion, if you like! Caboche was never a captain of war that I know of!'

'This is mere quibbling. Civil war was what I meant, and you cannot know what that is like, because in those days you were growing up in comfort in a noble castle, where the fury of Paris scarcely came! You do not know what took place in those days, when people here grew sick of Queen Ysabeau and her favourites, of wicked and extortionate nobles and rose up in the name of liberty! And even though it might be very painful to you, I must say that the murder, if murder it was, of the young Lord of Montsalvy was never a matter for indignation. Believe me, Paris will think it right that my lord Constable should take the life of a noble guilty of slaying a citizen, even one in the service of the enemy. For indeed, we were all so to some extent, whether from choice or necessity. The trial that my lord has so far postponed all too long because of certain political events must take place. Do you understand?'

Catherine looked at the old man and then at those about her, one by one. She saw Tristan's worried face, the Bastard's hopeless one and the Constable, whose tight lips and frowning brows showed his hardened resolution.

She saw, too, the men of Auvergne, their hands fidgeting for the hilts of sword or dagger, and she knew that in another moment it might be too late. All of them, brave men of a land she loved now more than her own native earth, were ripe for murder in order to snatch their friend from death and maintain their own seigneurial rights.

If Arnaud were sacrificed to the shade of Guillaume Legoix, there would be bloodshed here in the garden, and away in Auvergne a revolt that would blaze like a forest fire through the mountains. She could only prevent the tragedy and at the same time save Arnaud by making a sacrifice of her own pride and revealing herself for what she was.

The old Provost would not release Richemont from his word for the Lady of Montsalvy – but he might do it for Catherine Legoix.

She put up her hand to silence her friends who were already roaring their anger and disapproval, then she turned to Michel de Lallier.

'No, Messire, I do not understand. Rather, it is you who have something to understand, for there is a thing you do not know. At the time you speak of, I was not, as you so delightfully phrased it, growing up in comfort in a noble castle. I was in Paris, Messire, during those terrible days of Caboche's rising. In fact, I was actually on the Pont au Change that night when Guillaume Legoix murdered Michel de Montsalvy. Child as I was, my dress was splattered with his blood ...'

'But that's impossible! '

'Impossible? Those of my friends who are here present know that when Arnaud de Montsalvy married me, I was the widow of Garin de Brazey, Lord Treasurer of Burgundy; but Burgundians know that Garin de Brazey was married by Duke Philippe's command to the niece of a prominent citizen of Dijon who was not noble. You know that, don't you, Messire de Ternant?'

Thus directly appealed to, the Burgundian lord abandoned his detached attitude for a moment and regarded the young woman before him consideringly.

'I have heard it said, indeed. My master, Duke Philippe, being much enamoured of the young lady – a thing that one has only to look at you, lady, to understand – is said to have constrained the Lord Treasurer to wed the niece of – a draper, was it not?'

'You have a good memory, Messire. My uncle, Mathieu Gautherin, is a cloth merchant to this day, at the Sign of the Great St Bonaventure in the Rue du Griffon. He took us in, my mother, my sister and me, after we fled from Paris and from the fury of Caboche. I do not come from any noble castle lost in the depths of the country, Messire de Lallier. I was born in Paris on the Pont au Change. You may even remember my father, Gaucher Legoix, the goldsmith who used to make you such fine ewers ...'

The old Provost and the Constable were both seized with a sudden tremor.

'Legoix?' the Constable said. 'What does this mean?'

'It means that before I was Catherine de Montsalvy,' Catherine said, 'I was Catherine de Brazey, and before that, my lord, plain Catherine Legoix. I am cousin to the man whom you would avenge. His cousin and also his victim; for if my husband had not killed him, I myself would have come to you to demand his head!'

'On what grounds? I'll be bound the Montsalvys were nothing at that time to a goldsmith and his family – except perhaps customers?'

The faint note of disdain did not escape Catherine, and she could not bring herself to look at Tristan, remembering his warning about the dangers of revealing her origins. But she was not the woman to blush for her birth; and, having once revealed that it was not noble, she meant to cry it aloud and use it to the full in a last bid to save her husband.

So there was no trace of humiliation in her great violet eyes as she turned them on Richemont, but rather a kind of lofty pride that he recognised.

'No, they were not customers. They were, indeed, quite unknown to us; and it is not for the murder of Michel de Montsalvy that I should have called Legoix's life forfeit, but because he hanged my father, his cousin, from his own shop sign, and afterwards set fire to our house. What happened was that Michel, badly bruised, was being led out to his death when he escaped and took refuge in our house, where I hid him. The treachery of a servant betrayed him, and despite all my tears and entreaties I saw, saw with my own eyes – remember, I was only 13 – Guillaume Legoix raise his butcher's cleaver to slaughter an unarmed boy of 17, who was being torn to pieces by a mob!'

Encouraged by the murmur of horror and revulsion aroused by her words, she swung away from Michel de Lallier and directed a sudden attack upon the Constable.

'That day, my lord, as the people swarmed through the Hôtel de St Pol, I saw the woman who is now your wife but who was then the Duchesse de Guyenne, I saw her in tears, beseeching her father and the mob on bended knees to spare the life of a youth who was her page and very dear to her!

'That page, I, a weak, defenceless girl, almost managed to save! Madame de Richemont, if she were here, would be the first to entreat your pardon for the brother of her murdered page and beg you, with all the strength of her love, to abate your sternness!'

The Breton prince's blue eyes wavered, avoiding Catherine's.

'My wife ...' he muttered.

'Yes, your wife! Have you forgotten the lists at Arras, where Arnaud de Montsalvy submitted himself to God's judgement for the honour of his prince? Wasn't it the Duchesse de Guyenne herself, newly betrothed to you, who, with your consent, herself fastened her colours to my husband's lance? Remember, my lord! Her friendship toward our house is even older than your own!'

Richemont shook his head, as though to drive out unwelcome thoughts.

'Older? Not by much. It was at Agincourt that I first met Montsalvy and saw him fight.'

The revival of these memories had clearly left Richemont a prey to an inward struggle; a struggle that, Catherine knew, in his heart he longed to lose. But matters had reached a stage where it was no longer in his power to end the argument. The power of decision now rested with the fine-looking old man in the dark red velvet gown who was looking at her meditatively.

She turned to direct her entreaties at him.

'Sir Provost,' she begged, 'I, Catherine Legoix, ask you for justice against Guillaume Legoix, the murderer of my father and of one who was a guest in his house; a man whose crimes almost brought about my own death and have darkened my life ever since. And, seeing that justice has been done already, I would humbly beg your mercy for the man who was its instrument, a witting one to be sure, but blinded by so many years of hatred.'

There was a moment of absolute silence. All those present held their breath, conscious of the gravity of the hour and also, perhaps, stirred by the beauty of the woman before them, her eyes bright with tears and her delicate, white hands stretched out in a pretty, pleading gesture toward the old Provost of the Merchants.

He, too, was watching her with something at the back of his tired, old man's eyes that might have been pride, not unmixed with affection.

'So,' he said softly, 'you are the little Catherine I used to see playing with her dolls in our good Gaucher's shop in those days? Forgive me, I did not know of his cruel death. I was away from Paris in those dark days, and I never heard exactly how he died. There has been so much death of every kind since then ...'

'Then, for pity's sake, Messire, do not insist on one more!'

The Burgundian lords were also staring at Catherine with a kind of fascination, and now Villiers de l'Isle Adam spoke, as though unconsciously, and without taking his widened eyes from her face.

'You must pardon him, Lord Constable! I ask it of you in the name of my master, Duke Philippe of Burgundy, who, if he were here, would himself have demanded it in the name of justice – and of chivalry!'

An expression of bewildered inquiry crossed Richemont's stony face.

'Chivalry, did you say?'

'Most certainly!'

Smiling faintly, and still without taking his eyes from Catherine's head, Villiers de l'Isle Adam lifted his hand to touch the heavy chain of the Golden Fleece that lay upon his plain black doublet. His fingers toyed with the heraldic ram that dangled from it.

'No-one at the Court of Burgundy is unaware of the regrets of the queenly crown of golden hair that inspired Duke Philippe to found an Order that we, his vassals, are proud to bear, for it is the noblest that there is. That is why I ask for mercy in the name of chivalry – that, and because I deem the Lady of Montsalvy in the right in this.'

Richemont thought for a moment, frowningly. Catherine held her breath, striving to suppress the frenzied beating of her heart. Her fingers tightened painfully on the hand that the Bastard, sensing her need of support, had once more extended to her. And it was to him that Richemont suddenly addressed himself.

'My lord Bastard, what is your counsel?'

Dunois grinned back at him boldly.

'Why, pardon him, of course! I came for nothing else!'

'Yours, Ternant?'

The Provost of Paris shrugged. 'Pardon, of course, my lord Constable.'

'You, Rostrenen?'

'Pardon, Monseigneur! It is just!' the Breton captain said firmly.

Richemont did not look at the knights of Auvergne for their opinion, but these gentry did not mean to be overlooked. Their voices swelled into a vaguely menacing clamour, echoing the words of the three earlier speakers: 'Pardon! Pardon!'

'Come,' boomed Renaud de Roquemaurel. 'Let's free Montsalvy and be gone! We're needed at home!'

In the eyes of that blond giant, the issue was decided, and all that remained was to speed to the Bastille and release the prisoner.

Richemont did not see the matter in quite the same light, however.

'One moment. Sir Knight! There is still something to be said. Maître Michel de Lallier has not yet spoken, and you know that the verdict rests with him, and with him alone, whatever the rest of us may think. Come, my lord Provost,' he continued quickly, seeing the Roquemaurels' eyes bent gloweringly on the old man, 'what is your decision? Shall the Captain de Montsalvy live or die?'

'Live, Monseigneur, so please you. In such a case, it seems to me that no man has the right to condemn him. Nevertheless, I should like him to know that he owes your clemency and mine, not to his lordly rank, or even to the justifiable nature of his own revenge – but to the shade of a murdered worthy goldsmith to whom, in life, he would not have given a second glance and might well blush to call his father-in-law.'

'He shall know it,' Richemont promised. 'I pledge myself to that.'

'Then I will ask your permission to withdraw, for I must now go to the Maison aux Piliers to explain my decision to the Echevins. I am sure they will fully endorse what I have done.'

'Do you think the populace will do the same?'

The old man shrugged slightly and pursed up his lips tolerantly.

'I'll speak to the people this very evening and tell them it was my own suggestion to release you from your bond, Monseigneur, and to pardon the offender.'

'Will you tell them the reason for this clemency?' Catherine asked, almost timidly.

'Indeed I shall, my lady. I am acting in the people's name, and they must know my reasons. They will readily accept that one of their own should pay with his life for the death of another where, in their present over-excited state, they would probably not accept it where a young lord was concerned. Now, before I leave you, I should like, if you will allow me, my lady, to say that I am happy to have met you – and proud also to see that a daughter of Paris can become a lady so high and fair. May I kiss your hand?'

Impulsively, Catherine offered him her cheek and embraced the old man warmly.

'Thank you, my lord Provost! Thank you with all my heart! I shall not forget you, and I'll pray for you!'

As Michel de Lallier departed, escorted through the dappled shade of the garden by Jean de Rostrenen, with some of the men of Auvergne and two Burgundian lords who had bowed to Catherine with as much respectful solemnity as if she had still reigned over the heart of the Great Duke of the West, Richemont took her hand gently from the Bastard's and drew her down to sit beside him on the stone seat.

'Now that you've won your battle, my fair warrior, come and sit by me

168

and let me look at you. God, but you're beautiful, Catherine! You shine brighter than the gorse bushes of my own Brittany when the sun is on them and they set the heathland alight! If I didn't love my own sweet wife so much, I really think I'd be in love with you!'

He was smiling quite openly now, with a glad sparkle in his blue eyes, all trace of anger and resentment vanished, sincerely happy to be able to bask once more in the glow of old friendship.

Catherine, however, had not forgotten that word 'customers', and she was determined to exact a small revenge.

'How's this, Monseigneur? Will you indeed have a goldsmith's daughter sit beside you – one whose father may once have enjoyed the custom of your own family?'

He gave a shout of laughter.

'Touché! I deserved that! Forgive me, Catherine, but this business has been getting on my nerves. You know quite well that you are one of the few people in whom birth matters not a jot. You were worthy to be born on the steps of a throne, and in raising you to the rank you hold today, Fate has done you no more than justice. Now, tell me about yourself and about my goddaughter Isabelle and your beautiful country – to which I will send aid, just in case your ferocious escort should not be enough to relieve it.'

'I'll go, if you like,' Dunois offered. 'Montsalvy and I should be able to get the better of a band of brigands soon enough.'

'Out of the question. I need you, my lord Bastard! Don't rob me of everyone! In any case, it would be too much to send the bloods of Orléans to chastise a handful of filthy routiers! I'll deal with it in a moment, when the Lord of Montsalvy comes.'

'He is coming here?' Catherine cried, and the Breton prince smiled to see how she flushed with joy.

'Of course he's coming! Rostrenen has gone to the Bastille to fetch him. It's not very far. My poor child, did you think I'd have the heart to keep you here listening to my chatter when I know you're quivering with impatience to see him? I mean to give myself the pleasure of bringing you together. Methinks I've a right to some reward!'

'To any reward, my lord, and to all our gratitude! Thanks to you, I shall know rest and happiness and peace of mind again ...'

'But you won't be really happy until your husband is here in person,' the Constable said, seeing that Catherine eyes were already gazing up the garden, watching for the first glimpse of that tall, familiar figure.

She smiled in a little confusion.

'It's true. I am eager to see him.'

'Be patient. He'll be here in a moment.'

It was, indeed, no more than a moment before Rostrenen reappeared, but he was alone, and in a state of such evident agitation that Catherine rose to her feet automatically, gripped by a dreadful foreboding, as he came running through the orchard.

Almost as mechanically, Richemont had done the same, wondering to see how pale she had suddenly become.

'Well?' he said sharply. 'Montsalvy?'

'Fled! Escaped!' Rostrenen gasped, breathless from having run all the way from the Bastille. 'Some unknown monk helped him – and they have slain five men!'

The flower-filled garden, the cheerful spring sunshine were swallowed up for Catherine in a dark wave of despair. She was aware of an almost physical pain that took her breath away. She closed her eyes, wishing desperately that she could die the next minute, but heaven did not grant her even the mercy of unconsciousness. She was forced to endure to the end.

8: Chazay to the Rescue!

For an hour and more, Catherine had been shut up in her room at the inn, with her head buried in her arms, weeping herself into a state where she no longer knew if she were alive or dead. The blow she had received in the garden of the Hôtel du Porc-Epic, following so closely on a wonderful sensation of relief, had totally prostrated her, and ever since Tristan had brought her hurriedly back to the Eagle, telling her not to stir from there but to wait for him to bring her news, she had felt like one dead, indifferent to everything, unconscious of her surroundings, the only spark of life within her a small, piercing voice, sharp as a needle probing a wound: 'All is lost – all is lost!'

The words became a wearisome ballet inside her head, weaving themselves into such knots that they began to lose all meaning. Even then, she found a kind of bitter pleasure in repeating them.

Like a wounded animal, wanting nothing but the refuge of its own lair, she had declined the Bastard's invitation when, moved by her distress, he had offered her the hospitality of the Palais des Tournelles, where she might feel herself less alone.

But then, she told herself, she would have to get used to being alone once more. After his mad escape, which had cost a number of lives, Arnaud must be a proscribed outlaw, banished from the ranks of the nobility and a hunted man, as far as was possible in a land still ravaged by war and anarchy.

What would become of his wife and children then, if Richemont punished the offender by applying to the King to have them dispossessed of their lands – whether bestowing these on another or, more simply, quietly forgetting to oust the Apchiers? Where could they go for refuge when the Wolf of the Gévaudan debarred them from entering Montsalvy?

Even in the depths of her grief, Catherine could still hear the Constable's voice, so friendly only a moment before, saying with a return to his earlier tone of chilling menace: 'The fool! What madness drove him to do what cannot be undone? Men have died, our own men! Now I can do nothing, even if I would, except give chase and bring the lunatic back, dead or alive!'

Dead or alive! The dreadful words had struck like daggers, with such force that Catherine, exhausted by the strain she had been under, had been incapable of uttering or even thinking of a word in Arnaud's defence.

But for Dunois and Tristan, she might easily have died there in the garden, simply because she had no longer the heart to go on breathing. But these two had supported her tenderly back to the inn and handed her into the care of Mistress Renaudot, who had helped her up to her own room and would have undressed her and put her to bed had not Catherine insisted that she wanted nothing more of anyone.

She wanted to be alone, alone with the curse that seemed to hang over her life, setting war and men's violence in the way every time she thought she had found happiness.

A gentle hand raised her head, and a warm, fragrant steam assailed her nostrils.

'Drink this, my poor lady,' the hostess's voice said kindly. 'It will do you good.'

Catherine tried to refuse, but she no longer had the strength, and the mug was already at her lips and the taste of the hot, sweet wine, spiced with cinnamon, was on her tongue. Abandoning resistance, she clasped the tankard in both hands and, still without opening her eyes, began to sip cautiously at the boiling hot beverage.

'Sweet Jesus! ' Dame Renaudot exclaimed sorrowfully at the sight of the ravaged face turned toward her. 'What a state you've got yourself into, to be sure!'

With an instinctive tact, bred of long experience, she asked no questions but busied herself, with an agility amazing in one of her girth, in fetching water and a cloth of fine linen and bathing her guest's swollen features with a good deal of gentleness.

Catherine lay back with closed eyes, sipping her wine, and let the woman have her way, imagining it was Sara tending her with the motherly care she needed so sorely.

Never had she felt so appallingly lost. Everything had vanished in one swoop. She was alone in a hostile world that held no respite or refuge anymore. The only thing that was real was the fiery fragrance trickling down her throat, warm and friendly, bringing new life to the depths of her frozen body.

When the mug was empty, she half-opened her eyes and, fixing Mistress Renaudot with a heartrending gaze, demanded: 'More!'

'More?' that worthy woman exclaimed with astonishment. 'Don't you think you've had enough? That wine can go to your head very quickly.'

'That's just what I need – I'd like it to go to my head as quickly as possible, so that I can forget all about myself!'

'You want to forget all about yourself? Whatever for? Is it so bad?'

'Yes,' Catherine told her gravely, 'it is. I've had three names in my life. It must be much better to have none at all! Bring me some more of this wine. It's very good.'

The mugful she had drunk already was exploding inside her like a firework display, making her slightly lightheaded.

The hostess disappeared with reluctance to do as she was bidden, and Catherine opened her eyes fully and looked about her. A kind of mist seemed to have seeped into the chamber, blurring the whitewashed walls, the massive, dark beams, the small panes of greenish glass in the windows and the bed in the corner with its red cover, looking soft and comforting, like an enormous ripe strawberry. Catherine had a sudden longing to dive into it and bury herself in its soft, downy depths. Bed was still the best thing in the world for all those hurt in mind or body. You could lie there sweating with fever, groaning in pain, raving in sickness or ecstasy, forgetting in the sleep the world, wars, injustice and the folly of men; you could give birth there to the children begotten in the safety of sheets; you could make love …

When she reached this point in the cloudy meditation induced by the combination of weariness and wine, Catherine broke down again in compulsive sobs and made a dive for the tempting refuge of the sheets to weep her fill.

Love … Love, for her, meant Arnaud! Why, in all the whole world, did there have to be only that one man, that one, selfish, violent, jealous man to stand for love in Catherine's eyes? She had suffered so much through him already. From his hatred and scorn in the days when he had seen her as nothing more than one of the Legoix he hated; from his pride when, believing himself a leper, he had cruelly denied her the happiness of going with him into horror and death perhaps, but also into a terrible purgation and joy; from his fierce sensuality when, in Granada, she had found him in the arms of the perilously beautiful Zobeïda; and finally from his lust for battle and bloodshed when, to satisfy it, he had left her once more, after so many promises, to pursue the masculine adventures he loved more than anything in the world. And now, once again, had he thought of her, his wife, who had followed him for years and sought him to the ends of the earth and into the deepest depths of her own being? Had he thought of that for one instant when he had obeyed his own instinct for revenge in the face of express orders? Had he thought of it in the Bastille during those last hours when, instead of waiting for a judgment that his brothers in arms, out of their friendship for him, were almost certain to succeed in mitigating, he had condemned himself to proscription by escaping without so much as a thought for the consequences or for the trail of blood he left behind him?

She had sought him before in the besieged city of Orléans, in the dungeons of Sully and in the flower-filled snare of Al Hamra. Where must she seek him now? In some inaccessible cave in the volcanic rocks of

Auvergne, or on some black-draped scaffold?

But even while, in the depths of her weariness and despair, she brought her last remaining strength to bear in rejecting the idea of a return to her everlasting, soul-destroying quest, Catherine knew that in a day, an hour, a moment even, she would drag herself from her bed and go on, ever farther and deeper, in pursuit of her familiar mirage, until she dropped never to rise again; because while there was any breath left in her she would go on searching and calling for Arnaud's heart and Arnaud's hands and Arnaud's body, and because she was still ready to hazard her whole life for one single night of love.

When Tristan l'Hermite returned a few minutes later, he found the hostess standing in the middle of the room, a steaming mug in her hand, staring stupidly at the disordered bed, a red chaos broken here and there by splashes of black velvet and ermine trimming, a trail of white lace or a tangled skein of fair hair.

He directed a questioning look at Mistress Renaudot.

'What have you got there?'

'Some hot spiced wine. I brought her a mugful to do her good and she drank it all – but then – then she asked for more and I'm not sure that it won't make her ill.'

'I see. Give it to me, and then off with you. Oh, before I forget: the knights of Auvergne who were here this morning will be returning soon; ask them to wait a moment and then come and bring me word.'

When the door had closed behind her, Tristan began by swallowing half the contents of the tankard, at the same time keeping a wary eye on the bed from which a few hiccuping sobs were still emanating.

Judging at last that Catherine had indulged her grief for long enough and that a firm hand was now the best treatment for her, he set the tankard down on the table and, striding over to the bed, reached into it and hauled out a dishevelled Catherine, crimson-faced in part from weeping and in part from the dye of the counterpane staining her wet cheeks. The wide neck of her gown had slipped down as far as her armpit, revealing, above its subtle shadows, one golden shoulder and a breast so tempting that the Provost made haste to cover it, his face almost as red as hers. This was emphatically not the moment to fall victim to the charms of a violet-eyed witch who, even with her hair in tangles and her face daubed like an urchin who had fallen into the jampot, could still somehow manage to make one's blood run much too fast.

She, meanwhile, was regarding him with an expression half-doleful, half-offended. Then, extending a wavering hand toward the tankard, she demanded: 'Give me that drink, friend Tristan.'

'You've had quite enough as it is. Look at you! You're more than half drunk already!'

'Perhaps ... So much the better! I don't feel so unhappy. The wine does me good. It helps me to forget a little ... Give me some more, Tristan, my friend.'

'No.'

Then, as he saw the corners of her mouth turn down, he added in a gentler tone, for fear she should start to cry again: 'What is it you are trying so hard to forget, Catherine, and why ...? This is hardly the moment, you know... Don't you see that your husband needs you more than ever?'

She shook her head violently, as though striving against a storm, and the long strands of hair escaping from their braids writhed like golden tendrils about her head.

'Arnaud always needs me,' she cried. 'Always! But no-one ever thinks of asking if I might need Arnaud! I am his property, his rest and recreation, the mistress of his house and his chief vassal, his mistress and his servant, and everyone thinks it perfectly natural and fair and right that I should perform all this unflinchingly! Unflinchingly – and never indulging the wish that I might play another, unique role: the role of the woman he loves! Why must I never take but always be taken? Arnaud has made me a prisoner, bound me to him with his name, his lands, his children – and his caresses! I am *his* wife – to the point where, at times like this, he can forget me altogether and listen only to his own selfish folly! Why do you come and tell me he is my husband? He is wedded to war, and war alone!'

Without warning, she cast herself on Tristan's bosom and, flinging her arms about his neck, drew herself up on tiptoe to press herself against him.

'Such a love is slavery, Tristan, my friend, and the worst kind of slavery! There are times when I long to break out and be free! Won't you help me?'

The impassive Fleming felt a tremor run through him. He had been prepared to find a woman in a state of collapse, reduced by grief to a wreck of humanity, but not for this Catherine, more than half drunk with wine and anger, pouring out her torrent of bitterness and anger and her need for love, and with her clothes in a disorder that made his senses reel.

Disturbed by the womanly scents that were all about him, and angry with his own flesh for its instinctive response to the soft, clinging body, he strove to thrust her off, but she only clung more fiercely about his neck ...

'Catherine!' he whispered huskily, in torment, 'Are you out of your mind? There is no time!'

'I don't care! I don't want to know any more, I don't want to fight ... I don't want to be a leader in war! I want to be a woman – only a woman – and I want to be loved!'

'Catherine, pull yourself together! Let go ...'

'No! I know you love me – you've loved me for a long time – and I'm tired of being alone! I need someone to care for me, to live for me, and with me! What should I do with a man who thinks only of killing or being killed in the name of glory!'

'What should you do? Just at this moment you should try to save yourself and him from the worst in you, to keep a father for your children and for yourself – the only man you will ever call master! As for me, Catherine, you are making a mistake trying to tempt me. I do love you, it's true, but I'm of the same mould as Montsalvy. I am like him. Worse, perhaps, because I dream of power! Be yourself again and think of him! What would he think if he could see you now? That you are behaving like a great lady?'

She flung back her head, showing him a pair of drowned, melting eyes and moist lips, parted on a glimpse of small, bright teeth.

'I'm not a great lady,' she murmured, stretching herself against him like a cat. 'I'm a girl from the Pont au Change … Just a girl, Tristan, as you are just a man! We weren't born on the heights, either of us, so why shouldn't we love a little? You may even make me forget my stern lord …'

His breathing hard and his heart booming like a cathedral bell, Tristan knew that one more moment of this intolerable strain would finish him, that if he did not master his furious desire for her, he would reach a point at which it would no longer be possible to draw back.

She was putting him in the ludicrous role of an inhibited and over-anxious Joseph in the presence of an adorable Potiphar whose innocent depravity was wholly unconscious.

Only a few seconds more and he would probably rip off that disordered dress that hinted to his eyes at such delights and fling Catherine down on to the bed to lose himself, and even his very honour as a man, in seeking out the secrets of her woman-hood, taking advantage of a momentary aberration that would be regretted as soon as done. But even Tantalus could not endure forever, and Tristan felt himself yielding … blissfully yielding.

He was saved, just in time, by a discreet tap on the door. His forehead was running with sweat, sweat drenched his hair, and he was shaking as if in an ague.

Making a desperate effort, he tore himself free of the twining arms about his neck.

'That's enough!' he muttered furiously. 'Can't you hear? There's someone knocking.'

They were doing more than knock. Mistress Renaudot's voice, muffled by the door, was telling him that the gentlemen from Auvergne were waiting below, and they were in a hurry.

At that, Tristan went quickly to the pitcher of water, disregarding Catherine's protests, and when he had filled a bowl, began sponging her face and neck with a towel, calling out to the landlady as he did so: 'Give them some of your best wine to drink and keep them quiet for a moment longer! The lady fainted and I'm bringing her round!'

'Do you need any help?'

'No. It's all right.'

As he spoke, the Fleming was turning lady's maid. Gritting his teeth, but with an unsuspected deftness, he straightened Catherine's dress, shook out the creases and then turned his attention to her hair, combing it with an energy that drew howls from his victim. Then he plaited it swiftly into two braids that he coiled over her ears and, snatching up the veil from the hennin, long since cast to the floor, swathed it about her head and shoulders.

He held her briefly at arm's length and then declared: 'That's better. Now you're quite presentable.'

Except for her protesting cries of pain, Catherine had submitted to his ministrations with no more show of life than a rag doll; but, little by little, as Tristan worked, her eyes lost their misty, troubled look and became clear again. The effects of the drink, never very serious, were wearing off and giving way to a deep embarrassment very near to shame.

She saw now that her behaviour had been much more like that of a lovesick girl than of a decent wife whose husband was away facing the perils of the road. But her nature was too honest for her not to admit her mistakes, and when her companion would have led her to the door, she drew back.

'No, Tristan my friend, I don't want to go down yet – not without telling you – I'm ashamed of myself! The wine – being so angry – I lost my head, I think. And I dare not imagine what you must be thinking of me at this moment.'

He laughed and, taking her by the shoulders, dropped a brotherly kiss on her forehead.

'I'm thinking you've no need to be ashamed – and that, without knowing it, you spoke much that was true, my heart! It's true that I love you – and have long done so. Ever since Amboise, I think. And if you want to know the whole, I believe that if Dame Renaudot had not knocked, I should even now be begging your forgiveness. Now – we must forget all this. Nothing happened, and we are friends as before. Come, we must join the others, for indeed the time is short, and we have much to decide.'

In the common room of the inn, temporarily closed to its usual customers by a file of soldiers before the door, Tristan l'Hermite related to the grim circle of knights the results of the rapid inquiry he had carried out at the Bastille.

It took few words. At approximately the same time as Catherine was on her way to the Hôtel du Porc-Epic with Jean d'Orléans, a Grey Friar had presented himself at the Bastille with an order, signed and sealed with the arms of the Bishop of Paris, Messire Jacques du Chastellier, authorising him to visit the prisoner, Arnaud de Montsalvy, being his confessor and desiring to prepare his soul for a Christian repentance of his sins. As a result, the friar was admitted to the Bertaudière Tower, where Arnaud languished, and the door had been shut on the two of them.

A few minutes later, the gaoler had been attracted by the monk's cries, and had rushed to his assistance in the belief that the prisoner was throttling the holy man. He had opened the door and had been struck down immediately with a dagger in his heart. Two guards, alerted by the noise, had come running up and were promptly cut down with swords, for it seemed that the friar had been carrying a veritable arsenal underneath his robe, as well as a second habit, which Arnaud had put on.

Thus attired, the fugitives had reached the courtyard and then the guardroom, where two men had been on watch at the postern gate. They had been archers belonging to the Bastard of Orléans's company and well acquainted with the Lord of Montsalvy. One false move, just as he was about to set foot on the bridge across the moat, had allowed Arnaud's cowl to slip back and expose his face. He had struck as soon as they recognised him.

The guards' shout had been their last. In a matter of seconds, they had been dead, and the two men had leapt onto the horses being held ready for them by a band of three or four others and vanished in a cloud of dust in the direction of the village of Charonne.

'But who was this friar bearing an order from the bishop?' Catherine cried, when Tristan had completed his tale. 'Did anyone see him?'

'None of those who saw him close to are in any position to describe him,' Tristan said grimly. 'But the archers watching on the walls, who saw the two men's escape from above, say he was a fair youth of about 20 or so, and that the men waiting outside bore no distinguishing marks upon them.'

'It's little enough to go on,' growled Renaud de Roquemaurel. 'Is that all we know?'

Tristan's eyes rested compassionately on Catherine as he said, in what was almost an undertone: 'No, there is something else. The owner of the cook-shop by the Porte St Antoine was plucking geese outside his door and saw them ride by almost at arm's length. He heard one of the two supposed monks call out to the other: "This way, Gonnet! The road is clear!"'

A deathly silence fell, but only for an instant.

'Gonnet!' Catherine stammered in dismay. 'Gonnet d'Apchier! He has come – and he has succeeded! Oh God, Arnaud is lost!'

Renaud's great fist smashed down on the table, setting the goblets jumping.

'Wherefore lost? What is it that damned cur of a bastard has succeeded in?'

'I'm about to tell you.'

Facing the eager audience, Catherine described what had occurred outside the walls of Montsalvy, and the dishonourable mission undertaken by the Bastard of Apchier. Her voice was weary, but the account she gave was rapid and precise.

'Foolishly,' she concluded with a sigh, 'I believed that I had overtaken him. I hoped he would have stayed several days with the Castilian at Saint-Pourçain, but I was wrong. He was already here! He knew what had happened well before I did and was already laying his plans, setting the easy snare that Arnaud was mad enough to offer him – and that succeeded all too well! But as for how he managed to induce him to go with him, or how he obtained the order from the bishop – it must have been forged, I suppose …?

'No matter!' Renaud broke in, managing to override the indignant outcry of the other listeners, whose reactions had been as violent as instantaneous. 'How the villain did it will be a thing to be discussed later. For the present, we have better things to do. We must pursue and catch them; and, willingly or unwillingly, we must get Montsalvy away from this false friend who probably means to wring his neck in a wood one dark night! Come, all of you! To horse!'

'The Sire de Rostrenen is already hard on their trail,' Tristan said harshly. 'The Constable's orders were to bring them in dead or alive.'

The big Roquemaurel took a step forward to bring himself directly in front of the Provost, then bent a little to look him in the eye, since he stood a full head taller than Tristan.

'Dead or alive? And you think we'll stand for that? You might as well say that, between Apchier and your Rostrenen, Montsalvy has practically no chance of coming out of it with a whole skin! If that bastard cur doesn't find time to make away with him, then Monseigneur's emissary will do it for him; because if you think he'll suffer himself to be led back meekly, you can't know Montsalvy!'

'I know him, and …'

'I told you we were in a hurry, so if you've no objection … And now, Lord Provost, get this into your head. We want our captain back in one piece, and so we're going to give chase to these Bretons of yours as well as to the fugitives. We mean to overtake them, and we'll give them a drubbing if they get there first. You may tell that to the Constable!'

'I'll do no such thing. Unless, that is, you fail to give me your word to bring the prisoners back here …'

'Are you joking? You don't seem to remember we've two scores to settle with the Apchiers. So, when we've strung Gonnet up to the nearest tree, we're going straight on to flush the rest of the band out of Montsalvy; and to do that we must needs have our liege lord, who is Arnaud de Montsalvy! Once we've put all to rights again, your judges and councillors can argue the case to the end of time, and condemn him if they like. They can even come and hunt for him in the mountains if it amuses them. Understand?'

'Perfectly. It's a pleasure to listen to you.' Tristan said cheerfully. 'What I find harder to understand is why you are dawdling here – arguing.'

Renaud stared for a moment uncomprehendingly, then gave a shout of laughter. He dealt the Provost a slap on the back that all but broke it, and turned to Catherine.

'Go and get ready, Dame Catherine. We're taking you with us.'

'Oh no, you're not! ' Tristan exploded. 'What are you thinking of, Roquemaurel? You can't take a woman into the fight you've got ahead of you! Besides, she's tired to death and would only delay you. What's more – there is still something she must do for her husband. Off you go! When the time comes, we'll be sure to give her a sufficient escort to see that she reaches Auvergne safely.'

'I beg you,' Catherine cried, 'let me go with them! You know I can't bear it!'

He eyed her sternly, then said very clearly: 'It is your husband who will have lost all chance of a decent life if you do not remain here. But I am going to give you a choice. Either these gentlemen leave now, without you, and I close my eyes, or I summon the Watch and have them arrested on the spot.'

Catherine had risen to her feet, but now she sank back, defeated, onto the bench.

'Go, my friends,' she sighed. 'But, Renaud, I implore you, tell my husband ...'

'That you love him? By the mass, Dame Catherine, you'll do that much better than I! Farewell, until we meet again. Take care of yourself and leave it all to us!'

In a matter of seconds, the inn, which had been full to bursting only a moment before, emptied as explosively as a barrel that had burst its hoops.

The Auvergnats roared out into the Rue St Antoine, hurled themselves into their saddles and, without so much as a shout of warning, spurred their heavy mounts into gallop, riding down men and animals in their way and spreading terror in the path of their furious cavalcade. In a short time, nothing remained but a thick cloud of dust subsiding slowly about the feet of the Bastille towers and under the arch of the Porte St Antoine, and the victims of the charge getting, cursing, to their feet.

Catherine and Tristan, who had gone to the inn doorway to witness this tempestuous departure, turned back to the common room again. But the Lady of Montsalvy was not yet altogether resigned.

'Why did you stop me going with them?' she said reproachfully. 'You know I don't want to stay here a minute longer.'

'You will stay, however – tonight, to get your strength back. Tomorrow, I promise you, you shall go, but not to Auvergne, where you are not needed in the least.'

'Where, then?'

'To Tours, my child. To Tours, where the King will come within the week for the wedding of Monseigneur the Dauphin Louis to the Lady Margaret of Scotland, which is to take place next month. It is there that you will be of most use to your husband, for the King alone may pardon where the Constable has condemned. Go to the King, Catherine. A princely wedding is the best time of all to obtain a pardon in a difficult case. Montsalvy must have a written reprieve if he is not to live an outlaw for ever.'

'But will it be granted?' Catherine said doubtfully. 'You said yourself that the Constable has condemned Arnaud.'

'There was nothing else he could do, situated as he is in the midst of these ticklish Parisians. They'd scream like stuck pigs. But the King doesn't much care what the people of Paris might think. He's small cause to remember them kindly! He has forgiven them, certainly, on the surface; but you may be sure he's in no hurry to pay them another visit. He'll issue a pardon, if you ask him nicely. Montsalvy will retire discreetly to his mountains for a time, and all will be forgotten. He'll escape with a mild punishment of exile on his own lands, just to show willing, and in a year's time he'll be back at court again, where everyone will welcome him with open arms, and the Constable most of all!'

As her friend talked, Catherine felt her bursting heart subside. With a few words, a few optimistic phrases, he had brightened the horizon for her, driving the clouds away and bringing renewed hope.

Gradually, the dread in her mind was ousted by a feeling of infinite gratitude. She realised the true extent of Tristan's friendship. Strictly speaking, it had been his duty to have used any means to detain the Auvergnats, for they had made no secret of the fact that their sole object in pursuing the fugitive was to engineer his escape and bring him safely into his own lands.

With a pretty gesture, she took the Fleming's hand and laid it to her cheek.

'You always know so much better than I what is the right thing to do, Tristan, my friend! I ought to know that by now, and I'd do much better to follow your advice without question, instead of forever rebelling against it.'

'I don't ask as much as that! But since you are in such a biddable mood, suppose you ask Renaudot to let us have some dinner? I'm hungry enough to eat my horse!'

'And so am I,' Catherine said, laughing. 'As for Bérenger – but where is Bérenger? I haven't seen him all morning. In fact, I'd forgotten all about him.'

'I'm here.' The doleful voice appeared to come from the immense hearth on which an outsize stewpot was simmering gently.

There was a disturbance in one of the deep inglenooks on either side of the fire, furnished with stone benches where people could sit to warm themselves. The page's slight figure, clad in his brown woollen tunic, emerged out of the shadows and advanced into the meagre light of the small windows.

'Bérenger!' Catherine exclaimed furiously. 'Where have you been? I looked for you this morning, waited for you and ...' She stopped suddenly, becoming aware of the expression of deep unhappiness on her page's young face. His shoulders bowed, his head sunk on his chest and the corners of his mouth working spasmodically as if he were about to cry, Bérenger was the very picture of misery.

'Good God! Whatever is the matter? You look as if you'd lost your dearest friend!'

'Leave him alone, my dear,' Tristan said quickly. 'I think I know what the trouble is.' He turned to the downcast boy. 'Were you too late? Had something happened to him?'

Bérenger shook his head, and answered almost regretfully: 'Nothing, Messire. It all went very well. I gave them the letter you had given me, and they let him go at once.'

'Well, then? You should be pleased!'

'Pleased? Yes – of course. Oh yes, Messire, I am pleased, and I'm very grateful to you. Only ...'

'Suppose you tell me what all this is about?' Catherine protested. She had followed this dialogue between the page and the Provost with astonishment, not understanding it in the least.

'It concerns a student troublemaker called Gauthier de Chazay, whose arrest you witnessed yesterday. The boy's been taking an interest in him.'

Tristan went on to tell how, on the previous evening, when he had come to the inn to inform Catherine of her audience the next day, young Roquemaurel had spoken to him, and with a good deal of timidity, about the scuffle he and his mistress had witnessed a few hours earlier near the Petit Châtelet. He had mentioned the Lady of Montsalvy's interest in the red-headed student and her promise to try to do something to assist a paladin who was so obviously valiant and devoted to the service of distressed damsels. Graver problems had, not unnaturally, driven that promise from her mind, but Bérenger, full of spontaneous admiration for his 'light of the world', had not forgotten.

'Thinking to give pleasure to you both,' Tristan finished up, 'I obtained an order for Chazay's release from Messire de Ternant. He made no difficulty about it, but did it as a kindness to me. I sent it to the lad here so that he might have the pleasure of procuring his release in person. Which is why I'm somewhat surprised to find him looking so downhearted. I'll not deny I had expected to find him sitting at table, here or in some other tavern, getting himself thoroughly drunk with his new friend to celebrate the occasion.'

'It seems you were mistaken. Hadn't you better tell us exactly what happened, Bérenger, instead of looking as if you were about to burst into tears? Wasn't the young man glad to be set free?'

'Oh yes. He was very glad. He asked me who I was and how I managed to get him out of prison. So I told him. Then he embraced me – and after that he ran away as fast as he could go, calling out: "Thanks, friend! Perhaps we'll meet again some day! Just now you'll have to excuse me. I'm off to see Marion l'Ydole. She owes me something, and the sooner I can settle with her, the better!" Then he disappeared down the Rue St Jacques.'

'Well!' was Tristan's comment. 'That's not much by way of thanks! Put yourself out for people! What did you do then, to bring you back so late?'

'Nothing … I walked about by the river and watched the barges. I felt ever so lonely – and a bit lost. I wanted to see people. After that, I went and had a look at the colleges …'

'And then,' Catherine said, smiling, 'having failed to come across this young man who interests you so much, you thought you might as well come home! Don't let it upset you, Bérenger. You've done a good deed, and for no reward, since the friendship you desired was not granted you.'

'That's true. I did so want to be his friend! I know that compared with a Paris student I'm nothing but an ignorant little peasant, but…'

'You're a good lad, and you've done a great deal too much for an ungrateful braggart! Now forget him, as I shall. My only interest in him was because he reminded me of a friend I have lost. We'll not think any more about him! Tomorrow, as soon as the gates are open, we are leaving for Tours.'

'For Tours?'

'Yes. You might not have the friendship of a rebel student, but you might very well see the King,' Catherine said, smiling rather sadly. 'It's a fair enough exchange – even though our liege lord may not be much to look at.'

'The King? Yes … of course,' Bérenger said, with a sigh that showed he was not to be easily consoled.

For all that, his mind was not so set on higher things as to deprive him of his appetite, and he fell on his dinner every bit as voraciously as the day before. Afterwards, when Tristan had gone and his mistress was on her way to the church of St Catherine du Val des Escholiers to spend a long time in prayer, he set out again for another walk about Paris. This expedition was to be his last, for they were leaving the next morning, and he stretched it out for as long as he could.

With the coming of evening, the Eagle was filled with bustle and noise. The inn had rapidly made itself as popular with the relieving forces as it had been with the occupiers, and as twilight began to descend on the city, large numbers of soldiers settled themselves about the tables marked with wine and candle grease, to sup, to down innumerable flagons and to throw dice.

Wisely, Catherine and Bérenger had their supper served upstairs in

Catherine's chamber, and when the last mouthful had been swallowed and the servant girl was still clearing away the remains of the meal, Catherine dismissed her page and herself made ready for bed.

She needed a good night's sleep, for they were to start very early in the morning. Tristan l'Hermite would be with them at the crack of dawn, ready to escort the travellers as far as Longjumeau.

Catherine went calmly about her preparations for the night. Her long vigil in the dim and shadowy church had calmed her and fully restored her self-command. A priest, whom she had asked to hear her confession, had absolved her from the embarrassing memory of her brief intoxication and the attempt she had made to seduce the unfortunate Tristan. At last she had managed to quiet her heart.

She was able now to look squarely, and to some extent dispassionately, at the task that awaited her at Tours. All things considered, it did not look too difficult. She had complete confidence in her friends at Court, and in particular had not a moment's doubt, naturally, that her old protectress Queen Yolande would give her full support.

Her fears for Arnaud, too, were diminishing. She knew the knights of the High Auvergne too well, and especially the indomitable Roquemaurels, whose stubborn courage would move mountains.

All day long, her thoughts had followed them as they rode after the fugitives, and by now they might even have caught up with Arnaud and his dangerous companion. If that were so, then Gonnet d'Apchier would have ceased to live, and his intended victim would be riding peacefully in the direction of Montsalvy, once more in the company of his friends. It was even possible that the Bastard had died before he had time to spread his slanderous tale, accusing Catherine of adultery. A headlong gallop was not exactly conducive to an exchange of confidences.

Lulled by these comforting thoughts, Catherine got into bed even before the curfew had sounded, and was sleeping like a child almost as soon as her head touched the pillow. Not far away, Bérenger, tired to death, was already snoring as lustily as an old trooper. They did not hear the soldiers leaving the inn, cursing the regulations that compelled them to keep early hours, or the inn servants putting up the shutters, or the creaking of the stairs under the double weight of Master Renaudot and his wife as they made their way up to their conjugal bed.

The bell for matins had not yet rung from the nearby convent when the street filled with compact, silently moving shadows that gathered about the entrance to the Eagle.

There was a sound of metal scraping in the lock, but the door was stoutly barred within and did not yield. Then one of the figures shattered a window with a vigorous kick and another slipped quickly through. In another moment, the door was opened, letting the dark tide flow slowly into the inn.

When Master Renaudot, in his nightcap, with his candle clutched in one hand and holding up his breeches with the other, went down to see what was amiss, he recoiled in horror before the faces confronting him in the red light of the torches.

Broad and red, hairy heads capped with leather bonnets, those savage faces shared the same cold, ruthless eyes and the same cruel twist to what were often toothless mouths. The unhappy innkeeper was able to identify them at once by their bloodstained leather aprons and the gleaming knives and massive cleavers stuck into their belts.

'The butchers!' he gasped, in a voice that quavered. 'Wh-what do you want?'

One of the men stepped forward. His huge, bare arms were hooped with iron, like barrels, and his sweaty face was more repulsive even than the rest.

'Nothing of you, landlord! Get back to bed and stay there, no matter what you hear!'

'But I've a right to know! What do you seek here?'

'Not you, never fear! We seek a lady – a noble lady! You've one here, haven't you?'

'Y-yes, but ...'

'No buts! Our business is with her! So you just hop along back to your good wife – I'll wager she's sweating with fear between her sheets at this moment – and don't you take any notice of anything else at all; not if you want to keep this inn of yours intact! D'you understand?'

'M-my good wife? At her age?'

'What of it? We've seen worse! Nor do we care! Make love or say your prayers, so long as you keep to your room. If not ... we'll burn your house and you inside it! Understand?'

The wretched innkeeper's teeth were chattering, and it was all he could do to stand, but the thought of his guest, so young and fair and delicate, in the hands of these brutes, gave him a little courage. Nor was the thought of what Tristan l'Hermite would do to him, if any harm should befall the woman entrusted to his care, at all a pleasant one. He therefore attempted to argue.

'Listen,' he managed to say, 'I don't know what you've got against the young lady, but she's a sweet, gentle ...'

'That's for us to judge! Be off with you!'

'And then – Messire Tristan l'Hermite, the Provost Marshal, entrusted her to me! He's a hard man, and one without pity! He's not long been appointed, and you may not know him yet, for he's not of these parts, but they've already learned to fear him in the army! Take my word for it, and don't go against him ...'

'We're not going against him! And we're not afraid of any man! Now go, you, unless you want us to roast you slowly over your own fire. See there!

It's burning up nicely!'

One of the invaders was in fact engaged in stirring up the embers, which had been covered over with the hot ashes as they were every night. Already, flames were leaping up and catching the fresh kindling that was being piled on.

Faced with a horrifying vision of himself trussed like a sheep on his own spit, Renaudot crossed himself hurriedly three or four times and then bolted back up the stairs, praying desperately to St Lawrence, patron of cooks, to have pity on himself, his hostelry and his guest. It was already in his mind that he might be able to lower himself from his window with the aid of his sheets and run to fetch the Watch, when the man who had already spoken added: 'Go with him, Martin, and keep an eye on him until we call you! Just in case he should take it into his head to go and find his precious Provost! Come on, the rest of you! Four men come upstairs with me to get the wench!'

'We're making too much noise, Guillaume le Roux,' warned one of the butchers. 'We'll wake the whole *quartier*.'

'So what? If they do wake up, they'll not stir outside. Cowards, all of them! They'll stick their heads under the bedclothes so as not to hear.'

A moment later, Catherine, awakened by the horde that burst into her chamber with the sudden fury of a volcanic eruption, was plucked from her bed by half a score of callused hands that fastened roughly on her arms, legs and body and bore her downstairs to the common room and dumped her on the long table nearest to the fire.

At the appearance of the naked woman*, whose long, golden tresses in no way concealed a body evidently made for love, a kind of throaty murmur arose from the men gathered in the room. Lapped in the warm light from the flaming hearth, she seemed made of pure gold.

Still only half-awake, Catherine raised herself on her two hands and stared around her with eyes dazed with horror. She was surrounded by a ring of hot and gleaming eyes, of salivating jaws and hands already groping toward her flesh.

'By God, she's lovely!' someone said. 'Let's not kill her before we've tasted her! I want my share of the gorgeous creature!!'

'You're right there!' chimed in another. 'And so do I! Just look at those breasts, those thighs! We'll not get their like again!'

'Shut your mouths!' roared the man who seemed to be their leader. 'Time enough for all that later. I'd like to have a word with her myself. But first, she must be tried!'

By this time, Catherine had realised that this was not a nightmare. These

---

* Nightshifts were not commonly worn in this period.

men were real; all too real! She could still feel the bruising grip of their hands about her waist and on her legs.

A frantic terror seized her; the kind of mindless panic that paralysed the nerves and froze the blood in her veins. What were they going to do to her? Already the heat from the fire was scorching her.

She drew back along the table in order to escape it, but instantly the leader grasped her and held her still.

'Stay where you are, my beauty! We must have speech with you.'

Suddenly, Catherine recovered the use of her voice, which had deserted her in the extremity of her fear.

'What do you want with me? You say you mean to try me? But what for?' she asked in a small voice she scarcely recognised as her own.

'You'll find out. Now, Berthe! Come forward!'

Out of the crowd of men, a woman stepped forth. She was thin and swarthy, with iron grey hair and a sallow skin, and she was dressed all in black, enveloped so that the only thing visible was her long face, in which only the greenish eyes seemed alive. But the life in those eyes sprang not from desire but from hate; blind, implacable and unreasoning hate. It was the hatred of a mean and narrow-minded woman, soured by a life of outward piety and virtue and the slow, careful acquisition of wealth.

Catherine knew her at once, in spite of all the years. This woman was Berthe Legoix, the widow of Guillaume, the man Arnaud had killed; and she knew then that her own death was before her.

With a solemnity that would have been laughable if it had not been so filled with menace, the woman came to the table and, leaning forward, spat, like a snake discharging its venom, full in Catherine's face.

'Whore!' she snarled. 'You'll pay for what you've done, and for your husband's crime!'

'What have I done to you?' Catherine shot back at her in sudden anger. She had always disliked Berthe Legoix. Berthe must have been heartless, even as a young woman, and her servants had feared her as they feared fire, because she would beat them and starve them for the slightest fault.

'What have you done? You came here – you got round that great donkey of a Constable – slept with him as like as not – and then your husband just happens to escape from the Bastille! Well, you'll pay for it! If I can't have the murderer's skin, I'll have yours! By heaven, I thought I'd choke with fury when old Lallier gave out that he had released Richemont from his word, and then when the news came of the escape! So I got these good fellows together – it cost me something, but by good luck I've still some silver left – and you'll see what you'll see!'

'I'll see nothing at all!' Catherine cried, all the more furiously for the hideous fear that was beginning to gnaw at her vitals. 'This is Paris! There is a government, the Watch, the Provost! You'll be sorry for the rest of your lives if you touch me!'

'We're willing to pay that price, if you're dead first,' Legoix's widow sneered back at her. 'Besides, they'd have to find us first, and just as soon as we've dealt with you, we'll disappear! Come, you there, spill this woman's blood for me and give her to the fire!'

'Softly, Berthe, softly,' said the man they called Guillaume le Roux. 'There's no hurry. We've time for a little fun yet. You didn't tell us she was such a little beauty ...'

The woman shrugged angrily.

'You bunch of swine! I'm not paying you to fornicate with the woman, but to avenge me! What does it matter if she is beautiful? I'm telling you to kill her! We can't spend all night here, and unless you do it soon ...'

She made a sudden snatch at the cleaver in Guillaume's belt and, swinging it above her head, was about to fall on Catherine when the door, which the butchers had neglected to bar again behind them, crashed inwards with a noise like thunder and, through the broken windows and the open doorway, there burst into the inn a howling mob brandishing staves and axes. They were led by a tall, red-headed individual who flung himself bodily upon the butchers while at the same time bawling out his war cry at the top of his voice: 'Chazay to the rescue! Go at them, lads! Kick the scum out of doors!'

In an instant, it was a general melée. Berthe Legoix received a buffet that sent her flying backwards into the bread bin, where she collapsed into a semi-conscious daze, while on the upper floor Master Renaudot, who had been a helpless spectator of the events below, under the guard of the butcher Martin, as interested as himself, rushed to the window bawling: 'Help! Help! Fetch the Watch!'

This time, the street did waken to the din. Lights sprang up in the houses, and scantily-dressed citizens poured out to find out what was the matter.

Master Renaudot's inn was a blaze of light, and from the brightly-lit interior came the thuds and crashes and shouts of the combatants.

Catherine took advantage of the uproar to clamber off her table and slip upstairs for her clothes. Half-way up, she came face to face with Bérenger, who had been woken at last out of his first sleep and was coming down, yawning hugely.

At the sight of his mistress speeding upstairs, stark naked, his eyes popped open, and he gulped with amazement. But by then the extraordinary vision had dashed past him without a word and vanished through the door of the bedchamber, leaving him leaning speechlessly against the wall, already half-convinced that what he had seen was simply the effect of an imagination overheated by partaking too freely of the Cahors wine at supper.

He was roused from his thoughts by the sound of a joyous voice that set his heart beating faster.

'Ho there, friend! What are you doing, standing stock still on the staircase? You look as if you'd seen a ghost! Come and give us a hand!'

'Coming, Gauthier! I'm coming!'

And without the faintest idea of whom he was fighting, or why, Catherine's page plunged eagerly into the fray, hitting out impartially at all who came within his reach, with no thought in his head but to please his student friend.

The fight was growing so furious that Master Renaudot's hostelry might never have been the same again, but for the officer of the Watch, who chose that moment to appear with his men. The effect was magical. No sooner had the glint of the archers' helmets appeared at the end of the street than someone cried out: 'Here comes the Watch!' The ensuing flight was immediate and general, butchers and students scattering in all directions, like a flock of sparrows.

Only a few unfortunates, laid low by a blow from a cudgel or a knife, were left lying on the flagged floor at the feet of the bewildered Renaudot.

Guillaume le Roux was one of these. A whirling stool had caught him on the head and he was lying doubled up beside the hearth. Another was the widow Legoix, now being hoisted, none too gently, out of the bread bin by one of the archers. Both would be hauled without delay before the Lieutenant of the Châtelet, Messire Jean de la Porte.

In the presence of Messire Jean de Harlay, the current Officer of the Watch, all Renaudot's aplomb returned to him. He lodged a formal accusation against the two prisoners of breaking and entering his hostelry with the object of inflicting grievous harm on one of his guests, a lady entrusted to him by no less a person than the Provost Marshal, Messire Tristan l'Hermite (whom God preserve), in the pursuit of some nameless vengeance that, since it ran counter to the judgement of Monseigneur the Constable and Maître de Lallier (God's blessing on them both), was nothing less than outright rebellion! In all of which the worthy innkeeper demonstrated both the shrewdness of his mental processes and the excellence of his hearing.

In fact, thanks to the goodwill of the man named Martin, who had felt no desire to shut himself up in a stuffy bedchamber with a pair of innkeepers when such delectable things were going forward below, Renaudot had missed nothing of what happened in his common room. Content with keeping him in sight, Martin had permitted him to remain seated on the top step whence his view, if not perfect, was at least adequate. Acoustically, it was excellent.

Thus it was that Martin's generosity, and private inquisitiveness, enabled Master Renaudot to give a complete account of the night's events, an account larded with invocations to the Blessed Virgin and to every other saint with whom the worthy man appeared to maintain friendly relations.

When he had finished denouncing the 'cowardly attackers', Renaudot embarked on the praises of those saviours of his inn who, to judge from his enthusiastic description of them, could only have belonged to some legion of celestial beings expressly sent from Paradise on the orders of St Anthony, the patron saint of the *quartier* and of Renaudot himself.

Jean de Harlay listened gravely to the innkeeper's panegyrics, merely remarking that, as for angels, according to the two or three unfortunates left lying on the floor, whom he would see conveyed forthwith to the Hôtel Dieu, they were simply students from the College de Navarre.

'That's as may be, Messire,' Renaudot assented, sticking to his guns, 'but their leader was a youth with hair that flamed like the sun itself, and I could tell from his valour that he must be an archangel at least! What's more, he's vanished quite away, as you can see for yourself.'

The truth was that Gauthier de Chazay, having no love for Messire de Harlay in consequence of a slight disagreement that had occurred between them recently in the course of a fracas at a tavern known as the Mule, in the Rue St Jacques, of which Gauthier was one of the pillars, had deemed it best to abandon the field of victory in favour of a discreet withdrawal to the cramped but heartfelt hospitality of his friend Bérenger's cubby-hole of a bedroom.

As a matter of form, the Officer of the Watch heard Catherine's confirmation of the innkeeper's story and her generous plea for mercy for a woman who 'must have been out of her mind with grief for one who, little though he may have deserved it, was nonetheless her husband'.

Charmed by such magnanimity, Messire de Harlay tendered apologies on behalf of the Grand Châtelet and of the Provost of Paris and then withdrew, taking with him his still unconscious prisoners, leaving Renaudot lamenting over the damage to his property, which proved, in fact, to be not at all extensive.

No sooner had the footsteps of the Watch faded away down the Rue St Antoine than Bérenger and Gauthier reappeared as if by magic.

Confronted with the hero of the flaming hair, Master Renaudot was obliged to admit that he had not been favoured with divine intervention but, however earthly a being, Gauthier de Chazay was still entitled to his heartfelt gratitude, which took the form of a magnificent smoked ham, accompanied by a loaf of bread and an immense flagon of Chambertin. The generous innkeeper motioned the two lads to be seated, and they did not wait to be asked twice.

The student, for one, was so famished that he had carved the ham down to the bone in less time than it took to say an Ave Maria. It was a pleasure to watch him eat, and even Bérenger, the possessor of a very fine appetite indeed, could not compete with his friend.

Master Renaudot, his wife and the two servant girls stood gazing in open-mouthed fascination as the two lads ate their way through the quantity of food with a speed worthy of a brigade of white ants.

Catherine, too, watched, torn between amusement and pity for the half-starved youth. She waited until he was quite satisfied and then, when not a sliver of ham, a crumb of bread or a drop of Chambertin remained, she made her way to where the two friends sat and thanked young Chazay, very sweetly, for saving her from a hideous fate.

Gauthier de Chazay blushed violently, finding himself face to face with the woman whom he had seen, not so long before, in such a disturbing state of undress, and rose quickly to his feet.

'You owe me nothing – no thanks, I mean, noble lady,' he said awkwardly. 'I only – only paid my own debt. You got me out of prison.'

'Imprisonment for assaulting an officer of the Watch was not so very serious. You would have got out without me. In any case, it was Bérenger who obtained your release. But you saved me from a hideous death. Tell me how I may thank you.'

'But I don't want thanks!' the boy exclaimed, almost angrily. 'When old Lallier spoke to the crowd today from the Maison aux Piliers, I surprised the widow Legoix at her little game, soliciting the butchers right there in the Grève, with no more shame than a streetwalker in the Rue Pute-y-Musse*. I listened, and guessed they were up to no good. Then they mentioned your name – the name of the lady to whom I owed my freedom. So then I set about collecting some of my comrades – and God be thanked, we came in time!'

'And I thought you didn't care about us!' Bérenger wailed, almost in tears. 'I was calling you ungrateful, while all the time …'

'All the time,' Gauthier took him up, with perfect frankness, 'I was making love to Marion l'Ydole. It was afterwards, when the time came for me to take a stroll round the cookshops by the Porte Baudoyer, that I happened to hear old man Lallier's speech. I said to myself that now if ever was the moment to pay off my debts. And don't you start crying like a girl, either! If you want us to be friends, you'll have to show more spunk! Be more of a man, because that's the only thing that counts!'

'Quite right,' Catherine said, laughing. 'But you still haven't told me what I might do for you.'

The boy laid down the napkin with which he had been wiping Bérenger's nose and turned, with sudden seriousness, to look at the young woman. He met her eyes very squarely.

'Do you really want to do something for me, my lady?'

---

* Now, by a misnomer, the Rue du Perit-Musc.

'Of course I do!'

'Then take me with you. Bérenger has told me you are leaving tomorrow ...'

Catherine started.

'Take you with me? But – do you really want to leave Paris? What about the College de Navarre? Your studies?'

The student's face hardened under his freckles.

'I'm fed up – with college and with my studies! I hate Greek and Latin and all the rest! To be forever poring over dusty old grammars that weigh like the devil, to spend my days sitting in the straw, drinking water and going hungry ten months out of twelve, whipped like a schoolboy when the master's in a bad mood – do you think that's any life for a man? I'm 19, my lady, and I'm dying of boredom in this college! Of boredom and of anger!'

The student's outburst was answered by another, almost equally indignant, from the page.

'But it's the life I've dreamed of! To study! To become wise and learned! I've longed for that for years!'

'You poor fool!' Gauthier said scornfully. 'Easy to see you know nothing about it! A fine life, to be sure! You have the open air, the free skies, the mountains, valleys and streams, space to breathe! You're a page, you'll become a squire and have the right to bear arms, and then you'll be a knight, a captain maybe, which means that you'll be great and proud and dauntless – you'll be a man! While I and those like me will still be bent over our parchments, growing older and more lonely – and fatter, too, it's true, for those of us who have chosen the Church.

'Well, I hate war and weapons and all they stand for! I hate the captains for their arrogance and cruelty and the sufferings of the poor people!' the page cried, suddenly very red. 'How can anyone want to spend their lives fighting other people?'

'When they've spent years reciting Socrates and Seneca and Cato the Elder and made nothing of them! I've learned enough as it is, and since I've no ambition to be a cleric or a judge, I want to be off! Take me, my lady,' he went on in a pleading tone. 'I'm strong and brave, I think, and it's not for a lady of high degree to go travelling the roads with none but a babe to bear her company.'

'I'm not a babe!' Bérenger exclaimed hotly. 'I've fought in a battle, against real men-at-arms, too! You ask Lady Catherine!'

'It's true enough,' Catherine admitted with a smile. 'Bérenger bore himself most valiantly in a tight corner.'

'That's good to hear!' the student cried, dealing his companion an affectionate slap on the back. 'We'll be able to draw sword together – if your mistress will have me. And even if she won't,' he added, with a comical little grin that was not without a touch of sadness, 'I shall have to leave here all

192

the same – or take to a begging life!'

'But this is dreadful!' Catherine exclaimed. 'Why must you become a beggar?'

'Not because I want to, believe me; but if I would eat, even a little, it must come to that. The Master of the College de Navarre means to expel me. He says I'm no good, I'm a black sheep, because I like women and wine! As if I was the only one! The fact is that he doesn't like my face and, black sheep or no, he means to make a scapegoat of me! '

'Tell me one thing: what do your parents say to all this? If they sent you to college, they must have had some reason?'

'The very best – to be rid of me once and for all! I have no parents, gentle lady. Only a rich uncle who administers what little property I have left, for our manor of Chazay and the lands about it were burned and utterly laid waste by the war. Moreover, my uncle Guy has a son, and he's never tired of laying up riches, so he made up his mind that I should be a clerk and then, when the time came, take orders so that my property might go to swell his son's inheritance. Simple, you see ...'

'Very simple,' Catherine agreed. 'And to tell you the truth, I'd like very much to take you with me. But, do you want to make soldiering your life?'

'Yes, more than anything!'

'Then have you thought that in entering my service you will be entering also that of my husband – an escaped prisoner, an outlaw?'

Gauthier de Chazay laughed, a laugh so joyous that it did one's heart good to hear it.

'In the times we live in, today's outlaw may be tomorrow's marshal! A man may be an enemy in the morning and a sworn brother by evening, and last night's brother a hated foe by dawn! These are mad times, but one day things will be right again, the kingdom will be reborn and flower more gloriously than before. Before that time comes, there are blows to be struck on both sides, and I want to have my share! And whatever you might say, gracious lady, even at the risk of angering you a little – it is your service I would enter; you, above all, whom I would serve and defend!'

Catherine did not answer this at once. Something within her was deeply moved by the boy's unexpected declaration. He would never know how forcibly he reminded her of that other Gauthier, the mighty Gauthier Strongitharm, an encounter with whom had invariably proved fatal to every enemy in her path. He too had jibbed at the thought of serving Arnaud! He had wanted to be her servant, hers alone, and her rampart, none of which had prevented him risking his life many times for the master of Montsalvy, as he had done in Granada when the drums of Allah rolled.

A small voice, deep within her, murmured that this youth who bore his name had in him also a little of her old friend's spirit, that it was he, perhaps, who had sent him to her from beyond the grave ...

Gauthier, with his Viking blood, had more than any man the love of battle and of violence in a just cause, and Catherine found a strange kind of comfort in the thought that from now on she would have this boy at her side, reminding her so strongly of that other who, after all, had taken something of her heart away with him.

'It's settled then,' she said, stretching out her hand impulsively to her new follower. 'From now on, you are squire to the Lady of Montsalvy! Master Renaudot will find somewhere for you to sleep, and first thing tomorrow morning you and Bérenger shall go to the market near here to get you a horse and some better clothes to face the weather in.'

Gauthier's present garments certainly showed more holes than good sound cloth, but the student was far beyond the consideration of such sartorial refinements. His eyes were shining with joy, and he simply knelt at Catherine's feet, wholly unconsciously echoing the other Gauthier long before. And it was in very nearly the same words that he too dedicated his life to his new mistress.

Next day, as the sun rose high into the sky of a fine May day, it shone down on the windmills of Montrouge, their great sails turning slowly in the soft morning wind and, not far away, on a little group of mounted travellers riding southwards.

The Lady of Montsalvy, accompanied by Bérenger de Roquemaurel and Gauthier de Chazay and escorted by Tristan l'Hermite and a handful of soldiers, was leaving Paris after a stay of two days from which she had gained nothing but bitterness and disappointment and which left her with no wish ever again to revisit the city of her birth.

She was heading now for the River Loire, seeking at one and the same time Arnaud's safety and the right for herself and for the people of Montsalvy to live in peace.

PART III

AFFAIR OF HEARTS

9: The Dauphin and the Favourite

'No, Dame Catherine – it cannot be! I cannot grant what you ask. It is time – and more than time – that order was restored in the kingdom and for the nobles to learn obedience once again. I grieve for you, but I must refuse.'

Kneeling at the foot of the throne, in a posture befitting her suppliant role, Catherine raised a tearful face and clasped hands to the King.

'Sire, I beseech you! Be merciful! Who can pardon him if you do not?'

'The Constable, lady! It was his word that was given, his orders, and the escape took place under his jurisdiction. He is in absolute command of the army. Even princes of the blood must obey him. Have you forgotten the powers conferred by the sword of the lilies? It is my duty as King to support and maintain the powers of my military commander to the full!'

Duty! Maintain! What words from the lips of Charles VII! More astonished even than disappointed, Catherine stared at the King almost without recognition. What had come over him?

He looked the same as ever, the same long, pale, unattractive face with the big, drooping nose and pop-eyes. But where those eyes had once been dull and fearful, they now rested on her with a stern assurance. The lines of the face seemed less fluid, more firmly marked below the broad black hat, its brim turned up to reveal the gold embroideries beneath, which was encircled by a golden crown. It actually seemed as if the King had grown. It might have been because he held himself better, more upright, having at last thrown off the anxious, inhibited bearing that had been a part of him for so long. It was not just the heavily-padded doublet that made his thin, narrow shoulders look broad and strong.

Standing before his throne with a blue and gold canopy over his head, he held himself with authority, while allowing the great, snow-white hound at his side to lick his fingers.

Catherine knew, with a tightening of the heart, that this was a different man before her. But she had come to fight, and she meant to do so to the end.

'Then what can I do, Sire?' she asked. 'You see my grief, my distress – give me some advice at least.'

Charles VII seemed to hesitate slightly, reminding Catherine of the prince of other days. He appeared moved by the lovely, grief-stricken face raised to his. Making up his mind at last, he came down the three steps of the throne and raised the suppliant gently to her feet.

'You must go back to the Constable, my dear, and entreat him as charmingly as you can. His men will probably have caught the fugitives by now – indeed, already it may be too late.'

'No, I don't believe that! You mean, Sire, that my husband may even now have ceased to live? It is impossible! I know, I am sure, the Constable would never execute Arnaud de Montsalvy without first consulting you. I have been assured of it by his Provost Marshal, Messire Tristant l'Hermite.'

'I know this Tristan. He is a responsible man, not given to speaking lightly. Very well, then, take my advice and hurry back to Paris. Plead with Richemont, and perhaps ...'

'But Sire, remember I am only a woman, and for days I have been trapped in a vicious circle! If a pardon must come from Messire de Richemont, at least give me a few words from your own hand, counselling him – I say counselling, not commanding – to be merciful! If not, he may send me back again to you, and then where shall I be? I am alone here, with no-one to take my part. Her grace, Queen Yolande, in whom I had placed all my trust, is not yet returned from Provence, and they say that she is ill. All my dearest friends are with her, or making war in Normandy and Picardy. I have no-one – no-one but you!'

'It is true that my lady mother has been unwell of late, but word came yesterday that she is better and may even now be on the way here to be present at her grandson's wedding. You shall see her soon ... Then, suddenly, all his old nervousness, never very far beneath the surface, seemed to return, and he added in what was almost a scream: 'No, no more weeping, I beg of you! You are tormenting me, Catherine! You know the goodwill I have always borne you! You know the power of your tears – and you are using it to force my hand ...'

Sensing that that hand was weakening, and conscious that victory might be near, Catherine was about to seize it and press it to her lips when a voice spoke out from the back of the hall. It was a charming voice, soft and clear, but the things it said were terrible.

'None may force the King's hand, sire. It is high treason! My sweet friend, have you forgotten your lady mother's words? You must be firm, sire, you must maintain authority – at all costs! If not, you will never be the great ruler you should be!'

Catherine had turned and was staring wide-eyed at the dreamlike creature advancing slowly over the stone flags strewn with fresh flowers. She was a girl of perhaps 17, tall, slender and willowy. Her hair, of a light chestnut colour that was not quite red, with golden lights in it, fell from a pale coronet of roses about the milky-white shoulders that rose from a gown of azure blue taffeta, cut so low that it revealed the better part of two round, firm, snowy breasts that seemed at any moment about to burst from their blue silken prison.

Her eyes, which were very large beneath her long, fine lashes, were of the same celestial blue. Her brow was softly rounded, her cheeks plump and her small, red mouth as round as a cherry; but, above all, she possessed the whitest, finest and most transparent skin imaginable. It was this that gave her her almost ethereal glow, belied by the voluptuous fullness of her body. Knowingly or unknowingly, this girl was a continual, breathing invitation to love.

The King's face was transfigured. Like a page boy in love, he ran to the lovely child and clasped both her hands in his, covering them with frenzied kisses. She accepted it calmly, with a gentle smile.

'Agnès! My dear heart! Are you here? I thought you were out in the orchard, making the most of this sunshine.'

She laughed, a sound like the cooing of a dove.

'The sunshine darkens the skin and reddens the eyes, my sweet lord – and I was sad without you.'

'That was well said! You were sad, my lovely angel, and I, what was I doing? I languished, I died, for one minute without you is an age in hell! One single minute when I do not press your hand, or kiss your lips ...'

Petrified, Catherine stood and watched this unexpected love scene. Who was this girl? The King seemed mad about her – there was no other word for the emotion expressed in the burning gaze he rested on her and the trembling hands that sought the curve of her waist and her proffered breast.

Her own expression was luminous and carefree, but beneath the sweetness there was domination, and Catherine judged it dangerous.

Propriety might have dictated that the Lady of Montsalvy should withdraw on tiptoe, for Charles had Agnès in his arms by now and was kissing her passionately. But she knew that if she went, she would never obtain another audience. And so she waited until the kiss was over before she murmured, respectfully but firmly: 'Sire, won't you give me the letter I ask for?'

Charles shuddered like a man woken from sleep. Releasing his paramour, he rounded on Catherine irritably.

'Are you still here, Madame de Montsalvy? I thought I had made my wishes clear. See Richemont! I can do nothing for you.'

'Sire, for pity's sake ...'

'No. I have said no and I mean no! I am growing tired of pardoning your husband, lady! It was in this very room, remember, that I bade the executioner burn the decree that condemned him before! He should have thought of that before he committed fresh follies! Men of his stamp think that all is permitted them, and I mean to teach him to obey! You hear, lady? To obey! And so I bid you farewell.'

Slipping an arm round his mistress's waist, Charles VII strode quickly away toward the door leading into the castle orchard.

They were scarcely out of the door before Catherine heard them laughing. The sound hurt her. It was as if they were laughing at her. She took her handkerchief from her sleeve and wiped her eyes. Then she blew her nose and walked slowly to the great doorway that opened into the courtyard.

The vast hall, with its walls twenty feet high, hung with huge tapestries, and its massive hearth filled at this season with flowering broom, seemed to her like the setting of a nightmare. In its immensity, it was like one of those endless roads that stretch before one in dreams, always lengthening ahead as one walks and leading nowhere but to a painful awakening.

This one led to double doors of oak and bronze, guarded by a pair of impassive and apparently fleshless iron figures that moved automatically to throw them open at Catherine's approach.

The courtyard of Chinon lay flooded with sunshine at the foot of a broad flight of steps. As always, the Scottish archers stood guard at the doors and on the battlements, the herons' feathers in their caps stirring gently in the afternoon breeze. It might all have been no different from that earlier day when Catherine had climbed those same steps to a long blast of silver trumpets, to receive from the same king, in the same hall, the annulment of an unjust sentence.

The walls were the same, the weather was the same, the air and even the sun were the same, only on that day Catherine had been escorted by Tristan l'Hermite, and Queen Yolande herself had been waiting at the top of the steps to lead her through the whole court, respectfully assembled there, to the royal throne. That had been Catherine's day of triumph, whereas now she was leaving the castle alone and disappointed, with no idea what to do or where to go.

At the foot of the steps, she found Gauthier and Bérenger waiting for her, holding the horses by the bridles. Their questioning eyes had been on her from the moment she appeared, and they did not leave her now, although they had already read the answer in her face.

'Well?' Gauthier demanded in his gruff way. 'He refused?'

In spite of her grief, Catherine answered him automatically: 'The King refused! Yes, Gauthier – that's right. He said he has no right to pardon where the Constable has given judgement. That Monseigneur de Richemont is in sole command of his men and his captains. He said – oh, I don't even know what he said! But one thing is certain. I need look for no help from the King. I must go back to Paris and plead with the Constable again – unless it should be too late!'

'Go back to Paris?' Gauthier cried. 'Is he joking? Is this how a king treats a noble lady in distress? God's death, what kind of king is this? He counsels like a madman, not like a man of sense! Does he expect you to spend your life galloping the roads between here and Paris?'

The squire's anger brought a pale smile to Catherine's lips and comforted her a little. But she told him to lower his voice for fear of attracting the attention of the guard.

Bérenger was the next to speak. 'Let's not go back to Paris, Dame Catherine! What should we do there? Messire Arnaud won't have gone back. My brothers will have found him and taken him to Montsalvy! Why go and humiliate yourself by pleading in vain once more? These people don't care about us! Let's go home. Let's go and find Messire Arnaud and little Michel and baby Isabelle, and we'll wait in the mountains until the King is willing to grant us justice. And if he still refuses, then we'll hold out against him!'

Gauthier was regarding his young friend with admiration. 'Well, he talks like a book! You're right, lad. Let's go home to your country. I don't know it yet, but I ask nothing better than to learn! Something tells me I shall like it. In any case, we were wrong to come here!'

It was true, and Catherine blamed herself for having disobeyed Tristan's advice to go to Tours and await the King there, in order to take advantage of the wedding festivities.

But when she had reached the great city on the banks of the Loire, some fifteen days earlier, not only had the King not arrived, no-one had known when he would arrive. He was at his favourite city of Chinon and might only appear in time to welcome the Scottish princess.

Queen Yolande was in Provence, and it was not known even if she would be coming. As for Jacques Cœur, on whom Catherine had counted for a welcome since he now had houses and places of business in most of the royal towns, he too was absent from his shops in Tours. His people were expecting him, but he was probably still in Montpellier.

Catherine had waited then, but after ten days' idleness, with no word from Tristan in Paris, she had made up her mind to travel to Chinon to see the King more quickly.

Now that things had turned out as they had, she knew that she had ruined herself by her haste. She ought to have been patient, so as to appear before Charles VII with some firm support. Now it was too late! And yet she had been so near to success! But for that girl, who seemed to have the King on a string …

'Are we going back now?' Bérenger asked. 'It's nearly sunset and you need some rest, Dame Catherine.'

'In a moment. I want to go in there for a minute.' She indicated the little chapel of St Martin, tucked in beside the enormous keep of Coudray. She had often prayed and heard mass there in the days when she had lived in the castle after the downfall of La Trémoille, and she loved the pretty, intimate little shrine where Joan of Arc, too, had once prayed, as only she knew how. Prayer, for Joan, had been a bath of energy and faith, the sovereign remedy for grief and discouragement. She always emerged stronger, happier and more serene. And Catherine, on the edge of despair, thought that God might listen more readily to her if she appealed to Him in the place where His envoy had spoken to Him in the past.

The cool dimness of the chapel did her good. The dying sun shone through the rose window above the door, throwing blue and red patterns on the fine vaulting of the roof. The little stone altar, with its gilded reredos, took on a new brilliance.

The feeling in the interior of the little church was like being inside a reliquary; but, although beauty had always acted like a balm to Catherine, that day it was powerless to allay her disappointment or heal her lacerated heart.

She had built so many hopes upon the King, who until then had always shown her kindness and consideration. She had served him with all her heart. But he had always been the toy of more or less openly avowed favourites. Now, that favourite was a woman, but she would probably prove as baleful as her predecessors, Giac and La Trémoille.

When she had arrived at the castle, Catherine had thought to go to the chapel of St Martin after her audience with the King in order to give thanks; but her mood as she made her way inside was one of despair, to make her choice in silence between a problematical return to Paris or departure for Auvergne to join Arnaud in his rebellion.

But was there any real choice? She knew already that she had no heart left for more humiliating entreaties ... She was kneeling at the foot of a pillar, her bowed head resting on the stone of the communion table, weeping into her clasped hands and blind and deaf to all that might be going on about her, when a hand was laid on her shoulder and a voice said clearly: 'Praying is very well – but why so many tears?'

She started up, with the involuntary quickening of the heartbeats of one caught out in some misdemeanour, and stared at the boy who stood before her. He had altered a little since their last meeting, four years before, but not so greatly that she could fail to recognise Louis, the Dauphin.

The prince must be about 14 years old by this time. He had grown. But he still had the same thin, prematurely stooping figure, the same strong, bony shoulders, sallow, ivory skin and crisp black hair. It was simply that the lines of his face had grown more pronounced, stern and unsmiling about the jutting nose and deep set black eyes that sparkled with intelligence. He was ugly, but his ugliness was not without a forcefulness of its own. The boy might not be beautiful but he had about him a curious, subtle majesty and a peculiar charm that could have had its origin in those penetrating eyes.

For all his shabby hunting dress of coarse and well-worn Flemish cloth, the blood royal spoke through his imperious tone and the look of command on his face. While his words were those of a man.

Catherine sank into a deep curtsy, both surprised and slightly embarrassed at this unexpected meeting.

'Tell me why you are crying,' the Dauphin persisted, looking earnestly at her woebegone face. 'No-one, that I know of, wishes you any ill here! You are the Lady of Montsalvy, are you not? You were one of the Queen, my mother's, ladies-in-waiting.'

'Your Highness knows me?'

'Your face is not one that may easily be forgotten, Dame – Catherine, is it not? I see little to choose between the faces of the women around me. Most are either foolish or impertinent – or both. You were different – you still are.'

'I thank Your Highness.'

'So now, tell me. I want to know why you are crying.'

This was undoubtedly an order, and as such impossible to refuse. Reluctantly, Catherine told the story of recent events, not without some inward qualms, as she saw Louis' brows draw together at her account of Legoix's murder and, still more, Arnaud's escape.

'These feudal lords will never change,' he said crossly. 'They will go on doing just as they like until they learn who is master! Well, if they will be so headstrong, then their heads must fall for it!'

'Your father, Monseigneur, our lord the King, is master! No-one disputes that!' Catherine protested in alarm. Then, since she really had nothing more to lose, she dared to add: 'Alas, why is it that others who have not the right, not being of the blood royal, should rule through him?'

'What do you mean?'

'Nothing but what I have seen and suffered to my cost, Monseigneur!' And Catherine described her audience with Charles VII and the momentary hope that had come to her, to be so quickly dispelled by the intervention of the unknown beauty whom the King had addressed as Agnès. But no sooner had she uttered that name than a look of deep anger spread over the young face opposite her and his thin hands tightened on his riding gloves.

'That whore!' he snarled, regardless of the place where he stood.

But the sound of that outburst brought a man with a grave, bearded face out of the shadows. He did not speak, but his hand pointed toward the altar. Louis blushed, crossed himself devoutly and dropped to his knees on the floor to say a rapid prayer. However, this hasty mark of repentance had not made him lose the thread of his subject. Rising, he turned back to Catherine, who stood waiting speechlessly.

'I should not have used that word in church,' he said, 'but the fact remains. I detest the creature. My father is besotted with her!'

'Who is she?' Catherine asked.

'The daughter of one Jean Soreau, an esquire, Lord of Coudun and St Gérant. Her mother's name was Catherine de Maignelais. She comes of good, though not illustrious stock. My aunt, Madame Isabelle de Lorraine, paid us a visit a year back on her way to Naples on the affairs of her husband, Duke René, held basely captive by Philippe of Burgundy. This girl was one of her maids of honour. As soon as the King set eyes on her, he fell madly in love with her, like a man bereft of his senses ...'

Once again, the bearded man, who was the prince's governor, Jean Marjoris, intervened. 'Monseigneur! You are speaking of the King!'

'He should know that as well as I!' the Dauphin snapped back. 'I say no more than is the truth. The King is mad for that girl, and as ill luck will have it, my lady grandmother gives her her support and protection.'

Catherine opened her eyes wide. 'Who? Queen Yolande?'

'Oh yes! Madame Yolande is equally besotted over Agnès Sorel*. Tell me otherwise how she could have become one of my mother's ladies in waiting? Naturally, Madame Isabelle did not wish to take all her household overseas with her, but that in itself does not explain why she left this girl with us.'

'Was the Duchess of Lorraine to be gone for a long time?'

'I don't know. Several years, probably, since she went to accept the crown of Naples ... and the King couldn't bear the idea of being parted from his lover for so long! She rules him, as you said, and you have seen to your cost how it is! For my own part, I hate her for the grief she cannot help but cause my good mother.'

Catherine sighed. 'Then we are lost! There is nothing for me but to return home and await what fresh disasters may befall our house.'

'One moment. All may not yet have been said. In a few days, as you know, the King, the Queen and the whole court will be at Tours, where I am to be married to the Princess of Scotland.'

The thought of that marriage cannot have been much to his liking, because he grimaced as he spoke, as if the words had left a bitter taste in his mouth. However, he went on: 'The marriage is fixed for the second of June. The Lady Margaret is already in France and has been for some weeks, for she landed at La Rochelle at the end of April; but her progress is slow on account of the welcome she is receiving everywhere. By this time, she must be at Poitiers – very close now.'

---

* Feminine forms of masculine proper names were sometimes used at this period. Thus the daughter of Jean Soreau became Agnès Sorelle de Sorel.

This time it was he who sighed, and because of it Catherine permitted herself to ask softly: 'Your Highness would not appear glad of this marriage?'

'This marriage is no more repugnant to me than any other. I have never seen Margaret of Scotland. It is the thought of marriage that bores me! I have better things to do than dance attendance on a wife. But enough of that. The wedding is your chance. Be at the cathedral on the wedding day, just where the procession must pass. Address your plea for the Count of Montsalvy's pardon to me. Under the circumstances, the King can scarcely refuse it to me! Whether the Sorel woman agrees or not.'

Catherine dropped to her knees, overcome with gratitude, and would have taken the Prince's hand to kiss it but that he withdrew it hastily, as if he feared she might bite.

'Do not thank me! I am not doing this for you, still less to save that troublesome husband of yours, who had better take care in future not to give men cause to talk of him except on the field of battle – especially when I am king! For I shall know how to control my nobles, I promise you.'

'Then why are you doing it, Monseigneur? To get the better of this Agnès?' Catherine asked audaciously.

Louis smiled, becoming instantly the boy he was. It was the cheerful, mischievous grin of a child preparing to play a trick on a grown-up person.

'But of course,' he said happily. 'I'll be delighted to show that baggage publicly that she is not the only mistress of this kingdom. But that's not the only reason. You see, you were advised to come to the King by a man for whom I have a high regard. Messire Tristan l'Hermite is of the stuff of which great royal servants are made. He is stern, hard and of sound judgement. When the time comes, I hope to attach him to my fortunes … He is your friend, and it is him I would please. I would not have him send you here in vain. Now come. I must go in, and you must leave the castle, for the drawbridge will soon be raised.'

Side by side, the Lady of Montsalvy and Louis the Dauphin left the chapel. Then the Prince bowed courteously to his companion and she made her way back to her page and her squire.

'Who's that boy in the shabby clothes?' Bérenger asked. 'He looked ugly, I thought.'

'That was your future king. If, by God's grace, he lives, he will one day be Louis XI.'

'Well,' Gauthier remarked, 'no-one can say he'll make a fine-looking king.'

'No, but he will surely make a great one. In any event, through him I may obtain the pardon that the King has denied me. Let's go back to the inn, you two. I'll tell you what happened in a minute.'

'Are we – are we going back to Montsalvy?' Bérenger asked, a gleam of hope in his eyes.

'No. Not to Montsalvy, nor to Paris. We are going back to Tours, and we'll wait there until the wedding day, as we should have done all along if I had not been in such a hurry.'

They retraced their steps down the steep slope leading from the castle, built in past times by the Plantagenets, to the centre of the town, the Grand Carroi, where the inn called the Cross of Great St Mexme still welcomed travellers and where the gigantic Master Agnelet and his vivacious wife Permelle, two old acquaintances of Catherine's, still held sway over a world of serving maids, scullions and gleaming pans.

As they went, Catherine let the reins drop onto her horse's neck and allowed it to make its own way, while she sat in a dream. How beautiful it was that evening, how pure and clear the air!

A coolness was coming up from the river and a light mist hung over its curves. The rippled surface of the water had taken on an olive colouring, but the tops of the sallows were still gilded by the sun. The ancient walls and slate roofs of the town lying along the bank of the Indre had faded to the soft shades of an old painting.

Suddenly, two swans broke from a patch of sallows by the river and glided out into the stream. They swam together with wings neatly folded and curving necks, moving without regard for the current, which was strongest in mid-stream.

For a moment, Catherine's eyes followed their graceful, irresistible advance, and she saw in it a happy omen. There were two of them, certainly a pair, and because they were together they swam more strongly and they knew no fear.

She, Catherine, had a lesson to learn from them. She must go back to Arnaud and must never leave him again, wherever he might go. Only thus could they become indestructible. It was not good for either of them to be alone.

A kingfisher dived into the dark waters with a triumphant cry. Very likely he came up with a fish, but the three riders had reached the houses and were absorbed into their shadow.

Catherine was no longer looking at the river.

10: A Heart Smitten with Love ...

The house and warehouses belonging to Jacques Cœur at Tours lay alongside the River Loire, close by the barbican on the Grand Pont and immediately behind the wall that protected the city against the two-fold threat of enemy attack and the river in spate. His immediate neighbours were the Dominican convent and the fat towers of the royal castle that abutted on to the quays of St Libart.

There, as in other major towns, the furrier of Bourges, who had sworn to restore the kingdom to financial health and prosperity but who, for the present, was content with being its most powerful and imaginative man of business, had a house and shops where assistants and porters were busy from dawn to dusk.

He himself lived permanently on horseback, forever galloping from one establishment to the next: from Bourges to Montpellier, where the greater part of his business was conducted; and from Montpellier to Narbonne or Marseille, in which port he had interests; Lyon, where he had powerful friends; or Clermont, Tours or Angers.

At 36, Maître Jacques Cœur was a slim, elegant man possessed of a remarkable degree of energy and such an apparent gift for being in several places at once that his enemies, of whom there was already no lack, had been heard to whisper that he must have made a pact with the devil.

On her return from Chinon after her fruitless audience with the King, Catherine was overjoyed to find him at his house in Tours, which had become a scene of obsessive activity on that account.

Jacques would naturally not hear of his friend's returning to her inn. He had insisted that she and her two companions must stay with him, and had handed her over to Dame Rigoberte, the industrious housekeeper who kept his house in Tours in a state of constant readiness to receive him.

The two friends were deeply glad at their meeting. The affection between them was of long standing and rooted deep in their hearts, in a mutual esteem and some tenderness. It was a complex friendship, not without its sentimental side, for Catherine had always known that Jacques desired her and was in no way troubled by it, but woven also of the same strength and heartiness that characterised men's friendships.

Jacques Cœur had taken Catherine, Sara and Arnaud into his house when they had been pursued by the enmity of the all-powerful La Trémoille. Through him, they had been able to escape and regain their own lands in Auvergne. On the other hand, when Jacques had lost everything as a result of the shipwreck of the Narbonne galley bringing him back from the East, it was Catherine who had made it possible for him to start again and bring his business to its present heights by entrusting to him the finest of her jewels, the black diamond she had inherited from her dead husband, Garin de Brazey. Finally, it was on one of Jacques Cœur's ships that the Montsalvys had succeeded in leaving the Moorish kingdom of Granada and reaching France again.

All this meant that the first three evenings of Catherine's stay were fully occupied in the sheer pleasure of meeting again after more than a year, and of reviving their common memories.

Jacques marvelled to find his friend quite unchanged, as beautiful as ever, certainly, but also filled with the same appetite for life and the same courage in face of disasters that might have overwhelmed a woman of lesser courage.

'If I hadn't Macée and the children,' he said to her one night, 'and if you yourself were not a wife and mother, I think I should have carried you off and hidden you away, done everything to make you mine, noble lady though you are; because I do not fear the heights in which you move. I know I can join you there.'

'You will surpass us all, Jacques. You are going to be the most powerful man in France and one of the richest in Europe, if not the richest! The plans you have – the ports and mines you are starting, the way you send your agents to the four corners of the world – it is enough to make one dizzy!'

'It's nothing yet: you'll see, in a few years … I'll build a palace – though not, alas, to offer to you!' He smiled suddenly. 'But what I can offer you at this moment is several bags of good gold Saluts*, the income on your investment – and something else besides.'

He rose from the table where the two of them were seated over the remains of supper. The window of the room was open onto a small courtyard garden. Aromatic herbs grew there, as well as honeysuckle and jasmine, the scents of which overcame the pervading odour of the streets,

---

* So called from the picture they bore of the Annunciation, showing the Angel saluting the Virgin Mary.

with their gutters running with filth, and the aroma of river mud, with its lingering afterthought of fish.

Left to herself, Catherine leaned back in her cushioned chair and breathed in the perfume wafted on the evening air along with the chime of a distant bell.

She savoured the momentary peace. Ever since her arrival she had been allowing her nerves to relax and her body, cramped by long hours in the saddle, to rest and sleep interminably at the centre of this buzzing hive where she could feel at home once more.

Not once had she set foot outside the house or done more than sit occasionally with her elbows on the windowsill, watching the traffic of the street and the comings and goings of the clerks who, with goose-quills tucked behind their ears and rolls of parchment gripped in their hands, rode daily back and forth between the warehouse and the jetty outside the walls, where barges from upstream and seagoing ships from downstream had their moorings.

Most of the time, she was alone. Bérenger and Gauthier, neither of whom felt any need of extra sleep, spent their days exploring the town and the hythe. They took a keen interest in the business of the shop, which was full of goods and merchandise on account of the forthcoming marriage, not only for the backs of the ladies but also to deck the festivities.

Gauthier, who could write a fair hand, was also able to render Jacques Cœur some assistance, which was as welcome as it was unlooked-for. But, for the most part, the two lads roamed abroad, bathing in the Loire or setting forth, armed with rods and nets, to fish from one of the sandy, grass-covered islets when they did not install themselves on a mud-bank in imminent danger of being sucked down.

They would return at nightfall, dead tired and so sated with fresh air that they would gobble down the ample supper Dame Rigoberte provided for them in the kitchen and then tumble into bed in their attics to sleep like logs until daybreak.

But Catherine knew that such brief holidays, such moments of respite, could not last. In a few days, the city, still peaceful as yet, would fill with all the din and bustle of the Court's arrival. Already, the invited and the merely curious were beginning to pour in from distant parts. Soon, the castle, silent now, would be covered in banners and ablaze like a colony of glow-worms at night, to the sound of viols and rebecs.

In a few days, perhaps, she would hear news from Tristan l'Hermite, which he had promised to send if, as she hoped would not happen, Rostrenen were to return bringing Arnaud.

In a few days, moreover, it would be time for her to go and kneel in the path of a pair of children in the presence of a brilliant company in which she should have had a place. It would be one more humiliation; but that, she knew, was the price of Arnaud's safety. And she should be thanking heaven that this last chance had been given her.

'But it will be the last time,' she vowed. 'The very last! Never again will I kneel in supplication to any human being! Only to God!'

With all her strength, she thrust back the picture, so out of harmony with the softness of the late May evening, of a black-clad Catherine on her knees on the stone pavement outside the great door of the cathedral.

In any event, Jacques was returning. He moved out of the shadows into the yellow light of the branched candles on the table.

'Look,' he said.

It seemed to Catherine that what she witnessed then was a conjuring trick. The merchant brought his clasped hands close up to the light, then slowly parted them, and in the space between she saw a rope of pearls, the finest, purest and most beautifully matched she had ever seen. Perfectly round and indistinguishable in their perfection, they shimmered in the light with a delicate roseate flush. No setting marred their absolute small roundness; they were strung together only by a simple thread through the centre of each, and the effect was much prettier than if they had been, as they usually were, fixed into some heavy gold mount or combined with other precious stones, the more obvious glitter of which would have distracted the eye from their subtle sheen.

They hung between Jacques' hands like a softly-shining thread, a fragment of the milky way or a ray of rosy moonlight.

Catherine caught her breath, watching her friend's fingers playing with the jewels, turning them to catch the light.

'What is it?' she whispered, as though in the presence of a miracle.

'What you see – a necklace of pearls.'

'A necklace of pearls? But I have never seen such a thing!'

'No. No-one has thought of it until now. A charming idea; but not, it must be confessed, at all easy to match pearls of the same tint in this way. To do so, one would have to live by warmer waters than ours. This was sent to me recently by the Sultan of Egypt.'

'The Sultan of Egypt? You have dealings with him? With an infidel?'

'Fruitful ones, as you can see. You should not be so surprised to find me trading with the Infidel – have you forgotten our meeting in Almeria? As for the Sultan, I am able to provide him with a commodity he badly wants – silver.'

'So that is why you were reopening those old Roman mines you told me of, near Lyon?'

'St Pierre la Pallu and Jos sur Tarare? Yes, indeed. There is iron, kish, pyrites and some silver, in the first at least. The second has silver – and even a little gold, but so difficult to exploit that I prefer to leave it. In any case, for my purposes it is only the silver that interests me. But to come back to the necklace. Do you like it?'

Catherine laughed. 'What a question! Do you know a single woman who'd tell you she didn't?'

'Then it's yours. Your visit spares me the pains of sending it to Montsalvy – and gives me the unhoped-for pleasure of seeing it on you.'

Before Catherine could stop him, Jacques had moved like a conjurer once again, slipped the necklace round her neck and clasped the simple hook that fastened it.

'The Sultan sent the necklace, but he did not bother to give it a worthy clasp. I'll have one made for you that shall be worthy of it.'

Catherine had been conscious only of a fleeting coolness against her skin. Already the pearls had taken on the temperature of her body. It was a novel sensation, as if the pearls had suddenly become a part of her.

Amused by the childlike look of wonder on her face, Jacques handed her a mirror.

'They were made for you,' he said. 'Or rather, you were made for them.'

She touched the fragile globes almost timidly, with the tips of her fingers. They were as soft as a baby's skin. It was as if she was trying to convince herself that they were real. They were so wonderful! Jacques was right: next to them, her face, in repose, took on a new glow, while the pearls seemed to come alive at the contact with her delicately golden skin.

Abruptly, Catherine laid down the mirror and turned.

'Thank you, my friend; but I will not take these pearls,' she said firmly.

Jacques started violently and said quickly: 'But why ever not? They are for you and no-one else. I told you, they are not a present! They represent part of your profits.'

'Precisely. The Lady of Montsalvy has no business with new jewellery while her people are in want. I've told you what ravages we have suffered this spring. It has been so bad that I was intending to ask you to pay us our revenues in kind: in corn and seed, cloth, wool, hides, fodder and all the other things we may be short of next winter.'

The merchant's eyes, dark with displeasure the moment before, filled with affection.

'You shall have all that and more, Catherine. Do you think I'm such a fool I'd let you go with nothing between you and starvation and the rigours of a winter in the mountains but a fistful of gold and a string of pearls? I've taken some steps already since you told me of your needs the other day. You don't seem to have grasped that your wealth has been growing along with mine. You are my principal investor, and every year I reinvest a certain amount of your income. You don't know it, of course, but you now have an interest in a number of banking houses – with Cosimo de Medici in Florence, at Augsburg, with Jacob Fugger, and even, since the peace of Arras, with Hildebrand Veckinghausen of the Hanseatic town of Lübeck in Bruges, from whom I purchase Prussian wheat, furs, oil and honey from Russia, pitch and salted fish. Before long, you will have interests here in Tours as well, because I am laying the foundations of a clothworking industry that I hope may come to rival that of Flanders and even of England.'

He was off now. Nothing was more exciting to Jacques Cœur than his business ventures and his vast plans. Catherine knew that if she let him he was quite capable of talking until sunrise.

Already Dame Rigoberte, attracted by his ringing voice, was poking an inquisitive and disapproving face round the door. It was late. She had better cut her friend's eloquence short before he began to rhapsodise.

'Jacques!' she said, laughing. 'There was never a friend like you! And I suspect you of doing a very great deal more for me than that loan I made you deserved.'

Descending abruptly from the heights where he had been soaring. Jacques Cœur sighed dispiritedly.

'I'm afraid you'll never have a proper grasp of the value of money – or of goods. That diamond of yours was worth a king's ransom. And I got a king's ransom for it – or the equivalent. The interest is proportionate. In a few years' time you'll almost certainly be the richest woman in France.'

'Always supposing the King lets us enjoy our wealth.'

'What is lodged with me is no concern of the King's. Not unless he arrests me too and seizes all my goods! That is precisely the worth of those merchants the nobility despise so much. If you hadn't a single acre of ground or a single peasant left, you'd still be rich. That's what credit means. Now, put these pearls away in their little leather bag and stow them in your purse.'

He was trying to force them into her hand, but still she would not take them. The veins in the merchant's temples swelled in sudden anger.

'But why not? You are offending me, Catherine.'

'Don't take it so. I was thinking only that your pearls might have a better use elsewhere, and might even do me more good.'

'Elsewhere? But where?'

'Round the neck of that pretty girl the King loves ... that Agnès Soreau – or Sorel. You told me she was a friend of yours.'

It was a fact that when Catherine had described to Jacques her interview with Charles VII and the manner of its conclusion, the merchant had only laughed. Then he had remarked: 'You are mistaken in her, Catherine. She's a good girl. Only a little over- zealous.'

Hurt to discover so much charity in one whom she had expected to partake of precisely her own sentiments, Catherine had not pursued the matter, thinking privately, and not without some pain, that Jacques, like King Charles, might well have fallen victim to this new attraction. Since that time, she had not mentioned the favourite's name.

She did so now deliberately, watching its effect on Jacques through half-closed eyelids. But he showed no sign of embarrassment, or even awkwardness. He looked merely baffled. Moreover, what he said was: 'What are you about? I didn't get the impression, the other day, that you were exactly fond of Agnès, and yet now you want me to give her your pearls? I confess, I don't understand you.'

'Yet it's very simple. You are quite right in saying I do not like her. But I think that, bearing in mind her influence with the King, such a gift might ...'

'Encourage her to plead your husband's cause and obtain for you the pardon that means so much to you?'

'Not unnaturally, I should think!' Catherine cried with an involuntary toss of her head.

'Don't get up on your high horse. That's it, isn't it?'

'Of course it is. Give her these pearls – and make it clear to her what I want for them – what we want, I mean, because, after all, she's your friend, not mine.'

Jacques opened his mouth to retort, but thought better of it. Instead, he smiled and, taking Catherine by the hand, led her to a low seat covered with red cushions, which stood by the open window. He made her sit down and then went back to the table, where he filled two goblets with Malvoisie wine, one of which he handed to her. She continued to stare at him in some bewilderment as he pulled up a stool and sat facing her, his smiling eyes on her face.

'Let us get this business of Agnès straight once and for all. You know nothing about it. You are simply blundering about in a fog –'

'Is there anything to know except that the King has fallen passionately in love with her?'

'There's a very great deal to know. You said something to me the other day, a little bit spitefully, you'll admit, about the Dauphin blaming his grandmother for being besotted – that was the word? – over Agnès Sorel. At the same time, you seemed surprised, rather unpleasantly surprised, to find that I was on friendly terms with the young woman – and it is no more than that, by the way. But what neither you nor the Dauphin, who's a trifle young for such subtleties, can understand is that Agnès, like me and the Constable and the holy maid from Lorraine in the past, is only a pawn on Queen Yolande's chessboard. She has picked us up and allows us to play our parts because she thinks we are good for the Kingdom.'

'How dare you compare Joan with Richemont – and yourself and that girl, who does nothing but smile and let the King into her bed! Besides, Joan wasn't sent by anyone – except God!'

'To be sure. And I should be the last to deny it. But Catherine, have you never wondered how it was that a simple peasant girl should have come so strangely right to the King? Why, instead of dowsing her head in a bucket of water to cool it and sending her back to her sheep, did Robert de Baudricourt give her a horse and an escort? He certainly hesitated – but no captain would risk making such a fool of himself without direct orders from above. Well, the order came from Yolande! It was she who, realising how much help this girl who might be genuinely inspired, could do her, smoothed the way for her from the borders of Lorraine to Chinon and the King, to be sure, but also to herself, Yolande, so that she might form her own judgement. You know the rest. The King, my dear, like all those who lack love, has always needed favourites. He has seen them all killed, one by one, and rightly so, for each was a more pernicious influence than the last. Only La Trémoille, for whom he continues to feel bitter regrets, still lives. Queen Yolande was worried and did not know how to take Charles's mind off his brooding, when the Duchess of Lorraine came to court last year and in her train was – Agnès.

'The child had a stunning affect upon the King; and, for Yolande, it was like a revelation and a glimmer of light. A new favourite, especially one who inspired him to a great love, could rouse the King from his mood and possibly even help to strengthen his character. But it was necessary that this favourite should be a creature of her own. So she took the little girl and kept her with her when Madame Isabelle left for Naples. She had long been acquainted with her family and knew her character. She dressed her, decked her in jewels and set about forming her mind. Agnès is gentle but she is not a fool. She has a happy temperament and she became devoted to her protectress, who found her easy to train before delivering her into the arms of her son-in-law; a creature perfect in every detail who, while giving Charles the delights of her physical perfection could also instil in him, between kisses, the ideas and counsel of the Queen. You found Charles altered, didn't you?'

'I did, I confess. So much so that for a moment I wondered if it was the same man.'

'That is Agnès's work, and Queen Yolande's. And, think, this incredible result was achieved very simply. One evening, Agnès said jestingly that a fortune-teller had told her she would have the love of the greatest king in the world. "I shall have to go to England," she said, "and get myself presented to the King. For you, Sire, cannot be the greatest king in the world, since you do nothing while the English rob you of your inheritance."

'That small remark acted on Charles like a charm. You've seen the result, and now I don't think I'm exaggerating in saying that, in her own way and with her own weapons, Agnès is on the way to continuing the miracle wrought by Joan. She has made a new man of the King, and that was all Yolande wanted.'

'Very well.' Catherine sighed. 'The morality of it is somewhat dubious. It seems to me that Madame Yolande hasn't shown much feeling for her daughter, Queen Marie …'

'Come, come! You know quite well that Queen Marie could never have worked this miracle. The King is fond of her. He gives her a child at decent intervals. But apart from that, I imagine you must remember her face? I forget which ambassador it was who took one look at her and said: "The Queen's Grace has a face to frighten the English themselves!" Mother love is one thing. The resurgence of the country quite another.

'Stop blaming poor Agnès. I'll undertake to let her know she's blundered. In any case, Queen Yolande will be with us soon, and she will do it. Now, will you keep those pearls or won't you?'

Catherine drained her cup, then set it down on the table and laughed. 'You are more stubborn than your own mules, Jacques!'

'That's the way to succeed. Will you have them? Or must I throw them into the Loire? Because no other woman shall wear them, on my life! And I'll engage to obtain another necklace – for your friend Agnès, since you seem set on it.'

For answer, Catherine held out her hand, and he dropped the little leather bag into it. Then, pleased with his victory and with his innocent revenge, Jacques Cœur deposited a kiss on his friend's forehead and wished her good night.

'This is 30 May,' he said. 'The wedding is in three days' time. You'll not have to endure my whims for long.'

Two days later, however, Catherine returned from walking about the city and gazing at the preparations that were being made for the Dauphin's arrival and for the ceremony itself, to find Jacques in the little office at the back of the shop where he stacked his great parchment-covered ledgers. His face was grave.

'The wedding has been postponed, Catherine.'

'What? But – why?'

'The youngest of the royal children, the little Prince Philippe, who was born in February, is dying. The King, the Queen and all the court are obliged to remain at Chinon.'

'What about the Scottish princess?'

'She has gone to Chinon to wait with the rest of them. They can't leave the castle while the child is dying.'

'Oh my God!' Catherine groaned. 'This is the last straw! What if – suppose they celebrate the wedding there?'

Jacques had been moving the papers scattered on his desk, but he turned to face Catherine so abruptly that half of them were swept onto the floor.

'Where? At Chinon? No fear of that! The King would never serve his good people of Tours such a turn, or myself either, when I've been moving heaven and earth for the last month to make all ready here! Besides, good God, this is a foreign princess coming amongst us! You can't marry the daughter of the King of Scotland out of hand, like a goose girl! Stop worrying about it. The new date for the wedding will be decided on as soon as the poor child is dead, which can't be long, and we shall be the first to know of it. Aycelin!' The merchant turned to shout at one of his assistants, who was hurrying through the yard. 'Aycelin! Come here! Take this bolt of yellow Brabant cloth and put it away. It's in my way. Then ride to the strand to see if the Saumur barge is in yet.'

Realising that she too was in his way, Catherine slipped quietly out of the office and went for a long, melancholy walk beside the Loire to brood over her disappointment.

The time of waiting that she had believed nearly at an end stretched before her again, but for how long? It was undoubtedly a sin to wish for a little boy to die so that things might begin to move again; but, since nothing could be done to save him, wasn't it more Christian to pray God to shorten his sufferings?

Dissatisfied with herself and everything else, Catherine crossed over the bridge to the island called Aucard and sat on the grass under a willow to kill time watching a family of ducks dabbling in the water. The sight of the broad, slow-moving river she had known for so long and in which, on one morning of shame and despair, she had even thought to end her life, always brought her, not comfort perhaps, but a kind of peace. She let herself flow into it. She could only wait now for the Loire to bring her its usual small miracle.

Prince Philippe died the next day, 2 June. They learned soon afterwards that, in order to leave a small gap between the funeral and the wedding festivities, the King had fixed the wedding for 24 June.

'That means you will be my prisoner for another three weeks, Catherine,' Jacques Cœur said happily when they met that evening. 'But if you think you will be bored, would you like me to take you to Bourges for a few days? Macée would be delighted to have you.'

'And you to be rid of me! I'm afraid I am an embarrassment to you, my friend. After all, it may not be quite proper for me to stay with you, in spite of Dame Rigoberte's being here. The gossips ...'

'Will talk, even in a desert! As for being an embarrassment ...' His voice changed abruptly from its previous light tone to a low, serious note. 'As if you did not know what happiness it gives me to have you here with me – to myself, a little. Oh no, I don't want you to go – nor, if you will have it, have I the slightest wish to take you to Bourges, because I do not want to share you. These evenings we have spent alone together have become very dear to me, and will leave me, Catherine, when you do go away, full of regrets.'

The weather having turned very fine, it had in fact become their habit to sit out after supper on the bench in the little garden to enjoy the cool of the evening and watch the slow fall of the dark.

For the most part, they talked little, content to sit in a silence broken only by the murmur of the river and the night birds' cries, breathing in the scent of honeysuckle and watching the stars come out one by one.

But that night, Jacques was in no mood for silence. He, who was usually so grave, was suddenly as merry as a child. Gradually, the thought of his lovely guest's imminent departure had become intolerable to him, and this unexpected delay had filled him with a joy he could not conceal. He had proposed taking Catherine to Bourges, but in his heart he knew that this was pure hypocrisy, simply a wish to hear her say she did not want to go. If she had agreed, he would have found any number of excuses for staying at Tours.

He looked at her delightedly as she sat beside him on the stone bench. Because of the sudden heatwave, she had gone to the Queen's tailor. Master Jean Beaujeu, and acquired a light gown of mauve sendal with a white pattern that suited her to perfection and made her look like a little girl. With the simple white veil covering the hair coiled thickly on her neck and the pearl necklace gleaming softly against her throat, she looked like a vision from another world. But the scent that clung about her body, a heady attar of roses sent from Persia, which had been his gift to her, stole insidiously into Jacques' brain, reminding him that she was a creature of earthly flesh and blood.

She had made no answer when, a moment before, almost in spite of himself, his words had lost their light, jesting note and revealed a passion barely held in check. She had merely smiled and turned her head away a little so that he could see only her profile, blurred a little by her veil; but he could see the paler outline of her hands against the lightness of her dress, and it seemed to him that they trembled.

Driven by an impulse stronger than his will, he caught them in his own. They were cold and sought instinctively to free themselves.

'Catherine!' he said softly. 'You have not answered me. Have I offended you?'

He sounded so anxious that all of a sudden she could not help but smile.

'No, Jacques, you have said nothing that could possibly offend me. It is always pleasant for a woman to feel that she has been desired; but say no more.'

'And yet ...'

Swiftly, she freed her hand and laid it on his lips.

'No, don't say it! We are friends – old friends. That is how we should stay.'

He began passionately kissing the fingers so incautiously laid to his lips. 'That is nonsense, Catherine! Our old friendship is a delusion and you know it! For years now, I have loved you without daring to tell you …'

'Yet you have said it now – although I forbade you!'

'You forbade me! Do you know that all these years I have lived on the memory of one kiss – the one that passed between us in my cabinet at Bourges after you fled from Champtocé out of the hands of Gilles de Rais! I have never been able to forget it!'

'Nor I,' Catherine said coldly. 'But that was because I felt guilty. I have always believed that Macée saw us.'

'Yet you did not resist me. I even thought for a moment …'

'That I liked it? It's true. But now, please Jacques, let us leave it there! Otherwise, I can't stay with you any longer.'

'No! Don't go – I couldn't bear it! '

'I'll stay if you will promise me not to start again! You are not yourself tonight. It must be this garden, the scent of the flowers – the night is so beautiful! It troubles me also.' She had risen with a sudden nervous movement, as if she were anxious to leave this treacherous spot.

Jacques smiled painfully, yet still with a spark of affectionate irony. 'You see, you are still trying to delude us both! It's not the night, Catherine, it's you – and nothing else but you! In a broken-down hovel by a dungheap with the rain beating down, you could still drive me out of my mind! I think that must be what they mean by love … but, if you'd rather forget it, I'll try not to importune you further. Sleep well.'

She had already left the bench and was crossing the garden with quick strides, as though afraid of what she left behind her, but still the words reached her clearly, perhaps because she was still listening.

She slackened her pace as she moved out of sight round a rose bush, amazed to find herself so susceptible to the echoes of that voice, which roused a strange kind of happiness within her. It was as if her heart had long been waiting secretly to hear those words, as if it had expected them and so felt no surprise.

As she passed into the house, she had to force herself not to turn round for one last look at him, his strong face taut with desire and that funny little twist he had at the corner of his mouth, which made him look as if he were mocking himself. But if she once gave way to that impulse, the devil alone knew where this night would end!

Any woman, even the most elevated, might yield to the attractions of such a man! In him, brilliance and intellectual power were almost palpable, as vanity and foolishness were in others. He was a man of iron, with a dreamer's eyes, and for all his bourgeois birth, with the heart of a knight of chivalric romance. It was a very subtle snare for a lonely heart at grips with a cruel ordeal, a love not unpleasing …'

Stifling a sigh that held more regrets than she would admit, Catherine went up slowly to her room.

Round a bend in the stairs, she came abruptly face to face with Gauthier and Bérenger who, shoes in hand, were descending with infinite caution in their stockinged feet. They groaned aloud at the sight of her. Evidently Catherine was the last person they wanted to meet.

'Well!' she said. 'And where might you be off to?'

The stairs were dimly lit by a cresset stuck in an iron ring, but even that was enough to show her that the boys had blushed to the roots of their hair. Even young Chazay seemed to have lost some of his usual assurance.

'Well? Have you lost your tongues? Where are you going?'

It was Bérenger who spoke up at last.

'We were going – er – out! It's so hot upstairs, we couldn't sleep ...'

'Yes,' Gauthier chimed in, 'it's terribly hot!'

'Is it indeed? I hadn't noticed it. It has certainly been very warm all day, but the night air is really quite chilly.'

'Not up there,' Gauthier said earnestly. 'The sun has been beating on the roof all day and it's not cooled down yet. It's almost as if there's going to be a storm!'

But these barometric calculations were lost on Catherine. They did not explain the red faces of the two, not unless it really were as hot as a furnace up there, which she did not at all believe.

All of a sudden, she remembered Dame Rigoberte holding forth only that morning on the subject of a tavern that had opened recently near the Grand Pont, almost opposite the house, which she considered was not what an honest woman would wish to have in her neighbourhood. It drew its custom equally from men off the ships and from among the younger employees of the merchant houses. The housekeeper had added that the tavern keeper, a man called Courtot, had engaged the services of 'three brazen hussies' who were immensely popular with his clients.

Catherine studied each of the two lads in turn, dwelling particularly on Gauthier.

'You wouldn't have been thinking of taking a walk as far as Courtot's tavern? All this caution seems unnecessary just for a breath of air.'

Bérenger opened his mouth to deny it, but his companion silenced him.

'I do not tell lies,' he declared, with a certain dignity. 'It's true. We were going to Courtot's. I've never concealed from you that I like girls, Dame Catherine. This may shock you – but I'm the kind who can't do without them. So, I'm going to the tavern ...'

Catherine was not shocked by the young man's brutal frankness, just because she recognised it as, above all, frank. So she made no comment on it, but instead indicated the page.

'Bérenger has neither your years – nor your needs.'

'I know. I didn't want to take him ...'

'Only I threatened to make such a noise that he wouldn't be able to get out,' Bérenger put in, without heat. 'I might not be as old as he is, but I am a man as well, Dame Catherine, and to be quite honest ...'

'If you are alluding to your "fishing expeditions" to Montarnal, Bérenger, I might as well tell you straightaway that none of that is news to me. But there is a world of difference between that and going to sleazy taverns making a beast of yourself with loose women! I thought you were in love with your – your fishing companion?'

The page bowed his head.

'I am, my lady! I do love her, but that has nothing to do with it. I don't know when I'll see her again, and there's no reason why I shouldn't have some fun in the meanwhile. What the devil, after all, I am a man!'

'Leave the devil out of this; you've no call to meddle with him! Just answer me one question honestly.'

'What is it?'

'Those girls at Courtot's tavern. Do you really want to have anything to do with them?'

The boy cast his elder a beseeching glance, so full of ingenuous anguish that the student burst out laughing. He ruffled the page's hair with the back of his hand and answered for him: 'Of course not! But it's nice to think yourself grown-up, isn't it, youngling, even if you haven't got a hair on your chin as yet! Come on, up to bed with you.'

'No! I want to go with you ...'

'Then come on! I'm going to bed. That way you can be sure of acting like a man!'

Bowing somewhat awkwardly to their mistress, they retreated upstairs again.

Catherine watched them go out of sight with a profound relief. She was grateful to Gauthier for his brotherly sacrifice. It was a measure of the lad's quality. Young Chazay was brave and violent, he could be crude and vainglorious, but there were times when, by a word or action, he would reveal a side of his nature that was still determinedly boyish.

With Catherine, he could sometimes be so bold as to be almost insolent, and he had a way of looking at her now and then that made her think that in his eyes she was much more a woman than a mistress. But with Bérenger, although he often teased him, he was as thoughtful as if he and the page had really been brothers. More thoughtful, certainly, than any of the elder Roquemaurels would ever have been.

All the same, Catherine was worried as she made her way to her own bedchamber. She was not looking forward to the days that must still elapse before the wedding. The warm, late spring weather seemed to be bringing all kinds of secret passions into bloom, even more swiftly than the honeysuckle in the hedgerows. Inaction was not good for anyone. Those boys were capable of getting into some foolish prank if she did not watch them closely.

Then there were Jacques. Even after a hard day's work, would he be able to keep the promise he had just made her? Living together in such encouraging intimacy, would he succeed in checking the words that had risen so readily to his lips tonight?

And what of herself? She had very nearly let herself go just now, and she had needed to summon up all her virtue and the memory of those she loved to stop her ears listening pleasurably to what, after all, had been a far from disagreeable time. How could she tell that the temptation would not get worse? Ever since that day at the Eagle when, under the influence of that hot spiced wine, she had blatantly thrown herself at Tristan, Catherine had learned to distrust her own nature.

She undressed and brushed her hair slowly, an operation that, with no Sara to help her, became extremely wearisome. Then, after plaiting it for the night, she knelt by the bed to say her prayers.

Usually, she was able to draw some comfort from them. Her resolution emerged whetted to a keener edge. Tonight, however, though it may have been the heat that had something to do with it, she could not manage to keep her mind on the words she was murmuring. The prayers followed one another automatically, but her thoughts were far away. It got so bad at last that she stumbled, lost herself, began again and lost herself again, until in the end she gave up, snuffed out the candle and climbed into bed.

There, she lay stretched out on her back, her arms folded on her breast, shut her eyes and sought in vain for sleep.

On the other side of the dividing wall against which the head of her bed was placed, someone was walking up and down, endeavouring to tread softly, and she knew that it was Jacques. He was pacing his bedchamber slowly, regularly, and each time, the same board creaked underneath the carpet.

Catherine listened, dry-throated, caught up in the rhythm that so clearly betrayed her friend's state of mind. The creaking board spelled out the beat of his desire far more clearly than any words, and behind the dark curtain of her closed lids Catherine followed Jacques' mechanical pacing as if she had been in the same room with him.

He stopped for a moment, and she heard the sound of water. He must be trying to cool his brow, or else drinking something … Then the pacing was resumed, haunting, interminable …

Her body soaked with sweat, Catherine kicked off the bedclothes impatiently to let the night air cool her.

She wanted to cry out, to hit something, to tear herself apart to put out the fire that was mounting within her. Furiously, she pounded her pillow with her fists, then buried her head in it and clapped her hands over her ears so as not to hear, calling with all her might on her memories of Arnaud, her husband, the only man she truly loved, to help her!

How could Jacques have dared to tempt her? A woman whose husband was a proscribed fugitive, his very life in danger, should not, could not let herself so much as think of the love of another man! But when that other man was Jacques ... Catherine was compelled at last to realise that he was nearer to her heart than she had ever thought.

'Make him stop! Oh, my God, make him stop!' she moaned into the thickness of down. 'Can't he see he's driving me mad ...? Oh, I hate him ... I hate him! Arnaud ...! It's you I love! My love! My only love...'

But her unruly thoughts refused to hold tight to the familiar figure. God was deaf and the devil hard at work. Even while she strove with all her strength to recall hours of love spent with her husband, her memory, following the rhythm of those tireless footsteps, would bring her only one sensation: the warmth of Jacques's hand on her own so short a time ago.

Unable to stay longer in a bed that seemed to her to be on fire, so that she tossed and turned like St Laurence on his gridiron, Catherine got up and stared at her closed door. It was so near – and so near, too, the other room, where the man was pacing up and down like a beast in a cage.

A few steps and the door would open, a few more – and her hand would be on another latch. And then?

The blood tolled like a bell in Catherine's temples. The door hypnotised her. She took a step toward it, then another ... and another. The carved wooden panel was before her. Her hand touched the iron latch ...

In the next room, the slow steps had quickened. The door was jerked open and slammed to with no thought for the noise. There was a sound of rushing feet down the passage, running down the stairs, and then, after a brief interval, the front door banged shut.

Unable to control himself, Jacques had fled from temptation.

Something in Catherine snapped. She let herself slide to her knees, her head resting against the wood of the door. She felt utterly drained of strength but safe, while her mind was torn between gratitude and regret.

'Saved!' she sobbed out. 'Saved for this time! But only just!'

It was a pity, too, that her unexpected salvation should have held so little appeal for her – not to say an unpleasant taste of dust and ashes.

11: A Message from Burgundy

Catherine fell asleep at last, but it was a fitful sleep that left her with a pale face and shadowed eyes. In the morning, she felt so tired and drawn that she made up her mind, as she washed her face in a basin of cold water, that this state of affairs could not continue.

The ordeal of the previous night had exhausted her more than a long and arduous journey. Worse still, it had left her feeling depressed and heavy-hearted with a taste of ashes in her mouth.

It was impossible to go on living for another three weeks precariously balanced between Jacques' love for her and her own desire to remain faithful to her husband.

'I'm going to ask Jacques to keep Bérenger and Gauthier,' she said to herself, 'and I'll go myself to the convent of St Radegonde across the river until the wedding. It is too dangerous! It will take at least the breadth of the Loire and the convent walls to keep me safe! In any case, it will be more respectable! It's perfectly natural for a woman in my position to go into retreat.'

But when she went downstairs, fortified by this resolution, and inquired in the kitchen for the master of the house. Dame Rigoberte forestalled her.

Dropping a brief curtsey, she informed her that Master Jacques had been obliged to leave at dawn for Bourges on business.

'He left word, my lady,' the housekeeper added, 'that he hoped you would consider yourself mistress of the house in his absence and that all of us are commanded to obey you in all things. He trusts you will be comfortable, and he's taken the liberty of carrying those two young followers of yours away with him.'

'What an admirable idea! The boys were at a loose end here with nothing to occupy them. A long journey in the fresh air will do them a world of good!'

Dame Rigoberte smiled comfortably, revealing distressing gaps in her teeth.

'Isn't it? That was what the master thought as well. But here's a letter he left for your ladyship.'

As she ate the bread and honey dunked in warm milk that the housekeeper set before her, Catherine opened the folded sheet. Its contents were brief but to the point:

'I am going away, Catherine. I cannot keep the promise I made you. Forgive me. The house is yours. I'll return in time for the wedding. And just this once, my love, let me tell you I adore you ...'

Catherine read this missive over a second and a third time, deeply moved. At last she folded it away and finished her breakfast in silence.

Dame Rigoberte moved backwards and forwards nearby, the wings of her coif flapping like a gull's as she made ready for her marketing.

When she had gone, Catherine rose and, taking up the letter, read it once again. Then, with only the slightest hesitation, she went to the fire and dropped it in.

The scrap of parchment blackened, writhed and burst into flame, giving off a smell of scorched hide. In a little while nothing was left but a little ash on the biggest of the logs.

Catherine turned away then and walked slowly out to the bench in the garden where Jacques would not be coming again und where, from now on, she would sit alone and watch the darkness fall. She dared not ask herself why it was that she suddenly felt like crying ...

The days passed and the city swelled like a river after torrential rain. The delay to the wedding celebrations was the reason, for those who had arrived before 2 June had stayed, while those who could not come then were arriving now, delighted at this second chance.

The inns, although full already, tried to turn away as few as possible. Barns were turned into dormitories and the guest houses of monasteries and convents, as well as private homes, were full to overflowing.

Merchants arrived in swarms, by river and by road, and the entire nobility of Anjou and Touraine came flocking, encouraged by the brilliant weather. People had even brought out the great tents used on campaigns, and all the meadows around the city had burgeoned into blossoms of purple, saffron yellow, black and ultramarine, while forests of multi-coloured banners sprang up everywhere.

Then there were the mountebanks, dancers, singers, tightrope walkers, men with performing bears and dogs and jugglers who could send relays of flaming torches spinning like will-o'-the-wisps into the night sky. All these found billets where they could, out in the fields or underneath the shelter of the old, covered market, which at least gave them a roof over their heads.

And in the taverns by the waterfront, the harlots multiplied. They were to be seen as twilight dulled the surface of the river, lounging in the doorways of the brothels there, naked under the loose gowns that they would twitch aside at the approach of a man, showing the gleam of bare flesh. Their shrill voices filled the street, scandalising Dame Rigoberte, who had the shutters put up in front of the shop as soon as the sun set and barred all the doors as though she feared to find them squatting in her house.

Last of all came the sick. In memory of the child who had died and perhaps also with some idea of compensating his good people of Tours for the long wait he had inflicted on them, the King had given out that after the wedding ceremony was over he would go to the Abbey of St Martin to touch for the King's Evil.* The great news spread through the surrounding country like wildfire, for it was a rare occurrence.

They had been coming in from all directions ever since. Not the scrofulous alone but also cripples, cretins, those with sores and lame legs, a dreadful, pitiful tide of humanity in soiled rags, pouring into the city by every road.

They came in groups, in bands, in ragged bunches clinging to each other, crying aloud with a hope that was frightening. For so great was their faith in the mysterious healing powers of the King that none of these unfortunates paused to think that only the scrofulous might benefit from those powers. They credited him with the ability to cure all afflictions, as though God's anointed had been Jesus Christ in person. And so they came, even those who had lost an arm, a leg or an eye in the wars.

Before long the hospital and even the empty barns belonging to the religious houses were fully occupied. A stern watch had to be maintained at the city gates, because even the lepers were leaving the lazar-houses to come.

At the Abbey of St Martin, the overworked monks, assisted by the town's physicians, embarked on a rigorous sorting operation that all but unleashed a riot. The Watch had to be called in, and even the echevins of the city, to protect the monks, and there was some bloodshed.

Tours, decked out in garlands and streamers, with platforms and stages smothered in flowers for the tableaux without which no joyous entry was complete, began to look more like some delirious carnival, a grinning *danse macabre* in which ultimate wretchedness went hand in hand with luxury and splendour.

Catherine, for her part, no longer went out at all – except at daybreak, with Dame Rigoberte for company, to hear mass in the Dominican chapel

---

* The anointed King of France (like the King of England) was believed to possess miraculous powers of healing sufferers from scrofula, or King's Evil, by touching them with the words: 'The King touches thee, God cures thee.'

nearby. Sequestered in Jacques Cœur's house, confining herself to the little garden for sunshine and fresh air, she feared alike the wretched crowds that roamed the streets, incessantly demanding charity, often enough with threats, and the likelihood of meeting faces that she knew.

She considered herself excluded from the Court and had no wish to consort with her own kind, even those who were close friends like the Countess of Pardiac, Cadet Bernard's wife, Eléonore de Bourbon, who had given her children shelter at Carlat. This was due not to ingratitude or carelessness on her part but to a simple reluctance to compromise anyone. Until she had the King's pardon, she could not trust the future, and if no pardon were forthcoming, those who had given their support to Montsalvy or his wife might be involved in the same disgrace and find themselves under the King's displeasure.

The King's will is law; so ran the old adage. It was still true then, and Catherine, an outlaw herself, had no wish to draw her friends after her. The one exception was Jacques; but he loved her, and she could call on his help as she would on a brother's. Nor would he have had it otherwise. But the only ally Catherine really wanted had not come.

Every morning, when she got up, she ran to the window to look up at the castle keep, hoping to see the great blue, red, white and gold banner with the crosses of Jerusalem, the label of Sicily, the lilies of Anjou and the pales of Aragon, the banner of her protectress, Yolande.

But it was always the red sieve and the three gold clasps of the Sire de Graville, Grand Master of the Arbalesters of France and temporary governor of the castle, that flapped lazily over the heads of the slow-moving sentries armed with pikes and gisarmes. And Catherine, trammelled in the confined space of the shop with only an old woman for company, felt herself increasingly cut off from the world, more isolated than in the convent to which she had meant to retire. Time itself seemed to stand still ...

Then, quite suddenly, things began to move again. On 22 June, two days before the wedding, Jacques reappeared at the head of a train laden with aromatic bundles: the spices inseparable from any banquet worthy of the name. At the same time, barges laden with cargoes of eels and game began coming down the Cher from the lakes and forests of Sologne.

Catherine's heart contracted when she saw her friend. His drawn face, his pallor, spoke for him both of incessant work and nights without sleep. He smiled and kissed her, but his smile was sadder than any tears and his lips were cold on her cheek. With him came Bérenger and Gauthier, but there was nothing at all pitiful about them. Manifestly delighted with their travels, they exhibited such beaming faces and bright eyes that Catherine might even have been a little shocked if the page, with all the impulsiveness of his age, had not brushed shamelessly past Jacques Cœur and rushed to greet her the moment he got down from his horse.

'Dame Catherine!' he cried. 'We bring news! Montsalvy is relieved! Bérault d'Apchier and his sons have been driven off!'

The châtelaine uttered a joyful cry and seized the lad by his shoulders.

'Is that true? Really? Oh God, it's almost too good to be true! But, how did you hear?'

She was shaking Bérenger as if she would have shaken the news out of him like plums off a tree. But Jacques intervened.

'Wait a moment,' he said sternly. 'It's not as simple as that, and it was wrong of you, Bérenger, to put it in that way. Yes, Montsalvy is relieved, but all is not as well as you would have your mistress believe.'

'Neither is it all as grim as you would think, Maître Cœur,' protested Gauthier, who was very nearly as excited as his companion. 'It is good that Dame Catherine should know at once that the *routiers* have raised the siege and that her town is recovering from its wounds.'

'It is good, certainly, but nevertheless you two boys are talking too much, and too fast. Happiness is never really good unless it is complete.'

'For the love of God,' Catherine cried, 'stop talking and arguing! I can't wait another second to hear what you've learned! And first of all, who told you?'

'A messenger reached Bourges three days ago. He was half dead, having been set upon by a company of Villa Andrade's ruffians. He was wounded in the shoulder, but he managed to escape and hide in the woods for two nights before he was able to resume his journey. He had lost a lot of blood, but he was lucky and collapsed almost on my father-in-law, Lambert de Léodepart's doorstep. Before he lost consciousness he spoke the name of Montsalvy, and Lambert, knowing the bond between us, sent word to me at once. The man was not mortally injured, thank God, and we were able to revive him and make him comfortable ...'

'Who had sent him? My husband? Abbot Bernard de Calmont?'

'Neither. The messenger was coming from Burgundy. It was your friend the Countess of Châteauvillain who sent him with a letter, which I've brought with me for you.'

'I can't understand a word of what you're saying, Jacques. How could Ermengarde's messenger be coming from Montsalvy?'

'If you'll only be patient – the man was sent to Montsalvy, of course, by the Countess. He did not find you there, but Abbot Bernard and this lad's brother, the Sire de Roquemaurel, told him you were probably at Tours. Since his message was urgent, he set out again.'

Automatically, Catherine took the missive Jacques was holding out to her, but she kept it in her hands and did not open it. It was not what Ermengarde might have to say, however urgent, that interested her at that moment, but the implications of Jacques's last words.

'Abbot Bernard, you say, and the Sire de Roquemaurel? But where is my husband? Where is Arnaud?'

'Nobody knows,' Bérenger said quietly. 'There is another letter, written by the Abbot because neither Amaury nor Renaud even knows how to hold a pen. That letter we read and ...'

'You hold your tongue, Bérenger! Here it is, Catherine. As the child says, I read it, because I feared it might be bringing you fresh trouble. Trouble I would have spared you. But that was not possible. You will have to know it all ...'

Catherine's legs gave way beneath her and she dropped on to the bench before the house.

'Nobody knows where Arnaud is?' she repeated dully. 'Then – he is dead! Gonnet d'Apchier did what he set out to do. He has killed him!'

'Perhaps not ... Try to listen to me calmly, Catherine. You must think logically. You must not jump to the conclusion that your husband is dead simply because the Roquemaurels did not catch up with him on the road ...' He was crouching in front of her, gripping both her hands in his in his efforts to convince her. 'Let me read you the Abbot's letter.'

He let go of her and unfolded the parchment, while she slumped back against the house wall with half-closed eyes and tears trembling on her lashes.

To our beloved daughter in Jesus Christ, Catherine, Countess of Montsalvy, Lady of ... etc. etc., blessing and salutations. The knights who set out for Paris with your lord and our friend returned, by the signal grace of Almighty God, just in time to relieve our dear town, which had been reduced to its last resources and was on the point of yielding. Bérault d'Apchier, with his sons and his men, has returned to Gévaudan and we have been able to give most humble thanks to God, along with our returned brethren, for making you successful in your quest for aid. But we have sung no *Te Deum*, since Messire Arnaud has not returned with them ...

Messire Renaud de Rouquemaurel has told us what passed in Paris. He has described how he set out in pursuit of his friend and his perilous guide but failed to come up with them. Long before he reached Orléans, he met the Constable's emissary the Lord of Rostrenen and his men returning without sight of a living soul. And all along the road, he and his companions questioned everyone they met. No-one had seen those whom they sought, nor could they discover any trace of them. The general feeling is that it might have been a mistake to imagine that after leaving the Bastille, Arnaud's first aim would be to reach his own home and that he would head straight for Auvergne. In all probability, he has decided to hide himself in some secret place until the pursuit has died down. And I believe in all sincerity, my daughter, that you must arm yourself with patience until such time as your husband thinks that he might return to you without the risk of further peril either to himself or to us. For my part, I pray God with all my heart that it may be so …

'You see?' Jacques said eagerly as he finished reading and underlined the relevant passage with his fingernail. 'The Abbot thinks he is in hiding. And, after all, Catherine, it makes sense. A hunted man does not run straight to the very place where he is bound to be looked for; that is, his own home!'

But Catherine shook her head sadly.

'No, Jacques. Your reasoning would be all very well if we lived in some easily accessible castle in flat country, say, not far from Paris. But Arnaud knows very well that there is nowhere he would be better hidden, better guarded than in his own mountains. Believe me, the King and the Constable would pause before they sent troops into our narrow gorges or over our hard volcanic tracks! And even if he didn't want to go back to Montsalvy itself, my husband knows of a hundred hiding places in the neighbourhood where he might live for years, and even the Bailiff of the Mountains himself be none the wiser. Because there's not a man or woman on our lands who wouldn't shield him willingly, beginning with Abbot Bernard himself!'

'But he says himself …'

'He doesn't believe a word of it! He's only trying to keep my courage up a little. But he knows Arnaud as well as I do. I'm sure that in his heart he believes him dead!'

'But this is madness! Why do you keep insisting he must be dead?'

She gave him a bitter little smile.

'I'm not insisting, my friend – but I do fear it. Have you forgotten the man with whom he fled? Have you forgotten that Gonnet d'Apchier's aim was to kill Arnaud, after dishonouring him first if possible? Don't doubt it: that devil has succeeded, fully succeeded! He has slain an outlaw, an escaped prisoner – and tomorrow perhaps he will come before the King and claim the possessions of the man he has slain, all that belongs to my children …'

She had hidden her face in her hands and was weeping softly. The three men stood looking at her speechlessly, feeling clumsy and helpless in the face of her grief. Jacques took a handkerchief and began gently wiping away the tears that trickled through her fingers.

'Don't sit here, Catherine,' he murmured, uncomfortably conscious of his employees passing to and fro and casting them curious glances. 'At least let me take you indoors … Dame Rigoberte! Dame Rigoberte, come here!'

The old housekeeper bustled out of the house, wiping her hands on her apron. In the same instant, a fanfare of trumpets broke out from the direction of the Abbey St Martin, followed immediately afterwards by joyful shouts and cheers and the noise of hundreds of running feet.

Jacques looked up involuntarily to where the towers of the castle were crowned with men-at-arms, their weapons shining in the sun. A huge banner was climbing slowly up the flagstaff mounted above the keep. It was blue, white, red and gold, and its quartered arms unfurled against the blue of the sky.

Jacques Cœur trembled.

'The Queen …! Queen Yolande! Look, Catherine, she has come! Those are her trumpets you can hear!'

Now other trumpets were answering from the battlements, and in all the belfries of the city the bells rang out to welcome the Queen of the Four Kingdoms, suzeraine of this Duchy of Touraine. The cheering swelled until it seemed as if Tours would burst asunder with frenzied acclaim. But Catherine looked up at the castle with eyes misted with tears.

'It is too late … She can do nothing for me now!'

Jacques caught Catherine's arms and hauled her to her feet almost by main force.

'You do not know! You sit here weeping and despairing when no-one has told you yet you are a widow! Good God! Just because the Lord of Montsalvy hasn't reached home, that doesn't mean he's dead! And even if he were! You still need that pardon, don't you understand? You need it for your children, for your son especially! So you're coming with me to the castle this very evening. I know how to gain access to the Queen without attracting attention …'

'Jacques, it's no good! Leave the Queen in peace. There is no great hurry now. Why would you have me trouble Madame Yolande when the Dauphin has promised to help me? He has been kind to me, and I don't want to displease him by seeming not to care for his protection. You are thinking of my son,' she added, with a pallid smile. 'Remember that young Louis will one day be his king, and do not make him an enemy of our house at this stage. Besides, I've waited here for a month now – I can wait until the day after tomorrow …'

'No, Catherine, you cannot wait. You must leave tomorrow – for Burgundy.'

He held out his hand, and Gauthier put into it the letter from Ermengarde, which he had picked up when Catherine had let it slip from her lap. Jacques placed it in his friend's hand.

'You are forgetting this letter, Catherine. Yet it is important, for a man nearly died to get it to you.'

As he spoke, he was leading her gently into the house. Dame Rigoberte had taken her other arm as if she were too sick to walk unaided.

They sat her down very carefully on a well-cushioned chair beside the hearth. They were so solicitous that even Catherine noticed it at last.

'Good God,' she said, 'you're treating me as if I were suddenly very delicate! And yet you tell me I must go to Burgundy tomorrow? Must I indeed? I confess I can't see any sense in it myself. What do you want me to do in Burgundy?'

'Read! If we seem to be taking great care of you, it is because this letter, too, contains some bad news.'

'Bad news ...? Ermengarde! Oh God, she is not ...?'

'No, for it is she who writes to you. It is not she but – your mother.'

Rapidly, Catherine unfastened the rolled letter, recognising at a glance her old friend's extravagant hand and wildly exotic spelling. Ermengarde de Châteauvillain was too great a lady to be bothered with what she called 'clerkly fiddle-faddle'. But, good or bad French aside, what the Countess had to say was sufficiently startling. Catherine learned that her mother had quarrelled with her brother Mathieu. The cloth merchant of Dijon, feeling old age coming upon him, had suddenly discovered in himself a yearning for the married state. He had been assisted in this by a dressmaker by the name of Amandine La Verne, whose attractions were a great deal more physical than financial. This 'great godless wanton', as Ermengarde called her roundly, he had made his mistress and had installed her in his house in the Rue du Griffon. Since it very soon became clear that there was no room in the same house for both her and Jaquette Legoix, Catherine's mother had left the place in which she now felt a stranger. She had thought for a while of seeking refuge in the convent of the Benedictines of Tart, where her elder daughter, Loyse, was prioress, but she could not feel herself drawn to the religious life.

> Her real wish would have been to have gone to you, my dear Catherine, because really she stayed with her brother only to help him and keep house for him. She would have much preferred to live quietly with you and watch her grandchildren grow up. But it's a long way from Dijon to those mountains of yours, and her health would not let her undertake so long a journey. Instead, she accepted my offer of the hospitality of my old Châteauvillain, which you know so well. I gave her your room, and we would spend our evenings gossiping away like the old things we are, about you

and the children and your impossible husband! We've had some good times together. She's such a nice woman, your mother! But she caught a bad cold this year during Lent and I have watched her going downhill ever since ... and I am afraid, for each day she seems a little weaker. So I am writing to you to ask you to come. You are young and strong, and the road holds no terrors for you. You can make the journey she will never make now. But if you want to kiss her once more, I think you might do so if you do not lose too much time. Come, Catherine! I am asking this of you because she will never do it, and she loves you so much ...

The parchment slipped from Catherine's fingers and dropped to the floor, rolling itself again as it fell. Her face was wet with tears, but she did not comment on the contents of the letter, nor did she sigh or groan aloud. She merely bent and picked up the roll, then raised a tearstained but determined face to Jacques.

'This letter is dated the third of the month,' she said crisply. 'You are right, Jacques, I must leave tomorrow. I want so much, so very much not to – not to come too late! Poor Maman ...! I thought she was happy and content – I've neglected her badly!'

'You were not to know ...'

'What? That my uncle Mathieu was going to make a fool of himself in his old age by falling for a woman who was cleverer than most? Why can't he see she's only after his money? He dared to let my poor mother go, to turn her into the street like a beggar! His sister! His own sister!'

'Calm yourself, Catherine! I know the best way to make you forget your own troubles is always to give you a good cause for losing your temper; but, for the present, there is your departure to be thought of – and what you have to do first! I will make all the preparations for you. But tonight ...'

'Yes. I'll go with you to the castle! It's the last thing I shall be able to do for a long time for my husband, if he lives, and for my children if he is no more. Because after that I must put them out of my mind for a little while and think only of she who calls me and has need of me!'

Much later that same evening, long after darkness had fallen, Catherine and Jacques Cœur climbed the gentle slope leading up to the castle. A postern gate was opened for them on Jacques' showing the talisman he wore about his neck. Then, out of the hectic activity in the courtyard, a small, red door gave them access to a dark stone stair, spiralling upwards in the fitful gleam of an occasional torch.

At last, the two visitors found themselves in a little oratory hung with violet-coloured velvet fringed with gold. No-one had questioned their movements.

'You are expected,' Jacques explained simply, 'and I know the way. The Queen and I have frequent occasion to talk privately. She takes a great interest in my affairs, for already she sees that they can bring prosperity to the kingdom. But here she comes!'

A moment later, Catherine was kneeling to kiss the hand of a tall woman, very pale and thin, whose black veils were held in place by a high golden crown. Yolande of Aragon's face had been deeply marked by her recent illness. Her thick hair, once so black, was now as white as snow, and added a touch of softness to a face that was still strong and beautiful, although ravaged by suffering. Yet the black eyes had lost none of their liveliness.

She raised Catherine without a word and kissed her warmly. Then she looked at her shrewdly.

'Poor child!' she said. 'When will fate tire of tormenting you? Yet I know no-one who deserves more to live in peace and happiness.'

'I cannot complain, your Grace! Fate has tried me hard, it's true, but it has also given me the protection of those who are both powerful and generous!'

'Shall we say, it has given you the friends you deserve? For the present, I want you to leave this city with a quiet mind as far as your husband is concerned. The King shall pardon him.'

'Your Majesty – knows?' Catherine gasped in surprise.

The Queen smiled and glanced quizzically at Jacques Cœur.

'I have this evening read the longest letter Maître Jacques Cœur has ever sent me. Believe me, he left nothing out! Yes, I know it all. I know what your Arnaud has done to his family this time; and really, Catherine, it is at times like this that I find myself regretting that you did not marry Pierre de Brézé. He would have given you a life worthy of you! The Count of Montsalvy is impossible!'

'Your Grace!' Catherine protested, shocked. 'Remember that at this moment he may well be dead!'

'He? Dead? Come, come! You don't believe a word of it and nor do I! When that man dies, something is bound to happen – earthquake or flood, I don't know, but some extraordinary event there must be to tell the world! Don't look at me like that, Catherine! You know quite well I'm right. Men of his kind are like weeds – you can't get rid of them! On the field of battle they are heroes, but they will brook no control, and they are impossible in everyday life, because they are never content unless they can have sound and fury all about them! Discipline is the last thing they will tolerate.'

'Then, where is he?'

'I don't know. But a man who has been through what he has been through and survived, including even a spell in a lazar house and one as a captive of the Moors, isn't going to let himself be done to death by a country bumpkin on a lonely road! Believe me, Catherine, your Arnaud is still alive! Those who know me claim that I have power to see into the future, and that the mists will sometimes clear for me. It is not true – or not altogether true – and yet I say to you, go without anxiety. Go to your mother. She needs you more than anyone!'

Such was the force of this woman's will and the strength of her personality that Catherine found faith and hope flooding through her once more.

Yolande of Aragon was never wrong – at least, as far as Catherine knew! For so many years now, she had been dragging France slowly, with a visionary faith, out of the deep rut into which it had fallen. She had never hesitated over the choice of an instrument or of one to serve her, nor had events ever proved her wrong ...

'Then I may hope,' Catherine asked timidly, 'to receive a full pardon from the King?'

Yolande laughed. 'Receive it? Oh no, my dear! It is only right that Messire Arnaud should be put to a little trouble on his own account and not let it all rest on your shoulders. When you find him, or when you discover where he is, let him have this safe-conduct and send him to me. I will be responsible and he shall go himself to beg King Charles's pardon. He will get it readily enough, never fear. He need only bow his knee. One word more: you need not trouble yourself further about my grandson. I will tell the Dauphin of the bad news that has obliged you to go away. And I will tell him, too, that I am very pleased with his reception of you, and explain one or two things it is high time that he understood. He is a remarkable boy, and I have the greatest hopes for him, but those who would reach him will do better to address themselves to his intelligence, which is great, rather than to his heart, which is – secretive.'

Catherine knelt once more.

'My lady and my Queen,' she said, deeply moved, 'is there nothing I can do to prove my gratitude?'

The Queen seemed about to shake her head, then changed her mind and looked at Catherine thoughtfully.

'Whereabouts in Burgundy are you going? To Dijon?'

'No, my lady. To Châteauvillain, where my sick mother is a guest of the Countess Ermengarde; but that is not far from Dijon, and I had planned to go there. I have a bone to pick with my uncle!'

'Really? You will go there?'

'Beyond a doubt, and as soon as possible. I don't like to let my affairs drag on, and I mean to make that perverse old man listen to reason.'

'Well then –' the Queen hesitated again. Her eyes had brightened suddenly and a faint flush had mounted to her cheeks. Some idea had come to her that pleased her.

'My son, René,' she said at last, 'Duke of Lorraine and King of Naples, is, as you probably know, still held a prisoner by Duke Philippe. He is at Dijon, in one of the towers of the ducal palace.'

'That is so,' Jacques Cœur said. 'But I know, also, that the Constable de Richemont must be at St Omer at this very moment to meet his brother-in-law of Burgundy* in order to discuss the Prince's release.'

Yolande nodded rather dubiously.

'You are always the best-informed man in France, Maître Cœur. Your information is correct. It is quite true that the King and I have requested Arthur de Richemont to act as intermediary in this; but, to tell you the truth, I do not think he will be immediately successful. The Duke is attracted not even by the thought of a large ransom.'

'Yet he must need money. Isn't he preparing to attack the rebels at Calais?'

'Yes. But he has all the money he wants. The burghers of Ghent have made him free of their coffers and are arming themselves to assist him in his undertaking. I know the Constable will do his best, but I cannot feel in my heart that my son will soon be at liberty. And so, Catherine, if you do go to Dijon, you would gladden a mother's heart by agreeing to take a letter to him. You are still high in favour at the Court of Burgundy, even if you do not often avail yourself of it. You will surely be allowed to visit their captive and give him my letter.'

Catherine held out her hand.

'Give me the letter, my lady, and I swear to you it will reach its destination.'

Yolande went to her and, taking her face between her two hands, kissed her on the brow.

'Thank you, my child. You will be repaying a hundredfold what little I have done for you! Have no fear, I shall get your Arnaud out of this scrape, and he will not even have to come as far as this. It may be that he can make his peace with the King almost without leaving home.'

'How so?'

'The King will leave here soon on a journey through Guyenne, Languedoc and Provence. It took some doing, for he does not like travelling, but he has been – strongly urged to it. In any case, the death of the Count of Foix, who gave up his soul to God on 4 May, has made his going both necessary and urgent, since he must settle the matter of the succession. What's more, Languedoc is in need of help, because *routiers* and *écorcheurs* of all kinds ravage it at will … The King must go there to

---

* The Constable was married to the Duke's sister.

chastise them and restore order. He will pass through Auvergne. The rest seems to me obvious. Go now,' she finished, extending her hand to Catherine, who was already sinking into a curtsy. 'I will write the letter and send it to Maître Cœur's house tonight. You I shall see tomorrow, my friend,' she added, turning to the merchant. 'We will go over the accounts of these celebrations together …'

Catherine and her guide left as swiftly as they had come. As they went, Jacques bombarded his companion with instructions: he would do his best to provide for her journey, but she must be constantly on her guard. The country through which she had to travel was dangerous, full of traps, for the *écorcheurs*, the Skinners, were not ravaging the south of France alone.

'You'll be armed and have the two lads also. But I'd like to give you an escort …'

'She shivered and stared at him as if emerging from a dream. She had not, in fact, been listening, but that word 'escort' had penetrated.

'An escort? Certainly not! Three can pass unnoticed more easily than ten.'

'But you will have no-one with you but one boy and a youth who, for all his courage, is quite without experience in warfare!'

'I am not going to fight a battle. I know how to travel in such places. I have done it before, coming from Auvergne. In fact, I have even travelled the road from Châteauvillain to Orléans at the time of the siege! You need not worry. I know how to take care of myself.'

She fell silent, feeling disinclined for speech. In her hand, she clutched the safe-conduct that Yolande had given her for Arnaud. That was what mattered! That was what she had come for. Now she could hurry to her mother's side with a lighter heart and devote all her thoughts to her. Something of Yolande's confidence had taken possession of her mind, and she believed, now, with all her heart, that her husband was still alive.

Jacques was silent also. Dissatisfied, jealously aware that she was slipping from him once again and that Arnaud de Montsalvy was triumphing afresh, he watched her out of the corner of his eye with a dull despair. Her eyes were shining like stars, simply because she had saved the head of a man whose whereabouts, at that moment, she knew nothing, a man who would never stop at putting his wife and family in jeopardy! And the next day she was leaving to travel a road paved with dangers, and all for the hope of seeing her mother one last time, at the risk of coming too late and imperilling her life for nothing.

But she was like that: for those she loved, nothing was ever too hard or too much trouble.

He thought: 'If only she could love me like that one day – just for one day! I'd be the richest man in the world, and the happiest! But she loves another, and I envy him and detest him – I'd like to see him dead!'

Hidden by the sheltering dark, Jacques Cœur shrugged, and the smile he directed up at the starry sky was very bitter. It was true, he did hate Arnaud de Montsalvy – and yet the next day he would send his numerous agents scouring the kingdom with the object of finding him! Simply so that he need not see Catherine crying anymore.

Part IV

The Skinners

12: The Axe and the Torch

A part of the forest was on fire. A red cloud, streaked with brilliant tongues of flame, was mounting against the solid black arch of the sky. Thick smoke rolled over the treetops where the fire had not yet reached, driven by the rising easterly wind.

It was the very devil of a night! The air was stifling and filled with flying sparks and an acrid smell compounded of burning wood and charred flesh.

From nearby, toward the burning heart of the fire, the screams could still be heard, but they were feebler now and more heartrending. They were not, as they had been earlier, bellowings of mingled fear and pain, but long, gasping moans, the ghastly strangled sounds torn from bodies so replete with suffering that they no longer had the strength to cry aloud.

Away in the distance, thunder growled menacingly, like a warning from above, but it did not drown out for more than a moment the hideous clamour from the sacked village.

Catherine and her two youthful companions crouched hidden in the thick undergrowth, scarcely daring to breathe, as though the plunderers at their business could have heard them. Catherine had shut her eyes and held her hands clamped as tightly as she could over her ears to keep herself from seeing and hearing, overcome with horror and exhaustion. Never had she imagined that her headlong journey could turn into this descent into hell, this dreadful slide into the nethermost depths of horror, lasting for days on end –

The nightmare had begun after they had crossed the Loire at Gien. Before that, traversing the flats and level forests of Sologne, there had been only boredom. But later … Desolated lands stretching as far as the eye could see, villages reduced to blackened, empty shells; burned harvests; decomposing bodies lying rotting in the face of heaven while no-one so much as thought of giving them a Christian burial; monastery churches crumbling into the dry grass of graveyards; castles razed to the ground wherever their walls had not proved strong enough to stand up to the attacking hordes; polluted wells piled high with corpses; and all this horror and wretchedness was the trail left by those roving bands known by the dread name of *écorcheurs* – the Skinners.

Outdoing in ferocity, perhaps, even the Great Companies of the past, they had first made their appearance only weeks after the signing of the Treaty of Arras that had put an end to the war between France and Burgundy.

Men whose trade was war, who had been hitherto in the service of one or other of the captains: peace for them meant an ordered, tranquil life they did not want. A love of adventure, the inability to discover any other means of livelihood, added to the habit of living off the country by robbing, plundering and holding to ransom friends and enemies alike, transformed them from mercenaries into marauding brigands, ruthless bandits who would leave their victims with little more than the flesh on their bones. As Skinners, they were well named.

Their nationalities were French, German, Spanish, Flemish and Scots, but all were predators, and the country that had already suffered so much from war was to suffer yet more from the peace.

For these men, the Treaty of Arras was only a shameful scrap of parchment, and they flung themselves with renewed appetites upon the Burgundian territories, salving their consciences by declaring that the King had been cheated in the dealings at Arras. They found an even better pretext in the fact that a number of fortresses were still held by the English; and, in marching to attack them, they blithely ravaged all the countryside through which they passed.

The Burgundian side had its own Skinners, also, but they were of an older, more established breed. Their names were Perrinet Gressart, who had held La Charité sur Loire for many years past; François de Surienne, called the Aragonese, master of Montargis; and, still firmly entrenched, Catherine's old acquaintance, Jacques de Plailly, known as Fortépice, who yet ravaged the countryside around the castle of Coulanges-la-Vineuse, from where Catherine and Sara had once escaped with so much difficulty from his rapacious claws.

Taught by experience, Catherine had done her best to avoid those well-known danger points. Except for an occasional halt at one of the great abbeys or fortified towns such as Auxerre, Tonerre or Chatillon, she had chosen the more indirect ways, by hollow roads safe from observation, or wide, empty tracts of wasteland where there was nothing left to tempt even the most rapacious plunderer. Jacques had supplied the three of them with ample provisions so that they had no need to seek their food on the road.

The most dangerous, perhaps, were the forests where the unfortunate peasants, driven from their burned homes and deprived of all means of sustenance, had sought refuge. There they lived wild, more like wolves than those whose lairs they had come to dispute.

Twice, Catherine and her companions had owed their lives to the speed of their mounts. The third time, it had been Gauthier who had saved the day, by letting fall the bag containing his own provisions at the feet of the troop of ragged and bearded human spectres who pursued them.

'It was that or draw sword against them,' he had explained afterwards to Catherine, 'and I saw children amongst them, poor souls!'

A dozen times since they had come into these wretched lands, the young man had begged Catherine to turn back and go no farther into a region peopled only by ravagers and their victims, the second as dangerous as the first.

'We shall come too late,' he said. 'A dying woman cannot wait so long! It is a sin on your friend's part to make you go through such perils.'

'Are you afraid, my would-be captain?'

'Not for myself, my lady, you know that, but for you! How many women have we seen raped and disembowelled and left to lie by the roadside?'

'I know, Gauthier. But had I only a single chance to see my mother, I should seize it, however faint! And I believe that I shall see her. She will wait for me!'

And they went on, Catherine with clenched teeth, forcing herself not to look more than she had to, her heart wrung with pity and revulsion; Bérenger, dumb with horror; Gauthier grumbling incessantly.

The sight of what the borderlands of the Duchy of Burgundy were enduring had reawakened all Gauthier's old pro-Burgundian feelings. These had been somewhat dulled by his association with Jacques Cœur, but in the face of this desolation, which was in flagrant violation of the celebrated treaty, he breathed fire and flames all along the road, consigning the King, his ministers and his captains to all the cauldrons of hell, so that in the end Catherine lost patience and delivered a firm ultimatum:

'Gauthier de Chazay, either be quiet or I send you away! You can go where you like, I shall not detain you! In Paris, when you asked me to bring you, you swore to be faithful to me, despite what I told you about my husband. So remember this: outlawed or not, the Montsalvys serve King Charles, they have always served him and will always serve him! If you prefer Duke Philippe, no-one is forcing you to stay! Go into the next town and find out the governor and offer your services to him! He'll make you very welcome and give you a splendid green tabard with a white cross of St Andrew on it – and you can forget that you were born in the shadow of the cathedral at Chartres and draw sword against your rightful sovereign with a light heart!'

This tirade had its effect. Damped, Gauthier had relapsed thereafter into a silence as profound, though not as fearful, as Bérenger's. And so, arguing, hiding, fleeing or seeking the relief of a few hours' safety within the walls of some overcrowded town, they had worn away the journey until they reached the vast forest of Châtillon. They had barely three leagues to go before they would see the towers of Châteauvillain, perched on its rocky spur, when the thing happened.

The three travellers were following the course of a stream through the forest. Catherine knew it well, for it was the Aujon, the waters of which filled Ermengarde's castle moat. Darkness was falling, but they had decided not to stop that night until they reached their destination.

'We are so close now that it would be a pity to call a halt. We'll sleep at the castle!'

'We are close, but the weather's breaking,' Gauthier said. 'That's the second time I've heard thunder in the distance, and I think I can see some very black clouds over there.'

It had been as hot as an oven all day. More than once they had stopped when they found a stream that had not dried up, in which to cool themselves. The scorching air was charged with electricity.

Catherine shrugged. 'There was bound to be a storm, Gauthier; and for my part, I'd welcome one! I think a real downpour would do us a world of good. But in any case – I want to get there tonight, even if it does mean driving you both hard!'

'I ask nothing better,' Bérenger said. 'I'll be glad to arrive, and I'm with you about the rain.'

'Agreed as to the rain! ' Gauthier assented cheerfully. 'I feel dry enough to catch fire if anyone were to bring a torch within a foot of me! '

It was then they saw it, an ominous red stain in the limpid waters of the stream and, in amongst the tall, pale shoots of the reeds, the shaft of an arrow sticking up. It stood so straight that it could only have been buried in a human form.

Even then, accustomed as they were to such sights, they might have gone on their way, had it not been for the sound of a groan close by and some clamour that could have been men fighting in the distance.

Abruptly reining in his horse, Gauthier leapt to the ground; and, going down to the water's edge, bent over among the reeds.

'Come and help me,' he called to Bérenger. 'There's a man here and he's not dead.'

While Catherine was uneasily gathering up the horses' bridles and leading the animals into the shelter of the woods to fasten them to a tree, Bérenger ran to join his friend. Between them, they managed to drag the man on to the bank. He was a big man, clad in a smock frock and rough canvas breeches, now streaming with water. The arrow was embedded in his chest, and his bearded face was pale and twisted with pain. There was a bubble of pink froth on his pallid lips, from which a faint, persistent moan was now coming.

Catherine came to kneel beside them and wiped the injured man's mouth with her handkerchief.

'Is he going to die?'

'Yes, for sure,' Gauthier said. He had been examining the wound. 'The arrow is too deeply embedded for me to get it out. If there was a chance, I'd cut the shaft and push it through to make it come out at the back, but the hand of death is already on him …'

It was true: the man's face was turning leaden. Catherine fumbled hurriedly in the purse hanging at her belt, drew out a small phial and held it to the dying man's lips. It contained a mixture of wine from Cyprus in which herbs had been steeped with a small quantity of 'Maître Arnaud's ardent waters', a cordial highly esteemed for its almost miraculous properties, which Jacques Cœur had pressed upon her along with many other things.

The warming liquor trickled between the wounded man's lips. A tremor ran through him and he opened his eyes. There was a cloudiness about his brown gaze. It wandered uncertainly for a moment, then came to rest on the woman's face and widened. His hands clawed at the air, as though seeking a hold, and his lips moved, but to no avail.

'It's as though he's trying to speak,' Bérenger breathed.

Catherine gave him another drop of the cordial. At that, the wounded man gasped out: 'Fly! … Don't … go … village … the – the Skinners! '

'What, again!' Gauthier growled. 'Who is it this time?'

The man turned his darkening eyes upon him.

'I … don't know … A – a stranger! They call him … Captain … La Foudre! A … lieutenant of … Damoiseau de Commercy …! Go … away! Hurry … hurry …'

He gave a choking gasp and jerked backwards in a final spasm. Blood gushed from his mouth, and he did not move again.

'He's dead,' Bérenger said blankly, and laid the shaggy head down on the ground. Catherine closed the eyes reverently. Gauthier was already on his feet, staring down at the big body with a mixture of pity and anger.

'La Foudre!' he growled. 'The Damoiseau de Commercy! Who are these brigands?'

'La Foudre, I do not know,' Catherine said. 'But I can tell you something of the Damoiseau. He is as fair as a woman, noble as a prince, valiant as Caesar, young – as you yourself, Gauthier, for he must be about your age – and cruel as a Mongol torturer! His name is Robert de Sarrebrück, Count of Commercy, an archangel with the eyes of a maid and the soul of a demon! By him, you may judge of his lieutenant. But look – listen!'

It was dark, now, under the trees, and from the depths of the forest came sounds of screaming, while the first glimmers of fire were reflected in a bend in the stream.

'We can't go on,' Gauthier said decisively, drawing Catherine back to where she had left the horses. 'We must hide ourselves and the beasts and wait. When they have burned everything – then they'll probably go away, go somewhere else. It all depends if this village is a large one. Have you any idea, Dame Catherine?'

She frowned, striving to remember.

'It must De Coupray – or Montribourg!'

'Are they very big?'

'Big enough! Two hundred souls, perhaps.'

'Hmm! It could take a long time. In any case, we're bound to wait, if only to see which direction the fire will take. Because there's not only the village. The forest itself is burning …'

With the horses concealed in a brake, they had hidden themselves in the undergrowth nearby, and since then they had waited, with anguish in their hearts and souls in torment, for the village to finish dying.

The storm was coming nearer but did not really burst. Great, livid flashes of lightning swept across the sky, and the thunder rumbled almost continuously, but not one single drop of rain had fallen.

'If only it would rain!' Gauthier muttered. 'There's a chance it would put out the fire. The wind's in just the wrong direction. It's already cut us off from the road that would have taken us round the village. And on the other side there is the river, which looks fast and dangerous.'

'Better risk drowning than fall into those fellows' hands,' Bérenger argued.

Catherine said nothing. She was staring through the trees to where some lights flickered disturbingly. The shouts and oaths were coming nearer.

'Someone must have escaped,' she gasped. 'Listen! They are hunting them … Oh God! They're coming this way!'

'On horseback,' Gauthier said. 'That decides it. We can't stay here. We must cross!'

'It won't be easy. You can see the bank on the other side. It's almost sheer.'

'We'll cross diagonally. Look, there! Just below the bend in the stream, there's a little beach.'

Sure enough, at the point where the water was illumined by the reflected glow of the fire, a narrow crescent showed faintly at the foot of a grassy slope. Catherine regarded it doubtfully.

'Don't you think if we land there we'll be in sight of the village?'

'Maybe, but even so, there's no saying anyone will see us. Besides, these brigands will have to cross too to catch us, and meanwhile we shall be away. We could always turn back, of course …' He glanced round and uttered a smothered curse. 'By all the devils in hell! No, we can't go back now – the fire is there as well!'

And it was true. The infernal glow had broken out afresh in the direction from which they had come.

'We must get out,' Catherine said, 'or we'll be cut off! God help us!'

They remounted in silence. As they passed the place where the corpse lay, underneath the boys' hasty covering of branches, Catherine crossed herself and suppressed a shudder.

Then the three travellers edged their horses cautiously into the water. The brave beasts began swimming strongly upstream against the current, while their riders concentrated on keeping their heads above water.

Such noise as they made in swimming was amply covered by the continual rolling of the thunder and the clamour arising from the attack on the village.

They were nearing the little strand. Already the horses' hooves were out of deep water and scraping on the river bottom.

'We've managed to keep out of the light,' Gauthier said with satisfaction. 'That's lucky and …'

He never finished his sentence. All at once, the field above the strand and the surrounding hedgerows seemed to catch fire. A troop of men, some bearing torches, burst out of a coppice making for a fortified farmhouse that, Catherine saw too late, crowned the summit of the slope. In another moment, the travellers were caught full in the light.

'Ho there!' one of the men cried. 'See what's in the river!'

Uttering a series of bloodcurdling yells, he galloped down the meadow.

'We're lost!' Catherine groaned.

'There may yet be a hope,' Gauthier hissed contemptuously. 'If these men are for King Charles? Dog doesn't bite dog!'

'You young fool! The Skinners are for no-one but themselves …'

As they spoke, they were struggling to turn their horses back into the centre of the stream and go with the current, but already it was too late.

Still yelling, without a moment's pause, half a score of the brigands had plunged into the water and were grasping at the horses' heads. The two boys drew their weapons and strove desperately to use them, but their efforts were in vain. In a twinkling, all three of them were seized by demon figures with smoke-blackened faces and flung to the ground, where some began to bind them with a skill indicating long practice, while others took hold of the horses' bridles.

Bérenger had received a blow on the head and was mercifully unconscious.

'A good prize!' one of their attackers cried. 'Three fine beasts and wealthy folk by the look of them! Merchants, maybe …'

'Merchants!' growled Gauthier, struggling furiously. 'Do we look like merchants? We are gentlefolk, varlet, and with us is …'

He broke off. The man who appeared to be the leader had knelt beside Catherine. Her head had struck a root as she was thrown to the ground and she was still stunned from the blow. The black hood that covered her head had slipped back a little, and the man dragged it off roughly. Her thick golden hair emerged, gleaming almost red in the torchlight.

'Well, well!' the man said. 'What have we here?'

To make sure, he drew his dagger and, with one swift movement, slit the laces fastening her doublet, revealing the linen bands she was accustomed to swathe about her bosom whenever she dressed as a boy. The blade of the dagger had shorn through them in a moment, and the definitive proof of her gender was there for all to see.

The leader gave an admiring whistle.

'A very – very pleasant surprise! Let's finish peeling this tasty nut! It's certainly a woman, lads, and a rare one, too ...'

'Brigands! Savages!' roared Gauthier, almost choking himself. 'She's not a woman! She's a lady, a noble lady, and if you dare to lay a finger on her ...'

He writhed in his bonds, scarlet and choking with helpless rage. However, the leader drew back the hand that had been reaching out to strip Catherine and shrugged impatiently.

'Muzzle me that whining cur! I can't think with him shouting ... Now, tell me lads, am I right in thinking no-one's yet forbidden us to lay hands on noble ladies? All that matters is to know where they come from? So come on, sweetheart, wakey, wakey!'

While one of the ruffians stunned Gauthier with a blow of his mailed fist, another dashed the contents of a helmet filled with water into Catherine's face. She twisted, opened her eyes and, becoming aware of rough hands on her breasts, jerked upright and spat like an angry cat.

Thrusting with all her strength, she caught the man off balance and sent him sprawling. Then she sprang to her feet and, drawing the dagger from her belt, gripped it in her clenched hand, point forward.

'Brigands! I'll rip up the first man who touches me!'

A loud burst of laughter greeted this threat. The leader got to his feet, wiping his dust and sweat-grimed face on his leather sleeve.

'That'll do,' he said. 'We're going to have a talk. But only because we've heard that you're a noble lady. Don't flatter yourself that bodkin of yours would stop us having our way with you! Who are you? Where are you from?'

'From Tours, where I was present for the marriage of Monseigneur the Dauphin ten days since. I am a lady-in-waiting to the Queen!'

'Here, Le Boiteux! This looks serious! Hadn't we better take them to the captain?'

'When I want your advice, I'll ask for it,' the other said sharply. Then, turning back to Catherine: 'What's your name, fair lady?'

'I am the Countess of Montsalvy. My husband is well-known among King Charles's captains.'

Le Boiteux said nothing, but scratched his hairy head for a moment, then resumed his helmet and turned away with a shrug of his shoulders.

'So be it. Take them all to Captain La Foudre! For my part, I'd as soon not cross him – but make no mistake, my beauty, if you've been having me on, he'll know it, because he knows all the Court ladies! But you're a fine wench, and there's a fair chance you'll not be hanged for a while yet. He's fond of a fine, handsome wench, is La Foudre! Right, you lot, let's be getting on! You, Cornisse, put the two young 'uns on their horses, and you'd best be tying the lady's hands – she's a touch too ready with that knife of hers. Take them all down to the village. I wash my hands of them.'

While Cornisse lashed the still unconscious Gauthier and Bérenger to two of the horses' backs and then bound Catherine's hands, Le Boiteux and the rest of his troop made their way back up the hill and headed once more for the fortified house that still stood dark and silent on its hilltop.

Moments later, they were attacking the door with a tree trunk, making it ring in the darkness like a cathedral bell.

Cornisse took hold of the rope that bound Catherine, while one of his comrades led the horses by the bridle, and the whole party set off in the direction of the little stone bridge, not far from the bend in the stream that connected the village with the farther bank.

Catherine clasped her arms as tightly as she could across her chest in an effort to bring together the edges of her doublet, ripped open to the waist, but this was soon forgotten as her eyes were drawn irresistibly to the horrors before her.

With the exception of two or three houses that seemed to have been spared because they were better than the rest, the whole village was in flames. Already, some of the cottages were no more than heaps of glowing ashes with a few blackened beams still protruding from them. Others were blazing like torches with bright, leaping flames fanned by the wind. Even the middens were burning, giving off reeking clouds of noisome, stifling smoke.

But worst of all were the dead bodies that lay everywhere. Catherine saw women with their skirts drawn up over their heads and their bellies ripped open, dying in a welter of blood and refuse; an old man at his last gasp, dragging himself on his elbows while the blood spurted from his severed wrists; hanged men with purple, congested features and others suspended upside down over dying fires, whose faces were no more than huge, blackened cinders.

The village's single street had been transformed into a charnel house. Dying men, stuck full of arrows, were bound to the trunks of the trees. Before the door of a barn to which a peasant had been nailed like an owl, with outstretched arms, one of the marauders was raping a shrieking girl while another brought his mace down on the heads of a pair of children clinging to their mother's skirts.

Catherine closed her eyes to shut out the sight, stumbled and fell to her knees.

'Better look where you're going, my lady,' Cornisse advised her. 'You're not at Court now!'

'Look? And see this? What are you? Beasts ...? No, worse than beasts, for not even the most savage of them could equal your cruelty! You are brutes, devils with men's faces ...'

The other shrugged, without surprise.

'Bah! It's war!'

'War? You call this war? This murdering and torturing, this looting and burning?'

Cornisse wagged his finger at her with a sententious air that contrasted oddly with his flat, snub-nosed face.

'War without fire is like eels without mustard. It was a king of England said that, and he should know!'

Sick with disgust, Catherine made no answer. They made their way toward the church. Its door hung wide, torn from its hinges, and from the lighted interior came a lowing and bellowing of cattle.

Cornisse entered with his prisoner. Catherine saw that the place was full of cows, calves, oxen, sheep and goats. A *routier* wearing a mailshirt over a monk's habit was counting them with the aid of a big book lying open on the lectern. Bales of fodder were piled high in the side aisles, and in a small chapel, men were busy stacking quantities of provisions taken from the houses.

Before the altar, three young girls, stark naked, were dancing under the threats of a dozen men with drawn swords, who were laughing uproariously and beating them when they tried to hide themselves with their long hair.

Cornisse glanced round and then addressed the monkish scribe.

'Hi there, Reverend! D'ye know where the captain is?'

Without lifting his eyes from his writing, the scribe pointed to the other end of the church.

'The house just back there. It belongs to the bailiff. He's in there!'

'Right, then! We'll be off there,' the man sighed, giving a tug to the rope that bound Catherine to him. She glared into his dull eyes, her own blazing with anger and indignation.

'Curse you! Curse you all! If men do not punish you, God will surely do it! You'll rot in prison or on the gallows and then burn in hell for all eternity!'

To her immense surprise, the man crossed himself with patent terror, then told her angrily to be quiet unless she wanted to be gagged.

She turned her back on him with a contemptuous shrug and marched before him out of the desecrated church, her head held high. But as she set foot outside the porch, a tremendous flash of lightning lit up the entire village and, in that instant, the storm broke. Torrents of water descended with all the violence of a cataract, falling from a black sky in which the thunder crashed incessantly like the end of the world, quenching the flames and dowsing the fires so that they steamed like cauldrons.

Cornisse goggled wildly at Catherine and jabbed his hand toward her with first and fourth fingers extended.

'Witch! You're a witch! A daughter of Satan! Great lady or no. I'll tell the captain he should burn you!'

Catherine laughed shortly.

'A witch? Because the storm has burst? That's God up there showing his anger, you brigands! He is echoing my words, not the devil, your master!'

For answer, he dragged her at a running pace along the squat buttresses and through the puddles that were already forming underfoot. The rain lashed their faces and streamed down Catherine's unprotected chest.

One dragging the other, they darted into the porch of a somewhat superior house that was even furnished with glass in its windows. Frightful screams were coming from inside.

Leaving the horses and their burdens with their guards in the porch, Cornisse dragged Catherine over to a low door and kicked it open.

'Captain!' he called. 'See the gamebird I've brought you!'

But his words were lost in the screams that filled the room. He paused on the threshold, keenly interested, while Catherine choked back a cry of horror. This time, she knew she must have walked into hell itself!

The room in which she found herself was of handsome proportions, and its chief ornament was a broad stone hearth above which was a statue of the Virgin; but it was from here that the screams were coming. A bearded man in the prime of life was lying bound to a board that rested on two stools, his legs disappearing up to the knees in the fire. Four men were holding him down as he writhed in his bonds, and his mouth was open in a vast, unending howl of agony. The Skinners pulled him out for a moment while they repeated their question: 'Where's the goods?'

But although his eyes were rolling, his face scarlet and sweating and the great, purple veins in his forehead seemed about to burst, he still had strength enough to shake his head, and so the torture recommenced.

Like a kind of counterpoint, a woman's voice became audible, uttering screams and entreaties. It came from the other end of the room, where there was a big, red-curtained bed, just now creaking and shuddering under the burden of two struggling figures. In the shadows under the curtains, Catherine caught a glimpse of a bare arm and leg and a head with long, fair hair rolling frantically from side to side. There was a woman there, sobbing and moaning beneath the weight of the man possessing her with such barbarous violence.

Of the man, there was little to be seen beyond a large form clad in steel armour that added to the wretched woman's torments.

Tell them, Guillaume – tell them! ' she was screaming. 'Don't let them kill you!'

Appalled, her eyes wide with horror, Catherine stared in turn at the tortured man and at the woman, unable either to close her eyes or to drag them away. She was possessed by such an overwhelming revulsion that her body simply refused to obey her.

As though in a nightmare, she saw a fist smash into the woman's mouth, saw her lose consciousness and fall silent at last, while her tormentor uttered a short grunt and continued to take his pleasure of her.

Meanwhile, the tortured man's cries had ceased abruptly and his head fell back and lay still. The *routiers* hauled the body out of the fire.

'Captain!' one of them called out. 'He's fainted ...'

'That or died,' added another, with his ear to the man's chest. 'I can hear nothing in there!'

There was an angry growl from the depths of the alcove and a tall, grey figure rose with a clank of metal.

'You bunch of brainless oafs!' snarled a voice that made Catherine start suddenly.

Her dilated eyes widened still farther as Captain La Foudre stepped out of the shadows, straightening his embroidered leather baldric. He was bareheaded, his short, black hair on end and his tanned face distorted with rage as he bore down on his men, his fist raised to strike.

Cornisse coughed. 'Captain!' he said again. 'I've brought you some rare game here!'

The raised fist lowered. The man shrugged his steel-clad shoulders and directed a kick at the still body of the tortured man.

'Throw me this carcass on a dungheap – if there's any left!' he commanded. Then, snatching up a candle from the table, he strode toward the little group by the door.

'Rare game, eh?' he sneered. 'Let's see it, then!'

He raised the candle. The Lady of Montsalvy threw back her head. Her violet eyes, blazing with anger, met Captain La Foudre's black ones, which filled suddenly with a vast amazement. The candle clattered to the floor.

Catherine said: 'Good evening, Arnaud.'

13: The Damoiseau

The deluge! She was in the very heart of a deluge that must drown the world! God's anger was let loose on a guilty world in long, roaring torrents that battered the thatched roof, broke off branches, sent trees crashing to the ground and pitted the blood-soaked earth.

Face to face in the barn where he had dragged her without giving her time to speak another word, Catherine and her husband stared at one another. They seemed to be sizing each other up, like enemies on the point of battle.

On Arnaud's face, an almost insensate rage had replaced the anger of a moment before. He had grasped the fact that the slender black-clad form that had appeared so suddenly before him, like the avenging angel, was not a ghost, risen in some unexplainable way out of the acrid smoke of the fires or from the phantasmagoria of this hellish night.

It was a living creature, his own wife … It was Catherine herself, and his whole being cried out with anger at her. Never, not even during those endless nights when her image had remorselessly banished sleep and haunted his fitful dreams, could he have imagined he could hate her to this extent.

Like a man ridding himself of an unendurable burden, he had hurled her roughly from him into a corner of the barn. By good luck, there was still a little straw left to cover the ground at that point, but even so, she grazed herself on the tines of a fork that fell with her.

Then, suddenly, he vented his rage on her in a stream of varied insults the sense of which, however, was always the same:

'Slut …! Harlot …! Whore …! Strumpet …! So they sent you packing! Or was it he, your black sheep, who'd had enough of you and cast you out when he found that half his men had enjoyed you?'

Already, agile as a cat, she was on her feet again, nursing her injured wrist in her hand, dazed less by shock than by his flood of abuse, yet with her own anger instantly rising to match his.

'Who cast me off? What are you talking about? Because I caught you red-handed, because I saw you acting like the beast you are, you must needs leap to the attack and hurl baseless insults at me! It's much the best way!'

As she spoke, she was mechanically drawing her doublet together, using the ends of the shorn laces.

'I'm talking of my vassals, I'm talking of the people of Montsalvy who, I suppose, must have tired of watching you cavorting in the Apchiers' beds and driven you from their walls to roam the highways, reverting to your old trade!'

'Your vassals? Ha, I wish they might see you at this moment! You, their lord – almost their God! Covered with blood, burning, pillaging, torturing the innocent, and still hot from violating some wretched woman! Oh, they'd be proud of you! Brigand! Cut-throat! Skinner! Those are the Lord of Montsalvy's new titles! Ha! No, I was forgetting. Captain La Foudre, one of Robert de Sarrebrück's henchmen! That's what you are now!'

He went for her then, his fist upraised to strike as it had been earlier, but she did not flinch. On the contrary, she drew herself up and faced him boldly.

'Go on,' she ground at him through her teeth. 'Hit me! It's your trade, isn't it! The man who got you out of the Bastille and succeeded so completely in dishonouring you, Gonnet d'Apchier, has done his work well, I see!'

Arnaud held his hand. 'How do you know that?'

'I know more than you think! I know that when Bérault d'Apchier was laying siege to Montsalvy, he had spies within the town. He got the woman who betrayed us, Azalaïs the lace-maker ,to give him one of my shifts, on which she had to mend the lace, and part of a letter she had forged in my handwriting! It was for you – to convince you I had been base enough to deliver Montsalvy up to those swine! That's how it was, isn't it? But if you want me to say it to his face, go and fetch him and let him vent his spleen! Where is Gonnet d'Apchier? How is it I did not see him at tonight's little party? It was just the kind he should enjoy!'

'He's dead,' Arnaud said roughly. 'I killed him – when he gave me this.' His face expressionless, he drew out from beneath his hauberk a bundle of white linen, crumpled and stained with blood, and a scrap of parchment, and tossed them at his wife's feet.

'He got me out of the Bastille. He saved my life and yet I killed him. Because of you and because he dared to tell me – the truth about you! He was honest with me, like a brother – and yet I killed him!'

'Honest? A brother? All this in praise of Gonnet d'Apchier? Honest, the man who fed you with such shameless lies? Brotherly, the fellow who carried on him poison that he got from your local witch, La Ratapennade, and meant to use to end your life? Arnaud de Montsalvy, have you lost your wits?'

He burst into a fresh fury, but now there was a hint of doubt and uncertainty in his waves of anger.

'Why should I believe you rather than him? How do I know that what you say is true? It's natural you should attack him to defend yourself, especially now that I've been fool enough to tell you he is dead!'

'You don't believe me?' she said coldly. 'Well then, will you believe Abbot Bernard?'

'Abbot Bernard is far away, and so you know!'

'Not so far as you think. Read this.'

She drew from her purse the letter she had received at Tours. The stout leather had kept it safe from the water and it was not even damp. She thrust it briskly before her husband's eyes.

'I think you know that writing? Do you think Bernard de Calmont d'Olt would address as his beloved daughter in Jesus Christ a slut whom his servants had flogged from his gates?'

He cast her a glance in which uncertainty was now tinged with anguish; then, moving to where he had placed the candle on a beam, he began to read slowly, half under his breath, pausing over certain words as though endeavouring to weigh them correctly.

Catherine caught her breath and watched him with despair. She saw that the strong, manly lines of his face seemed to have thickened and coarsened with a kind of brutality that was new to her but was brought out all the more sharply by the poor light of the candle. His cheeks were covered with four or five days' growth of beard, the filthy stubble destroying all trace of beauty in his face, and his eyes were pouched and swollen from his excesses.

With pain she saw, behind the image of this mailed ruffian who, in her memory, loomed fierce and menacing against the background of a burning village, the familiar figure as she had seen it last, so proud and cheerful beneath the shimmer of bright, silken banners against the spotless canvas of the snow-covered plateau.

It was only six months since, and the man she loved more than anything in the world had changed into this! Her grief was so great that she could make no effort to contain it. Tears filled her eyes and poured in silence down her cheeks, without so much as a sob.

Arnaud, however, had finished reading. He had dropped the letter at his feet and was staring at it blankly, as if trying to learn something from its shape. His hand went involuntarily to his breastplate, discarding it and the shoulder pieces and unfastening the mail hauberk to free his powerful neck, like a man finding difficulty in breathing.

Suddenly, he wrenched out the hatchet that was stuck into a chopping block and hurled it away, then seated himself with his elbows on his knees and his head sunk between his hands.

'I don't understand ... I don't get it ...! I can't understand! I think I'm going mad!'

'Won't you let me explain?' Catherine said softly, after a moment's silence. 'Then I think you'll understand everything.'

'Explain, then,' he said grudgingly, still with a trace of anger that was only strengthened by the unpleasant sense of having been in the wrong all along the line.

'One question first. Why, after you left the Bastille, didn't you go straight back to Montsalvy?'

He shrugged his shoulders irritably.

'The Abbot understands why! And so should you! It's easy enough. When you're on the run, you don't go straight back home.'

'You could have gone somewhere in the region, at least. There are plenty of places to hide, to say nothing of castles belonging to those who would gladly undergo battles and sieges for your sake!'

'I know,' he cried angrily. 'But that accursed bastard, may God damn him, told me I was under sentence of death and was to be executed that same night! He even came as the monk who was to shrive me! When we fled, I wanted to make for Auvergne, in fact I wanted nothing else, only he told me the King was already sending troops to invest the town and seize my goods. And then afterwards -- when he told me - the thing you know of, I no longer wanted anything, except to vent my rage on all who came within my power! What was the good of going back? If the King's men had already taken possession, I'd not even have the satisfaction of ripping out Bérault d'Apchier's guts. So I came to join Robert. I knew he had made his escape from the prison where René of Lorraine's people were holding him. I'd known him for a long time, and moreover he was now like me, an escaped prisoner, an outlaw. Only he was powerful and leader of a strong force. So I joined him. And his friendship did not fail me. The Damoiseau welcomed me with open arms!'

'And turned you into this brigand with a name that's all too apt! You'll forgive me if I'm not exactly grateful to him! And now, if you like. I'll tell you all about it.

She squatted down beside him and began.

As clearly and as calmly as she could, Catherine described the events that had led her from the caverns under Montsalvy to this village in the uplands of the Marne. She told of her encounter with Richemont, of her audience with the King, her meeting with the Dauphin, the help Jacques Cœur had given her, and finally of her visit to the castle of Tours to see the Queen of Sicily.

He listened without a word, his hands clasped between his knees and one iron-shod foot pawing the earth now and then, like an impatient horse.

At last, she rose and, feeling in her purse once more, took out the safe conduct.

'There!' she said. 'This is what the Queen gave me for you. Go back to Montsalvy. Very soon now the King, with the two Queens and the Dauphin, will be travelling south to arrange the succession to the County of Foix and to ...' Her voice faltered imperceptibly, then she made up her mind and spoke even more clearly, to make a greater impression, 'and to put down the excesses of the Skinners!'

He shuddered, and his dark eyes rested on her. She was expecting a reaction, and he did not fail her.

'I disgust you, don't I?'

'Yes,' she said crisply. 'You disgust me. Say, rather, the man I see before me now disgusts me, because I can't believe it's really you.'

'Who else? I make war, Catherine, and this is what war is! All war is like this, however much it hurts you to believe it. I'm doing no more than I've always done, what they all do: La Hire, Xaintrailles and all the rest you are so fond of! What do you think those two are doing at Gisors this very moment?'

'They are fighting the English! They're fighting the enemy ...'

'And so am I! The English? Where do you think they are, then? On our borders? No, ten leagues from here, at Montigny le Roy, where your Duke Philippe takes care to leave them unmolested, but where at this very moment the Seigneur de la Suze, René de Rais, is laying siege to them.'

'René de Rais? The brother of ...'

'Of Gilles, the monster of the blue beard, yes! But René is a goodly knight and my brother in arms, even if he does resort to methods you'd not like any more than mine! As for me, I fight against Burgundy – because Burgundy is the worst of all our foes!'

'Our foes, you say? What foes? Whose foes?'

'The King's – and France's! Were you so much in love with the Treaty of Arras, that shameful rag that bound the King to ask Philippe's pardon and released the Duke even from the duty of paying homage? Not one of us accepted it, or ever shall! We want none of peace at that price! And this is Burgundy!'

'Burgundy? Yes, indeed it is, but I have seen no walls, no men-at-arms or engines of war! I have seen only old men, women and children murdered, unarmed men put to the torture to make them disgorge their wealth!'

'War knows neither age nor gender! The enemy is all one! Strike at those who supply the army and you destroy it as effectively as if you cut them down in battle!'

They were quarrelling again, violently, each feeding it with their resentment and their own beliefs. Faced with the ruthless feudal lord, accustomed to despise almost without exception the countless ants of city and countryside, Catherine found herself solidly on the side of the suffering people, oppressed and bled white: she was one of them, and not the least ill-used.

'Come, it's not the first time I've seen war, since you claim this is one! I know it's horrible. But not like this! What has changed you, Arnaud? You were valiant, stern, ruthless sometimes, but you were never cruel or ignoble! Don't you remember what you once were – what you all were when you followed Joan the Maid?'

At the name, his face took on a look of joy, suddenly, almost of release.

'Joan? But I follow her still! Indeed, I serve her now better than I have ever done, for I have seen her – and she has given me her blessing!'

Catherine stared at him in amazement.

'What are you saying …? Joan, you have seen Joan?'

'Yes, alive! And beautiful and hearty and stronger than ever! I have seen her, I tell you! I saw her when I joined Robert at Neufchâteau. She had just come from La Grange aux Hornes, not far from St Privey. There were two men with her, and all the lords of those parts were flocking to see her.'

Catherine shrugged impatiently. It was bad enough that her husband had become like a wild beast without adding imbecility to his failings.

'I began to think you must be right. You are going mad! Joan alive! How could that possibly be?'

'I tell you I have seen her,' he said stubbornly.

'You have seen her? And I suppose you didn't see her at the stake in Rouen when the executioner fanned aside the flames so that all the world might see that it was truly her? For my part, it's not something I shall ever forget! Her poor body, stripped naked by the fire, all raw and bleeding! And her face, with the eyes closed, already lifeless – but untouched! I suppose that wasn't her?'

'It was someone else. A girl who looked like her. They got her away.'

'How? By the tunnel under Saint-Maclou where you were waiting for her, or by some tunnel in the prison itself, where the English kept a constant watch on her? If anyone had been able to get Joan away, it would have been us who were on the spot, with all the help it was possible for anyone to have! It's you, Arnaud, who have been taken in by a resemblance.'

'That's not true! Joan's brothers, the Seigneurs du Lys, recognised her also.'

'Those two!' Catherine said scornfully. 'They'd recognise anyone so that the blessings that came to them through their sister might continue to fall! Those wretched creatures were scrubbed clean, ennobled and made rich while poor Joan perished in the fire! Why weren't they at Rouen, with us, trying to save her? I don't believe a word of their recognising her! As for you, you're like all the others, yearning so much to see her again that you fall for the slightest resemblance!'

'It was her to the life! I knew her well!'

'And so did I know her well. And I'd go to the stake if need be swearing that I saw, with my own eyes, Joan of Arc die in the fire!' Then, suddenly recalling the words Arnaud had used a moment before, she added: 'But what was it you said just now? You told me you were serving her? And better than ever? That she gave you her blessing …? So it's with her blessing that you're burning and plundering and torturing, and turning God's house into a stable and a bawdy house? And you dare to tell me this imposter is Joan?'

'We are avenging her! Burgundy gave her up and Burgundy must pay!'

'You poor fool!' Catherine cried, beside herself. 'When did you ever see Joan call for vengeance? Urging men-at-arms to kill poor folk? And, if you're so set on vengeance, why don't you go and make war on Jean of Luxembourg? He's the one who gave her up, and he even refused to sign the Treaty of Arras! You've a real enemy there! But he's a hard nut, Luxembourg! He has power! And strong castles, and soldiers who know how to fight! It's not as easy as slaughtering poor, defenceless peasants! Oh, she's a beauty, is this Maid you've found yourselves! And you're a splendid bunch of heroes! '

'When you see her, you'll think differently. And, by the way …' Arnaud turned to his wife, an arrested look in his eyes. The thought that had just occurred to him was a perfectly simple and natural one but, strange to say, caught up as he had been in the heat of the argument, it had not crossed his mind before.

'By the way, what?'

'Would you mind telling me what you are doing here? Where were you going?'

Arnaud's voice had taken on a deceptive silkiness, but Catherine did not heed the warning.

'I told you. I am going to my mother. She is dying.'

'In – Dijon, is that?'

'No. She is not there. My uncle has taken some hussy to wife, and my mother was obliged to leave his house. Ermengarde gave her a home. I thought I had told you already. She is at Châteauvillain.'

'At Châteauvillain? Is that so …? Well, you know, my dear, I could have sworn it!'

His eyes had narrowed so that he looked like a cat watching a mouse in the instant before it springs. He was smiling, his lips drawn backwards in his unshaven face, giving him a ferocious look.

Catherine stared at him in bewilderment and incomprehension.

'What is it you could have sworn?'

He moved suddenly like an uncoiled spring and grasped her by the throat.

'Yes, I could have sworn it! And I know now that you're a strumpet! And worse than all the rest! Do you think I don't know who is waiting for you at

Châteauvillain? Who it is you're going to meet? Eh?'

'Let me go!' Catherine gasped, fighting for breath. 'You – you're hurting me! I can't breathe …'

'You won't get round me this time, damn you. When I think that I nearly fell for your explanations and your tears, when I think that I was blaming myself – that I was ashamed, yes, ashamed! And all the time you were talking away, lashing me with your scorn, and with just one idea in that dirty, stubborn little head of yours, to pull the wool over my eyes so that you could be off to join your lover!'

'My – my lover?' Catherine croaked. 'But – what …'

'The one and only – Duke Philippe himself, who was seen arriving five days ago in secret with a small escort to visit that old bawd Ermengarde, the devil damn her! Eh? What do you say to that …? You see, I know a thing or two as well!'

Barely conscious and struggling desperately for air, Catherine hung limply between the hands, which were shaking her, as she made no more effort to defend herself than a rag doll. The answer to Montsalvy's question came from a small voice that spoke up clearly, if somewhat quaveringly, behind his back.

'I say you lie, Messire Arnaud. The Duke of Burgundy is not here, and you are strangling your lady wife!'

Arnaud's hands relaxed involuntarily, and Catherine, released, collapsed onto the damp earth floor. Arnaud turned to look at the group now standing in the doorway of the barn. It consisted of Bérenger and a red-haired youth, both bound and soaked to the skin, and four men-at-arms holding them.

It was the page who had spoken, driven to it by an indignation stronger than the terror that his lord had always inspired in him.

Arnaud folded his arms and regarded the group with an astonishment he did not attempt to conceal.

'Young Roquemaurel! What are you doing here, my lad?'

The boy put up his head proudly as he answered: 'When you went away, Seigneur Comte, I was already Dame Catherine's page. I am so still, and I have followed her wherever she has gone, to serve and aid her as best I could. But you, Messire – are you still the man she loved so deeply?'

Beneath the clear, childish gaze, Arnaud blushed and looked away. The boy had power to make him feel uncomfortable, and the disappointment and reproach that he read so clearly on the tired young face stung him.

'Mind your own business,' he growled. 'Boys should not meddle in the affairs of grown men and women.'

He nodded at Gauthier, who had not spoken so far, and added: 'Who's this?'

The student drew himself up, meeting the captain's eye challengingly, and said with a defiant curl of his lip: 'Gauthier de Chazay, esquire in the service of the Countess of Montsalvy, may God preserve her from all evil and deliver her out of the hands of base cowards who dare to lay rough hands on her!'

Arnaud's hand caught the younger man a blow on the cheek that made him stagger.

'Hold your tongue if you value your life, my lad! If you are in her service, you are thereby also in mine. I am the Count of Montsalvy, and I am quite within my rights to beat my wife.'

'You – her husband?' He turned incredulously to look at Bérenger, who, seeing that Catherine had not risen, was now weeping with mingled grief, rage and helplessness. The page uttered a heartbroken sob.

'It's quite true …! All too true! And now – he's killed her! My poor lady – so good – and gentle – and lovely …'

'That will do!' roared Arnaud who, however, had gone down on his knees beside his wife and was studying her with more anxiety than he cared to show. 'She is not dead. She is still breathing … Bring me some water!'

'Untie me!' Gauthier said. 'I can revive her.'

Montsalvy nodded to the men to cut the two boys' bonds, and Gauthier came forward and knelt by the unconscious woman, examining her bruised and swollen neck.

'Only just in time! Another moment and she would have been past help.'

His fingers moved lightly over the bruised flesh while he assured himself that nothing in that slender neck was broken. Then he felt in Catherine's purse and brought out the little crystal phial and unstoppered it.

Arnaud was watching him with interest.

'You're an odd kind of squire! Are you a physician, friend?'

'I was a student when Dame Catherine rescued me from a tight corner and took me into her service. Medicine interested me more than anything else, but that's not to say I was wild about it … Look, she's coming round!'

Catherine had opened her eyes. The sight of her husband's grim face bent over her brought a moan of terror to her lips, and she shrank away. He was on his feet in an instant, the anger and resentment back on his face. But she, too, had risen, recollection of her purpose returning with her strength.

'My mother is dying.' She brought out the words with difficulty. 'I must go to Châteauvillain.'

Her voice was strangely harsh, emerging agonisingly from her strangulated vocal cords at the cost of an immense effort.

Arnaud's fists tightened.

'No. You are not going to Duke Philippe. I shall find a way to stop you! That Châteauvillain woman has set a trap for you – if indeed you have not planned this between you.'

'The duke … is not there! I know! He is at St Omer where … even now he is to meet … the Constable!'

'Lies! He is there! He has been seen!'

'There must be some mistake. He is preparing to lay siege to Calais. What should he be doing here?'

'Waiting for you! The Châteauvillain woman hates me. She must have arranged all this to restore herself to favour. Things have gone ill with her since her son has gone to serve the Duke of Bourbon! It would be very like her!'

Catherine's face twisted with pain. She leaned heavily on Gauthier's and Bérenger's supporting arms and forced herself to stand erect and meet her husband's eyes.

'I am going, whatever you may say,' she said, adding again, 'My mother is dying! Remember your own!'

Unable any longer to bear the sight of the weak, dishevelled woman proclaiming in that terrible voice her right to go to her mother, a woman whose every glance was a reproach and an accusation, Arnaud de Montsalvy turned and fled.

A gust of wind and rain blew in through the wide open door of the barn, making the wisps of straw on the ground lift and swirl. But already the storm was passing over and leaving behind the collapsed roofs and still-smoking ruins of what had once been a village.

Dawn came like a thief, poking its grey fingers through the ramshackle timbers of the barn.

Catherine sat up in the straw, where she had slept for a few hours like an exhausted animal. Her whole body ached, and the skin of her face felt drawn where the tears had dried on it. She felt weak and vulnerable, but it was only her body that had suffered, for her spirit, lifted out of its comfortable rut by the terror of those last hours and by the appalling shock she had experienced, was already eager for the fray.

If she died for it, she would not yield to the demands and the unjust suspicions of a man whom she had loved past all the limits of endurance and in whom she now discovered a tyrant and a brute capable of giving free rein to his worst instincts! Even if Arnaud were to kill her for it, she would proclaim to her last breath her right to perform the ultimate duty of love toward the woman who had given her birth ...

The light was growing stronger and, on the other side of the barn, she was able to make out the sleeping forms of Gauthier and Bérenger, lying huddled together against the cold. The elder lad's cheek was marked by a bloody streak, a reminder of the blow Arnaud had dealt him, but apart from that both faces shared, in sleep, the same look of youth and delicacy. And yet, to her, they had surely been the best and most faithful of companions.

Outside, a watchman sounded his horn. It must be still raining, because trickles of water were finding their way through the timbers of the barn, and from somewhere came the gurgle of a gutter overflowing.

Catherine got up, shook the creases from her clothes as best she could and went to dip her handkerchief in a puddle, taking care not to disturb the layer of mud at the bottom. When she had dabbed her face with it, she combed out her hair, braided it after a fashion and tucked it into her silken hood.

She was hungry and thirsty, but worst of all was the sense of desolation that possessed her. She felt utterly alone, in spite of the presence of the two boys sleeping nearby, alone despite the fact that her husband, the man who had sworn faithfully to love and cherish her, was only a few yards away. But there was a gulf between them now, an abyss she dared not even contemplate, because the depth of it made her giddy.

People were moving about outside. There was a clatter of mailed feet on the ground, followed by voices, laughter and a whinnying of horses. Men came in at last, backs bent against the rain. Catherine recognised Le Boiteux and Cornisse.

'Oh, so you're awake!' said the former, holding out a pitcher and a chunk of bread, while his companion, who carried similar provisions, went across to wake the boys.

'Here, drink some of this! Then come with me. You can stow the bread in your pouch and eat it on the way.'

Catherine took the bread and swallowed a deep draught of the water. It was cool and sweet. Then, after a glance at her youthful companions, who were staggering to their feet, their eyes still heavy with sleep, she said, addressing her words to the Skinner: 'Where are we going? Where is – your captain?'

'He's waiting outside. So bestir yourselves. He's not a patient man.'

'I know that. But you've not answered my question. Where are we going?'

'Back. Back to Châteauvillain, I mean. We came here only on a foraging expedition. The Damoiseau is waiting.'

Bérenger came toward them, already gnawing at his bread, a glimmer of hope in his eyes.

'To Châteauvillain? Messire Arnaud is going to let us go there?'

'He has no choice,' Catherine answered dryly. 'He does as he's told. Or so it seems.' There was a world of anger, contempt and humiliation in those few words. She picked up her riding cloak and slung it round her shoulders. 'I am ready,' she said.

'Come, then. Your horses are outside.'

They left the barn. Rain was still falling. In the single village street, or what was left of it, the company of Skinners was drawn up in a long line like a scaly, iron snake, still half-asleep. Waiting …

Le Boiteux cupped his hands, awkwardly, to assist Catherine into the saddle, but she disdained his help. Placing the toe of one boot in the stirrup, she mounted easily. Taking a firm grip of the reins, she turned her head to look for Gauthier and Bérenger, but they were already waiting, sitting on their horses rigidly, with a curiously blank look in their eyes.

'Go on. I will follow,' Catherine said to Le Boiteux.

They moved up the column. Holding herself erect, with her head high and a scornful curve to her lips, Catherine showed the long line of men an impassive profile. She would not look at the pitiful remains beyond the line. She would not look at the ferocious faces of the men-at-arms or at the spoils that were everywhere to be seen. She would not look at the bodies, piled into a rough heap by the roadside shrine to rot there, perhaps to breed plague or some other scourge as soon as the hot weather came again. She would not look either at the herds penned in the entrance to a field where, among the baggage animals, a handful of chained men stood with bowed heads, wretched human cattle, enlisted by force, who must now become more savage than the wolves or be devoured.

Right at the end, ready to take the head of the column, Arnaud, too, was waiting.

Armed cap-à-pie, motionless on his black charger, he sat silent and withdrawn, revealing nothing of himself beyond the two-thirds of his face that showed beneath the raised visor of his uncrested helm.

As Catherine came up with him, their eyes met, but no word passed between them. But one glance had been enough to show Catherine that her husband was very pale, with deep black rings under his eyes, but that he had shaved. Possibly with a somewhat makeshift implement, to judge from the blood still oozing from the cuts on his face.

They moved off in a north-westerly direction along a narrow road in which the rain had left deep, muddy holes. The country lay sodden under a grey sky. It looked utterly dead. Nowhere was there rising from a chimney the slender column of smoke that would have betrayed a sign of life. Not even a bird sang or a frog croaked. Nothing stirred. The only sound was that of the horses' hooves and the heavy, iron tread of marching men. Sated and still drunk with the previous night's slaughter, the Skinners were making heavy weather of the march.

They rode for a long time in silence. They went at a foot pace on account of the cattle, which could move no faster. The day was heavy, hot and humid. The air was stifling, for the high winds of the night before had dropped. It was like travelling through a waterlogged sponge. In a little while, they entered the forest, and the atmosphere grew more oppressive than ever. Catherine felt weary in body and sick in mind. She kept her eyes on the road ahead, without ever looking at Arnaud. Now and then, looking down, she caught sight of his mailed thigh and knee joint, but they were as stiff and empty-looking as the suits of armour in the armoury at Montsalvy. It was like a bad dream that clung and would not be cast off.

Could this man now riding like a shadow at her side really be the same as he who, for so long now, had been her whole reason for living? Was this the man who had held her in his arms, had clung to her in a delirium of love, and was the father of her children?

He was there, close beside her, and yet far more inaccessible than when huge distances and the walls of the Bastille had lain between them, for then at least Catherine had been able to believe that their hearts were as one. What had happened? There was some mystery there that was beyond her travel-weary mind to unravel. A man did not change so much and in so short a time without some outside agency, or person or event, to work the change.

Certainly, the ghastly night just past had shown her that she did not know him; or rather that she knew little of this world of men at war.

For all her adventures, she still had a lot to learn about the magnificent captains, so valiant in battle, who ever since her childhood had passed before her wondering eyes like a cheerful pageant painted on a wall. She knew now that they were capable of both the best and the worst, that they were all too rarely the defenders of the widow and the orphan, unless these belonged to their own caste, and that their attitude to the common people, the great mass of the kingdom, was very much that which had existed in ancient Rome between the patricians and their slaves. She could still hear Arnaud's voice in the ill-lit barn, objecting: 'What do you think those two are doing at ... this very moment ...?'

What mattered was to live, at all costs, and live well if possible; to feed the men and pay their wages and let them slake their instincts without troubling overmuch what that might cost in terms of human misery and pain! And yet, for his own people, the people of Montsalvy, Arnaud was ready to shed the last drop of his blood. They were his: there lay the difference ...

So, how had it happened? It was not, it could not be the outcome of his arrest for the murder of Legoix, not even if Gonnet's lies had led him to believe his death was imminent.

When, once before, the power of the Montsalvys had been broken by order of the King, at the instigation of La Trémoille, Arnaud had not reacted by taking to the roads ... Was it, then, this woman, this adventuress who, aided by some evident physical likeness, was daring to pass herself off as Joan of Arc? When he had talked of her, it was with a kind of fanatical faith, and with a light in his eyes that was like love. Yes, that was it: love! This creature had only to appear, it seemed, to draw the heart of Arnaud de Montsalvy to herself and turn him into another man, something brutal and bloodthirsty.

'She's a witch!' Catherine raged inwardly. 'She must be a witch, and she deserves nothing better than a pyre of logs and faggots in a village square!'

Of course, there was an element of jealousy also. Arnaud's brutal reaction when he had found himself unexpectedly face to face with his wife had left her in no doubt that it was so. He could have killed her because he believed her guilty, and that said little for the trust he had in her. Then, just when she had succeeded in convincing him of her innocence, he had to bring up this absurd tale about Duke Philippe! Was there really any likelihood that he could be at Châteauvillain, when there were such pressing affairs to keep him in the north? If it were a matter of the workings of Ermengarde's mind alone, the thing was possible. She had never liked Arnaud and had always done everything humanly possible to throw Catherine back into Philippe's arms. The business of the hospice at Roncevaux had not yet faded from Catherine's memory. Ermengarde was an obstinate woman, capable of going to great lengths to carry her own point of view; but not to the point where she could make use of something as tragic as a mother's death to draw Catherine into a snare. Unless it were all true.

While she was turning these thoughts over and over in her mind, the journey was nearing its end. Even so, it was almost midday before the towers of Châteauvillain rose before them as they rounded a bend, looming out of the river mists in its lordly eminence, with the village clustering about its feet. In fact, the little township was divided from the castle by a loop of the Aujon, and was defended by walls of no great height that, in the event of an attack, would offer nothing like the security of the formidable curtain walls about the seigneurial keep.

Catherine recognised the grey walls, the dark wooden hoardings and the tall pepperpot towers, their roofs of blue slate gleaming from the rain. It was all just as it used to be, and high up on the keep the red banner of Châteauvillain hung limp and wet. But that was only on the surface, for all along the river bank, by the little Roman bridge, a camp had sprung up, with its faded tents and its cooking fires; a camp that was like as two peas to the one the Apchiers had made before Montsalvy, except for the banner.

This one was a lion argent crowned or rampant on a field azure and flanked by crosslets fitchy – or, the arms of Sarrebrück. Catherine greeted them with a sardonic smile, for although the colours might change, the hearts of men remained curiously alike. If, that was, one could talk of hearts under the circumstances!

At first sight, the village seemed not to have suffered from the Skinners. All the houses were still standing and undamaged. But as they came nearer, Catherine saw that all the people had vanished. The figures that appeared in the doorways as the company rode up were all soldiers who, moreover, had the air of being very much at home there.

The inhabitants of Châteauvillain must have fled in time, for there was not a single corpse to be seen anywhere, and the trees bore only leaves, unmixed with any more sinister fruit. Most probably they had been flushed out by the arrival of the *routiers* and had gone to earth in the woods, or else – and this was the more likely – had sought refuge in the castle, the massive bulk of which reared up on its rocky spur as if mocking the tribe of vicious ants that crawled about its feet.

The company's arrival was greeted with enthusiasm by the *routiers* on account of the booty it brought with it. The Damoiseau's men came running, baying a welcome larded with oaths and obscenities to which the newcomers were not slow to respond in kind. Indeed, no sooner were they inside the place than they broke ranks and sought out their particular cronies, to launch into tales of their hideous exploits, told with much boasting and loud, braying laughter and triumphant back-slapping, interrupted only by frequent calls for drink.

Their leader, however, seemed barely conscious that they had arrived. He rode on steadily, in taciturn silence, his gaze fixed straight between his horse's ears, indifferent to the uproar that greeted his return, locked in his own silent withdrawal.

Only a handful of the riders, taking their cue from him, followed after, hemming in the mounts of Catherine, Gauthier and Bérenger as if to prevent them escaping.

In this way, they came to the bridge, the mossy arch of which spanned the swift-flowing current where the weeds streamed out like long, green hair. The castle rose above them like a cliff. It gave no sign of life. Mute, dark and close as a tomb behind the massive seal of its oaken drawbridge, it had the formidable dignity of a god asleep.

Then Arnaud, who had not opened his lips throughout the journey, rode up to Catherine. He was even paler than when they had set out, and his face, beneath the shadow of his helm, was grey as a ghost's. His gauntleted hand pointed to the silent castle.

'There is the object of your journey,' he said without expression. 'There is where you are expected. And there is where we part …'

Startled, she turned her head sharply to look at him. But he was not looking at her, and she saw only an obstinate profile, set hard, and the bitterness about his mouth, which was drawn into a tight, thin line.

'What do you mean?' she asked dully.

'That the time has come for you to choose.'

'To choose?'

'Yes, between your past and present life. Either you renounce your purpose to enter that castle, or you renounce your place at my side – forever!'

She was frightened, appalled by the prospect that had opened so suddenly before her and by this choice that nothing, in her eyes, appeared to justify.

'You are mad,' she cried. 'You can't ask that of me! You have no right!'

'I have every right where you are concerned. Just now, you are my wife!'

'You have no right to stop me seeing my mother for the last time when she is dying, to pay my last respects to her.'

'No, so long as it is to see your mother. But I know it is no such thing. It is not she who awaits you. It is your lover.'

'It's not true! I swear to you it's not true! My God! How can I make you understand? How can I convince you? Listen, let me go inside, only go inside and kiss her once more, for the last time ... After that, I swear to you on my children that I will come out again.'

For the first time, he looked at her. His eyes rested on her for a moment, and the tragic emptiness of them made Catherine afraid. He shrugged wearily.

'You may mean what you say. But I know that if you go in there, you will not come out again. They've gone to too much trouble to get you this far. They'll not let you go!'

'Come with me, then! After all, she is dying, and you are her son, too, although you might not be very proud of it. You treated her kindly once, with courtesy and even affection. She would be doubly happy to see us together. Why won't you come with me and bid her a last farewell?'

She had warmed to the idea. A faint flush had mounted to her pale cheeks, and her eyes were shining with hope. But Arnaud only laughed, and it was the harshest, most tragic laugh imaginable.

'Now, Catherine, use your head! Where are your wits? I go in with you, when for three days we have been besieging this castle in order to take the fox in the trap? Are you jesting? I'd not come out again alive. It would be too good an opportunity for Philippe: to hold the wife and rid himself of the husband!'

'You're mad! ' she groaned. 'I swear to you you're mad! Duke Philippe is not there, I'm certain! He can't be ...'

'Nevertheless, he is.' The words were spoken in a cool, assured voice by a man who had just ridden up beside Arnaud.

From his appearance, even more than from the coat of arms emblazoned on his surcoat, Catherine recognised the Damoiseau de Commercy.

He was astride a great, roan stallion, and he wore no helm. His handsome head was bare and crowned with hair as fine and as golden as Catherine's own. He had large blue eyes, shaded by improbably long eyelashes, a delicate, mobile mouth, just now parted a little over very white teeth in an engaging smile that was belied by the calculating hardness of his gaze. His whole elegant person was scented faintly with musk and contrasted strikingly with the plain, warlike accoutrements of the Lord of Montsalvy, who looked, beside the fair Robert, more than ever rough and soldierly, like some rude mercenary smelling of goose-grease and horsedung.

Yet of the two, it was the young man of almost feminine beauty who was the more dangerous and the more to be feared. Chewing idly on a clove, as was his habit to sweeten his breath, the Damoiseau waved the butt of his gilded riding crop in Catherine's direction.

'Ravishing!' he said appreciatively. 'Horribly dirty, but ravishing … Who is she?'

'My wife,' Arnaud retorted, in a curt tone that could by no stretch of the imagination be termed an introduction.

Robert's big eyes opened inordinately wide.

'Well, well! How delightful. And – er – what might such a fair and noble dame be doing in this mudbath?'

For all his elegance and charm, Catherine felt in no way drawn to the Damoiseau. Indeed, the feeling he inspired in her was chiefly a kind of revulsion mingled with loathing. But for him, Arnaud would probably have gone to seek refuge at Montsalvy and she herself would not now be caught in this hideous coil. So it was in a very stiff tone that she answered him.

'My mother lies dying in the castle there, which I am told I may not enter and which you yourself are apparently besieging in defiance of all the laws!'

'Besieging? And what gave you the notion this was a siege, gracious lady? Do you see here any engines of war, any sappers at work, any ladders or weapons of war? I am not even wearing a helmet. No, we are merely sitting down beside this charming stream and – er – waiting.'

'What for?'

'For Duke Philippe to make up his mind to come out, of course; for, to revert to what I was saying when I took it upon myself to interrupt your conversation, the Duke is there, I am quite sure.'

Catherine shrugged and curled her lip disdainfully.

'You are daydreaming, my lord count. But, just supposing he is there, which I do not at all believe, you should know that when he became aware that you were staying here, he would scarcely have remained. Châteauvillain, like many of its kind, possesses an underground exit, and by now the Duke must be far away.'

'The castle does in fact possess two underground tunnels, fair lady,' Sarrebrück answered, unperturbed. 'Fortunately, we know where both come out and have naturally placed a guard on them.'

'How do you know?'

The Damoiseau smiled and stroked his horse's neck. His voice became, if possible, even silkier than before.

'You can have no idea of the effectiveness of a nice, bright fire – or of a little lead judiciously employed. In that way, it is possible to obtain all the information one requires.'

Catherine's spine shivered with disgust. Fire! Again ... The image of the previous night was still too vivid in her mind for her to be able to recall it without pain. Gritting her teeth to keep herself from screaming her revulsion at the youth whose extraordinary beauty repelled her as much as if he had been the most hideous of monsters, she looked from one to the other of the two men.

'You are monsters, both of you! In you, my lord count, I am not surprised, for your unhappy deeds are well known, but my husband ...'

'Enough!' Arnaud broke in harshly, having so far appeared to pay little attention to this passage of arms between his wife and his colleague. 'We need not go over that again. You have heard what we have told you, Catherine. The Duke is there. What are you going to do?'

She was silent for a moment, searching desperately for the chink in his armour, the slightest crack through which it might be possible for her to reach a heart so strangely sealed against her. But he was like a wall, locked up in his bitter jealousy and rancour even more closely than inside his armour.

She gave an anguished sigh and murmured: 'I implore you! Let me go in, if only for ten minutes! On my soul's salvation and our children's lives, I swear to you that I will not stay longer. Ten minutes, Arnaud, and not one more ... and I ask those only for my mother's sake. And afterwards I will turn my back forever on this land of Burgundy and we will go home together.'

But he was not looking at her, refusing to meet those beautiful, beseeching eyes that possibly held more power over him still than he was willing to admit.

'I am not going back to Montsalvy now. I have work to do and I am needed here. The Maid ...'

'The devil fly away with the witch and with this madness of yours!' Catherine burst out, with a fresh surge of anger. 'You will lose everything, rank, honour, even your life perhaps and your immortal soul, to follow an adventuress who is bound to end on the scaffold! Be yourself again, I implore you! You have a safe conduct. Go to the Queen ... I

'When I go to the Queen, Philippe of Burgundy's head shall be my safe conduct. And as for you ...'

He did not finish, for at that moment the silent castle came alive. In the twinkling of an eye, the towers sprouted a crown of archers and crossbowmen while, with a noise like the crack of doom, the great drawbridge came crashing down.

Some fifty horsemen poured out from within the fortress, waving lighted torches.

'To me! Sarrebrück!' the Damoiseau yelled, drawing his long sword, while Arnaud de Montsalvy swung the heavy mace that hung at his saddle bow and was already thundering to meet the enemy, his men at his heels.

Catherine and the two boys found themselves pushed back against a wall. Bérenger tugged at his mistress's hand.

'Come away, Dame Catherine. Please, let's fly! Messire Arnaud is mad, for sure, and he will never let you enter the castle! Come away! Think of the children, Michel and Isabelle – they need you!'

'Besides,' Gauthier added, 'you might be fighting for nothing, my lady! Your poor mother might be buried by now. If so, she sees you from Paradise and knows that you tried to go to her. Bérenger is right. You must not stay here!'

But Catherine was incapable of movement. She could only stare in fascination at the battle taking place before her eyes. Hemmed in by four attackers, Arnaud was fighting like a demon. A mighty stroke from a mace had shattered his helm and he, too, was now fighting bareheaded, roused to madness by the pain of the blow.

It was the first time she had seen him fight, except for their encounter with the bandits of the sierras while escaping from Granada, and some of her old admiration revived. There was no doubt about the man's valour. Far from avoiding battle or seeking to get in a calculated stroke not strictly in accordance with the laws of chivalry, he rushed openly straight at the enemy. His mace whirled about him, beating down the steel-clad wraiths; but if ever in the course of the combat one of his adversaries chanced to turn his back on him, he would refrain from striking.

The Damoiseau also fought well. From time to time he glanced uneasily at his camp, part of which was burning, set alight by the torches flung by the men from the castle, but he still managed to deal some shrewd blows with his battleaxe. Moreover, the fight was less uneven now than it had been to start with. The Damoiseau's cries had alerted those of his men who were off duty and they were now hurrying to the bridge, their numbers growing visibly.

Seeing that they would have to deal with strong opposition, the knights of Châteauvillain were falling back in good order up the slope to the castle, impelled by their horses' powerful hocks and covered from pursuit by the watchers on the battlements.

'Enough!' the Damoiseau cried. 'Fall back! We must put out the fire!'

Arnaud, however, either could not or would not hear. Instead, he hurled himself in pursuit of the retreating horsemen, galloped over the bridge and flung himself at the slope as though drawn by the tall gateway that yawned above him, leading to the lair in which he believed his enemy lay concealed.

A single mad idea had stubborn hold of his fevered brain: to reach the hated Burgundian by any means. His hatred had the bitter taste of stale beer or bad wine. It could be satisfied only by the blood of one or other of them.

'Come out! Philippe of Burgundy!' he bellowed. 'Come out and let me cross swords with you at last. Traitor! Lecher! Seducer!'

The rage that drove him on had no limits now. In his mind there could be no more doubt that the Duke was there within the walls; for, of those engaged in the foray, the greater number had borne the highly recognisable quarterings of the Burgundian arms.

Catherine had also recognised Philippe's arms, and a doubt had entered her mind. Was it possible these men were right? That Ermengarde had set this shameful snare for her? Everything she knew of her old friend and her intransigent sense of honour cried out against such a thought; but, on the other hand, the Countess of Châteauvillain had always longed to restore her young friend to the affections of a prince whom she loved as if he were her own son.

From the shelter of the substantial buttress of a small chapel, from which she automatically resisted the attempts of her two youthful companions to dislodge her, she watched Arnaud's crazy ride in agony. She saw his horse rear up under rowelling spurs and almost fall with him upon the steep slope. That it recovered its balance was due only to the strength and skill of its rider. She heard his voice crying out, but the wind was against her and she could not understand the words he spoke.

'He's mad!' said the Damoiseau's voice beside her, still breathless from the heat of the battle. 'He'll get himself killed!'

She clutched instinctively at his arm.

'Don't let him go alone! Send men to help him, or he'll …'

She broke off with a cry of horror. The crossbowmen, perched high on the projecting turrets, were firing to arrest the madman's frenzied charge. Catherine saw her husband keel over slowly and fall like a stone. The horse was down also, but scrambled up again at once and galloped back down the road to the village, dragging Arnaud's lifeless body by one of his steel shoes, which was caught in the stirrup.

Catherine would have started forward, but the Damoiseau held her back. She cried out.

'Stop that horse! He'll be killed …'

'He's almost certainly dead already. And there are men still ready to fire up there.'

Crazed with anger, she hammered at his chest with her clenched fists, while he made no effort to defend himself.

'Coward! You're nothing but a coward!'

'I'll go,' a resolute voice said beside her.

Before she could stop him, Gauthier de Chazay had leaped forward. She saw him dash toward the bridge to meet the runaway horse. With a catlike bound, he sprang for the creature's head, got a grip on the bridle and pulled with all his might. The destrier did its best to throw him off, and dragged him along the river bank while he hung by his full weight from the leather traces until the additional burden slowed the horse down.

Then two men ran forward and held it, foaming and wild-eyed. The men-at-arms on the towers had stopped firing and were following the spectacle with interest.

Gauthier picked himself up, wiped his sweating forehead on his sleeve and made instantly for Arnaud. One of the soldiers had released his leg from the stirrup. It was broken and lay twisted at an unnatural angle.

Then Catherine, who had stood for a moment breathless and petrified, ran forward also and dropped on her knees in the dust beside her husband, uttering a heartrending cry and struggling not to give way to dizziness at the sight that met her eyes.

'Go away, Dame Catherine!' the student cried. 'Don't look ...!'

But it was impossible for her not to look at that broken body, with its face covered in blood and its terrible wounds. Arnaud had been struck by two crossbow bolts. One had pierced through his armour and the seam of his leather shirt and entered his right armpit. The other had struck the captain full in the face, below the left cheekbone, causing an extensive wound from which the shaft still protruded grotesquely.

'He's dead!' Catherine wailed. She crouched down with her head in her hands, not daring to touch that mutilated form.

'Not yet,' Gauthier said, 'but he's not far off!'

He had worked swiftly to detach one of the couters from the wounded man's arm and held it to his parted lips. A faint mist appeared on the burnished steel.

The young man looked down for a moment at the blood-stained figure, with a far from hopeful expression, and shook his head. His eyes, filled with pity, moved to rest on the sobbing woman huddled on the dusty ground at his side.

'We should have a priest,' he said quietly, 'if there are any left in this benighted land.'

'There's a monastery church not far from here,' the Damoiseau said, coming up to them. 'But before we could drag one of those shivering rats out of their hole, Montsalvy would be past needing him! All we can do is to carry him inside the chapel. At least he can die before the altar ... Ho there! Four men and a stretcher – anything will do!'

Dead! Past help! The words struck like knives through the abyss of suffering into which Catherine had fallen. She stirred, lifting up a face that was no longer simply a mask of grief and clutching at Gauthier as he tried to raise her.

'I won't let him die! I won't! He can't! It mustn't end like this between us, in hatred and anger! God cannot do that to me! He is mine – only mine! I've spent my whole life for him, for love of him! It's not possible ...! Save him! Oh, please ... save him! I'm the one who's dying.'

Gauthier was staring at her disbelievingly. Never before had he beheld despair so naked and heartrending. He knew little enough about the lives of these two, but he knew that the man who now lay dying had subjected this woman to every possible form of earthly suffering, and more than ever in the hours just past.

Yet she seemed to have forgotten all that: the merciless contempt, the insults and the cruelty. She was there on her knees to him, Gauthier, with her face contorted with grief and so racked with anguish that she was on the point of blasphemy. Was this love? This torment, this fever and this madness?

He bent over her. 'Lady,' he asked softly, 'can you still love him after – after all that he has done to you?'

She stared at him dazedly, as if he had spoken in a foreign language.

'Love him …? I don't know … I know only that my body is broken, that my shoulder is on fire … that my head is in torment … that there is not a fibre of my being that does not bleed … I know I am dying!'

Her face was livid and her breath came so fast that he really believed that she was going to die there at his feet at the very moment when the man she loved beyond all reason, beyond what was humanly possible, should cease to live.

The soldiers had improvised a stretcher out of two long shields and placed the motionless form upon it. They began to carry him away.

Uttering a cry like a wounded animal, Catherine plunged after him, dragging herself on her knees, too deeply shaken even to get to her feet.

'Arnaud! Wait for me …'

In sudden rage, Gauthier grasped her under the arms and hauled her to her feet by main force. Then he hurried after Robert de Sarrebrück.

'Don't carry him into the chapel,' he said. 'Take him to a house, the best you have – where he may be cared for.'

The Damoiseau lifted his eyebrows.

'Cared for? You're wide of the mark, friend! He's dying.'

'I know; but, all the same, I mean to do what I can to the end – for her sake.'

'What is the use? He's already unconscious. To tend him is to torture him. Let him die in peace.'

'He doesn't deserve to die in peace!' Gauthier shouted. 'He deserves to die a thousand deaths, and so he shall if there is only a bare chance, one single chance of saving him for that unhappy woman!'

The Damoiseau shrugged, but he ordered his men to carry the wounded man to the house in which he and Montsalvy had set up their quarters. He did so with an ill grace, and had been on the point of refusing, for he was a man who saw no good in hindering the approach of death. Tending such a gravely wounded man was a waste of time, and very likely a sin, an offence against heaven, which had decreed that his hour had come. But the arrogant woman of a moment before had been transformed before his eyes into a pathetic image of Our Lady of Sorrows, and her ravaged face had made a deep impression on him. It had also given him an idea that required some thinking about.

Arnaud was still breathing when they reached the house the two leaders had made their own, which was, it went without saying, the best in the place, and formerly occupied by a ducal notary.

The soldiers laid him down on the big table in the kitchen. Catherine had followed like a walking puppet, revived only by Gauthier's promise to her to do everything to try to snatch her husband back from death. She set herself quite naturally to do whatever her esquire told her and to help him to the best of her ability.

While Gauthier, aided by Le Boiteux, who had volunteered his services, was unbuckling the various pieces of armour, taking infinite care as he removed the breastplate not to disturb the bolt that had pierced it, Catherine went to draw water from the well and set it to boil in a big cauldron on the fire that blazed brightly in the hearth. Then, taking from a coffer some of the linen that had been the pride of the notary's wife, she began tearing it into strips. Next, she hunted for oil and wine, in obedience to the self-appointed physician's instructions. It kept her hands occupied, and she found some comfort in the activity, which attached her to the world of the living; but all the time her eyes would keep turning anxiously to the big table where Gauthier was now gently exploring the injured man's scalp, trying to find out if it had sustained any fracture when he was dragged by his horse.

'It's quite incredible,' he said after a moment, 'but there seems to be none! He has a tough skull!'

'The toughest of any I know,' Le Boiteux assured him. 'I tell you, lad, I've seen him hurl himself at an oak door and go right through it without so much as a scratch! He's an Auvergnat! Like me!'

Catherine looked with astonishment at the man who had so terrified her the night before. It had not occurred to her that these dreadful ruffians could even have a Christian birthplace, own to a region, a village, a home. Such was their terror that only hell could have spawned them, and this specimen, with his brutish features, broken nose and prognathous jaw most certainly looked the part.

Almost without thinking, she asked: 'Are you from Auvergne? Whereabouts?'

'Saint-Flour. But it's long since I last saw it. I was 16 when I ran away to escape from that damned bishop who would have strung me up for killing a deer on his lands. Right now, boy! We'd better see about getting those dirty great bolts out of him,' he added, with what was almost a comradely tone for one possessing some skill in healing.

'I don't know if he can even bear the operation of extracting them. He is so weak ...'

Gauthier was cleaning the wounds with a little wine as he spoke. The one in the shoulder was not too serious, and he could tell, after feeling the shaft gently, that he would be able to remove it without too much trouble. But the terrible wound in the face filled him with dread, for the bolt was embedded as firmly as a rock. The bleeding had stopped, but the flesh showed livid where it had been cleaned.

Gauthier looked up with a face of anguish.

'I can't get it out,' he stammered. 'The point must be stuck in a bone.'

'If you can't get it out,' said the Damoiseau, who was standing with folded arms and one foot on a stool, watching grimly, 'he will be dead in an hour. No-one can live with a crossbow bolt in his face. It's a miracle he's still alive now! Don't tempt God!'

'What do you know of God?' Catherine said savagely. 'How dare you even speak His name? Gauthier, I beg you, please try ...'

'There's not much to get hold of ... and I can't tell if in taking it out I might not hasten his death.'

'He'll die either way! Try ...'

The young man crossed himself and then, after wrapping a piece of linen round the shaft, took a grip on the bolt and pulled, gently at first and then more strongly. But there was no movement. Only the wounded man gave a long groan.

The sweat was rolling in great drops down the youth's lean face.

'I can't,' he wailed. 'I can't ... I need ...' He left his patient abruptly and turned to the Damoiseau. 'You have a smithy here! Get me a pair of pincers, the longest you can find.'

'Pincers?' said Le Boiteux.

'Yes. As long as you can. Hurry!'

But the man had already gone. He was back in a few seconds with a pair of pincers not less than three feet long. Gauthier regarded them with approval, cleaned them with a cloth soaked in hot water, and then again with oil, to take off any particles of dust or iron filings that might be left. Then he returned to the wounded man and grasped him by the shoulders.

'Help me!' he commanded Le Boiteux. 'We must lay him on the floor.'

The Skinner did as he was told, without a word. Between them, they lifted Arnaud and laid him down on the warm flagstones before the fire. The big, half-naked body looked almost bloodless, already like one of the frozen stone figures that men carved piously on tombs.

Gauthier bent down and turned the head gently so that it rested on the undamaged cheek.

'Do you want me to hold him?' offered Le Boiteux.

'No. I need to get as much purchase as possible. Dame Catherine, turn round. You won't like what I'm going to do.'

'Whatever you do, I could not dislike it, since it is to save him. Forget I am here.'

He did not insist, but took a firm grip of the pincers and then set his foot deliberately on the wounded man's jaw.

This was more than Catherine had bargained for, and she crammed her fist into her mouth to stifle a cry. The pincers grated on the metal bolt.

'Pray!' Gauthier said in a low voice. 'I'm going to pull.'

Time seemed to stand still. Catherine had dropped to her knees at her husband's feet and was murmuring a continuous stream of prayers. The rest held their breath. The veins in Gauthier's temples stood out with the effort.

'It's coming!' he gasped.

The murderous weapon yielded all at once, bringing with it a thin trickle of blood, and everyone breathed out again. Instantly, Gauthier was on his knees, listening for the patient's heartbeats.

'It's slow and very weak,' he said, looking up with a face radiant with relief, 'but it is still beating!'

'You make a good surgeon, friend,' the Damoiseau complimented him. 'You shall serve me henceforth.'

'I serve the Lady of Montsalvy.'

Robert's handsome face smiled, one of his slow smiles that made him seem more formidable than in anger.

'You will not be offered a choice. Nor will the lady need you for much longer.'

'What do you mean?'

'Nothing. Go on. I suppose you mean to cauterise the wound?'

'No. He could not bear it. I have done everything possible to save his life, but even so, it hangs by a thread. I am only going to bandage him with oil of St John's wort, of which Dame Catherine has a phial in her baggage, and then splint his broken leg. After that, we can only pray with all our might that he will live. If God wills, he will be saved – but only if God wills.'

Catherine could tell from his tone that he placed little reliance on divine indulgence toward a man who had sinned against it so gravely, and that in spite of all that he had tried to do, he did not believe that Arnaud would recover.

The injured man had been carried back to the table, and the student began to bandage him as he had said. His deft hands moved lightly and gently over the tortured body, from which all consciousness had fled, leaving only the almost inaudible breathing that might cease at any moment.

Catherine sat on the end of a bench by her husband's lifeless head and, gently, with an infinite tenderness, stroked the short black locks emerging from the white bandages.

Ever since he had gone so far away, almost beyond recall, she had forgotten everything but her love. She would not think of anything but him. She had forgiven and forgotten everything else, even the dreadful scene she had beheld the night before. He was slipping through her fingers, and out of her arms, like some lovely dream that one strives in vain to recollect. Was he, after all, only a mirage, to vanish as soon as reached? Yet, before this day of wrath and disaster, there had been so many happy moments, so many wonderful nights! She would not, she could not even imagine a life without him … All the evil memories, all the horrors of the previous night, were lost in the overwhelming shadow of death.

She had almost died of grief when they had torn him from her and sent him to the lazar house at Calves, but she had recovered then because, in spite of everything, he was still alive. And that had made all the difference. For if he were to die now, in an hour or in the night, there would be nothing left for her, nothing to cling to in times of wretchedness, but a low mound of earth in some grass-grown churchyard or a slab of carved stone in a chapel, with a cross, the symbol of an eternal life in which, in her misery, Catherine could no longer bring herself to believe. What mattered a life after death, if in this world she could no longer hold him in her arms? The promises of the Church seemed suddenly empty and hollow.

Happiness, for Catherine, took the form of a man in his prime, his hair streaming in the breeze of a sunny morning, sitting on his great black horse and laughing at the clumsy efforts of little Michel as, his nose wrinkled in concentration, he endeavoured to mount the old grey donkey that browsed placidly among the daisies in the castle orchard. And now, that pleasant picture was ending here, on this bloodstained table, where the same man was breathing out his life.

Who could believe that the skies above Montsalvy would be as blue again, or the spring as happy when its lord was no more than a shade, a pair of gauntlets, an empty helm, golden spurs upon a black cushion and a great sword hung up forever on the armoury wall beside that of the last lord, Amaury?

Gauthier completed his patient work with a sigh. He tried to smile at Catherine over the still form, about which the pungency of aromatic oils had replaced the stale, sickening smell of blood, but could not manage it. The sight of that slight, tragic figure with its eyes like great shadowy pools was too much for him.

He wiped his hands on a scrap of linen and, with an automatic gesture, tossed back the lock of red hair, damp with sweat, that hung over his eyes. It was only then he noticed that his hands were shaking with relief now that the terrible nervous strain he had imposed on them was over.

He was simultaneously pleased with his work and furious at his own impotence, because in that moment he longed to possess all the knowledge in the world, so as to wrench from God the secrets of life and death. True, he had done all he could for the man whom he had detested from the first moment he saw him. But what miracle could he hope for, what medicine could he offer to this woman whose grief was a mute thing, like that of some gentle hind beside the body of her fallen mate?

'Take him away,' he said, and sighed again as he turned away. 'Put him to bed, if he has one. He'll be best there.'

Then, in a lower tone, he asked that someone should be sent to the nearby monastery to fetch a priest. He was watching Catherine's face to see the effect of his words, but she did not even tremble. Her hand continued to stroke her husband's hair.

When Le Boiteux and the other two men lifted Arnaud to carry him up to his chamber, she rose quite naturally to go with them, but the Damoiseau motioned her to remain.

'Stay, lady. I must speak with you.'

Catherine's eyes moved slowly in her set face. They were as hard as ice.

'I have nothing to say to you, and it is my wish to stay with my lord until the end.'

'He does not need you. They will fetch some monk or other to him, willy nilly, and for the rest, this lad here, who has been striving to mend him, can quite well watch over him. In any case, he'll not last the night out.'

'Precisely. I wish to be there …'

He was barring her way. She tried to slip round him, but those of his men who had come in to watch Gauthier operating were still there. Catherine found herself at the centre of a ring of grim, blank-faced automata ready to close in on her if she made the slightest attempt to struggle.

From beyond, she heard the stairs creaking as the men carried Arnaud's body up it, but she knew also that she could not fight, and she sat down again, apparently resigned.

'What do you want?'

'Merely to recall to your mind that this tragedy has caused you to forget another. What has become of your haste to go to your dying mother?'

Catherine did not answer at once. She dipped a piece of rag in water and dabbed at her burning face. What he said was true. Seeing her husband dying, she had forgotten all about her poor mother; but she had already abandoned her intention of crossing the threshold of Châteauvillain of her own accord when she had caught sight of the Burgundian arms.

'I cannot go,' she said at last. 'Arnaud was right, and you also, my lord count. It may be that Philippe is indeed here. If that is so, I will not go to bury my mother. I will have many masses said for her in our abbey at Montsalvy …'

He nodded, and it seemed to Catherine that he approved her decision. He turned away for a moment, and when he came back it was with a piece of parchment and an inkstand. He set these on the table before her.

He smoothed the sheet with his hand. 'Write,' he said.

'I, write? To whom?'

'To your friend, the Lady of Châteauvillain. Say to her that you have arrived in the village and were amazed at the welcome you received when you approached the castle. Add that you are travelling with your esquire and your chaplain – and that you would have them open a gate for you.'

'But I tell you I no longer wish to go! What is all this about? My esquire and my chaplain? You can't imagine that I …' She broke off suddenly, seeing in a flash what it was that this fiend intended. The esquire and the chaplain would be men of his own, who would infiltrate the castle in her company.

His mocking smile told her that she was right.

'Why, yes,' he said softly. 'Indeed I do imagine just that. When the devil puts a key to the castle into my hand, you wouldn't expect me to ignore it? Write, lady fair, and then we will see how your message is to reach them.'

'Never!'

She had risen so abruptly that the bench crashed over behind her. Her hand moved to brush away the parchment, but the Damoiseau reached out and pinned it to the table. His slim fingers were suddenly like steel.

'I said write! '

'And I said never! Base brigand! Do you think I am as rotten as you? You want me to betray my friend's house into your hands, the place where my mother lies dying? You have succeeded in bringing my husband down to your level, but he would never resort to so base and cowardly a means to get at his enemy!'

'That is possible, indeed most probable! Montsalvy was prone to absurd scruples that I have never understood. But he no longer has a say in the matter, and in a little while that Abbot of yours will be able to sing masses for him to his heart's content. So let us leave him out of it. You, however, are thoroughly alive, you are here, and you provide me with a means of entry up there. I mean to take it.'

'You mean to take it? Do you indeed? My will is as strong as yours, and you will not force me to write what I do not wish to write.'

'Are you so sure?'

'Quite sure.'

Very well … But I think you will change your mind.'

He snapped his fingers to summon one of his men who was standing near the door.

'Bring the page to me here,' he said in a level voice.

It was then that Catherine observed that Bérenger was not in the room. She realised that she had not seen him since they had picked up Arnaud along the river, although, wrapped in her grief, she had not thought of him before.

In any case, the page seemed to possess the faculty of appearing and vanishing at will, like the fairies, and with scarcely more fuss. But when she saw him come in with his hands bound behind his back and flanked by two men-at-arms, she understood something of the peril in which they both stood.

The boy was very pale, although he was doing his best to put on a brave face and biting his lips until they were white to keep them from trembling.

'Why have you bound him?' Catherine said with difficulty. 'What are you going to do to him?'

The Damoiseau walked over to the fire, poked it with a long rod of iron and threw on a few more logs and an armful of brushwood, which flared up at once. Tall, yellow flames shot up inside the dark chimney. He brushed a few twigs off his silken tunic and smiled pleasantly.

'Why, nothing … Nothing at all, if you are sensible.'

Catherine's throat was suddenly dry and her heart missed a beat. She had known as soon as she saw the child that she was to be coerced into some hideous bargain; but, ugly as the Damoiseau's reputation was, she still refused to believe that a man who bore the golden spurs could so dishonour himself.

'And if not?' she asked in a strained voice.

'Ah, well, then … we shall replace this big cauldron with that gridiron there and lay this youth upon it, having first basted him with oil so that he roasts nicely.'

Catherine's gasp of horror was lost in the howl of sheer terror that came from the wretched Bérenger. The page was writhing and struggling in his captors' arms in an agony of fear.

'You would not do that! Have you no fear of God?'

'God is a long way off, and the castle is here. I'll deal with the Almighty when the time comes. A few statues, an acre or two of land given to the Church and I shall be as pure and spotless as a new-born babe to enter into heaven. As to my threats, know that I never threaten what I will not perform. Strip the boy and oil him well!'

One of the men had his hand over Bérenger's mouth to stifle his cries, but the poor boy's eyes were rolling in his head with terror.

The thought of what would happen to him if she did not comply was more than Catherine could bear. The page could look for neither mercy nor pity from these hell-born blackguards. She refused to prolong his agony.

'Let him go,' she cried. 'I will write.'

Bérenger had swooned with terror. They carried him away, and Catherine seated herself at the improvised writing table.

14: The Man of God

The message had been sent. The way it had been sent was very simple: a trumpet blast that summoned a watcher to the battlements, a white cloth brandished on the point of a lance to indicate a wish to parley, and then the best archer in the company notched an arrow to his bow with the letter rolled tightly round its shaft and tied with a thin thread of hemp.

The man had some skill and a powerful weapon. The arrow sped easily over the battlements to fall on the wall walk. Since then a party of the Damoiseau's men had been waiting at a point beyond the drawbridge for an answer from the castle.

Catherine had been permitted to go to her husband's bedside. Having once got what he wanted, the Skinners' captain had no more reason to prevent her.

'You will be able to bid farewell to him and say a prayer for the repose of his soul,' he told her by way of consolation, bowing with exaggerated courtesy.

She made no answer. Still shuddering from the atrocious scene he had just forced on her, she had climbed the narrow stairs, passed through a room so full of booty that it resembled a merchant's strongroom and entered another chamber, bare of all furnishings except a bedstead big enough for four people, a coffer and three stools.

Very little light penetrated the oiled vellum that covered the windows, and a candle was already burning on one of the stools beside the bed where Arnaud lay.

But the first thing Catherine saw was Gauthier kneeling on the floor of small, red tiles and endeavouring to revive Bérenger, who had been released from his bonds and dumped there without ceremony. The boy's thin face had a waxen pallor, and he seemed to be breathing very unevenly.

The student turned as the door creaked under Catherine's hand. 'Let me have your flask of cordial,' he said. 'I can't bring him round. What did they do to him?'

She gave him the flask, and as he took it, Gauthier said hotly: 'If there

282

was any justice in the world, that villain ought to suffer the tortures of the damned! Not that I can think of any bad enough for his desserts! This Damoiseau is inhuman! To dare to force you to betray your friends, basely to make use of you while your husband lies dying! When your husband is his own brother in arms!'

'Such men own no brothers, of any kind. The Damoiseau would skin his own mother if it suited him.'

She spoke calmly enough, in a level voice that seemed to come from very far away. She had just delved so deep in horror and pain that she still felt only half alive. Physical sensations reached her as though through a thickness of cloth, and her brain seemed unable to grapple with them. There was a delay in her reactions. She remained standing in the middle of the room with her eyes fixed on the bed where her husband was lying stretched on a grimy mattress, but covered with an embroidered silken coverlet that must have formed part of the Skinners' plunder. Its strident pink clashed with its dismal surroundings, like fancy dress upon a corpse. The bandages in which Arnaud's head was swathed were already stained with blood, and he was lying so still that Catherine thought he must be dead. Even the agonising tensing of his jaw that had been apparent earlier had ceased.

She threw a frightened glance at Gauthier, but he shook his head.

'No. He is not dead yet. His breathing is scarcely perceptible, but he is still alive. I think he has entered that stage of insensibility that the Greeks called coma.'

The page, meanwhile, was coming to himself. As he recognised Gauthier bending over him, his clouded gaze cleared and he started to smile. Then the memory of all that had occurred came back to him suddenly, and he flung himself on to his friend's chest with a shriek and began sobbing convulsively.

The older lad made no attempt to quiet him, knowing that often, after unbearable tension, it was best to let the floodgates open. He merely stroked the boy's curly head with an affectionate hand, while at the same time returning Catherine's flask to her with the other.

'Drink some yourself,' he recommended. 'You look as though you need it.'

She obeyed him mechanically and put the flask to her lips. The liquor was very strong. It made her shiver and cough as the fiery stream coursed through her body. But she felt more alive, and her mind was more alert.

'What are you going to do?' Gauthier asked, when the page's sobs had subsided a little.

Catherine shrugged. 'What can I do?'

Just then, the door opened and the Damoiseau came into the room. The angelic face with its foxy eyes bore a satisfied expression.

'Tomorrow at sunrise you may go up to the castle, lady,' he said. 'You will be expected.'

'Tomorrow?'

'Yes. The day is overcast. It will be dark earlier than usual, and it seems that your friends are unwilling to run any risks. They want to see you coming in broad daylight. Let me wish you a good night. Food will be brought to you in due course.' He indicated the tall figure lying motionless beneath the ridiculous pink coverlet. 'When all is over, inform one of the men who will pass the night outside your door, so that I may pay my last respects. I sleep in the next room. Ah, I nearly forgot …'

He opened the door again. In the doorway stood the ghostly black shape of a Benedictine monk in his funereal habit and scapular, his cowl pulled low over his face and his hands tucked into his wide sleeves. The only thing about him that seemed human and of this world was the pair of large, bare feet, grey with dust, that showed through the plain leather straps of his sandals.

'Here is the prior of the Good Men of the forest. Their hermitage is less than a league from here. He came most – willingly to assist our friend on his last journey. I will leave you now.'

The monk came forward and, without glancing at any of them, walked toward the bed. He was a frightening figure with the cowl pulled forward, revealing nothing of his face, and Catherine crossed herself superstitiously and withdrew into the shadow of the bed-curtains. It seemed to her that she was looking at the shadow of Death himself, come to take Arnaud away.

When he reached the foot of the bed, the Benedictine gazed at the dying man for a moment and then turned to Gauthier, who had left Bérenger sitting on a stool and come to him.

'Will you draw that chest closer to the bed, if you please,' he said in a low voice. 'I have brought all that is needed for the last rites …'

He put back his hood as he spoke, revealing strong, ugly features adding up to a face that, for all its ascetic leanness, was both energetic and cheerful. The wide mouth, curving slightly upwards at the corners, and the rather snub nose suggested a naturally optimistic temperament, and his tonsured head was encircled by a crown of unruly, grizzled dark brown curls. But when he moved into the light of the candle to bend over the dying man, Catherine uttered an exclamation of amazement. She stepped out of the shelter of the grey curtains where she had been hiding, unable to believe her eyes.

'Landry!' she whispered. 'You, here?'

He straightened up and looked at her without surprise, but with a joy that brought a glow into his brown eyes so that she saw in them again, unaltered, all the eagerness of her childhood friend.

Standing on the other side of the bed, she stared at him open-mouthed, as if he had really been the ghost she had thought she saw entering the room a few moments before. Her astonishment was so obvious that he smiled, despite the gravity of the occasion.

'Why, yes, Catherine … it is I! How long you have been!'

'Long? Do you mean – you were expecting me?'

'We have been expecting you. The Countess of Châteauvillain, who is generosity itself, has made to my brethren and me, their unworthy head, a gift of a tract of forest land on which to build our priory. She is our benefactress, and in return we take it upon ourselves to administer to the service of God up at the castle. She told me, naturally, that she had sent for you. That is why you were expected.'

As he spoke, he was laying out on top of the chest that Gauthier and Bérenger had carried close to the bed, a crucifix, two small candles, a box twig and two small flasks, the one containing the oil, the other holy water. He asked for a basin of water and a towel.

Catherine, meanwhile, was kneeling by the bed. She kept looking at Landry, unable to take her eyes off him, as though she feared to see him vanish in a puff of smoke. Whatever he might say, it was so extraordinary to find Landry Pigasse, the boy she had known on the Pont au Change, here, when she had last seen him at the Abbey of St Seine! Although, when one thought about it, the Abbey was not so very far away.

'My mother?' she whispered.

'She could not wait for you, Catherine. It is a full week now since she fell asleep in the Lord. Do not distress yourself,' he added, seeing her face pucker up. 'She died with no pain, talking to the end of you and her grandchildren. But I think she was glad to be going to join your father at last. She was not sorry to quit this life …'

'Yes, I think she never really got over his death,' Catherine murmured. 'I didn't realise it for a long time, because one never thinks of such things in connection with one's parents … One sees them as people apart, not altogether human … Yet I think they were very much in love.'

'Never doubt it. Theirs was a quiet, humdrum love affair, very simple and ordinary, and might have endured for many years, but for the tragedy we unloosed on them.'

Catherine's eyes filled with tears. She had never thought of her parents as lovers. She had known them as a quiet, tranquil couple, living together with few words, perhaps because they had needed no words to understand one another. It was an undemonstrative love, but very real, and it had lasted to the end, for although Gaucher's life had been wrested from him in the sound and fury of an angry mob, Jaquette's had continued, day after day, in silent resignation, until the time came when she too was able to set out on the great journey to which she had looked forward for so many years. How she must have welcomed it at last!

Burying her face in the satin coverlet, Catherine began to pray at once for her who was gone and for him who before very long would take the same dark road. Their own love had been woven of contrasts: tragedy and happiness, violence and gentleness, joy and suffering. But the Lady of Montsalvy knew that when her lord was no more, her own life would become like her mother's, and like that of Isabelle de Montsalvy, her mother-in-law, and of all women left behind on earth by a husband they loved: a long wait, a long wearying-away of time, a gradual progress toward the dark doorway that should yet open on an eternity of light.

While she was praying, Landry had finished his preparations and donned the silk stole over his frieze habit. He was looking down at the dying man.

'Who is he?' he asked gently.

Catherine shivered, realising suddenly that he could not know, for although Ermengade had told him to expect Catherine, she could not have imagined or foreseen all that had happened. Nor would the men-at-arms who went to fetch the monk have bothered to mention his name; or, if they had, would the name Captain La Foudre have meant anything to Landry?

She took the big hand lying on the coverlet, startled to find it so warm when she had been prepared to feel the chill of death already on it. But he was burning with fever.

'My lord,' she said with a sigh. 'The Count of Montsalvy.'

She saw that Landry had not understood, but he asked no further questions. Only his eyes, filled with compassion, rested in turn on the fair head and on the other, lying there, half-hidden in bloody bandages.

'You shall tell me later,' he murmured. 'There will be time enough.'

Then, as they knelt, he dipped the box twig he had brought with him in the holy water and sprinkled the room.

'*Pax huic domi,*' he began in a loud voice. '*Adiutorinum nostrum in nomine domini ...*'

The simple, soothing Latin phrases of the ritual of Extreme Unction purred through the room. Landry bent over Arnaud's body and with a little holy oil anointed the wounded man's orifices, his eyes, his ears, his lips, as far as the bandages allowed, the palms of his hands and his feet, while Gauthier and Bérenger, suddenly remembering their early religious training, intoned the responses and embarked on the litany for the dying.

When the last 'Amen' had died away, Landry rinsed his hands and wiped them on the towel that Bérenger held out to him, took off his stole, put out the little candles and returned all the things he had been using to the bag he carried slung from the cord round his waist. Then he turned to Catherine, who had gone to open the tiny window.

It was quite dark by now, but the heat in the room was like an oven. Their clothes stuck to their skins and sweat ran in shining rivulets down all their faces.

The noise from the little square floated into the room. It was little enough: only a few of the men were about, moving between the houses and what remained of the camp. A few lights shone in windows, giving the impression that everything in the village was as it always had been, and up on the turrets of the castle there were braziers burning to light the wall walks and leave no shadowy corners to encourage a surprise attack. The effect was like a flaming coronet in the sky.

'Now, tell me everything,' Landry said quietly. 'I am listening.'

'What do you want to know?'

'All that I do not understand. Why have you taken so long to answer Dame Ermengarde's summons, and why do I find your husband here with you, gravely wounded? Were you attacked by these brigands? I was told of an injured man with some name like thunder or lightning …?'

'La Foudre. Yes. It's right that you should know. In fact, if I hadn't lived through it, I doubt I should believe it myself. But these are dreadful times …'

The tale of all that had happened at Montsalvy and afterwards in Paris, Chinon and Tours was easy and soon told. Catherine was beginning to know it by heart now. Of her life up to the time of the siege, Landry had already heard from Ermengarde. But it was difficult when it came to the events of the previous night. It was not easy to find words to describe the shattered village, and harder still to utter them, for each conjured up its own frightful visions.

'I know what it was like,' the monk interrupted her. 'It is not, unhappily, a sight that is new to me. I've nearly met my death in similar affairs several times before now.'

'Several times?'

He shrugged fatalistically, and there was a melancholy twist to his mouth.

'Oh yes, that is war, apparently! But, go on, please.'

'Go on? The hardest part is yet to tell, my friend.' She could not bring herself to look at him as she described the ravaged house, the man tortured and the woman raped, and then, burying her face abruptly in her hands, she went on: 'It was then I saw their leader – Captain La Foudre. It was – my husband! It was Arnaud!'

There was silence. Landry said nothing. Gauthier and Bérenger had withdrawn discreetly to the other end of the room, where they were more or less hidden by the curtains round the bed, and were trying not to breathe.

After a moment, the monk leaned forward and tapped his old friend on the knee with one finger.

'What were your feelings then, Catherine?'

She parted her hands and looked at him desolately. 'I don't know …! I don't know anything anymore! Horror, yes, and disappointment – no, that's not the word, but I can't express it. It was hideous, you know … A bit like that night when Caboche killed Michel outside our house. Did you see what the mob had done to him before Legoix finished him off? Some indescribable thing, a bloody mess that bored into my sight like an arrow. Well, I felt something like that when I found Arnaud last night. He was there, before me, looking just as he always looked, and yet it was as if the man I knew had been slain as well. I think I felt sick, but I didn't have much time to think about it, because the next moment we were fighting. We quarrelled and said things to each other as if we were strangers, enemies! I tried to make him understand what I felt, but he was past all reason, almost beyond proof! It seemed as though some unknown power, some hostile force possessed him. It showed me that Arnaud had no real faith in me ...'

'It showed you, you say? Are you sure you had not known for a long while?'

She thought for a moment and then, with characteristic honesty, assented.

'You're right. I think I've always known. He doesn't trust me. To start with, I was a daughter of the Legoix family, and that was enough to make him shrink from me. And then there was my – my connection with Duke Philippe, whom he had always regarded as his greatest enemy.'

'All those who serve King Charles with any loyalty think that,' Landry observed. 'Only, in your husband's case, political hatred is strengthened by a private grudge, a hatred as man to man. The evil force you were speaking of a moment ago, don't you think its first name is jealousy?'

'Was it jealousy that made him burn a village, violate a woman, torture a man? When I remember that, I feel myself hating him again.'

'Because you, also, are jealous. The thing you find it hardest to forgive him is his unexpected admiration for this woman from St Privey, isn't it? The one passing herself off as the Maid? That – and his rape of that woman! A woman with fair hair, like your own, didn't you tell me?' Landry turned to look at the man lying on the bed. He studied him attentively for a moment or two.

'I could have wished that he had not been too far gone to confess,' he sighed. 'In souls like his, where pride rules more than God, there are many strange corners, and dark as all such corners are. A passion of jealousy, a deep disgust with mankind – or womankind, if too much idealised – can lead them into the worst kind of excesses, in which the need to destroy is only a reaction, the desire to cause suffering only a way of alleviating their own! I have seen other examples ... But tell me, Catherine, before the fight broke out today, what had you decided to do?'

She answered without a second's hesitation. 'I wanted to see my mother. No force on earth could have prevented me, because it was natural, and I had every right to do so. I made this whole journey with that one object. Besides, the choice Arnaud put before me was wicked, hateful ...'

'Not from his point of view. He, I believe, had but one picture before his eyes, the unbearable one of you, his wife, entering the gates of that castle and finding within them, waiting with outstretched arms, the man he hated most in all the world, your former lover. He could see nothing else. Nothing at all! And he was seeing it still as he hurled himself so furiously to meet his death …'

'Do you mean … that he meant to die?'

'No, no. He was, as you say, beyond all reason. Look, I am trying to help you, to explain. Don't think I am excusing or condoning the excesses of such men, brought up to the taste of blood; but in the course of a life spent delving into the human heart, I have learned many contradictory things. As for him, in giving him absolution in *articulo mortis*, I have pardoned him in God's name. But now, my interest is in you, and it is you I would understand. How is it with you, Catherine? Did the thought of finding Philippe of Burgundy up there play any part in your determination to enter Châteauvillain even at the risk of cutting yourself off forever from your home?'

A slow flush spread over Catherine's neck and cheeks as she realised exactly what it was that Landry was saying. But her eyes did not falter.

'You want to know if I felt any – any pleasure in the idea of seeing the Duke again? No, Landry, none! I swear to you, as I hope for salvation! I never truly loved him. All I wanted was to see my mother – and to protest against the violence being done to me! I cannot bear to be constrained, and Arnaud had no right to …'

'Oh yes, he had! Every right!' Landry said firmly. 'As well you know. Even the right to forbid you, purely and simply, to enter the castle. Even the right to compel your obedience by force. He is your husband before God and men, by whom all laws are made.'

'I know all that,' Catherine said bitterly. 'Men have all the rights and leave us only one – the right to obey unconditionally! And if they abuse those rights, so much the worse for us! That is what Arnaud did, and what I could not forgive him for!'

'And now?'

'Now?' Great tears welled up in Catherine's eyes and overflowed, and with them all her grief. 'For me, there is no now! How could I not forgive him in the moment when I am about to lose him forever? Perhaps I am the one who should ask for forgiveness, if my rebellion has caused his death … I love him, Landry. I love him as much as ever – even though now I am afraid of him – and that love is my whole life. You do not tear out your life because a dream is ended …'

The monk rose and went to the bed. Bending over the wounded man, he took his hand and looked down at him for a long time, frowning, as though seeking for something he did not find. Then he shook his head.

'He is very close to death,' he said. 'But – what if he were to recover?'

'What do you mean?'

'Nothing. It is only a hypothesis to make you look into your heart. This man, this dying man whom you forgive in his last hour, would you also forgive him if God were to decide that this hour should not be his last?'

She dropped to her knees and stretched out her arms to the monk, seeing him at that moment only as a man of God whose prayers might have power to wrest mercy from heaven.

'Only to know that he was alive, I could submit to anything – even separation, even to obey in silence!'

'Do you love him so much?'

'I have never loved anyone else!" she said, almost savagely. 'I implore you, if there is any hope, any chance, however small, even one chance in a million that God will let me keep him, only tell me!'

The monk gave her a smile filled with sadness and compassion.

'You speak as if you see me as some kind of ambassador or intermediary, able to negotiate with the Almighty.'

'You said so yourself – He is the Almighty, and you are His priest!'

'But I cannot work miracles. Do not dream, Catherine. It is true that once before, at the Abbey of St Seine, I have seen a man survive a wound such as this. That one was caused by a lance, and the man, like this, was strong. But the physician was skilled – and here we have in our poor priory only one of our brethren, who is a little simple but who has a great love of herbs.'

'What does it matter!' Catherine cried, filled with a hope she could not contain. 'You must go quickly and fetch this brother of yours – or, better still, we must take my husband to St Seine! It's not far, and if he could endure the journey ...'

'Hush! I put the suggestion, I tell you, only to test your heart. There is no way by which we can leave this house before tomorrow. And tomorrow – the Damoiseau is not a dog to let go, once he has a hold! Have you forgotten what tomorrow holds for you? Are you not compelled, upon pain of seeing a child tortured to death, to enter the castle accompanied by two men? Two men who will be neither your real esquire nor the chaplain you do not possess, but two men-at-arms whose mission will surely be to open the gates to their friends ...'

Catherine brushed her hand across her eyes with a dazed expression. Landry had brought her brutally back to earth just as she was bestriding the mettlesome steed of hope. She had no choice. She had no means to save her husband, even if there was a chance! She could only stay where she was until allowed to go up to the castle she was to betray. Her eyes went to Landry's, questioning, beseeching him for some hope, however vain.

'Surely they can never succeed,' she murmured to herself. 'With the Duke there, and his guard ...'

'The Duke is not there,' Landry cut her short impatiently. 'It was the Seigneur de Vandenesse who arrived, with a company of the ducal guard. The Skinners were deceived by a slight resemblance, like the people of the region. Châteauvillain is one of the important fortresses of the Burgundian borders, and the Countess had few men to defend it. She was alarmed by the nearness of the remaining English strongholds and by the movement of troops that has been taking place there since the Treaty of Arras. She asked for reinforcements. That is all.'

Catherine gave a deep sigh of relief. It gave her some comfort to be able to exonerate Ermengarde from the charge of having set a trap for her. Her mother was dead, Philippe was not there. That being so, what business had she with the castle?

She had made her decision in an instant. Getting up suddenly, she walked to the door.

'The Damoiseau must be told! He must be told at once! He'll believe you, because you are a man of God. Tell him what you know, especially that the Duke is not there. I'll call him now ...'

But he stood in her way.

'Don't be a fool! I told you Châteauvillain was one of the keys to Burgundy. It makes no difference to Robert de Sarrebrück whether the Duke is there or not! What he wants, and what he expects you to do, is to help him to take a place he can never enter except by a trick! Whatever we tell him, up you will have to go to the castle tomorrow at sunrise, to ease their work for them. You can guess what will follow.'

A long shudder ran down Catherine's spine. She closed her eyes. Yes, she knew what would follow. Ermengarde's home would become a battlefield and, after that, the Damoiseau would install himself, and from the shelter of those mighty walls he could defy the Constable himself ... Her old friend would be murdered, and all her people with her. How could she bear to think of it? But the thought of little Bérenger dying a hideous death was no more to be borne.

She opened her eyes again and found the monk watching her closely.

'What can I do?'

'Fly!'

'Do you imagine we've not thought of it?' It was Gauthier who spoke, with some asperity, judging that the time had come for him to take some part in the discussion. 'But how can we fly? The room next door is full of soldiers, and the only other way out of this one is by a little window even Bérenger could not squeeze through! In any case, we'd only land on the Watch in the square! So think, father, before you say things like that,' he finished tartly.

'If I tell you to fly, it's because I know a way, stripling! Look ...' He crossed to the wall facing the window. There was a small door in it, opening onto a tiny lumber room.

'That hole?' Gauthier said disgustedly. 'We explored that earlier. There's nothing there but old clothes and empty jam-pots, distaffs and some hemp for spinning ...'

'You haven't looked properly. Bring the candle.'

Landry fetched a stool, took it in to the closet and stood on it, stooping a little to avoid banging his head on the low ceiling.

'Look,' he said, placing both his palms flat against the ceiling. 'This lifts up when those two bolts there are undone.'

'A trapdoor?' Bérenger breathed. 'But where does it go?'

'To the hayloft, of course, just underneath the ridge of the roof. Master Gondebaud, whose house this is, is an extremely capable man unfortunately possessed of an appallingly jealous and shrewish wife. She made him sleep in this room, from which he could not escape except by passing through her own. Or, at least, so she thought. But the ducal notary, who's as busy as he is cunning and will go after a petticoat as soon as after a rabbit, built this trapdoor with his own hands to give him a way into the loft. There's an opening at the other end by which the hay is brought in. It overlooks the orchard that leads down to the river. I don't know if the ladder is still there, but you're young, all three, and the grass is long. You can easily jump.'

'And then?' Gauthier, who had been listening intently, asked him softly. 'How do we find horses and get through the gates?'

'Don't try, you'd be bound to get caught. Swim the river and climb the rock to the castle. There's a thick clump of bushes near the barbican. You can hide there until daylight and then, when the drawbridge is lowered ...'

'Take refuge in the castle, do you mean?' Bérenger said in astonishment. 'But wouldn't it be better to keep to open country?'

'How could you? You'd be recaptured before noon, and then I don't know what would become of you. Believe me, the castle is your only chance. You'll be safe there and can wait until the Skinners tire of this and go away or until help arrives.'

The two boys found it hard not to exclaim aloud in their eagerness and delight at the prospect before them, but Catherine said nothing. She had listened to Landry's plan in silence, glanced briefly into the closet, and had then returned to the bed, where she was standing with both hands clasped round one of the posts, as though afraid of being torn away.

'I can't! I can't go!' she gasped. 'Don't you understand, I want to stay with him until the end? You boys go! It's Bérenger who's in danger. Once he's safe out of the way, the Damoiseau cannot force me to do anything.'

'You think not?' Landry said dryly. 'You want to stay until the end, you say? The end of what?'

'Why ... of his life?'

'He is not dead yet, and may not be tomorrow morning. What do you think the Damoiseau's reaction will be when he learns that the boys have fled? Will he put you to the torture? Oh, no! He's a cleverer devil than that! It's your husband, wounded as he is, who will take Bérenger's place. Do you feel strong enough to see him stretched on a gridiron?'

The scream burst from her before she could prevent it. 'No!' In a more moderate voice, she added: 'He would not dare! They are brothers in arms!'

'You little fool! Have you learned nothing yet? A man of his stamp will not hesitate between such a scruple as that and Dame Ermengarde's great castle! I doubt if there's a spark of ordinary human feeling in that handsome devil! But if you are brave enough to face the risk ...'

Catherine bowed her head and released her grip on the bedpost. But she could not bring herself to answer and only shook her head. She was beaten. Landry was right. She must go with the others and leave the man she loved behind, with no means of even finding out what might become of him. It would not be she who would be present when he breathed his last or, in the unlikely event that God might prove merciful, would be the first person on whom he rested his eyes.

Her grief was so heavy and her heart so full of pain that she could not resist making one last effort.

'How do I know that they won't kill him after we've gone? I cannot leave him alone, Landry – I can't leave him helpless at the mercy of these brutes!'

'He will not be alone. I shall stay.'

'You're mad! They'll kill you!'

'I think not. Our talkative young friend here shall gag me and tie me up thoroughly. He can tear up the bedcurtains for ropes. He might even give me a little tap on the head to make it look real. After that, it is up to me.'

Already Gauthier and Bérenger, agog for action, were taking down two of the curtains and tearing them into long strips, which they twisted together like strands of hemp. In no time at all, the monk was thoroughly trussed up, while Catherine could only look on helplessly, incapable of offering the smallest help.

She had her husband's hand in hers and was nursing it to her breast. It was burning hot, but it was still the hand of a living man, and the blood that throbbed in it belonged to the man she loved. She knelt and laid her wet cheek against it and touched it with her trembling lips. She knew that after the next few moments, she would not see him again, that she could not fight the inexorable march of fate ... This look and this caress were her last.

'My love,' she whispered. 'I want so much to stay, to stay with you always – even in the grave! I wish I could die too! But there are the children, our children – they need me, you see! I must go back to them – to our home – for their sake! I must go away and leave you, my darling ...'

She laid her head down on his hand, wishing desperately that she could die there, in that instant, never to rise again.

'Dame Catherine!' It was Gauthier's voice speaking gruffly. 'Everything is ready. We must go.'

She looked at them. There were tears in their eyes but also a fierce determination.

Landry was securely bound but still on his feet, and his mouth was still free.

'I wanted to say goodbye to you before they gagged me,' he said quietly. 'Have faith, Catherine! Go without fear along the road that lies before you. You know that I am your brother and always loved you dearly.'

At that, she flung her arms round the monk's neck, hugging him fiercely, and kissed him several times.

'Take care of yourself, Landry,' she said in a choked voice. 'And take care of him, and pray God to have mercy on us ...'

'Hurry,' Landry said impatiently, reluctant to give way to emotion. 'You must lose no more time! The gag now ... and then a blow with the stool. Only take care you don't kill me, young man! I will pray for you all! Farewell, Catherine ...'

A moment later, the monk whose name had once been Landry Pigasse was lying on the floor, stretched unconscious by Gauthier. A little blood showed against the brown skin of his tonsured scalp.

'He'll have an enormous bump,' the young man observed, 'but he's breathing normally. I did my best. Let's go, now.'

Catherine had been drawn back irresistibly to her husband's still form. Gauthier dragged her away almost forcibly and urged her toward the cupboard.

Her last sight of Arnaud was of his face in the yellow light of the candle, looking as though set rigidly for all eternity beneath its blood-soaked bandages.

The long night came to an end. As dawn rose over the spreading forests all around, in answer to the summons of a raucous cock or two, the sky, where a few bright stars still lingered, turned grey-blue, then mauve, then pink. Sunrise came triumphantly, heralding a beautiful day, and the three fugitives, huddled amongst cornels and brambles, watched the light grow.

They were tired and frozen stiff in their wet clothes, which the chill of the early morning had turned to ice. The crossing of the river had been awkward on account of the swift current, nor had the ascent of the castle rock, bypassing thickets and loose stones, been any easier. When they came to the foot of the massive walls, they had flung themselves down into the bushes as though into a haven. They were invisible and very near to safety. Even so, they waited with impatience for the castle gates to open.

The village down below looked very small and unimportant, yet out of all the terracotta rooftops, Catherine was able to pick out one: the one particular roof under which lay the husband she had been forced to leave behind.

Was he still alive or had death, so adept at stealing into the tired bodies of the sick in the black hours of the early morning, already done its work? Had Landry recovered his senses yet? Had their flight been discovered?

The village was very quiet, almost too quiet. In the square, a few soldiers, naked to the waist, were making for the well to wash away the mists of sleep, while others were already under arms and on their way to relieve the sentinels. A waft of smoke was coming from the chimney of the notary's house.

Catherine felt Bérenger's breath against her cheek and saw that the page was looking at the village, and there were tears in his eyes. Touched, she asked him: 'Weeping, Bérenger?'

He turned his tired little face toward her. Fear and exhaustion made him look younger than ever, but the sadness in his brown eyes belonged to a man. Bérenger might still be no more than 14, but he had aged in these few days.

'Messire Arnaud ...' he murmured. 'Will we ever see him again? Will God be merciful to us?'

'To us? Would you still want to serve him – after all that you have seen?'

'Yes. Because of you, Dame Catherine. You love him so! And yet you agreed to leave him for my sake, without even knowing whether or not he would live!'

'It was not only for your sake, Bérenger. The Damoiseau would have found some other way of forcing me.'

'You're saying that to make me feel better, but I am guilty also, because he is my lord and I have abandoned him. If he dies – I'll go back to the canons of St Projet and become a monk!'

The boy's unhappiness, his need to sacrifice himself, and also the form of bargain he intended to strike with God, touched Catherine deeply. She turned her head and touched her lips softly to the page's wet cheek.

'Don't be foolish, Bérenger. You were not born to be a monk.'

But something in her heart contracted. Landry had not seemed cut out for the cloister either when he was Bérenger's age. The call came sometimes in devious ways ... But she knew that Bérenger had not heard it. He wanted only to repay what he thought of as a debt, and to enter the Church in order to expiate his lord's lonely death.

She looked up at the sky, as though asking it for a sign. It was clear and lovely, so serene that it seemed as if there could be nothing below it but peace and happiness. It was not in the least a sky for despair, and in the warm, golden light that was beginning to flood the world, Catherine thought she read a kind of promise.

She seemed to hear from afar off, Sara's voice saying, in a tone of utter conviction, as she had said it on the first night of the siege: 'Messire Arnaud will come back to Montsalvy!'

Alas, she had not said how he would return. Her prophecy had been confined to telling Catherine that she had more to suffer yet on his account.

The chapel bell rang for prime and, slowly, the castle's sleepy heart began to beat again. The watchmen called to one another from tower to tower and a horn rang out somewhere to summon the men to their daily duties.

Gauthier, who had dropped asleep at last, stretched himself and yawned. 'Is it time?' he asked.

For answer, Catherine pointed to the sun now rising above the wide green sea of trees. Yes, it was time. The beginning of a long time to come ...

What future did that sun proclaim for the Lady of Montsalvy? A future of love rediscovered, renewed, reborn in a man's arms? Or the austere future of a woman dressed in black, alone in her mountain fastness, set halfway between heaven, which was her last hope, and the earth where its heir was growing up and where a proud, stubborn and hot-blooded people would still write the history of Auvergne in their blood and sweat?

The answer lay not with Catherine, but this time she did not try to influence fate with fresh entreaties. The time for that was past. Simply, and humbly also, she placed herself at last in the hands of One more powerful than herself.

'Thy will be done, Lord,' she murmured.

Then, bravely, she turned her eyes away from the notary's house as, with a thunderous roar, the great drawbridge descended.

About the Author

Juliette Benzoni was born Andrée-Marguerite-Juliette Mangin on 30 October 1920 in Paris, France. She spent her childhood in Saint-Germain-des-Pres until she was almost 15 years old, when her family went to live in Saint-Mandé. She was educated at College d'Hulet, then at the Institut Catholique, where she studied philosophy, law and literature. In 1941 she married a doctor from Dijon, Maurice Gallois, and was soon mother of two children, Anne and Jean-François. In her twenties, she spent many hours in libraries, studying the history of Burgundy in Medieval times. One day she came across the legend of the Order of the Golden Fleece, which would later inspire her to write the *Catherine* series.

After her husband died in 1950, she went to Morocco to visit a relative of his, and ended up staying for two years, joining the editorial staff at a radio station called Radio-International. She then met Colonel André Benzoni, who in 1953 became her second husband. After her return to Paris, France, she launched into journalism, writing for several newspapers. At the beginning of the 1960s, a literary editor who had seen her make a television appearance invited her to write a historical romance in the style of Anne Golon's *Angelique*. The outcome was *Catherine: One Love is Enough* (original title, *Catherine, Il Suffit d'un Amour*), the hugely successful first entry in what was originally intended to be a five book series.

Next came another big success with the *Marianne* series, set during the Napoleonic period, beginning with *Marianne: A Star for Napoleon* (original title, *Marianne: Une Étoile Pour Napoleon*). Juliette was then asked if she would write two additional *Catherine* books, due to their sensational popularity. She agreed, and the series' seventh and final entry, *La Dame de Montsalvy*, appeared in 1979.

In 1983, the French company Antenne 2 adapted *Marianne: A Star for Napoleon* for television, directed by Marion Sarraut. This led, three years later, to a television adaptation of all seven books in the *Catherine* series, again directed by Sarraut; the end result pleased Juliette far more than a substandard movie version produced in 1968.

Juliette died on 7 February 2016.

For more information about Juliette and the *Catherine* books, see this official website: www.catherinedemontsalvy.ch.

Other Titles from Telos Publishing

Printed in Great Britain
by Amazon

81313675R00169